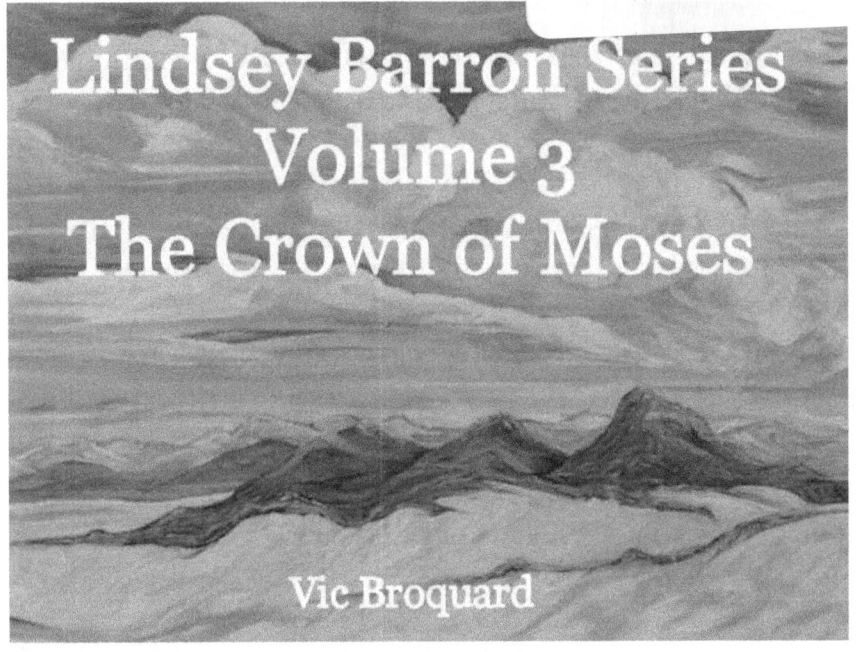

Lindsey Barron Series
Volume 3
The Crown of Moses

Vic Broquard

Lindsey Barron Series
Volume 3
The Crown of Moses

Vic Broquard

Artwork by Crooked Willow Studios.

Published by:
Broquard eBooks
http://Broquard-eBooks.com
author@Broquard-eBooks.com
103 Timberlane
East Peoria, IL 61611

For Morgan and L. Ron Hubbard

Table of Contents

Chapter 1—Prelude

God spoke to Moses, "The time has come for you to lead your people to freedom. Cross the Sinai to the land I have promised thee."

"Lord, how shall we survive the desert?" Moses asked.

"I give thee thy Crown and Staff. When you have finished, cast them into the waters off Sidon. Thy Staff shall part waters; thy Crown shall control the weather. Go now and lead thy people to safety."

Several millennia later, Underwater Archaeologist and wizard, Professor Jacques Flambois checked his diving gear and rolled backwards off his ship into the blue waters of the Mediterranean Sea. Looking for ancient sunken ships this summer, Jacques already had found seven to excavate. He was diving some hundred twenty miles east of Larnaca, Cyprus. The suspected ancient ship was nowhere to be found, but a glint of gold caught his eye. Pushing away the silt, Jacques found a crown, heavily encrusted from its long submersion. Excited, he used the remaining air in his tank to locate the vessel, which was possibly associated with this magnificent find. Finding none, he returned to the surface.

Later, as he cleaned the crown, he noticed that it radiated strong magical energies. An Identification spell later, he sent off a flurry of email messages back to his base in Nicosia and to his department at the Bordeaux University, Bordeaux, France. The magnitude of this find was such that he immediately ended his explorations a month early, sailing for home near the end of August.

Arriving near September 1, he took his priceless artifact into his office and began to clean it carefully. He spent hours studying the proper location and action for each Clean spell he intended to cast, working long hours into the night. Mornings, he spent answering the many email queries from various colleagues, historians, and Biblical scholars. All wanted to see this relic first hand. Hence, Jacques arranged for its first public showing on September 25.

Over a dozen well-respected men arrived at the university at the appointed hour. However, Professor Jacques failed to appear. The university police discovered his dead body in his office a little later. The crown was missing. There were no clues.

Chapter 2—Late Summer

"It's organized chaos, that's what it is," Lena Compton said, laughing her head off as the children made a mad dash to the front room teleportation device that took them over to the Whitewater ranch. It was Saturday mid-July. She and her husband Lloyd, along with Polly and Fred Betts, sat at the kitchen table sipping their late morning coffee. "How did I ever get along without it? I'll miss them something awful when they all go back to school." She was referring to the last week of August when all the children would be returning to Arthur Bradbury's School of Magic.

Lloyd Compton, who worked for the Department of Defense, Magical Branch, Denver, Colorado, smiled. "I know. I've never had so much fun in my life. I'm so glad that I met you, Lena. Look what you've done for my life!" He had been assigned to protect Lena Barron from retribution by the evil wizard, Dominus Malefic. Her first husband, Samuel Rabnor, had been instrumental in his capture many years ago, as one member of the famous Rat Pack, a group of four who finally brought Dominus and his Death Stalkers to justice. Back then, he swore vengeance on those who captured him. Some of his men still on the loose had murdered the remaining family of Mabel Pruit, the Diviner of the Rat Pack. Sam had changed his last name and gone into hiding along with the other two members. Calling himself Sam Barron, he'd married Lena, and they had a child, Lindsey. Sam was murdered some five years later, though until last year, his death had been attributed to an unfortunate farming accident. With Lindsey's identity now known, Lloyd had been sent to protect Lena and also Lindsey, when she was home from Bradbury's. Lloyd had also fallen in love with Lena, and they married last summer.

During these past two years, Lindsey had repeatedly demonstrated the budding skills needed to become a Dispeller, one who can easily counter nasty spells so that others could apprehend the evil doers. Lindsey was born without hands and lived a perfectly miserable childhood, completely friendless.

However, during her first year at Bradbury's, Doctor Caterwall had re-grown her hands, and she had made lasting friends, for the first time in her life.

One of those friends was Pam Betts, a homely girl with black hair and hazel eyes. Her two front teeth had a noticeable gap in them, only adding to her lack of self-image. Pam, however, was a computer genius and had already demonstrated that she had a knack for sleuthing. Indeed, her sleuthing last year had been instrumental in uncovering a dire plot to have the head master of Bradbury's fired. None other than the Governor General Albright, a crony of Dominus Malefic, had been behind it. Her testimony led to his arrest and lengthy jail term.

He, too, swore revenge on Pam and Lindsey. In fact, Dominus supporters attacked Pam's home in Sterling, Colorado, ransacking it. Her father, Fred Betts, was the director of the Department of Magical Misuse, Sterling. Her mother, Polly, had narrowly escaped the thugs who broke into their home. Because of the ever-growing crime wave being fostered by Dominus, the department's forces were now stretched very thin. As a result, the Betts family moved in with Lloyd and Lena, so that their families could more readily be protected.

In these hard times, Lena and Lloyd opened their home to another young girl in Lindsey's class, Audrey Lemon, whose parents had been killed by Dominus many years ago. A very levelheaded orphan, she had managed to get by on her own, living with many foster families. Now, she was staying with the Compton's, which she loved. She was an incredible wood carver, producing absolutely fabulous carvings of animals from blocks of wood. Fred had helped her set up a Web site from which to promote and sell her carvings. For the first time in her life, she had money coming in; carvings were selling from one hundred to five hundred dollars each. Audrey also was a plant expert, as plants had been her only true friends for much of her childhood until now. Audrey fit in perfectly here, helping Lena with the many garden plots.

Their new ranch and home was on a five mile square of rangeland, just north of the tiny high plains town of Arapahoe, near the Kansas border. Their nearest neighbors, the Whitewater ranch, lay on the small Indian reservation, north of Arapahoe. The Whitewater family was Apache, and their four children were also close friends of Lindsey.

Amanda had long black hair, thick lips, and black eyes. She was demonstrating Tracker skills, the ability to see residual magical energies left from the casting of magical spells. Amanda was Lindsey's very best friend. Amanda's sister, Fern, a year younger than Amanda, was also a plant lover, and was now a close friend of Audrey's. Her two older brothers, Jim and Tom, were also good friends. All were on the Bradbury track and soccer team. Indeed, Jim, Tom, Amanda, and Lindsey were the long distance runners and had helped the team win second place in the National Track Meet last May. Their specialty was the twenty-mile relay race. Fern ran in the mile relay race portion.

Tom, now a sixth year student, had just announced his engagement to Sandy Rains, an Arapaho who lived in the tiny town. She worked part time at the Indian casino in town, the biggest moneymaker for hundreds of miles in all directions. Both Sandy and Tom were Yellow Hall Floor Monitors, helping the new students during orientation week and at all other times.

Jim, now a fifth year student, had a crush on Lindsey from the first day he had met her, two years ago. However, this summer, his world was turned upside down. Another Special Needs student had been accepted on a full scholarship to Bradbury's, Ashley Stokes. Lindsey had agreed to become a Yellow Hall Floor Monitor especially to assist her. Indeed, she would be bunking with Lindsey, Amanda, and Pam in their school dorm.

However, Ashley, an orphan since the horrible car accident when she was two, had been kicked out of every foster home she had live in, and now had been kicked out of the Twin Cities School of Magic as well. Having nowhere to stay for the summer months, Governor Alister Broadwell, head of Bradbury's, had asked Lena and Lindsey if Ashley could spend the summer months with them. Both had agreed.

Ashley was fiercely independent, taking nothing from

anyone. When she arrived, she had numerous black and blue bruises from the fights she had recently gotten into at Twin Cities. She had no money and wore only a tattered school dress, badly mended. Ashley had a violent temper when she arrived, along with her physical disability, no arms. She had lost them in the car accident, which killed her parents.

During her first six weeks here at the Compton ranch, Ashley, at last, found people that she could respect and would respect her as well, so much so, that her entire attitude towards life began to soften. Lena was the only non-magic user here, yet Ashley found that she could talk about her deepest feelings freely and openly to this normal woman. Lena gave her the love and encouragement that no other woman had been able to do. Lindsey, who had assumed the responsibility for her as Yellow Hall Floor Monitor, because of her childhood, knew how to handle Ashley with dignity and respect. A strong bond of love sprang up between them as well.

Three weeks ago, Ashley volunteered that she wished that Lena could be her mother! For Ashley, this had been an enormous change of attitude, and Lloyd had already begun the formal adoption process to make Ashley part of their family.

Yet with the constant increase in crime, due to Dominus Malefic and his now famous manifesto declaring that wizards ought to rule the world, no one was safe anywhere. Hence, families began to band together for mutual protection. Indeed, Running Bear Whitewater, or R. B., had helped design the new ranch home for the Compton family, based upon his own unique design. Totally energy efficient, the home was mostly underground, with three feet thick earthen walls and a sod roof that was really part of the ground. The new Compton ranch home was only forty feet by twenty on the outside, but five times that size inside, a magically altered space.

Further, since his children and those at the Compton ranch were together nearly all the time, R. B. created a permanent teleportation device in both their front rooms, allowing them to go back and forth with ease and safety, though often they all chose to ride their horses back and forth as well. R. B., Lloyd, and Fred were planning for the future. If things got worse, which everyone predicted, they would have a secure home base from which to operate and take in others who may need their assistance.

When Ashley first came to live with them, Pam used her sleuthing skills to inquire into the past of Ashley. She discovered an old bank account of Ashley's mother, and Lloyd had helped her obtain her inheritance, a little over ten thousand dollars. A byproduct of this was Ashley learned that she had paternal grandparents, Samson and Bertha Stokes, who were now living in an Assisted Living complex. Once a week, Lloyd took her to visit them.

During this summer, Polly and Lena decided that, since their girls were now fourteen, it was time that they learned how to keep house: specifically, how to plan, cook, and serve meals, deal with housecleaning, laundry, and other domestic duties. Ashley was very proud that Lena allowed her to learn how to do these herself, letting her have the time to work out how she could accomplish these things in her own way. Ashley continued to insist on her independence, fiercely so.

Additionally, Lena obtained the majority of her income from their ranch crops and horse breeding. Lloyd, a city slicker, was slow to learn the ways of ranching. Hence, Lena also had given the girls various chores to do. Pam and Lindsey were in charge of the many animals, milking the cows, collecting the eggs, feeding and watering the animals, cleaning out the stalls, and so on. Pam's experience at milking cows convinced her to make a deal with Lindsey. She'd collect the eggs, if Lindsey would milk the cows.

Audrey, the plant expert, was put in charge of the several garden plots. Ashley was given the chores of cleaning the house and doing the laundry on Fridays. Of course, Fern dropped by nearly every morning to help Audrey with the plants and garden. By now, Audrey and Fern had become close friends, sharing many mutual interests.

Already this summer, Ashley had demonstrated several times her uncanny ability to sense when someone was in trouble, a key aspect of a Diviner. She had sensed that Lloyd was in trouble when some irrigation pipes fell on him, pinning him to the ground. Later, she had sensed that R. B. was in dire peril, when he had gone off to help the reservation police capture the men responsible for beating up Grey Eagle. She also told them just where to find the man had taken R. B., that is, in an abandoned line shack. Lindsey, Amanda, and Pam suspected that lovable Governor Alister Broadwell already knew that Ashley displayed Diviner traits and had worked to get her to their school and into their lives.

However, Ashley's appearance created a new problem for Jim, who had a crush on Lindsey for the last two years, ever since he had met her. Now, he just could not keep his eyes off Ashley! She was so much fun to be around, so feisty, so independent, so like himself, rowdy and playful. He had a large photo of each girl posted on his bedroom wall. Jim was confused; he liked the two girls very much. In fact, he had kissed Lindsey twice now, after the last dance of the Formal End of Term Dance at Bradbury's. Twice, Amanda had chided him for trying to have two girlfriends. Still, he just couldn't bring himself to choose one over the other.

Mid-July was exceedingly hot there on the High Plains. Nevertheless, the track runners continued to race every third day, pushing themselves to run at least twenty miles. All four long distance runners were intent upon winning first place at the Nationals this year. Jim had even convinced Ashley to try becoming part of their mile racing team, along with Fern. Indeed, with two of their team members having just graduated, they had to find two new replacement runners or they would not be able even to field a track team or soccer team.

Around ten each morning, either the girls came over to the Whitewater's ranch or vice versa. Chores done, today, Lindsey, Audrey, Pam, and Alison headed over to Amanda's. On days when they were not running, Pam and Audrey came too, for neither was interested in running. Today, however, Sandy had scheduled time to meet with Lindsey to go over her duties as Yellow Hall Floor Monitor.

Sipping sodas, Lindsey took notes on her laptop, while Sandy outlined all her new duties. "With the first years, it is pretty clear. You go with them a week early, show them to their rooms, and show them around the dorms, where the bathrooms are located, and those sorts of details. Next, you take them to the Bookstore and help them get their supplies and schedules. The House Mother usually hands out the new laptops and cell phones, though you ought to be with them as well, in case of troubles. Next, you take them around to their classes, just as they will be doing on the first day. You are allowed to do anything that you believe will help ease them into the school routines."

"On the bus, at each stop, you do a head count. I'll have the official boarding list with me, and I check off each student as they get aboard. Now, in your case, you will also be responsible for getting Ashley familiarized with the campus. First, though, go to Cho Lin to get her schedule, since this is the first year that students have the option for an elective. Ashley might want one instead of a Study Hall, though I found them very useful. I swear each year the courses get harder and harder. Also, you will need to assist her at meal times. Actually, anytime there is something that you think she may need a little help with, then you should be there for her."

"Now, anytime that there is trouble, as you have seen, Governor Alister puts us monitors in charge, so be alert for that too. Also, third years go on many field trips, US History trips. You get to see many historic places. It's rather fun. On those bus trips, you are responsible for making sure all Yellow Hall students are aboard and none is left behind. If anyone gives you any guff, you have the right to assign them detention."

"We didn't know about the field trips. That sounds interesting," Lindsey replied, finishing typing in Sandy's list of things for her to do.

"Oh, there is one more thing that has just come up, Lindsey. Perhaps you would take this one for me as well. We have another new third year student who has just transferred to Bradbury's. Since I will have my hands full with a hundred first years, could you also handle this new third year as well?"

"Sure, glad to," Lindsey replied. "Who is it?"

"Andy, Andy Rains." Sandy said rather quietly. Lindsey looked up at her, she added, "Yes, my little brother. He wants to be an archaeologist and spent his first two years at Boston School of Magic. He's been on two school digs with their archaeology faculty. He's rather weird, you know. I don't think he liked Boston at all. He's, well, you will just have to meet him and see for yourself. I've asked him to come over here and meet his new Floor Monitor, unless you don't want to deal with him."

"I guess I should meet him first, Sandy. After all, it does make more sense for me to handle all the new third year students, since you have a hundred first years. When is he coming by?"

"If he follows orders, which he seldom does, he ought to be along anytime now. I told him to come around 10:30 so I could have time to hat you up on your duties," Sandy explained, clearly relieved that Lindsey would handle him.

"Is Andy an Arapaho too? You two don't get along?" Lindsey asked the obvious.

"Yes, he is and no, we don't. He's always bringing in dirty things into the house, making a mess, and I have to clean up after him. Just be glad that you don't have a little brother around."

Just then, the magical owl announced, "Friendly visitor arriving at the corral." The two girls headed outside, after Sandy said it was probably her brother. Lindsey's first impression of Andy was mixed.

He wore his hair overly long, for a boy. Thick black hair came down to his shoulders. Andy had the same slightly darkish skin tone as his sister and the Whitewaters as well. He was about the same height as Lindsey, tall and thin, but he wore blue jeans and a western shirt, both were slightly dirty.

"Andy, this is Miss Lindsey Barron, your Yellow Hall Floor Monitor. She's going to be your guide when you go to Bradbury's. I'm warning you, if you give her any trouble, I'll see that you get detentions," Sandy said slightly antagonistically.

"Hello, Miss Lindsey Barron. I'm glad that you will be my Floor Monitor and not my stupid, bossy sister." Sandy glared at her brother. "You into archaeology?"

"Er, no, I'm afraid that I don't know anything about it, Andy. What is it anyway?"

"Oh no, Lindsey. Now you've done it! He'll talk about

old bones for hours now. I'm off to find Tom. See you later."
Sandy quickly headed back inside, as the other girls were
coming out to see Andy.

"Oh, here are more of our third years. Andy Rains, this
is Pam Betts, Audrey Lemon, and Ashley Stokes. You already
know Amanda and Fern, I suppose." Lindsey did the
introductions. "Andy is going to be a third year with us this
fall."

"Pleased to meet all of you. Gee, Ashley really doesn't
have any arms! Wow! I didn't believe Sandy when she told me.
Sorry," Andy replied.

Ashley's face took on a distinct look of anger, though
she forced herself to remain calm. Lindsey was pleased that
Andy was observant. He hastily added, "Ashley, don't
misunderstand me, I think that it is just fabulous that you
have carried on and become a third year witch. You must be
better than the rest of us to have gotten so far. After all, casting
all those grade 0 and 1 spells in forty-five minutes was tough
for me, and I've got two arms."

"Thanks, I think. Usually, they ask me if I cheated and
didn't do all the spells or if someone gave me a pass on having
to cast some. I'll have you know that I did get all them done in
the forty-five minutes my first year. Last year, I got them all
but the necromancy ones. I hate necromancy," Ashley replied,
still on the defensive.

"Wow! You mean others think you got a pass on doing
spells? Not doing them all? That's down right idiotic of them,
Ashley. At least I think so. After all, we are supposed to be
learning how to do magical spells. What's the use of giving
someone a free pass on them? Makes no sense. You must be
using your feet like we use our hands," Andy observed.

For once, Ashley was taken aback. Andy was on her
side, most unusual, especially for a boy. She had always been
on the defensive, especially when changing schools. Maybe
things would be different at Bradbury's, she thought.

Andy continued chatting, "Say, are you the Pam Betts
who got the Governor General arrested for all those crimes?
We heard about it on the news in Boston," Andy asked,
genuinely interested.

Pam blushed, "Yes, that's me."

"Way cool! Some of us cheered when we heard about it. Say, can I ask you all something? I've heard all sorts of rumors, bits from the news, and Sandy's emails. Are you a Sleuth, a Tracker, and a Dispeller?" Andy inquired. "I mean beginning ones or whatever."

"We are," Lindsey decided to answer for them. "This fall we get an elective or Study Hall. Pam is taking Sleuthing Theory I, Amanda is taking Tracking Theory I, and I am taking Dispeller Theory I. Ashley is already a Diviner, at least we think so, and I will be seeing if I can get her some theory course for Diviners, if there is one."

"Cooler than cool! Say, do you all hang out together, like studying together and all that?" Andy asked.

"Sure, Audrey here is the resident plant expert. There is nothing that she doesn't know about plants," Lindsey put in a good word for Audrey as well.

Andy grinned. "Can I join you? I mean studying together. I'm good at math and science, naturally, though I'm really most interested in archaeology. Not many are, you know."

The girls looked at each other, Pam answered for them. "Sure. I could use some help with these folks. We have Algebra II this fall, and I'm about the only one around who can do it. You have to promise to help the others though, especially Emilio and Kathy. They are really bad at math."

"Sure thing. Say, do you have chemistry this fall? I know back at Boston, I was supposed to have chemistry this fall," Andy asked. All nodded that they did. "Good, maybe I can help out there too. I already know quite a lot about chemistry. I did a lot of playing with chemistry sets when I was in grade school. All the field trips to excavation sites have taught me more. You know that I've been on two school-sponsored digs? That's how I normally spent my summers, on archaeology digs with the professors. Rather boring this summer because I'm not. Does Bradbury's have any archaeology digs or even classes?"

"I have never heard of either, but then that is my job to find out, Andy. When we get there, this fall during orientation week, I'll check and see if there is anything like that. Is that what you would want for your elective?"

"You bet! Thanks. Say, does Yellow Hall have a soccer team? I played goalkeeper in PE class," Andy ventured.

Amanda let out a war hoop! "Eureka! We just lost our goalkeeper; she graduated. We've been looking all over for a new goalkeeper. You absolutely *have* to try out! Unless someone crawls out of the woodwork, you're it! Wait til I tell Jim and Tom!"

Lindsey added, "You are looking at more than half the team here. All four Whitewaters are on it, plus me. Jake and Emilio are also on it. We have two openings. Ashley is going to try out for one, and you can try out for the other. If you can play at all, you're probably on the team."

"Cool. Golly, Ashley, you play soccer too? Now that is impressive indeed!" Andy praised her.

Ashley smiled for once, "Well, I play, but no one ever wanted me on their team. I've been practicing for the mile relay race too. I think I will be better at that than sprinting the short distance."

"Cooler than cool, Ashley. I think I would be better at sprinting short distances. I really don't like to run around that much. That's why I like being the goalkeeper," Andy admitted.

Already sweating, Amanda took them all inside. Drinking sodas, they congregated in the living room. Lindsey asked him, "How come you left Boston? If they had all those digs, how come you are coming to Bradbury's?"

"Er, I'm a Native American. I just didn't fit in at all well with those Bostonians. I found them awfully stuffy and picky. Snobby, really, like they were God's gift to mankind or something. I also got into a few too many fights, too," he admitted sheepishly. "They didn't like my hair either."

Ashley giggled. "Me too. I got into so many fights that I got kicked out of two different magic schools already."

"What? You? Little old you? Fights?" Andy asked, very impressed.

"Yes, I don't take anything from anyone, not even professors. I kicked our necromancy professor in his privates when he was giving me a hassle about learning those awful spells of his."

Lindsey vouched for her, "Yes, she had all sorts of bruises when she first came here. So you better watch yourself around Ashley. No monkey business, Andy." He grinned and promised that he would do no such thing.

Pam then made the mistake of asking him about archaeology. He began telling them all about it, for the next hour! However, he was so passionate about it that the girls sat there listening to him, until Jim and Tom finally interrupted them, asking him about becoming the goalkeeper.

A bit later, Andy asked them, "Say what do you all think of the trouble that is brewing in Arapahoe?"

"What trouble?" asked Pam, suddenly curious. Perhaps there was a mystery here to solve.

"Sandy hasn't taken you to see our house? She hasn't told you?" he asked incredulously. Even Amanda shook her head no.

"It's all this Dominus Manifesto bunk. You see, Arapahoe used to be a tiny town. Heck, it still is! Like there are four east west streets and four north south streets, but half of those don't go all the way through town. Population is only a hundred or so. It used to be nothing but a train grain elevator stop, back in the old days. My dad, he runs the grain elevator company there. It's been in our family three generations now, but I sure as heck am not going to take it over. Then, the government came and confiscated some mostly worthless rangeland just north of the town. All the irrigated farms lie to the south, well mostly so. They put the Apache reservation there, you see. That rather angered most folks, but then the real reason for doing that surfaced, the Tall Wolf Casino. Big gambler draw, it provides good, steady work for over half the town. Sandy works there."

"Anyway, these days it's a mess. Hot heads on the reservation think that they ought to control everything and have been causing no end of trouble, vandalism mostly. Half of the town thinks that the reservation should go, while the other half thinks it should stay. Hot heads think the town should go. It's like a three way battle that's going on. I think it is stupider than stupid to be fighting over *the* gas station, *the* hardware store, and *the* tiny grocery store. But then, they think I'm now an outsider, a Bostonian."

"Say, what are you all doing for fun around here?" Andy finished and then asked.

"Oh we get together for a formal dance every Saturday night," Amanda replied at once. "We also play a lot of Scrabble, listen to records, watch movies, and eat pizza. Want to join us, Andy?"

"Sure. Any time. I have my old Monopoly set if you want to play that too. That reminds me, I've been looking for a job, but there's nothing around here, excepting the casino, and I refuse to work for them."

"Maybe mom could use another hand in our fields," Lindsey suggested.

After lunch, she took Andy over to visit her mother and see about the chances for a job. Since he would work for minimum wages and knew about ranching, Lena gave him a part time job clearing the brush from the edges of the fields. The circular centers were irrigated. The former owner ignored the land outside these circles letting them grow wild. Lena had long range plans to alter the irrigation to make use of these areas. However, they needed to be cleaned up first.

For the next month, Andy rode his horse over around nine in the morning and worked until noon, clearing the brush. Of course, Lena insisted that he stay and have lunch with them as well.

At the next Saturday night dance, Andy showed up dressed in his soft suede suit, brown of course. He had his long hair tied back into a ponytail. Jim now danced almost exclusively with Ashley, who wore her beautiful, long, blue silk gown. Thus, Andy shyly asked Lindsey to dance. She loved the feel of his jacket, and he danced far better than Jim did, she noted. Although no one paid much attention, Andy always chose Lindsey as his dance partner after this. Of course, when Monique appeared and danced exclusively with Pam, Andy became very curious about the pair, though he said nothing. Lindsey caught him watching them several times.

On August 1, Audrey took Lena aside and said, "Mrs. Compton, if I were you, I would lay in a large store of food and fodder for the animals. I have a feeling that the winter will be bad this year." Lena knew enough not to pressure her for additional facts or for reasons why. Even if she had pressured her, Audrey wouldn't have been able to say much more. It was just those self-preservation premonitions Audrey occasionally had. By now, Lena knew enough to trust both Ashley and Audrey's future hunches. She agreed to stock up, and Audrey felt relieved.

Chapter 3—Back to School

At last, the last week of August came. For days, Lindsey and Ashley worked on packing their things, deciding just what they should take back to school with them. Always before, this was extraordinarily easy for Ashley. If she took everything, it fit in one duffle bag, mostly her old school books. Now, she had dresses and so many new things that she needed three duffle bags. At first she was petrified over how she could carry so many bags—one was challenging enough. However, Lindsey, who took five back with her, explained that she couldn't carry all of hers either and that the Floor Monitors would transport them for the students.

As with last year, because of the heightened security, Audrey and Pam would be returning on Friday not the following Monday. Hence, the girls spent considerable time saying their farewells. They would be apart for nearly a whole week, while Lindsey performed her Floor Monitoring duties. Having said their goodbyes and with many hugs and kisses, the two girls waited on the front porch for the bus to arrive. Of course, Pam and Audrey waited there with them, if only to chat a while longer. At last, the yellow bus appeared before the porch, preceded the familiar popping sound.

The four security men hopped off first, followed by Jimmy. Conveniently, the men took the many duffle bags to the bus for the girls, but only after first checking to be sure that the girls were in fact who they were supposed to be. Ashley was very annoyed at being challenged, though Lindsey calmed her down by explaining the need for this extra security. After all, it was herself that Dominus had magically become during her first year at Bradbury's.

Jimmy was his old self, "Pleased 'o mee' you again, Miss Lindsey and Miss Ashley. I'm Jimmy, in case you forgo'. Climb onboard, only 'hree on board so far."

"Thanks, Jimmy," Lindsey replied. "Say when are you going to get your teeth fixed anyway?" Jimmy merely smiled back at her.

As they climbed on the bus, they spied Tom, Sandy, and Andy sitting at the back of the bus. Sandy waved, and the two hurriedly walked to the back to join them. "Don't forget to put your seat belts on," Sandy reminded Lindsey. Then, she showed Lindsey her clipboard, showing the names of those they were to pick up along the way. She had placed a checkmark beside their five names.

Tom was about to offer Ashley a hand fastening her belt, but correctly hesitated. She slipped off her shoes and awkwardly used her feet to get the job done. Tom rightly concluded that she had done this several times before. The bus began moving but stopped almost at once in the nearby town of Cheyenne Wells, where a first year boy climbed onboard. Sandy greeted the Brown Hall student and helped him get situated. In Colorado Springs, ten more boarded. Lindsey lent a hand with these.

Another twelve got on board in Pueblo, including Emilio's brother, Francesco Lopez, the Brown Hall Floor Monitor. Six were added from Canyon City, while five more were added at Colorado City, just south of Pueblo. Two more joined them from Monte Vista. Then, the long haul began in earnest. The southern route bus would pick up others from the Durango area.

They shot along US 160, while Ashley enjoyed the magnificent scenery flying by the windows. She had never seen the mountains before. However, she was not impressed with the magical bus flying through the heavy traffic of Durango. She had seen far worse traffic in Chicago and the Twin Cities. At Cortez, they took the state route 145 up towards Telluride. Ashley stared at the magnificent mountains, so close that you could almost touch them—her words.

Lindsey, Sandy, and Tom, began to worry. It was along this nearly deserted road that their bus had been attacked twice now. Lindsey prayed that nothing would happen today! Up the San Juan Highway they flew. Finally, the Ophir Loop came and went, and Lindsey relaxed. All the likely ambush locations were past them. Bradbury's was nearby. A few minutes later the bus pulled into the parking lot of Arthur Bradbury's School of Magic, with many of the first year students oohing and ahing.

"Okay, first thing, when you get off the bus, congregate around your Floor Monitors," Sandy announced.

Andy whispered to Ashley, "Congregate around Miss Lindsey, shall we?" She grinned. Only two years ago, Ashley, too, was a first year, very frightened of what she had gotten into by accepting the scholarship. Now, she was still a bit nervous. This was a new school, and one that she knew she should be attending, if only she didn't blow her chances, as she had done at Chicago and the Twin Cities.

"Let's let them get off first, shall we? Less hassles for us," Lindsey suggested. Watching the nervous boys and girls, she whispered, "Gosh, I remember when I was just like them, only more so. I had no hands. I was terrified. Always before if things got bad, I could run the mile from my school in Plano back home. Here, I had no idea even where I was at, dependent on others for nearly everything. I was anything but independent, Ashley, scared and frightened. That seems so long ago now."

"If the others wouldn't stare at me so," Ashley admitted to Lindsey, though she didn't finish her sentence. Both Lindsey and Andy knew what she meant.

Andy whispered, "Ashley, when you see boys looking at you, they are really thinking what a gorgeous young woman you are. That's true, by the way." She blushed, but said nothing.

Finally, the pile of first years entered the gates, led by their Floor Monitors. The three finally exited the bus. Jimmy had piled their bags neatly for them. Lindsey looked at her papers, "Let's see, we are in room eight this year." Using her new spell, she moved her bags there first, followed by Ashley's bags. "You are in room eight too, boys side, not girls side," she added, flushing for a moment. She moved his bags there for him. "You are supposed to say thanks, now," Lindsey teased them.

"Now, I'm supposed to give you a short tour as we head for the dorms. This is the only entrance gate, for students. It is enchanted so that only students may pass. Notice that there is a high stone wall entirely surrounding the campus, also designed to keep non-students out. The campus is in the shape of an enormous pentagram; we're standing at the southeastern corner. This is the Admin Hall, where Governor Alister has his office and the computer system is located. There is a trophy display room in there as well, where our new trophies are on display. Follow me."

A little ways beyond that building, she pointed out, "This is the Infirmary. On beyond it at the southwestern corner is the Hall of Necromancy. Our dorms lie in the dead center. Follow me. Here is the swimming pool, but there are some others located underground so we can swim in the wintertime." She continued to describe the buildings as they appeared. Soon, however, they reached the tall dorm, which also was in the shape of a pentagram.

"Black Hall is the bottom section. Yellow Hall is at the northwestern corner. You can enter any of the entrances, signs point out the directions to all the halls. Of course, there are lots of shortcuts, but first, let's get you used to our hall and work from there." She led them to the first floor of Yellow Hall.

"Here is our commons room; back here is our study room, where most of us meet at night to help each other out. Actually, any student is allowed in here. Audrey of Brown Hall is always studying with us and sometimes Monique of Red Hall comes here to visit with Pam. Now then, see those doors that indicate the restrooms? They are in the basement. Only boys can enter the boy's restrooms, while only we girls can enter the girl's. If you try to enter the wrong one, an alarm sounds; it's very embarrassing. The same stairs lead up to our rooms. Again, only the guys are allowed into their section and the same with us girls."

"Now hang on a second, while I look at the rest of this for you, Andy." She flipped the paper over, "Hey, cool! You are in room eight as I said. One of your roommates is Emilio Lopez. That's really going to be convenient! Okay, so let's go to our rooms, unpack, and visit the restrooms. Although I can't go with you, if you run into trouble, you can Message me or Message Tom. If it is a guy thing, try Tom first." Andy chuckled.

"When you are all settled in and have checked out the

restrooms, Message me, and we three will meet here in the commons for the next step. I want to beat the rush on the Bookstore, if possible." Lindsey led Ashley up the steps to the second floor.

"Oh, I nearly forgot to tell you, Ashley. Governor Alister says that all the doors that have knobs on them have been adjusted to open when you say, 'Door: Open.' I think it's a spell he put on them for you. That way, you can more quickly move around. Is that acceptable to you?"

"Well, actually, yes. I got tired of trying to open doors by myself. I can do it, only it takes a long time and is a lot of trouble. I have to sit down, take my shoes off, and open them with my feet. Then, I have to keep it open while standing back up. Sometimes that is embarrassing, and I would often wait until someone else opened a door, pretending to be arriving just in time. I'm ready to accept this assistance, I guess," she admitted.

"Cool Ashley, because with us, you don't have to prove anything! Come on. Let's find our room. When I was first here, this room was ours. Now we are all the way down to room eight. We were in number six last year. Here's ours. Want to try the open spell? Let's see if it works."

Ashley whispered, "Door: Open." It did as instructed, "Excellent, I don't have to yell it out. That would be so embarrassing that I think I would sit down and open it myself. Oh, this is a really elegant room!" She stepped inside. To Lindsey, it looked just like the other two rooms she had had. Their many bags were sitting on the floor, neatly arranged. "Which bed is mine? I don't want to take Amanda's or Pam's or yours, Lindsey."

"Well, I always like this one by the left of the windows. Pam likes the one on the far side. Amanda has always been in the one next to me. She used to help me with everything when I had no hands, you see. Ever since then, we've always bunked side by side. So that leaves that one for you. Is that one okay with you?"

Ashley said it was and promptly bounced upon the bed. "Gosh, this is super luxury! Wow! Incredible. The other two schools were nothing like this!"

"Cool. This is your dresser, table, chair, and mirror. Let's unpack, unless you need to use the restroom." The two began unpacking their things. Lindsey made sure that Ashley could manage the drawers herself, which she did. She marveled at how efficiently she unpacked her clothes, carefully placing them into her drawers, while seated in front of the dresser. Her feet were indeed her hands. After placing her laptop on her table and plugging in the power supply, she was finished.

"Now, let's check out the restrooms, shall we?" Lindsey led her down the stairs to the basement. Ashley was shocked at the incredible luxury before her. Many showers, baths, power jets—every imaginable luxury was here for her use.

"This is utter heaven!" Ashley repeatedly commented. Lindsey wondered just what these other schools must be like. Just then, Andy Messaged her that he was done and was waiting for them in the commons. The two used the facilities and then headed off to rendezvous with Andy.

"Hey, are your bathrooms as incredible as ours?" Andy asked, but then realized that she had no way to answer that one. "This place is three times fancier than Boston. I like it already."

"Me too. It is ten times better than Chicago, which is a slum compared to this place," Ashley added.

"Oh rats! I forgot. We have to go visit with Professor Cho Lin to work out your elective before we can go to the Bookstore. Ah well, we might have to put up with all the first years after all. Come on; let's go by the dining room and courtyard on our way to the Hall of Illusion, where her office is located.

"Well, the dining room layout is the same as Boston," Andy remarked as they entered.

"Yes, same as the Twin Cities and Chicago," Ashley added.

"It is self-serve buffet style here during orientation week, until Friday night, when everyone is here. Saturday and Sunday mornings and afternoons, it is also self-serve. Obviously, these are the Yellow Hall tables," she pointed out the long tables with the yellow tablecloths. She led them out the doors into the courtyard, where many potted plants grew. "Sometimes we eat out here during nicer weather. There is our dorm on our right." Next, she led them outside and both saw the huge stadium, just north of the dorms.

Lindsey led them across the grass to the Hall of Illusions, which marked the eastern most corner of the pentagram of buildings. She marched them up to the second floor office of Professor Cho Lin and knocked.

Cho Lin opened the door and said, "Welcome back Lindsey. Good to see you again. Ah, these must be our new third year Yellow Hall students. Miss Ashley Stokes?"

"Yes professor," Ashley replied timidly.

Cho Lin wore her Chinese print, long yellow silk dress. She had long black hair and deep blue eyes. At once, she opened her arms wide, indicating a hug for Ashley, who allowed her welcome and then added her leg to it. "Golly, Alister did not say that you were gorgeous, Ashley. Let me be the first to welcome you officially to our school of magic. We are all honored to have you. I'm your Hall Counselor. If there is ever anything that you need, any questions you might have, any problems, why, just come and see me. Acceptable?" Ashley nodded.

"And you must be Sandy's brother, Andy, right?" She shook Andy's hand firmly. "Welcome to Bradbury's School of Magic. I hope you find us superior to Boston. That's a joke, by the way. Come on in. I was having a cup of tea. Would you care to join me?"

"Well, I wanted to get their electives sorted out so that we could beat the rush at the Bookstore, but it looks like we won't. You two mind if we have some tea?" Lindsey asked.

Cho Lin poured them each a cup, using her fine china cups. She watched as Ashley used her legs and feet to take a sip. "Now then, electives. Normally, I discuss these with each student privately. However, we could save time and just discuss it here, unless you would feel far more comfortable with a private conversation."

"It's fine with me," Andy volunteered. Ashley agreed.

"Well, then, who wants to be first?" Again, Andy volunteered.

"I'm into archaeology and that's why I went to Boston. I got to go on two summertime digs with the professors. I was hoping that there might be some archaeology elective I might take," Andy said, half expecting a "no."

"Well, actually our resident doctor has a minor in archaeology. Of course, no one would believe that a medical man would be so inclined. I've checked with him, and I can tell you that he is elated to have you as a student. So yes, you can take Archaeology as an elective with him. Actually, according to Doctor Frank Caterwall, you should plan to take this as an elective each year, if you wish to gain the fullest background in the subject."

"Wow! Incredible. Terrific! I'll do it!" Andy replied, nearly jumping out of his seat. "I never expected this." Cho Lin smiled.

"Now then, Ashley, what did you have in mind? Governor Alister has made a suggestion if you are unsure of what to take. I told him that you might need a Study Hall to keep up with the heavy study load here."

"A Study Hall is a complete waste of my time," Ashley said didactically. However, she was very curious about just what this Governor Alister would be suggesting for her to take. Ashley just had to know, thinking that it might yield a clue as to how she was being seen around here—Special Needs student and all that that connoted. "Can I ask what Governor Alister suggested that I take?" she asked timidly. She found that asking timidly often got others to do what she desired.

"Of course, he suggests that you take Divination Theory I from Professor Mary Ann Thornby. How does that sound to you?"

Ashley's mouth fell open. She was not expecting this course of study. "There is such a course?" she finally managed to say.

"Yes, there most certainly is. However, it has not been taught to a single student here at Bradbury's School of Magic since Mabel Pruit took it, darn near twenty years ago. Professor Mary Ann would dearly love to teach you, Ashley. How does that sound to you?"

"I keep doing it, you know, predicting things that are

true. I've gotten into a lot of trouble doing it, though recently I've been saving lives, I think. It would be wise of me to learn all I can about it, don't you think?"

"Yes, Ashley I most certainly do. I think that is a very wise decision on your part. Then, that's settled. I'll enter those courses into your schedules immediately. Won't take but a minute." She waved her wand and shortly two papers floated down and landed on the table before the two students, such that they could easily read them. "A copy has also been sent to your email addresses as well."

Lindsey looked over their shoulders, very curious to see their schedules. "Hey, they look the same as ours," she commented.

"Of course they are, excepting the electives, of course," Cho Lin replied with a smile.

"Oh yes, do you all have your signed notices from your parents or guardians so that you may be allowed visits to Telluride this year?" she asked.

Andy handed over his. It was crumpled up in his pocket. Lindsey produced hers and Ashley's from her pocket. Theirs were neatly folded. She added, "Mom signed for Ashley, you see, we are adopting Ashley. By Christmas, I hope to officially have a sister!"

"You're kidding?" Cho Lin asked, quite surprised.

"Nope. Dad already has sent in several of the forms, and we have been granted foster parents rights, until the adoption is finally approved."

"Well, congratulations to both of you. This is wonderful news indeed! I've been assailed with bad news all summer long. It is so nice to hear such wonderful news for a change. Yes, Lena's signature will do just fine. Wait until Alister hears about this! That willy old fox. He said that obtaining Ashley Stokes as a student here at Bradbury's was the coup of the century, that those other schools had no idea of what they had with Ashley. Amazing, simply amazing."

"You mean that Governor Alister knew that Ashley has great talent as a Diviner?" asked Lindsey.

"Yes, but how he ascertained that from her school records is beyond me. I saw the very same records, since she was Yellow Hall. I guess that's why he's the Governor and I'm only a professor," Cho Lin admitted. For the first time in her life, Ashley felt somehow special, not because of her lack of arms, but for her unique abilities. She radiated pure joy.

"Well, I've kept you long enough. May I suggest that you go visit the House Mother to obtain their computers and cell phones first? By the time that cycle is done, the lines in the Bookstore ought to have diminished somewhat."

After thanking her, the three left. On their way back to Yellow Hall, Andy continually chatted about how lucky he was to get four archaeology courses, while Ashley chatted about having a chance to learn what she was doing with all her foresight of things. Lindsey merely wondered how Alister had figured out that Ashley was really a fledgling Diviner and had somehow gotten her to his school.

The three climbed the steps to the penthouse located at the very top of Yellow Hall. Here lived the House Parents, who really handled the domestic duties of so many students. Lindsey recalled having met her only once, when as a first year student, she had gotten her laptop and cell phone from them. As they entered, Lindsey saw a matronly woman, whose hair was tied back in a tight brown bun, and her husband, a tall, just as stern looking man. Both were in their forties.

"I am your Hall Mother for you girls, Ann Bitterroot. You are to call me Hall Mother, got it? Now, then, my husband Fred handles the boys for your Hall." She spoke with a commanding and stern voice. Lindsey thought that she would tolerate absolutely no nonsense at all.

"Now then, if you have any problems, worries, concerns, anything at all, you are to come and see me. I live here in the penthouse suite just above your floor."

"First, the School Rules. No students are every allowed on the campus grounds after midnight, ever. No excuses allowed. Instant detention. Second, all first and second year students must be in their own Halls at ten o'clock every night. I guess that you need not worry about this rule now. For you older students, curfew is midnight, no exceptions. Third, no boys are ever allowed in the girl's quarters and vice versa. Instant detention for both parties."

"Fourth, unless you have a written pass from the Hall Parent, no student is ever allowed to venture beyond the stone walls of Bradbury's, nor are they allowed onto the mountain to the east."

"Why all these severe rules? We are totally responsible for your safety while you are here at Bradbury's School of Magic. We want you to have a safe environment in which to learn. All of us Hall Parents, as well as all the faculty and staff here at Bradbury's, take this responsibility for your safety quite seriously, especially in light of all the nasty business that has been going on here these last two years."

Fred took Andy aside and gave him his new laptop and a fancy cell phone. Meanwhile, Ann said, "I see that Alister has already sent you your new laptop, Ashley. We need to get you a new cell phone. Now, as a Special Needs student, honestly, Ashley, I just don't see how I can help you with the phone. Now with Lindsey here, she could push a button, so I rigged a number of phone numbers that could be dialed simply by pushing the speed dial button. Perhaps with a stick held in your mouth you could push a button."

Ashley's face grimaced, as anger swelled within her. Ordinarily, she would be lashing out at this ignorant woman about now. Lindsey sensed this and immediately interceded, "Ashley does everything that we do with our hands, only she uses her feet. I believe that the best thing is to program my mother on speed dial number one. You see, we are in the middle of adopting her so she will soon be my sister, and anyway, mom is now her temporary guardian. When we get back to our room, I will show her all the fancy features and fix up the other speed dial buttons for her." Lindsey held out her hand to take the cell phone from Ann, alleviating yet another potential awkward moment for the two.

"Oh, I didn't know. Now that is so generous of your mother and father. Ashley, please accept my heartfelt best wishes!" Ann completely forgot about the cell phone, mechanically handing it to Lindsey. Ann felt very ill at ease around Ashley. She was unsure how to handle this Special Needs student.

"Thanks, House Mother. We'd better be going now. I

have to take them to the Bookstore to get their books and supplies," Lindsey added, nudging Ashley towards the door. Andy, carrying his new computer and phone, saw how angry Ashley had become and quickly opened the door for the two girls.

Once outside, Lindsey complimented Ashley, "Well done, you didn't kick her."

"Well, I was just about to do just that when you spoke up. I, I'm glad that you did. I love it here, so far anyway, and I don't want to get kicked out so soon," she admitted.

Andy soothed the waters a bit, "Look, she just feels horribly uncomfortable around you, that's all, Ashley. She probably has never seen anyone like you. Since she is supposed to be helping you out, she probably feels terribly upset that she has no idea of your real needs." Lindsey was grateful for his attempt, and Ashley calmed down.

"Well, I like the speed dial feature, it is easier to push one button than seven," Ashley admitted. "Does it really take pictures like she said?"

"Absolutely. When Pam gets here, she will fix up your computer so that you or anyone else can somehow phone your pictures to your computer. I don't have a clue how to set these things up to do that. We just have to wait on Pam."

A short while later, they entered the Bookstore. However, unlike the first year students, they only needed to get their new books and a few supplies. Lindsey showed them where they could receive any mail, normal or magical, and where they could cash a check. A while later, using her new spell, Lindsey whisked their new, large pile of books to each one's bedroom.

On their way back to the dorms, Lindsey explained, "Supper is at five, about a half hour from now. It will be the meet the teacher's night for the first year students. That means it will be a formal dinner, not the self-serve most other nights until school starts. We should probably go change into our school clothes and meet at the Yellow Hall tables around five, okay?"

Back in their room, Ashley wiggled out of her pants and allowed Lindsey to help her with the school skirt. Fortunately,

Lena had made her a matching blouse done in her special style, where there was no hint of armholes or sleeves. Ashley had fallen in love with this new look that Lena had devised for her. Besides, the dangling armless sleeves of her other school blouses kept getting in the way. Finally, the two headed down to the dining hall. Andy was already there and had joined his sister, Sandy, and Tom. Ashley and Lindsey joined them.

Soon well over a hundred first year students, their Floor Monitors, and the Hall Mothers and Hall Fathers gathered at the five different colored tables. All eyes started at the long table at the head of the dining room.

Sixteen adults sat at the professor's table, discussing things among themselves. All student eyes focused on the man in the middle, the oddly dressed man in his fifties. Lindsey whispered to Andy and Ashley that this was Governor Alister Broadwell. While everyone else wore their wizard robes, he was dressed in an out of style, by several hundred years, black business suit complete with a top hat that a norm magician might use to pull a hare out of a hat.

Lindsey had grown to love his kindly look, with his black moustache and goatee beard and long sideburns. At last, he rose, and a complete silence fell in the dining room. Alister spoke clearly and slowly, as if each word held some kind of magical power behind it. Lindsey realized it was nearly the same speech she had heard during her first year here.

"Fellow professors, Hall Mothers and Fathers, Floor Monitors, and first year students, welcome to Orientation Week at Arthur Bradbury's School of Magic. I'm the Governor, that's head man to you students. . ." That last was a sort of joke and the many adults present chuckled.

"I'm Governor Alister Broadwell, and it's my pleasure to welcome yet another class of first year students to Bradbury's, even if it is in these most difficult times. You must forgive my appearance. I have just come from an important meeting with the Department of Defense. It seems Dominus Malefic has given everyone the willies." Again, many adults chuckled, Lindsey thought it must be a joke or pun, but didn't understand it.

"I assure you all that you are all going to be quite safe

here at Bradbury's. I know you have heard we were the target of several bombings last year, but I point out that not a single student suffered any permanent damage."

He grinned broadly and said, "Now Professor Elaine Mac Elroy, your English and Literature teacher, has accused me of not being romantic enough, so I dressed for this occasion. How is this, Elaine?" He looked at one of the older teachers, who grinned back and shook her greying head at him. "Oh, you mean I'm several centuries off?" Now the whole group of teachers chuckled. Even Lindsey smiled; he did look terribly old-fashioned, but it was the same joke he had played two years ago when she was first here.

"Ah, then how's this?" He waved his hand and in a flash, he was wearing his wizard robes, looking much like the other teachers.

Alister continued, "Ah, still not romantic enough for the professor, so try this." He waved his hand and thousands of small candles burst into flames high over the heads of everyone, while the normal lights turned off. The room took on a distinctive yellowish glow, a warm glow at that. Several students cheered and broke out into a clap.

"Allow me to introduce our faculty to you," Alister continued. "Starting here on my right is Professor Blake Smith, Conjuring-Summoning. Girls, you have no doubt noticed just how handsome Professor Blake is, but unfortunately he is married to Professor Janice Smith, sitting next to him. She is your Charm-Enchantment teacher. She also will be teaching you your Grade 0 and 1 level spells this year. She is also in charge of the Red Hall." Lindsey looked at her; she continued to present the appearance of a glamor queen or model. However, her smile appeared forced or faked.

"Next to her is Professor Jerry Thalmus, Abjuration. He also will be your History of Magic teacher and is the head of Blue Hall." He looked to be around fifty years old and was quite bored with this whole meeting. "Next to him is Professor Mary Ann Thornby, Divination." Her hair flew off in all directions, as if she'd just had an electric shock or something. She seemed very nervous. Lindsey could see her trembling slightly, which she now knew was normal.

"Next to her is Professor Delius Dogs, Necromancy and head of Black Hall." He had a dark complexion and an antagonistic stare. However, he received a round of applause from the twenty-some, Black Hall, first year students. He managed a smile. "Next to him is Professor Arthur Thornby, Alteration, and head of Brown Hall." Several Brown Hall students clapped for him, but again Lindsey wondered why he was not sitting beside his wife.

"Now on my left is Professor Huan Su Sung, Invocation-Evocation, and beside him is Professor Cho Lin Sung, Illusions and head of Yellow Hall." Not to be outdone, those around the Yellow Hall including Lindsey began loudly clapping. Cho Lin looked directly at Lindsey for a moment and smiled.

"Next to her is Professor Herbert Mac Elroy, your Math teacher. Students take note; he is not a wizard. He will tolerate no monkey business in his classroom. Next to him is Professor Elaine Mac Elroy, English-Literature; she is a witch, mind you." Several on the staff chuckled, but Lindsey wondered what was funny. She still did not know that answer.

"Next to her is Professor Jasper Jones, Science. He is also not a wizard. Let me warn you all. Do not call either Professor Jones or Mac Elroy a norm or you will find yourself in detention." This was a stern warning.

"Next to him is our Librarian, Lillian Angel Jones, who will assist you in finding your research and study materials. She would like me to remind you that the library closes at ten p.m. Next to her is Doctor Frank Caterwall, our resident physician. Let us hope that none of you need to visit him this term." He grinned and many chuckled, for who wanted to see a doctor? Andy now did, but for an entirely different reason: archaeology.

"Finally, at the far end are Hank and Betsy Walls, your PE teachers. First years," Alister winked at them and leaned forward as if he was letting them in on a secret, "let me warn you in advance, those two are fitness freaks! They are even trying to get me to lose some weight!" At that, the staff all chuckled.

"You see, Bradbury's has a very wide and talented set of professors, perhaps one of the best in the United States. I suspect that is because we are in the Rocky Mountains. After all, isn't this the vacation spot of the country?" Everyone chuckled. Even Lindsey knew that Colorado had huge revenues each year from tourism. In the wintertime, people flocked to the many ski slopes.

"Now let the feast begin." He waved his hands and piles of food suddenly appeared on the tables before the students and teachers. Everyone began picking dishes and eating, though many stared at Ashley, to see how she would manage. Purposely, Lindsey took no note of Ashley's unusual methods of eating with her feet. Likewise, Andy, Tom, and Sandy followed suit. Ashley noticed this subtlety as well. She grit her teeth and endured their stares. After all, this would be the third year in a row that hundreds would be staring at her every move at meal times. Ashley took some comfort, remembering that after about two weeks at the other two schools, no one bothered to watch her any longer.

When they finished eating, Lindsey asked, "Well, do you want to take the grand tour yet this evening or wait until first thing in the morning?"

"Hey, let's do it now," Andy replied. "Are you up for it, Ashley?" She was eager to see the entire campus as well. Lindsey gave them each their detailed map, though Ashley only put it into her dress pocket.

Outside their dorm at the north point of the pentagram building, Lindsey pointed out, "To our right is the Bookstore that we went to a while ago. If you need any supplies, clothes, or such, just go there and ask. Due north of us is the Stadium. Our PE classes will meet at the Stadium. Due west of us is the library. It looks small, but it is huge inside, magical expansion. Due south of us is the swimming pool."

Lindsey led them around the Stadium to the northern point of the Bradbury pentagram of buildings. "Here is the Math and Science Hall. Our first two classes, chemistry and algebra II, are in this building. Math classrooms are on the third floor and the others are for science classes." This building looked just like any normal college science building, lots of steel and glass windows, rather modern looking.

She led them southwestward to the next building. "This

is the Hall of Alteration Magic. As you can see, this building continually changes its appearance each day. Yesterday, someone said it looked like a castle, but today I'd say it looks like a rocket ship or something. Cool building to look at, anyway." She led them on southwestward to the next building in the line, which marked one of the five corners.

"This is the Hall of Illusion Magic. Each day, it changes its color scheme." The building looked like a grand old mansion, today constructed of red-brown bricks. Ivy grew up one side of it. She led them along the southeast line to the next building.

"Here is the Humanities Hall. Here is where we have our English and US history classes." Lindsey thought that this stately building looked like an English manor house. Ivy completely covered all sides of the building. She walked them further along this southeast line to the next building.

"Here is the Hall of Invocation-Evocation Magic. It looks like a dragon, so you can't mistake this building." Indeed, the main entrance was through the dragon's gaping mouth. "Here is where we begin learning our Grade 4 spells and have evocation theory class."

Lindsey led them on southeast. "Here is the bottom east corner of the pentagram of buildings, the Administration Hall. This way. Here is the Infirmary building. I guess your archaeology elective will be in here, Andy. Yes, it looks like a norm hospital. Now let's continue going east to the bottom east corner building." The two followed her.

They all disliked this next one. "This is the Hall of Necromancy, the dark arts." The building was entirely black. Stone serpents climbed up the walls on either side of the doors. Human skeletons were carved into the stone walls at periodic intervals. Lindsey commented that it gave her the creeps.

She hurried them on northeastward. "Here is the Hall of Divination Magic. Kind of a strange looking building isn't it? It's supposed to be a crystal ball sitting in the ground." Indeed, a giant translucent sphere rose from the ground. Ashley, your elective class will be in here."

From here, she led them on northeastward to the next

building. "This is the Hall of Abjuration. It always looks like a miniature castle. Now let me point out the Dark Woods. See this dense patch of woods here? It stretches from here all the way to the mountainside and all the way down to the outer ramparts wall that surrounds Bradbury. First years are not allowed to go into the woods without a professor with them. It is dangerous, primarily because wild animals sometimes come down from the mountains around us, but we can take care of ourselves now."

"Now from here on northward and all the way to the eastern ramparts wall are the Formal Gardens. They are fabulous. One path is called Lover's Lane. I'll show you after bit." She then led them to the easternmost corner building.

This is the Hall of Charm and Enchantment Magic. I know that it looks like a small English cottage, but that is only its enchantment. Inside, it is large. You will soon see what I mean. Okay, only one more building to go. This way." She led them northwest.

"Here is the Hall of Conjuring and Summoning." The building resembled a Greek building with many marble columns and arches. Part was out in the open, part was enclosed. She explained, "If you summon something, it has to have someplace to stand, so hence the big open areas." She led them back to the Math and Science Hall.

"On nice days like today, most of us walk to and from our classes, just like we are doing now. However, when it rains or snows, we all go a different way," she added rather spookily, remembering how Sandy had done it.

She led them into the entrance doors of the Math and Science building. "Now let's go down the stairs," a teasing note in her voice. Soon the stairs opened into a long tunnel deep underground. Five could walk abreast in here. Periodic lamps provided good illumination, however.

"You see, there is a vast tunnel network connecting all the buildings on campus. When it is cold out or deep snow, we all go from place to place following the tunnels. Notice that at each entrance point, the signs are clearly marked." Lindsey pointed out one direction arrow, which said "To Hall of Charm and Summoning," while another directional arrow said "To

Hall of Alteration." A third tunnel arrow said, "To Stadium and Dorms."

Lindsey explained further. "The outer line of tunnels goes from building to building in a giant pentagram of tunnels. However, there are numerous cross tunnels—the shortcuts, as we call them. Here is the shortcut tunnel that leads to the Stadium and then to our dorms. Let's say that you are here in the Math Hall and you need to get to, oh the Infirmary. You could walk the long way around either side of the giant perimeter pentagram tunnels. However, if you take the shortcut tunnels, here to the Stadium and the dorms, and then the tunnel from the dorms south to the Infirmary, you can cut the walking distance nearly in half."

"Be careful, you can also get yourself messed up down here. Let's say you are here at the Math Hall and need to get to the Charm-Summoning Hall. The shortest way is along the outer perimeter tunnel. Just follow that sign there. It leads directly to it. However, you could walk on down the shortcut to our dorms in the middle of the entire campus and then take the shortcut tunnel from there, which leads to the Charm Hall. If you went that route, you would walk nearly four times the distance you needed to go!"

"Now follow me. We are going to the most confusing location on campus: the tunnel hub underneath our dorm!" Part way along the tunnel, a sign pointed to a side stairs that led up to the Stadium. At last, they reached the huge hub below the dorm pentagram building.

"Wow!" exclaimed Ashley. Andy echoed her sentiments.

They stood in an underground room nearly as large as their dining hall above them. All around the perimeter of the room shortcut tunnels sprang, all twelve of them were clearly labeled. Hence, one could not get too lost down here. "See, in bad weather, you just go down here and find the right tunnel and off you go. Only problem is that there's going to be six hundred of us coming down here at the same time. It gets to be a big mess at certain times of the day, as you can imagine," Lindsey stated from her two years of experience.

"I will say this," Ashley finally spoke up. "Bradbury's has the coolest looking buildings and campus that I have ever seen!"

"Yes, Boston is nothing compared to this place," Andy added. "Are you going to walk us through a day of classes?"

"You bet, we'll do it above ground first and then pretend it is wintertime and do it using the tunnels. Actually, we can do it as many times as you want. We've got scads of time on our hands," Lindsey explained.

"Can we do it tomorrow? I'm exhausted," Ashley asked. A bit later, the three sat around the commons, chatting. Andy decided to get his things organized and gave them a good night hug, which surprised both girls, who also headed up to their room afterwards.

"Andy's rather nice, don't you think?" Ashley said when the two were in their room. "I've seldom allowed anyone to hug me before, but since I came to your house, everyone's doing it to me."

"It's your lovable personality," Lindsey teased. Ashley whipped out her wand and sent a pillow flying at Lindsey. Soon, a pillow fight erupted between the two girls.

"That's no fair, you are not using your wand, and I have to," Ashley finally stopped and complained. The two hugged.

"You know. I wonder if you could learn how to cast some spells non-verbally and without your wand? Honestly, if you could, that would really be darn convenient for you," Lindsey speculated.

"Sure would be, but I don't know how. I guess I had better get things better organized." The two began sorting out their books and arranging their section of the room. Lindsey already missed Pam and Amanda and promptly sent them emails telling about how the day went.

The next morning, the three met in the dining room for breakfast, self-serve style. They had arisen early, and only a few first years were here. Ashley felt more relaxed as a result. "Hey, I have an idea, Ashley. Why don't I cast Levitate on your tray, doing it non-verbally, no wand. Then, you can just push it over to the table. It will draw less attention, don't you think?"

"Hey, that's a cool idea. I do wish that I could learn to do some spells that way." The two experimented with the tray, and Ashley soon got the hang of merely pushing her tray about. Over breakfast, Lindsey produced a copy of their daily class schedules.

```
 8:00 Chemistry
 9:00 Algebra II
10:00 English/US History
11:00 Physical Education
12:00 lunch hour
 1:00 Spell Casting—Grade 4
 2:00 Evocation Theory I
 3:00 Illusion Theory I
 4:00 Study Hall/Elective
 5:00 Dinner
```

Lindsey, Andy, and Ashley spent the entire morning going through their schedule of classes, walking from room to room. After doing it twice from above ground, Lindsey had them do it three more times using the tunnels. "Now, it's solo time. We are at the dorms. I want each of you to walk through your whole schedule by yourselves. Andy, you go first; we'll give you a five-minute head start. If you run into trouble, just Message me. Ashley, I will go Invisible and tag along somewhere behind you, just in case any trouble arises. After all, that is part of my responsibilities this week. That way, for all practical purposes you are on your own. I will only intervene if you call out for help. Is that okay with you?"

"Actually, Lindsey, I appreciate it. It is always a bit daunting to find myself alone on a new campus. This way, it will look like I am, but I'll know you are around if I get confused or something. Thanks for suggesting it. I guess I'd better start; it's been at least five minutes." Lindsey watched her as she began walking north toward the math and science hall. Silently, she cast her spell and trailed along behind Ashley.

Indeed, it was a bit of a challenge for her. Once she arrived at the building, she had several doors to manage. Since no one was around, she had to sit down, take off her shoes, and open the door, completely refusing to try the Open: Door spell. Next, while keeping it open, she had to get her shoes back on and get to her feet to continue. Inwardly, she felt grateful that Lindsey and the others, her close friends, would be traveling from class to class together. She could avoid this bit of awkwardness, at least until it was elective time. Then, she would have to deal with the Hall of Divination doors herself. If all else failed, she would use the Open: Door spell.

When they all arrived back at the dorm, Lindsey had them repeat the whole thing. This time, they had to use the tunnels exclusively. Now there were even more doors for Ashley to navigate, plus she ran into several first year students making their way around the campus, just as she. Some of these opened doors for her. They were impressed that she was really a third year student. Ashley felt a surge of pride when they uttered their exclamations of surprise.

After this trip to their classes finished, it was time for lunch. Lindsey gave them both a pass on finding their way around campus. After lunch, she took the three for a long walk through the formal gardens, one of Audrey's favorite places on the campus. Not interested in the gardens, Andy took his leave of the girls. The two finally sat down on a bench overlooking a bed of magnolias.

For a time, the two merely sat and reflected. Then, Ashley asked, "I'd like to learn how to cast spells like you do, Lindsey. Do you suppose that I could learn to cast non-verbally and without my wand? I heard that in our sixth year we are encouraged to try, but hardly anyone can."

"Well, we have almost nothing to do for the next three days so why don't we try?" Lindsey said encouragingly. "We should pick the simplest ones first. Let's start with Clean, shall we?" She used her foot to spread a little compose from the flowerbed onto the paving stones at their feet. "First, use your wand to cast the Clean spell and observe how you are doing it."

Ashley said, "Wand to Me," catching it with her toes of her right foot. "Clean," she stated as she made the proper wand motion. The compost vanished.

Lindsey put more back and said, "Now concentrate really hard, wave your wand, but don't say the words, think them." After a number of tries, Ashley again vanished the compost. After an exuberant outburst at her success, they continued doing it many more times. Finally, Lindsey had her attempt it without using the wand. Again, it took a lot of coaching on Lindsey's part but finally the compost vanished. Ashley had cast her first spell non-verbally and without a wand! She was so excited that she danced around the garden for several minutes.

For another half hour, Lindsey kept her at it, until both were confident that Ashley could do it when she desired. Armed with success, Lindsey next had her working on tying and untying shoestrings, dress sashes, and similar small things. By suppertime, Ashley now could cast three spells in this manner. They raced off to the dining room to tell Andy, who had Messaged them that he was heading down to eat.

Ashley proudly told Andy what she could now do, but asked them to keep this to themselves. She didn't want everyone to know about this yet, not until she had more confidence. Andy gave her a hug, saying, "Ashley, now you can do three things that I can't possibly do! Very well done, hot shot!" Ashley was very pleased with his compliment.

"Now I've got something to tell you," Andy began, once she had calmed down. "I've finally been catching up on my archaeology news. Guess what? The Underwater Archaeologist, Professor Jacques Flambois, a Frenchman from Bordeaux University, Bordeaux, France, has made an astounding discovery. This is a fabulous area for wizard archaeologists you see, underwater digs. We can cast water breathing spells, you see. He was diving off the coast of Larnaca, Cyprus, looking for a sunken ship to excavate. Instead, he made the find of the century! He first reported that he had found a golden crown. We heard about that two weeks ago, but I didn't pay much attention to it then. Now he is back in his office and has made the startling discovery that this crown is magical. He suspects this might be the legendary Crown of Moses!" Andy waited for the girls to react. Neither did.

"I've never heard of this crown," Lindsey replied. "Is it important? Who did it belong to? What does it do? Is it somehow valuable?"

Andy threw his hands through his long, black hair in exasperation. "Valuable? If this really is the Crown of Moses, it would be worth millions and millions of dollars, a priceless artifact and magical relic. According to all the historical myths or legends, possibly even obscure Bible passages, God gave this magical crown to Moses, when he was to lead the Israelites out of slavery, across the Sinai. No one knows for sure exactly what it does. No one has seen it for three millennia at least! Professor Flambois is keeping everyone updated on his progress via his Bordeaux University website. Of course, you both know how terribly difficult it is to properly Identify all the magical properties of an item, right?"

"Yes, we spent a whole week last year trying to Identify all the properties of Professor Mary Ann's rings. That was quite a chore," Lindsey replied.

"Anyway, his latest entry says that he suspects the Crown of Moses does something about the weather. At least, he is making progress. This is the coolest archaeological find in years. I wish I could be there with him. How he must have felt when he pulled this crown up from the bottom of the sea where it had been for millennia! Gosh, it's so exciting." Lindsey had not seen Andy quite this exuberant before. He was very animated, talking rapidly.

"Well, I wish that I knew about that in my first year," Lindsey replied. "We had to list out all the jobs what wizards and witches could have once they graduated school. I can see that this one, Underwater Archaeologist, would have been a good one. Even Pam didn't have this one on her list. Golly, you could even do excavations of sites that are impossibly hard to reach as well."

"Now you are talking, Lindsey. That's just what I hope to do when I graduate," Andy added full of enthusiasm for the future. "Who knows, maybe one day I will get lucky and find something really powerful and cool?" He sighed, "Honestly, usually, is it just more old bones, bits of pottery, stone tools, and garbage pits that are found. Still, it can happen, like it has with Professor Flambois."

The next day, Lindsey and Ashley worked on some more spells. Unlike Lindsey, Ashley could only learn how to do certain spells in this special manner. During the morning hours, Ashley learned to handle Warm and Chill without her wand and non-verbally. In the afternoon, she was able to add

Open, Lock, and Unlock to her small repertoire. During the evening, she learned to do Move Object and to Gentle Fall as well. All other Grade 0 spells did not seem to work for her this way. By now, Lindsey had figured out some methods t she could use to tell rather quickly whether Ashley would be able to do a specific spell in this fashion.

The next morning, Ashley added Light, Magical Missile, and Sleep to her small collection of special spells. Lindsey now ascertained that was all the Grade 0 and 1 spells that Ashley could readily master in this fashion at this time. She speculated that perhaps later on, Ashley might be able to pick the others up as well. With the bus due to bring all the other students scheduled to arrive just before noon, the two had to stop. Both wanted to be there to meet Amanda, Pam, Audrey, Fern, and Jim, to say nothing of Lindsey's other friends, Emilio and Kathy.

On their way to the main gates, Lindsey noticed that Tom had already plastered several signs in their commons asking for tryouts for the track and soccer teams. His notice announced tryouts would be on Saturday afternoon. He wanted the team solidified early, she gathered. The three chatted about tryouts as they walked to the gates.

"How long will it be? I'm getting hungry," Ashley asked.

As if in answer, they heard the popping sound of the bus materializing in the parking lot. Sandy and Tom ushered them through the gates, allowing Lindsey to lend them a hand with all the returning Yellow Hall students. All their bags needed to be moved to their bedrooms. Sandy called out, "Yellow Hall—over here." One by one, the exiting students found their way over to their Floor Monitors.

Lindsey waved at Pam and shortly, Pam, Amanda, Audrey, Fern, Jim, Kathy, and Emilio all came over to Lindsey, Andy, and Ashley. Lindsey quickly introduced Emilio and Kathy to Ashley. Both had been warned not to mention the phrase Special Needs and to give a hug to Ashley, if she seemed to welcome it. "Golly, you are much prettier than they have been telling me," Kathy said as she greeted her. "You could be a model!"

Ashley blushed, but said, "Kathy, I'm sorry that they

moved you out so that I could be with Lindsey."

"Hey, anytime, besides, I'm right next door, in nine. What's all this about—you're soon to become Lindsey's sister? Is that true?" Kathy asked, guessing this might please her.

"Well, yes, Lena and Lloyd are adopting me," Ashley replied quietly.

"Hey, don't I get a hug?" Emilio butted in. "After all, she is my relay race team member, well she is, if someone doesn't beat her out of that position." He gave her a hug as well and then shook hands with Andy. As usual, they chatted, giving the many other students time to get their bags sorted out and moved. When the crowd had lessened, Sandy, Lindsey, and Tom set to work moving their friend's many bags to their rooms. Then, together they all walked to the dorms, chatting all the way.

"We have a Pam emergency," Lindsey said. "Computers and cell phones help is urgently needed." Pam merely laughed.

"I told you so, didn't I?" Pam giggled to Amanda and Audrey. "Bring them all to the commons, and I'll get them going, but can I go to my room first?" she teased them. An hour later and after they all ate lunch, Pam had her laptop in the commons, along with Andy and Ashley's computers and phones.

"First, I'm fixing the phones up to speed dial and transmit pictures back to your laptops. While I'm doing this, Lindsey, please enter all our phone numbers into their phones. I'm emailing Andy's and Ashley's to everyone else. They can add his and hers themselves." Lindsey began pushing the buttons, while the two watched what they were doing.

"I'm just saving you time, Ashley. I know that you could just as easily do this yourself, but this will go faster since I'm doing both at once," Lindsey suggested, giving Ashley a way to save face. She knew that Ashley might insist on doing it herself.

"Does this computer take my external drives?" asked Andy. Pam asked to see them and Andy showed her one.

"Yes, it's completely Plug 'n Play with those. Why do you need so many drives?"

"Well, all the archaeology photos I have got. I kept

filling up my old machine, and they said this was a good alternative," Andy replied.

"Slow, but it works. I may have a better way for you. Let me check on it first," Pam replied. "Okay, Andy, yours is working. Give it a try."

Andy took a photo of Lindsey with his cell, punched #9, went to his laptop, and watched as the image arrived in his Agent mailbox. "Great. Guess what I'm doing with this pic?" A minute later, the photo of Lindsey became his desktop background. "You look good," he teased her. Lindsey blushed.

"There, Ashley. Yours is ready too. Give it a try," Pam announced.

"Okay, thanks. I want to get a picture of each of you," she ordered. Pam was very curious how she could possibly use the cell phone. Many others were equally curious. Ashley sat down, took off her shoes, and opened her phone. Using her toes, she pointed and clicked. One by one, she got a picture of them. Then, she sat up and asked for directions. As each picture appeared, she pressed #9, followed by 9 representing the letter 'Y' for yes, meaning delete the photo from her cell phone's memory. Using her feet, she opened her email Agent and watched the photos appearing, one per each email. "Cool! Thank you Pam!"

Pam grinned, "Say, I could also put some helpful voice activation software on your computer too. I did it for Lindsey, when she had no hands and needed to use the computer. You give it orders, and it can type notes and papers for you as you speak the words. I don't know if this is something you really want or need, though."

Ashley, who at first began to ridge up at the suggestion she needed voice software, softened her attitude as she heard the rest of Pam's words. "Would I have a choice of which to use? I mean, once it is on there, can I still run everything as I'm used to running it?"

"Sure, to get it going, you have to double click one icon on the desktop or use the mouse to select VAS, Voice Activated Software. You can also stop the program from running anytime you want and go back to typing everything yourself. It is merely something that you might, at times, find a convenience. It certainly isn't necessary in your case, Ashley, just something you might find useful, perhaps." Lindsey admired the way that Pam was presenting this, definitely allowing Ashley to be right in her choice.

"Well, I can see there might be times this would be more convenient. Thanks for doing it, Pam," Ashley decided. Pam went to work loading it up from her computer.

"Hey, I'm not done with yours either, Andy. These come with tons of services loaded and running that you will never need, and they slow your computer down. They are always checking to see if they have anything to do, which they don't, you see. I want to disable those services, and your computer will not be so sluggish, especially as it boots up." Andy left his on the table, while Pam finished up with Ashley's computer. "Okay, Ashley, yours is done. Try a reboot and see how much faster it is."

Ashley grinned, "I sure am glad this one has a reset button. The Control-Alt-Delete is incredibly hard for me to hit with my toes. Wow, it does start up faster! Thanks, computer genius."

With the "Pam emergency" handled, they all began to chat, particularly Kathy and Emilio, who they had not seen all summer. Kathy admired Pam's hair, "Gee Pam, you've let your hair grow longer this summer. I like it, makes you look more mature." Pam blushed. She had intentionally allowed it to grow, trying to emulate Lindsey and Amanda.

Kathy then suggested, "Ashley, you ought to let yours grow a bit longer, say down to your shoulders, not to your waist like Amanda's though. These are the latest styles," she showed all the girls her latest fashion magazine. "You would look even more attractive if yours was a bit longer, don't you think?"

"Well, it's short so I can manage it myself," Ashley immediately went on the defensive, but almost as quickly changed her mind. "You really think so? If it is too long, I can't easily get into my clothes."

Kathy definitely so insisted, and Ashley decided to try it. Besides, she realized that she could have it cut if it didn't work out.

Emilio became bored with all the girl talk. He thought they all looked just great the way they were and changed the subject, "Say, Fern has been telling me how you two have been practicing all summer on the baton passing, Ashley. Normally, I start the race, because I'm not the fastest runner, and Fern, who is, runs last. I wonder if maybe you ought to start the race and then I take the baton from you second."

Ashley giggled. She and Fern had already discussed this point. "You're assuming that I make the team. We best wait for tryouts and see if I do. Besides, shouldn't Tom be helping us make such decisions?" Emilio's face flushed slightly and agreed.

Lindsey interrupted them, "Come on you guys; we ought to get you all to the Bookstore so you can get any last minute things. We got most of our books last May, but I still need some pens." After taking their things to their rooms, off they all went to the Bookstore.

Chapter 4—School Begins Again

Saturday morning, the Yellow Hall track team met at the stadium for tryouts. Lindsey was prepared to help Ashley into her running outfit, but Ashley was able to manage it all herself, primarily because she could now cast Tie. With a great deal of pride, she got her spike track shoes on and used two spells to tie them. While she was wearing them, she felt self-conscious, because she knew that she was helpless without the immediate use of her feet. In addition, she was nervous, never having tried out for a track and soccer team before—besides, she was going to be judged by her friends as well.

Andy showed up as they walked out of the dorm, heading for the stadium. "Hi Ashley, Lindsey. I guess we two are the guinea pigs this morning. Nervous?"

"A little," Ashley found herself admitting. Never before would she ever have openly admitted such. She wondered why she had just done so. *What is happening to me?*

"Me too. I've never been on a track or soccer team at school before, though I have played a bunch in PE," Andy admitted as well.

"There might not be any competition," Lindsey began to explain. Prior to the last two years, Yellow Hall had always finished dismally. Few ever wanted to be on their teams. However, the last two years, things had changed. Lindsey wondered if there would be others who now wanted to try out.

She need not have worried. As the nine of them stood around waiting for ten o'clock to come, they kept looking for other arrivals. Finally, Tom took charge. "Well, looks like you two are it. Andy, let's see how you do at the hundred meter dash. Jake, will you race against him? You are probably our best other possibility at such a short run."

"Sure, but I would hate to give up my spot in the mile relay, boss," Jake teased Tom. Both smiled. Tom took out his stopwatch, and had Lindsey move out to mark the ending line.

"Gosh, this is an awfully short run," Jake commented. Tom gave the countdown, and the two boys raced to Lindsey's

46

location. Andy beat him by a step.

"I haven't even got going," Jake complained.

"Congratulations, Andy, you are our new 100-meter dash runner," Tom said cheerily.

"Great, now I don't have to run anymore," Andy replied, and everyone laughed at him.

"Now then, I already know that Ashley can do the mile relay race. As Fern had told me repeatedly, Ashley has to start the race. When we took on Lindsey two years ago, we checked the rulebook. There is nothing in there that says the runner has to hold the baton in their hands, merely that the runners have to exchange batons. Hence, Ashley is wearing the belt pouch we made for Lindsey, who started the race for us. Whoever runs second must get up to her speed and retrieve the baton from her."

He continued, "I know that Fern and Ashley have been practicing this all summer, but I really need Fern running last, since that's the most critical runner, and she's the best of you milers. Hence, it is either Emilio or Jake that has to run second, retrieving the baton from Ashley. It is my decision to go with experience. Jake, you now run second. Your task is to retrieve the baton smoothly."

"Now I know that last year, Becky had us all running five miles. I think that is silly. We should use this time to practice what you are going to be doing, the mile relay. So you four get warmed up and into position. Oh, Ashley, you run half way around this track before handing off to Jake. Twice around is a mile. Action, ladies and gentlemen. Let's see how you do."

While they were warming up, Ashley admitted to Lindsey, "I'm really nervous. What if I mess up, fall down, or something?"

"Hey, I was spooked my first time too. Just do your best. That's all anyone can ask of any of us. After all, last year Emilio over ate at noon just before our race and ran slow, costing us the race. Anyone of us can mess up. You'll do fine."

Tom got them into their places and then gave Ashley the countdown. Admittedly, Emilio and Jake stared at Ashley as she began her run around the track. Neither had seen an armless person racing before. Soon, Jake forgot about the novelty and began getting up to speed, matching Ashley. He easily slipped the baton from her and sped on down the track, while she slowed down. A bit later, he handed off to Emilio, and finally, Fern took it from him. As she blazed across the finish line, Tom punched his stopwatch.

"Eureka! 5:30, great going. While that isn't any speed record, it is good enough to win a good percentage of the time. Ashley, you're on the team! Okay, five milers, we're up. We ought to give it a go, just once. Jake, time us, will you?"

Ashley watched the major event: the twenty-mile relay race. She'd not yet seen the three Apaches and Lindsey in a race before, though they had been running all summer. Their speed made a distinct impression on her as she watched all four. "Why does Amanda run last?" she asked Emilio. "Tom's the oldest."

"Amanda can beat both Jim and Tom every time. All three routinely beat Lindsey, though just about no one else can take her. The last runner is always the team's best, since often the race is on the line at the finish line. Amanda really can take the heat. She's about the best runner we have ever fielded, at least I think so," Jake answered her.

When Amanda crossed the finish line, Jake called out, "106:30. Fabulous time, if we can do that once here, we are off to the Nationals in May! That's a certainty!"

Once they had caught their breaths, Tom suggested that they next experiment with their soccer game. "Last year, Becky called it right. It's best not to shuffle players from position to position, if it can be avoided. Andy, at your request, you will be our goalkeeper. Ashley, the other opening is our LFB, left full back. Your job is to defend our goal. Jake is your partner, the RFB."

"Now you three take your positions. Actually, Fern, Emilio, you take your positions too; they are the middle fielders, the LMF and RMF. We four are normally the various forwards. Today, we four will pretend that we're your opponents, trying to score against you. I want to see how Ashley and Andy work out at their positions. Remember, Ashley, the full backs are never to go beyond the quarter field spot. Stay close to our goal, but on either side. Okay, action."

Amanda and Lindsey took their usual positions in the middle, while Tom was on the far left, Jim, far right. Tom began bringing the ball down the field. As he approached Fern, cleverly, he passed over to Amanda, dodged around Fern, and had Amanda pass back to him. He wanted to test Ashley, Lindsey realized as she moved on down the center of the field. Ashley put her body in blocking position as she had been taught in PE class. Since Amanda had moved closer to the goal, Tom decided to see if Ashley could block a hand pass. He attempted to toss it over Ashley to Amanda, who would make the score attempt. To Tom's surprise, she jumped at the right moment and head butted the ball fairly well so that Fern could retrieve it.

"Great move, Ashley," Tom praised her. They restarted again. This time as Tom came at Ashley and tried to kick it by her. As he was getting his feet ready to kick, nimbly, Ashley beat him to it, knocking it towards Fern. "Another good move, Ashley! Good defense! You get a full pass, Ashley."

"Now, let's see how our goalkeeper does. Jim, see if you can get it by him." Jim raced the ball towards Andy and gave his usual violent kick. Andy simply caught it and tossed it to Ashley, who head butted it over to Fern.

"Okay, okay! It's time to call out our heavy scorers. Amanda and Lindsey are our top two scorers. Lindsey, will you get this ball by Andy somehow?" Everyone laughed. She back up and began to bring it down the field at Andy.

Just as she neared prime kicking position, Andy suddenly saw five Lindsey's coming at him. He concentrated on the original Lindsey, but she saw what he was doing and had the images co-mingle, just before she kicked. Andy made a valiant dive, but missed it by inches.

"Okay, miss hot shot. Let's see you do that one again," Andy called out, tossing the ball back to her. She grinned and repeated her performance. This time, Andy was prepared, wand at the ready. Just as she was about to kick, he dispelled her multiple images, blocking her ball successfully. "See, it only works once." Everyone laughed.

"Okay, let's see how you do blocking a penalty shot.

Remember, usually these are kicked very hard," Tom pointed out, moving to the penalty shot line. Wham! Tom gave the ball his hardest possible kick. Andy reacted and deflected it out of the way. "Good block!"

Just then, the Black Hall team showed up en mass. Tom called out, "Okay our time is up. Black Hall has the field next. Let's hit the showers."

All nine walked off the field. However, Ashley felt the stares of the other nine on her back as they walked back towards the dorms. She felt uneasy as usual. Tom was in excellent spirits, "You are all going to work out just fine. We certainly have a shot at first place in the Nationals and maybe even winning the school soccer cup. I'll let you all know the schedule as soon as it comes out. I've been lobbying for an earlier than normal start this year, so we can avoid the bad weather games."

As they entered the dorms, Lindsey was careful to make sure the doors were opened as Ashley entered. She knew that Ashley was feeling a bit helpless, since she was still wearing her track shoes, but she didn't want to make it obvious that she was helping. At last, they entered their room. Ashley finally untied her shoes and regained the use of her feet. They gathered some clean clothes and headed for the showers.

Instead, they took a very long bath in the huge tubs, which held six at one time. "I can't believe that I'm on the track and soccer team," Ashley said. Only now did she allow herself to become excited about what had just happened to her. "Tom was testing me, wasn't he?" Lindsey nodded. "But he actually wants me on his team! No one has ever wanted me on their team, not even in PE classes. I was always the last one chosen, well not really chosen. I was just put on the last team."

"Yes, you have the skills, and we definitely need you. I thought you did well today."

"Did he mean what he said about you and Amanda being our top scorers?"

"Er, yes, she and I scored most of the goals last year," Lindsey admitted.

At last Monday arrived, none too soon for Pam, who was anxiously counting down the hours. She was ready for the classes to begin last June 1! As the girls were getting ready for their first day, as usual, Pam reminded them, "Remember to pack your algebra book, chemistry book, and English manual this morning. Tomorrow, bring the history book not the English manual."

"Yes, mom," Amanda teased her, but Ashley double-checked to make sure she had stowed the right ones. The four grabbed their school bags, Ashley wiggling her long strap over her head. They headed down to breakfast. Their normal routine was to pack the morning supplies, eat breakfast, then head to class. Over lunch, they would re-pack their bags with the afternoon books. Andy and Emilio were already done eating and waiting for the girls to arrive.

Self-serve breakfast was organized chaos as usual, six hundred students wandering down to the dining room shortly before eight. Jim arrived slightly late, but in time to wish Ashley a great day. The group of friends headed off to chemistry class together.

As usual, Pam wanted to sit as near the front as possible, which met with Andy's approval in chemistry class. Pam, Andy, Lindsey, Amanda, Audrey, Ashley, Kathy, and Emilio all sat close to each other.

Slowly the others arrived, including Deiter Cross and his Black Hall friends. "Hi Lindsey," Deiter called out, as he took his seat. What a change, Lindsey thought. Her first year, Deiter continually made fun of her at the start of each class. Now he was being down right friendly. She smiled back at him.

Of course, all the other students began staring at Ashley, whispering madly about her. Lindsey prayed with all her might that no one would start to make fun of Ashley. Her prayers were answered, as Professor Jasper Jones walked in. "Good morning everyone. Welcome to your first class in chemistry. I already know most all of you. However, we have two new third year students with us, transfers from the Twin Cities and Boston schools. Would Andy Rains please stand up and let your classmates have a look at you?"

Andy's face flushed, and he rose hesitatingly. Yet, he knew that Ashley would be next. He quickly said, "Well, how do I look?" It was a tease. He had forgotten to brush out his long hair. Someone called out, "Like a hippie." The class roared. Andy had accomplished his goal and sat down.

"Would Miss Ashley Stokes please stand up and let your classmates have a look at you?"

Ashley found this was less embarrassing, because Andy had gone first and make a joke out of the embarrassing situation. Of course, everyone stared at her as she expected. Following his lead, she said, "Well, how do I look?"

Various replies echoed, most of which were "Wow! Incredible!" However, two replies were, "Really cute!" She actually blushed. The last two years she had gotten very angry when being introduced, especially in the Twin Cities.

"Well, there you have our two new additions. Now I have a short warning for you. If I catch anyone picking on Ashley, I will assign you double homework, that is, after Ashley is finished kicking you. I have it on good authority from her former schools that Ashley is quite the fighter, so my advice, boys, is that this is one girl that I wouldn't tease." Ashley flushed, but thought that was quite funny. At least they were warned that she wouldn't hesitate to kick in her defense.

"Now then, let's get down to business. Chemistry is the study of substances and the changes that take place when they combine to form other substances. You must pass this course with at least a C if you wish to go onto potion making next year. Chemistry is divided into two groups: inorganic chemistry and organic chemistry. Can anyone tell me what the difference between these two are? Yes, Miss Betts?" Pam's hand shot up at once. She had already read the first five chapters of the textbook over the summer.

After the bell rang, they all headed upstairs to their math class. Deiter came up to them and said, "Hi, I'm Deiter Cross, Ashley. I helped Lindsey and the others capture the Mad Bomber last year. Congratulations on being Floor Monitor, Lindsey. Ashley, you're in good hands with Lindsey, here."

"Thanks," Ashley managed to say, accepting his pronouncement without becoming angry. She thought he meant well. Nearly all the other girls in their class came over to meet Ashley, since they had nearly ten minutes to climb one set of stairs. Most were curious and wanted to see her up close. Her blouse left nothing for their imagination: no trace of arms did she have. Ashley endured a number of sympathetic comments from the well-wishers.

Professor Herbert Mac Elroy began Algebra II class by saying, "I know most of you, but I need to call roll for our two new additions. Andy Rains, Ashley Stokes? Ah, I see you. Good. Okay, I see that you all are just *dying* to learn more advanced math so let's not waste time. Open your books to page one and away we go." Emilio wished that he had wasted a little more time; the class was beginning much too soon for him.

The late summer morning was sunny and warm as the group all headed down to the Hall of English. Professor Elaine Mac Elroy began by identifying Andy and Ashley for her own benefit. "On Mondays and Tuesdays, we will be going over English. The rest of the week will be on US History. Please take note of this unusual schedule. The reason for this is that I would like to take the class on a number of field trips to see firsthand some of the famous historical sites in the US. Yes, we will be taking quite a few trips, and I know that you will enjoy the outings. Now then, open your English books to chapter one. It's time that you learn where all the commas actually belong."

Later on, they all headed for the stadium and PE class. As usual, they were divided: the girls went with Betsy, while the boys went with Hank. "Girls, this fall until the weather changes, we will be practicing our swimming. Later on, we will tackle diving, but will use the heated indoor pool. I expect to see some pretty swan dives from some of you. So from now on, report to the swimming pool not the stadium." Lindsey appreciated the nice walk down to the pool.

As they walked, Lindsey whispered to Ashley, "Can you manage swimming?" She suddenly wondered if Ashley could handle it.

"Barely. At least I don't drown," Ashley whispered back. Indeed, while the other girls swam well, Ashley, using her legs only, managed at least to stay afloat, frog kicking. She was more comfortable floating on her back, however.

When they finished, Betsy confidentially said to her, "Very good Ashley. I'm glad that you can manage. Good going. Let me know if you encounter something that you are going to have difficulty with, and perhaps we can work out better ways for you to do them."

On their way to lunch and book swapping, Ashley commented, "It's funny, but so far none of the teachers have introduced me as their Special Needs student like they did in Chicago and the Twin Cities." Lindsey suspected Alister had a hand in this.

"Good afternoon, welcome to Spell Casting Grade 4. I'm Professor Huan Su Sung. I'll be up front with you. These spells are much more difficult to master fully, which is one reason only one grade of spells is taught. In addition, you will be taking many field trips in US History, which will cut into our available time. This year, you will have seven of us teaching you your spells. This is because they are more difficult, and we wish you to have the most appropriate professor for each type of spell. We are beginning with the new evocation spells, while the weather is still cooperating. No fun launching a fire spell in the rain." Many giggles replied to his tease.

"Now that you are all settled in your seats, please pack up everything. We are going outside for the rest of this week and next. Yes, meet here, and we will go out as a group. Today, we are going to provide a service for our ground keepers. Along one wall where the Dark Forest meets the Formal Gardens, they wish us to cultivate a section of the ground. Hence, we will be learning our Dig spells and putting them to good use at the same time."

"Finally, a note about wand activation. I've talked this over with the other professors during the summer. We have all agreed that as far as the final exam goes, all that matters is that the spell works properly. This means our Lindsey may cast hers non-verbally and without a wand, if she can actually learn to do these this way. However, until you can demonstrate for your professor that your spell works properly when you speak the command, your wand must also activate properly as well. In other words, learn the spell correctly, and then you may move on into the realms of non-verbal and sans wand."

"I see that you are all packed up, so let's go outside and enjoy this fine late summer afternoon, shall we?" Huan then led them across the campus to the stone wall on the south side of the gardens. Naturally, everyone wanted to see just how Ashley could possibly cast a spell. Most of the class either stared openly or continually glanced over at her as she began to try to figure out this new spell. Lindsey saw that Ashley was getting rather annoyed and distracted, but Huan beat her to the handling.

"Okay, okay. Class, it seems that you have never see a witch cast her spells. Ashley, please cast a simple spell of your choice at the wall, and let everyone watch how you do it. After this is done, it will be detention for any of you that I catch putting your attention on Ashley rather than your own spells." Ashley actually smiled; for once a professor understood what she was fighting. She cast a Magical Missile at the wall, which made some sparkles as it hit. She swivelled on her rear to face half of the class, as if to say, "There, are you satisfied?"

With that out of the way, everyone got down to the job at hand. Audrey and Amanda teamed up, so that Lindsey could work with Ashley. Before long, Ashley commented, "Say, this is an incredibly useful spell! I can really dig this way. I never could really handle digging in the ground. Maybe now I can grow some plants." Lindsey complimented her, and Ashley now coached Lindsey until she got the hang of the digging.

A little later, Amanda traded places with Ashley. Audrey and Ashley really wanted to get the indicated plot dug for the grounds keepers and together they both went to work. Meanwhile, Amanda helped coach Lindsey, who wanted to get the spell down non-verbally and preferably also without her wand. The hour passed altogether too quickly for everyone. Reluctantly, the entire class headed back indoors for Huan's Evocation Theory I class.

After that, they had Illusion Theory I. Professor Cho Lin Sung greeted them. "This is the first year that you will be learning many illusion based spells. This is why we are covering the basic theory at this time, before I take Huan's place and we try out these many new spells." Even though the

Yellow Hall students rather adored Cho Lin, Lindsey, Pam, Amanda, Ashley, and Andy were most anxious for the next class, their elective.

The group split up for their last class of the day and many went to the Library for their Study Hall. Lindsey went to room 303 Admin Hall, as directed on her class schedule. All the way there, she wondered who would be teaching her first real Dispeller theory class. When she walked in, her mouth dropped, so startled was she to see none other than Delius Dogs waiting for her. Lindsey utterly despised his subject, necromancy. After last year, she also didn't like him as well, even though he was head of Black Hall. He was an imposing man, around forty. He had a dark complexion and an antagonistic stare. His black hair was long, but smoothed, and he sported a tiny moustache.

"Good afternoon, Lindsey. Welcome to Dispeller Theory I. I must say, it has been many years since we were able to offer this class here at Bradbury's. However, ever since your first year here, I have been anticipating this day. And here we are. Let's get the record straight right from the start. I know that you and I have not gotten along well, particularly last year. Yet, we must lay aside our personal feelings and learn the art of Dispelling, shall we?"

"Yes, sir." This was the only thing Lindsey could think of to say to him.

"Now then, you are probably wondering why I am your teacher," She nodded. It was as if he was reading her mind. Instinctively, she touched her father's ring and pin. Both were in their places; he could not be actually sensing her thoughts, she concluded and relaxed slightly.

"Real world, Lindsey. Honestly, do you think that you will be facing combat situations with witches such as Professor Janice Smith and her charms? Ha! Never! I'm sure that she would rather teleport away than to engage in a combat, unless there was no other acceptable way out for her. No, Lindsey, you have already faced Death Stalkers and even Dominus. It is my task this year to help give you insight into the art of Dispelling, for an art it actually is, *not* a science."

"By the way, I've heard about how you and Lloyd faced

down the renegade who had captured Running Bear this summer. Let's begin with that one, shall we?" Lindsey wondered how he had learned about that one.

"Okay, when you were standing there with your father, what did you actually do?"

"Well, I sucked up several spells, sir, into my staff. Later, I helped dispel other spells that were entrapping my friends," she replied.

"Yes, but did you know in advance what spells were being cast and thus which spells ought to be either absorbed or dispelled immediately?"

"No sir. I just have my staff absorb nearly everything."

Delius actually smiled, "Typical of those who do not know what they are doing. Absorb everything that comes your way. Well, that is crude, but effective only when you are facing one opponent. What are you going to do when four of you are facing four other wizards who are all casting away?"

Lindsey smiled, not because she found anything humorous, but rather because this was the very worry she had always had about dispelling. "Am I going to learn how to handle this kind of situation? If so, I'm very eager to learn. I've always wondered how my dad could have done it, when there are so many casting at nearly the same time. I've sort of depended upon having some protective spells on me and my friends to help, though that cannot be the real solution."

"Wise, very wise of you, Lindsey. You have reached the first important milestone of the art of dispelling. Yes, it is an art. You have to have a feel for the spells, predict what is being cast, and then act. You have only tiny fractions of a second to make these observations and then act upon them. That's why it is an art and not a science. There are no hard and fast laws with dispelling, no set of rules, such as first you do this and so on. It is all about prior knowledge of your opponents, their skill levels, and their psychology, if you please."

"Today, we are beginning an adventure into instant spell recognition. I'm going to cast attacking spells at you, and you're to try to identify what spell I'm casting. Don't worry. I will always kill the spell by using the wrong final command word. No actual spells will be cast. The instant you recognize what spell is coming your way, yell it out. Got it?"

At supper, Lindsey eagerly began relating what an exciting class she'd just had. "I can recognize a Ball of Fire spell before someone is finished casting it!" She chatted on and on about this most exciting class.

"I've got Alister for Tracking Theory," Amanda chatted excitedly. "This is going to be an incredible year!"

"Really? Wow," Pam interrupted, "I've got Cho Lin for Sleuthing. She is terrific at setting up mysteries for me to solve. Gosh, I have to use every wit I have, and I have to know so much about spells and their effects! It's the most incredible class I've ever had!"

"No, that would be my archaeology class," Andy interrupted them all. "We spent the whole class studying the significance of Professor Jacques Flambois and his incredible discovery of the Crown of Moses. We've just learned that it can even be used to control the weather. Professor Jacques believes that it was used to temper down the extreme heat of their desert crossing or to perhaps bring rain to quench their parched throats."

"You don't need no crown to survive in the desert," Emilio interrupted him. "I've got Japser for Desert Survival. Incredible class. Do you know that there are all sorts of plants that you can use to obtain water in the desert?" Audrey interrupted him, rattling off several such species.

Ashley was the only one who was still silent. She had gone to the Hall of Divination for her special elective class. Because of the many doors in her path, she had to use the Open: Door spell three times before finally entering room 300, where Professor Mary Ann was waiting for her. Yes, she still looked frazzled; her eyes continually darted around the office, but as soon as Ashley had entered and the door closed, her eyes focused upon Ashley. "Come in, my dear, come in. It has been ages since I was able to teach Diviner Theory. I haven't had the opportunity to meet you in person, Ashley. I must say you are such a pretty young girl and so incredibly talented too. Come, take some tea with me or would you prefer a soda? I keep forgetting that you younger folk so prefer sodas."

"Tea will be fine, Professor," Ashley timidly replied,

taking off her book bag and sitting down across from her at her small table. She slipped off her shoes, ready to deal with the cup that Mary Ann was pouring for her.

"Sugar? Cream? Plain?"

"Plain, please."

Ashley noticed that Mary Ann didn't pay any attention at all to how she was using her feet to sip the hot brew. Instead, she launched immediately into the business at hand. "A Diviner must be *at cause* over their premonitions. Governor Alister has told me that you have already had many such premonitions, some of which have saved lives. Is this correct?" Ashley nodded. "Please, tell me about some of the more recent ones you've experienced."

Ashley liked this kind, old woman, who was accepting her as she was, not even paying attention to her awkward methods of sipping tea. She began relating the most recent one with R. B. Soon, she found herself telling about the time with Lloyd, and then many that had happened at her other two schools. "Honestly, I told them to warn them, but they laughed at me. Then, when it happened, they cursed me and called me names. Of course, that's when I kicked them and got into so many fights."

"Of course, of course, others fear what they do not understand. Please, forgive me for making you relive those unpleasant times. It was necessary for me to ascertain truly the depth of your native ability as a Diviner. Honestly, Ashley, you have incredible potential, perhaps the greatest potential this world has seen in eons. Yet, we must work on its control. A Diviner must be able to focus and obtain premonitions that others can use to accomplish their tasks. For example, I will pick on the world famous Rat Pack, who originally captured this devil of a man, Dominus and his Death Stalkers." Ashley noticed that she shivered something fierce as she mentioned his name. She remembered that Lindsey had mentioned that Dominus had attacked Mary Ann many years ago, which probably accounted for her strange behavior now, she reasoned.

"Mabel Pruit was her name, the Diviner of the Rat Pack. She would get inside the head and mind of Dominus and predict what he would do next, where he would strike, that sort of thing. Using these premonitions, the others in her group acted, ultimately leading to their capture. Ashley, what we must work on first is your control over your inborn ability, so that it is there as a tool for your use, much as your wand is there for you to use when you need it."

"Wow, this is possible? I mean, until now, they just come to me, usually when I least expect them to come," Ashley replied. For the rest of the class period, the two began to work on the principles of control. Although she soon realized that this would not be easy, she now had set a goal for herself, something for which to strive. When the altogether too short a session was over, Ashley was truly serene, which is why she did not interrupt all the others, as they excitedly tried to describe their exciting elective classes.

After dinner, Tom gathered his track team together for a brief word. "Got the schedules; mark down these dates. A week from Saturday, we race against Brown Hall. The following Saturday, we have our first soccer match against Black Hall." He rattled off the other matches, which would take place during the subsequent four weeks. "I like the schedule; we got the best positioning, probably because we took second at the Nationals." Lindsey relaxed, after two Saturdays, they would be free of track and soccer worries until springtime.

In spell casting class the next day, Huan announced, "Today, we are going to begin to learn a series of spells that you can use to protect yourself a bit and harm others if they try to hit you physically. These spells are particularly effective against normal thugs, so you girls take note of these. The first one operates two ways; it is the Shield of Defense. When you cast it on yourself, either your body is surrounded by shimmering flames or waves of coldness. Of course, you are not affected in any way. However, if a thug attempts to hit you, they will take burning damage or freezing damage. How much damage depends upon how much damage they are delivering to you. The more they harm you, the more they are hurt in an equal amount."

"But what if you don't want to get hurt at all?" Audrey

asked.

"Well, we'll get to that spell tomorrow, Audrey. Now then, today, let's work on casting the shimmering flames version." Everyone was outside on the lawn, enjoying the sunny afternoon, though the temperature here in the mountains was definitely getting cooler; fall was rapidly approaching.

Suddenly, Ashley had another of her premonitions. "What's his name is going to get horribly burned, I know it," she said to Lindsey. In the past, Ashley would have simply rushed to the person and blurted out her premonition. However, based upon her lessons with Mary Ann, she sent a frantic Message to Huan.

Just then, Lyle, one of Deiter's buddies, cast his Shield of Defense, only he goofed the spell. Real flames completely engulfed his body. As he screamed, Huan immediately dispelled the flames, before Lyle suffered horrible burns. Still, he was in pain from first-degree burns.

Huan acted immediately. "Class, thanks to the timely warning by Miss Ashley Stokes, I was alerted to Lyle's goof. Still, he has suffered bad burns. I will take him to the Infirmary at once. While I'm gone, none of you are to cast any more spells; please study the text until I get back." He levitated the crying boy so as not to touch his burned skin, created a magical door, and stepped through it.

Suddenly, everyone began whispering and looking at Ashley, who felt very uncomfortable. Her anger began building, though she saw no immediate threat.

A minute later, Huan reappeared. "He is being attended to by Doctor Caterwall, who says he will be fine later today. Again, I want to thank our budding Diviner, Ashley, for alerting me in time to prevent more serious injury. Now let's review this spell further. I don't want anyone else making such a mistake. Remember, students, these are Grade 4 spells, not Grade 0! They command far more magical powers, so please be most attentive to your casting."

Indeed, by three o'clock, Lyle rejoined them, looking much more subdued than normal, but otherwise all right. He did not thank Ashley, however, but Deiter had already thanked her when they all were walking to their next class.

The next day, they learned how to Charm by Fire. Essentially, the caster turns any normal source of flames into a dancing column of flames, and those who observe it have a good chance of becoming charmed into standing around and watching the flames, forgetting all else. This Audrey appreciated far better. This was followed by Setting a Fire Trap upon some container, such as a chest of valuables. If another tried to open the chest, a fire explosion encompassed the person, causing major burns, though not harming the container it was protecting. Again, Audrey thought that this was a useful spell. The next day, still outdoors, they learned how to create a Wall of Fire. Similar to a stone wall, this wall was entirely composed of burning flames. Anyone who attempted to pass through it sustained major burn damage. While the total amount of damage was variable, no normal person could pass through it without dying. At last, Audrey was satisfied, here was a real protective spell, and she worked hard on mastering this one quickly. Many others also saw the great benefit of this particular spell.

The following week, Huan taught them the opposite of the Wall of Fire, the Wall of Cold. Unlike the flames, the sheets of ice could be formed in any number of ways by the wizard or witch. Anything from a simple wall to a hemisphere could be constructed. Naturally, with a spell this complex, the caster had to be very specific in his or her commands. Lyle, who loved cold type spells, excelled at this spell, being the first to create a large igloo dome over the whole class. Huan explained that if a normal person would attempt to break through the wall, the cold shock would very likely kill him. Next, Huan had them all creating Hail Storms, in which large hailstones fell down, again very likely killing normal people, if the stones hit them on their heads.

Lindsey now realized that these Grade 4 spells were indeed vastly more powerful and could easily kill those who did not use magic. Their week ended with another useful spell, Alter Voice. With this spell, their voice was amplified to the desired degree stated by the caster. Indeed, many now realized this was the spell that Professor Blake Smith used when he announced the track and soccer meets. However, if the caster increased the volume even more, he could actually deafen another person, at least temporarily.

Pam's comment at the end of their second week spoke for all them. "Gosh, these new spells are awfully powerful, aren't they?"

Chapter 5—Surviving Sports

On Saturday morning, when Ashley arose, she thought to herself, "If I can only survive these next eight days!" The track meet was this afternoon and next Saturday was their soccer match. She now realized that by being on the team, she would be center stage. She would be being stared at and watched by all the students, her worst possible scenario. Ashley hated being stared at more than anything else.

Indeed, by the time to get ready, she was so nervous that she could not tie her shoes and had to let Lindsey tie them for her. "I know I was very nervous when I first ran, Ashley. I had no hands then and everyone was staring at me. What I did was concentrate all my attention on my running and tried to block the announcer and crowd completely out of my mind. It works mostly. I still get nervous, especially at the Nationals."

Together, the two headed for the Stadium, joined by their team members and the rest of Yellow Hall supporters. Tom explained, "There may not be a big turnout for a track meet, most find it's boring. Soccer, well that's far more interesting." She tried to take heart from this. Unfortunately, as they approached the Stadium, a fairly large crowd was already gathering.

"They are all coming just to see me," wailed Ashley. "I'm getting really scared about this."

Tom saw that Ashley was really beginning to freak out from his point of view. "Ashley, I'm going to cast a little helpful spell on you, okay?" She nodded. He waved his wand and said, "Emotion: Calm." Instantly, Ashley felt calm and tranquil. *Whatever am I worrying so about?* She had completely forgotten about it. They entered the Stadium and took their warm up jogs, awaiting the beginning of the meet. Tom cancelled the spell, as Ashley moved up to the starting line. On the opposite side of the track, Jake was in position to take the baton from her side pocket.

Professor Blake Smith opened the meet, "Welcome one and all to Bradbury's first track meet of the year. This afternoon, it is Yellow Hall, fresh from their second place finish at the Nationals in May, taking on Brown Hall." He began to introduce the team members. As he got to Ashley, Lindsey got a flash of the joke he was about to say. She realized this would totally upset Ashley. If he said, "And here to prove to you all that you don't have to have arms to run is Miss Ashley Stokes." Without thinking, Lindsey cast dispel magic on him and his shout spell instantly ceased, causing him to lose track of everything, as he hastily recast his spell, wondering what had happened. "Oh, yes, Miss Ashley Stokes, and Mister Andy Rains." He then introduced the Brown Hall runners. Lindsey smiled to herself and thought, "Plus one to me!"

First came the 100-meter dash, which Andy promptly lost, though he was grinning about it. Then, Ashley took her count down and her ordeal began. She was still somewhat calm, thanks to Tom and she sped down the track, concentrating on doing just what she and Fern had practiced all summer. Before long, Jake was running beside her, and she felt him fumble a bit for the baton, but then she felt it leave her bag. Baton in hand, Jake pulled out in front of her, and she gratefully slowed down, ending up beside Lindsey.

"Well, I didn't make a complete fool of myself by falling down or anything," she whispered.

"You did just fine. Watch, Emilio is handing off to Fern now. Can she ever fly!" They watched along with everyone else as Fern sped across the finish line several feet ahead of the last Brown Hall runner.

"There you have it, Yellow Hall wins ten points. Ashley can run, yes indeed. The score now stands at Yellow Hall: 10, Brown Hall: 5. As always, it all comes down to the grueling twenty-mile relay. Remember, each contestant must race five miles before handing off the baton. Lindsey will lead off for Yellow Hall." He continued with the announcements as Lindsey moved to her starting position.

"Remember, we want to set a good speed record to ensure we go to Nationals," Tom reminded Jim, Lindsey, and Amanda. Then, the race began. Lindsey quickly found the Apache pace and concentrated on maintaining that pace, ignoring the Brown Hall runner. As far as she was concerned, this was a race against the clock, not Brown Hall. Sometime later, she passed off to Jim and began her cooling down jog.

"I just now realize how long you have to run! You four are incredible," Ashley commented, as Lindsey finally joined the others, watching the rest of the race. She smiled.

At last, the race was over; Yellow Hall had broken their own record from last year, 105:12. The crowd of Yellow Hall supporters cheered loudly, and Ashley's first meet was finally over. On their way back to the dorm and showers, Pam told Ashley, "I thought you ran great." Audrey added her praise, as well as Kathy. Inwardly, Ashley now began to worry about the soccer game next Saturday. At least, she had not gotten into any fights over the track meet.

However, during the week, Ashley forgot about the upcoming soccer match, at least during the daytime hours. Tom insisted on holding soccer practice each evening for an hour after supper. He claimed that there would be no more practices after the match on Saturday, which made them more amenable to the nightly practices.

In spell casting, they now had Professor Arthur Thornby for the many alteration-based spells. In fact, the entire class was ecstatic over their first spell, Magical Door. Everyone had seen the various professors using this spell on numerous occasions. Essentially, one created a magical door, which when you stepped through it, you stepped out the other side some distance away. While that distance was not huge, as in a teleport spell, it was still highly useful as a shortcut way to cross distances. However, it was anything but easy to master. Most worked on the spell all week before they could confidently cast this one.

By now, they discovered that their larger study group was paying benefits. Kathy and Emilio had an awful time with the more advanced algebra assignments and needed more than normal help. Pam, Andy, and Ashley picked up the math quickly, coming to the aid of the others. Kathy was horrible in chemistry, but for once, Emilio was doing well. Andy, of course, was outstanding, even aiding Pam a bit. Ashley, however, was having a hard time performing the experiments, primarily because so many of them required things to be added at a precise time, which she found difficult to do. Using her feet, she was always very slow at it.

Kathy and Audrey surprised everyone by having a knack for US History, tutoring all them on this subject. Pam and Lindsey had to assist others with the magical theory assignments. So all in all, the extended group working late in the study hall of Yellow Hall produced excellent results.

At last came the day that Ashley had been dreading, the soccer match. As before, Tom cast his calming spell on her to good avail. She definitely needed calming; indeed the entire school was on hand for this first match. Everyone knew of the bitter rivalry between Black Hall and Yellow Hall these past two years. Nearly six hundred students, many with loud stadium horns, crowded onto the stands at the south side of the field.

Blake began by welcoming everyone to the match. "For Black Hall, this is a trying year. They've lost many of their players and are fielding three first year students. Let's give them all a rousing welcome. At goalkeeper, second year Fran Jacks. At left full back, second year Jen Bloom. At right full back, third year Ben Dingle. At left middle field and controlling the action, sixth year and captain Herman Freeze. At right middle field, fourth year Henry Fielding. The forwards, sixth year Phillip Royston, and the three first years, the Royston twins, Harriet and Annie, along with Len Smith. Let's give them a loud round of support." Stadium horns drowned out the cheering and clapping.

"Now for the hot Yellow Hall, reigning soccer champions two years in a row. At goalkeeper and straight from Boston, third year Andy Rains. At left full back, third year and straight from the Twin Cities, our own armless Ashley Stokes, proving anyone can play soccer." He meant it as a compliment, but Ashley fumed! Tom had to restrain her from dashing up to the announcing platform and kicking Professor Blake in his privates.

"At right full back, fifth year Jake Rattlebeam. At left middle field, second year Fern Whitewater. Yes, get ready, the entire Whitewater clan is here." Quite a few laughs were heard before he continued, "At right middle field, third year Emilio Lopez. At forwards, team captain and sixth year Tom Whitewater, fifth year Jim Whitewater, third years Amanda Whitewater and Lindsey Barron. Let's give last year's winners a welcoming round of applause." Again, another set of stadium horns blared loudly, and Lindsey saw Pam and Kathy cheering wildly in the stands. She smiled.

The two teams prepared to take the field. However, as before, Lindsey began casting defensive, protective spells on her team members using her staff. "Remember, these guys will kick you purposely in the legs to knock you out of the game. These Skin of Stone spells will not allow their kicks to hurt you, but instead hurt them." While the others took their wands onto the field with them, Ashley and Lindsey did not. Lindsey didn't need it, and Ashley couldn't use hers, because her feet were bound tightly in her soccer shoes. Besides, she was terrified of making a complete fool of herself anyway.

Blake's baritone voice called out, "And there's the toss. Rattlebeam snags it and passes over to—no wait, Freeze intercepts, brilliant move. He brings it down the field. Nice pass over to Phillip, their top scorer. Now he is one on one with Stokes, driving her back. Both of his twins are in the open. Will he pass?"

Phillip played with the ball, taunting Ashley. "You stupid idiot bitch. You actually think you belong on the soccer field? Soccer is for real people, not helpless, armless cripples." Ashley could scarcely control her anger and fought hard to restrain herself from kicking him hard, knowing that would be a foul. Phillip saw his twin sisters in the open and decided to lob it over Ashley's head, since she had no arms with which to stop it. He made a simple lob toward Annie.

No one expected Ashley's move, except herself. She saw his arm pull back and knew he was going to toss the ball. She jumped straight up and intercepted the ball with her head, bouncing it to Fern at left middle field. Fern in turn whipped the ball far down the field to Tom.

"You bitch!" Phillip screamed, and he kicked her hard in her legs and deliberately pushed her backwards. Three things happened at once. Ashley had no way to keep from falling, but had the presence of mind to cast her Gentle Fall spell, non-verbally and without a wand. She landed on her back, violently angry, cursing and swearing at Phillip. Phillip's foot connected with the Skin of Stone, and he was hopping around on one foot, yelping in pain. Hank, who had been warned to keep a sharp eye on Ashley, blew his whistle madly, throwing his hands up indicating a foul on Phillip.

Ashley rolled over and began her awkward movement to regain her feet, furiously angry, fully intent upon teaching Phillip a lesson he would never forget. Fern saw her expression and raced to help her up, trying to restrain her a bit. Hank also saw what was about to happen and raced to put himself between the hopping boy and the livid young girl. "Foul! Foul! One more like that Mr. Royston and you will be thrown out of the game. Free running shot for Ashley! Get into positions. Free running shot." Hank ordered, with Betsy attempting to force the other players to get to their positions instead of enjoining a free-for-all battle.

Henry pulled Phillip back and out of the way. The boy began rubbing his foot, trying to lessen the pain. Nothing was broken however, much to Ashley's dismay; she'd hoped he'd broken his toes. Blake's voice drowned out the yelling and booing coming from the stands. "Deliberate foul by Phillip Royston, nasty foul. Let me tell you, Stokes is roaring mad. Good thing the referee is between them or Phillip might find himself in real trouble. Miss Stokes certainly is mad about his deliberate foul. Now they are lining up; Stokes gets a free running shot. Let's see how she does this."

Fern tried to calm Ashley down, "Okay, it's okay. The refs have warned him. Come on; you get a free shot so make it count. Put us on the boards."

Ashley was fuming mad. She stormed around the free shot line, glaring at the goalkeeper, Frank Jacks. At last, she began running towards the ball. Her kick was not what Frank had expected. Usually, the free kickers merely gave it a straight shot, hard and fast. Not Ashley. She angled her blow to the ball sending it obliquely towards the net. Worse for Frank, she put all of her anger into her blow. Her powerful legs and feet connected with the ball, driving it harder than normal along this unusual trajectory. Frank dove to his right; his hands caught the ball, but the momentum of this hard kick forced the ball on out of his hands and into the net. The buzzer sounded.

Blake's voice yelled, "Goal. Brilliant kick by Miss Stokes! Yellow Hall: 1, Black Hall: 0. Now Herman's bringing the ball down field for Black hall. Long pass to Anne who is in the open. Rattlebeam moves to block her. Nice pass to Harriet, who takes a kick. Oh, good block by Rains. He lobs the ball back into play. Stokes has it and kicks over to Lopez, who is bringing it down the field. Oh, he is being double teamed. He passes to Amanda. She is quickly double teamed as well. Look at the solid defense of these Black Hall marvels. Look at that flying interception by Freeze! Now Black Hall brings it down once more."

"Fielding has the ball. Look at his fancy footwork. Emilio is definitely being confused by it. Nice pass to Smith who moves the ball into classic scoring position. No, Stokes is on him, blocking him nicely."

Ashley kept her eye on the ball, watching her chance. As Henry looked to see where Annie was at to pass off, her right foot kicked the ball back between his legs. "What an intercept!" Blake announced. In the mad scramble for the loose ball, Emilio came up with it, kicking hard over to Fern to avoid being triple teamed by the rushing Black Hall students. She long kicked over to Amanda, playing center forward just now. She moved the ball on down into scoring position. Ben Dingle rushed to intercept her, and at the last moment, she kicked the ball to her right into the feet of Lindsey who now appeared to be five Lindseys, each with the ball. All began to kick for the goal. However, Fran Jacks, having just learned her Dispel Magic spell, began to cast it. Lindsey timed her action; while he was slightly distracted attempting to remove the multiple Lindsey images, Lindsey kicked hard. Fran frantically dove to block it, but the buzzer sounded as the ball flew into the low net.

"2 to 0!" Blake announced. "Now Phillip has the ball, bringing it down into scoring position. Stokes is all over him. Wow, look at that pass over to Annie, who kicks for the score." Indeed, she faked out Andy and drove the ball into the net, getting Black Hall on the scoreboard.

A while later Phillip had the ball once more, as he got into scoring position, five Phillip's appeared. While Andy worked on dispelling the magic so he could see which one to block, Phillip drove the ball past him, tying the score. Lindsey realized what had happened and Messaged Andy her new strategy. As the ball moved down the field, the whistle blew once more. Hank gave the signs and Blake announced, "Illegal tripping on Phillip. Stokes gets a free running kick once more."

Indeed, after scoring, he had boisterously charged at Ashley, intentionally tripping her, laughing, as she had no way to break her fall or regain her balance. "You need arms to play soccer," he yelled at her. Ashley, seething with anger, struggled to get to her feet. It took the intervention of Fern, Emilio, and Jake to keep her from attacking Phillip.

As Ashley angrily stormed around the shooting line, Lindsey Messaged her. Silently, Lindsey cast her Multiple Images spell on Ashley. Suddenly, Fran had five images of Ashley. As a result, she blocked the wrong one; Ashley scored once more. As they all took their field positions, Ashley yelled angrily to Phillip, "Keep it up, buddy, and I'll keep scoring, you idiot!"

Now the game got more serious. Phillip continued to try to dominate the scoring for Black Hall, ignoring his often open other three forwards. He tried various spells from Multiple Images, to Jumping, to Levitation. Each time he was ready to shoot the ball by Andy, Lindsey dispelled his magic in time for Andy to block it. Worse for Phillip, he could not tell who was cancelling his spells!

On defense, the Black Hall full backs continued to press both Tom and Jim, figuring they were the older ones and thus the ones to stop. Hence, both continued to pass off to Lindsey and Amanda who remained in the open. When the game ended, the score was Yellow Hall: 8, Black Hall: 3. Lindsey and Amanda each had scored three goals, while Ashley had two to her credit.

As the stadium horns blared and the crowd yelled and whistled, the Yellow Hall team members rushed together and began holding each other and jumping up and down, pounding their fists into the air in a victory celebration. Jim grabbed Ashley and hoisted her onto his shoulders.

"Put me down!" she called out. "What are you doing?" she demanded.

"Showing you off! You got two goals!" he called out, as the many Yellow Hall students rushed on the field to mob their team. At last, Jim sat her down on the grass, but Pam, Audrey, and Kathy began hugging her at once, throwing accolades at her.

"I don't take nothing from nobody," she tried to explain, but that was now obvious to everyone.

As the crowd thinned and they headed to their dorms, Tom complimented the team and Ashley especially. "Way to go Ashley! Great shooting. Two goals from a back fielder! You don't see that very often!"

Jim had his arm around her shoulders all the way back to the dorms. "You are a hot soccer player, Ashley. Dynamite. You sure showed Royston. You are my kind of gal." Ashley blushed; no one had ever said that to her before.

She could only think of one answer, "I don't take nothing from nobody." After she said it, she wanted to retract it, since there must have been something better she ought to have said, she thought.

Tom added, "Good job on keeping your anger under control, Ashley."

"I didn't. Fern, Emilio, and Jake stopped me. I intended to kick Phillip where it hurts, but they wouldn't let me get near him."

"Good thing, then you would have also drawn a foul," Tom pointed out.

"Yes, but he might get the message to leave me alone," Ashley protested.

"Don't worry; only Black Hall plays dirty," Amanda explained. "With all the other halls, they are out there for a fun time and an enjoyable game. Black Halls just think they are God's gift to the world, the idiots."

"They made no use of their three first year forwards," Tom pointed out. "Many times one of those three was in the open with a good shot, but Phillip wouldn't pass to them to let them have a chance. On the other hand, we are a team."

Jim added, "Yes, Ashley, did you see the way that their fullbacks always thought Tom and I were the ones they had to stop? We just set up Amanda and Lindsey. Who cares which of us forwards scores, only that we score. Teamwork. We are the team to beat now! Glad you are with us, Ashley." She smiled. She'd never really been a part of any team in her entire life before now. She noted that she did feel very good about it. She felt even more strongly that being at Bradbury's was the right place for her.

Even after a bath and a snack, Ashley's anger had still not completely left her. Sipping a soda in the dining room, she saw Hank come in, helping himself to one as well. She got up her nerve and approached the PE teacher. "Excuse me, Professor Walls, can I ask you a question?"

"Sure, but it's just Hank, dear. Say, mighty good game you played today. I was very much impressed with your skill and agility on the field. Where did you learn those moves?"

"In my PE classes. I had to learn to watch closely; otherwise I was mostly useless on the field. What I wanted to know is there a pool table anywhere on campus that we can go to shoot some pool?"

"Yes, bottom floor of the Stadium building, room 404. Five tables. Why? Do you shoot pool too?"

"Yes, I love to shoot pool, sir."

"Incredible. Well, go have some fun. Got to run, Betsy will wonder where I've gotten to by now." He left with his soda.

Just as Ashley finished hers, Jim wandered in, looking for a sandwich or more. "Hey, hi there Miss Hotshot. What's up? I'm starving. Thought I'd get a snack before supper."

"I'm going to shoot pool. Hank told me where the tables are," Ashley replied.

"No kidding? Pool? Now this I have to see. Come on; I'll join you. I've played a bit of pool in my day. One of the norms in Arapahoe has a table. That's where I learned. Mind if I join you? I didn't know that we even had a pool table here."

"Why do you got to see this?" she asked defensively, still troubled by Phillip's two attacks on her.

"Cause I like to see the balls cracking. Hey, bet you five dollars that I clear the table before you do," he teased her.

"Huh? Well, buster, thanks for giving me a free five bucks! Come on. I'll take your money," she replied a bit huffily. The two headed for the Stadium. As they walked along enjoying the crisp cool air of the late afternoon, Jim slipped his arm around her waist. Ashley didn't protest, however.

They found the basement and then located the right room. She found a bar stool and pushed it over to the table while Jim racked up the balls. "You want to crack or should I?" Jim asked.

"Age before beauty," she retorted, allowing him to crack. Actually, she couldn't hit with enough force to crack effectively, that was her weakest part of her game. Jim sent the balls flying wildly, but none went in a pocket.

Ashley, with the barstool now near the table, walked to the cues and using her teeth pulled one out. With difficulty, she got it nestled between her head and shoulders and brought it to the table, allowing its bottom to slide to the floor, and then leaned it against the table. For a minute, she studied the lay of the balls. "Want me to call each shot?"

"No, just the eightball."

"Okay, the first five shots are plainly obvious. Have to see about the rest," Ashley said, becoming very serious in tone. She pushed the barstool to where she wanted it and sat down, picking up the cue stick in her toes. She put her left foot onto the side of the table to support her shot and laid the cue on top of her foot. With her right foot, she latched onto the center of the long wooden cue between her toes. She took her time and lined up the first shot. She propelled the cue with her right leg, and the cue ball flew across hitting the one ball into the side pocket with the cue ball moving right into position for her next shot.

"Lucky shot," Jim suggested.

"Little off," Ashley growled. Now she moved her stool to the other side and retrieved her cue. After sitting on the stool and placing her left leg in its proper position, she struggled to get the cue in the right place as well. "I'm really slow at this," she added. She lined up her shot carefully and again tapped the cue ball, which rolled nicely, knocking the five ball into the corner pocket. The cue ball came to rest where she desired. Again, she had to move the stool to the other end, positioning it just right, and then went back for the cue stick.

Jim watched, as she hit two stripped balls into the two opposing side pockets, with the cue ball lying nicely for the next shot. Once more, Ashley moved first her stool and then her stick. She studied the table for a minute. "I guess I'd be better off if the ball is in position for the seven ball after this shot." Jim knew that he could not make that happen, though he could drive in the nine ball that she was shooting. He watched fascinated as she tapped the ball and got precisely her desired result, for the cue ball was now in position for the seven ball.

"Unbelievable," Jim commented.

As he watched, Ashley continued to make shot after shot. Key to her strategy was cue ball position after it stopped rolling. It had to be in position for the next shot. At last, Ashley announced, "Eight ball, corner pocket." One more tap and the game was done. "You owe me a five."

Handing her the bill, which she took with her toes and stuffed into her dress pocket, Jim exclaimed, "Where did you *ever* learn to shoot like this? My god, are you are a pro or something?"

"Willie's Hangout," she replied. "It's really more of a dive. Chicago. I spent most of my childhood hanging around Willie's, both before school, after school, and all summer long. Sometimes, I even cut classes to hang out there. He's a fat, kindly old man, and he used to give me lessons and let me play whenever he wasn't busy, early mornings and afternoons mostly."

"How about another game? You crack this time," Jim suggested.

Sure enough, her crack was not great; the balls were not far apart. "I can't hit it hard enough for a proper crack," Ashley admitted, reluctantly.

Jim now proceeded to knock two balls in before he missed. Ashley got four in before she had to waste a shot attempting to break the bunched balls apart. This was a far closer game, as Jim then got another pair sunk. However, with the balls nicely broken, Ashley finished the game, stating "Eight ball, corner pocket." The black ball rolled nicely into the pocket.

"Rematch, I call for a rematch," Jim faked a mock protest.

"Well, I can tell what the outcome will be," Ashley declared. "You play pretty good for a beginner, but I believe that I'll take you each game. This is my worst game, when I have to crack. I can't hit the ball hard enough, you see. Would you please rack them up for me again, please? I have an awful time getting the balls out and up onto the table and into the rack."

Since she had asked, Jim did so at once. "You are darn good at pool, Ashley."

"Thanks, it is my stress reliever. When I get all tensed up, like today, I play pool, and it slowly calms me back down. I like having someone to play with me though. It's not often anyone would, you see."

"Why? I think you are a terrific player," Jim asked.

"Cause I'm so slow and really can't break properly. Hardly anyone would every play against me. Well, they might just once, until they discovered just how slow I am. I have to move the stool each time, fiddle with the cue stick. Honestly, it is terribly slow, and I have a devil of a time getting the balls out and back on the table. Always have, cause it's hard," she admitted, though she had never admitted this openly to anyone before, not even Willie.

While Jim didn't know this for sure, he suspected that she had just told him something very personal. His reply was tempered by his suspicion. "Yes, I see that, but the important thing is that you can do it, no matter how long it takes. You can play with me anytime you like. If we play long enough, maybe I will get better and be more of a challenge to you."

"Really? You can be that patient with me?" she asked timidly.

"You bet; you are one hot girl!" Jim replied sincerely.

Just then, the door opened and Deiter and Lyle entered. Both looked very surprised to see Jim and Ashley here. "Hi, I didn't think you knew about our pool room. Very few do," Deiter said.

Jim answered, "We just found out about it today."

"Say, Ashley, I want to apologize for Black Hall's conduct on the soccer field towards you today. Please don't judge all of us Black Hall guys by what Phil does. I thought that you were really a good player. Besides, Phil was being a ball hog today. Anyone could see the new first year players were often in the open, and he refused to pass to them," Deiter said, looking as if he meant what he said, at least Ashley thought so.

"Thanks. You are right. The first year forwards should have gotten lots more passes than they did. Why does Mr. Royston hate me so?"

Deiter squirmed. He had never been around someone like Ashley, and he feared upsetting her. He now knew about her temper too. "Cause you are a girl, and you are so different." He wanted to add "with no arms," but thought better of it. This was a wise move on his part.

"Well, I *am* different," she stated flatly and a bit annoyed. "I don't take anything from anybody, but I can see the girl thing," she admitted. "You boys think you are so hot. I guess that it makes sense why he didn't pass to the twins."

Deiter decided he had better change the subject, "Say, do you play pool?"

"Yes, we were just setting up another round," Ashley replied.

"Hey, how about a game, though I ought to warn you, Lyle and I are pretty darn good at this. You won't get upset if I skunk your butt, will you?" he teased with a grin, but beneath that facade, he was serious. He certainly didn't want to get into a fight with her or get her angry with him.

"I'm quite slow, but it may well be that I'll do the skunking. You won't be mad if I win?" she turned the tables on him.

"Nah, if you can beat me, then obviously you are a better player," Deiter replied.

"Okay, you can go first, crack away," Ashley suggested. Jim realized that she had just gotten him to play to her strongest game by having him crack. Jim smiled.

Deiter grinned, assembled his own cue stick, and hit the cue ball hard. Balls flew in many directions. A stripped ball went into a pocket. Deiter was off and running. He got three more balls sunk before he missed and Ashley's turn began. She knew that both would be staring at her, curious about how she could possibly play pool. Indeed both boys did, marveling at her dexterity.

Solid ball after solid ball fell into pockets, as Ashley began cleaning up the board on Deiter. "Amazing, how did you get the cue ball to stop precisely there? Incredible setup, Ashley," Deiter exclaimed.

"That's where I wanted it." She continued to slowly move her stool, then handle the stick, then reposition her body, then line up the shot, and finally taking it. "Eight ball, side pocket," she announced, and the ball went precisely there. "Game," she announced.

"That was incredible, Ashley. You skunked my butt!" Deiter exclaimed. However, instead of getting angry, he said, "You are darn good! I would never, ever have suspected that, not in a million years. Where did you ever learn to shoot like this? I mean, you are close to a professional shooter!"

Once more, Ashley explained about Willie's in Chicago. "I'm a little rusty. I haven't been able to play in months. They had a worn out table in the Twin Cities, only I got into too many fights there and got banned from the pool room for fighting."

Lyle finally spoke up, "Deiter's the best shooter on campus, well, until now anyway. I suppose that I ought to thank you for alerting him when I caught fire. Thanks." He looked mostly at the floor, unable to face her directly.

"Accepted," Ashley replied.

"Not the best—that's Professor Jasper Jones," Deiter changed the subject. "He usually comes down to shoot a game or two with us Saturday afternoons. He should be here pretty soon. You should shoot a game with him."

"With whom?" the voice of Jasper came from the doorway. He'd just arrived, carrying his cue case. "Hello, Jim, Ashley. Playing a bit of pool are we?"

"Yes, Professor. You won't believe this, but Ashley just skunked my butt!" Deiter told him.

Jasper's eye brows raised. "My, the things that we do not know about our students. Is this true?"

Jim and Lyle confirmed it. "Would you mind shooting a quick game with me?" he asked. "Mind you, I have been known to run the table on my turn."

"So has Ashley," Jim countered, Jasper smiled again.

"Okay, Miss Stokes, you are on. Would you like to crack?" Jasper asked kindly.

"No, you crack. If you run the table on me, so be it," Ashley replied, knowing better than to crack first, not when he was known to be able to run the table.

Jasper took aim and whacked the cue ball solidly; the balls flew well, and a solid fell into the corner pocket as he had intended. "I like the solids better," he said quietly. He proceeded to run five more balls straight before just barely missing one.

Ashley knew she was in a game! She knew that she had to run the board because Jasper was sure to finish on his next turn. She studied the table for several minutes before awkwardly scooting her stool to the first position. Of course, Jasper watched her every move, as did the others. She focused her attention on the table and began her turn. True, she was painstakingly slow at this, but ball after all went in to the pockets.

When she was down to her last two stripped balls, she misplayed the cue ball, which rolled out of position from where she had intended, though the other ball fell into the designated pocket. "Goofed that one," she said.

"How so? Looked fine to me; went in," Deiter asked, not understanding her comment.

"Cue ball is too far over to the right, Deiter," Jasper answered for her. "Now she has a tough shot. Let's see how she chooses to take this one."

After studying the board for a couple minutes, Ashley pronounced, "Stripped nine into corner pocket; eight ball into side pocket."

"Now that is a tricky shot indeed," Jasper commented.

"May I ask you why?"

"Because it is the only way I can win. You will likely run the table on me next. The only other possibility is for me to put the cue ball totally out of position for your next turn and hope for the best. I hate to do that, so I'm taking a gamble on the hard shot," Ashley replied. "I'd rather lose by my own shot."

Everyone held their breath, as she took twice her normal time to line up her legs and the shot. She gave it a gentle tap and the cue ball hit the nine ball, which rolled slowly and dropped into the corner pocket. The cue ball bounced back and tapped the eight ball, which rolled ever so slowly towards the side pocket. Ashley held her breath. It slowed down and, just as it started to come to a stop, it hit the dip and rolled into the side pocket. "Whew, that was a close one!" she exclaimed.

"Congratulations, Ashley, you are the first pool player to run the board on me here at Bradbury's! Incredible game!" Jasper complimented her. "I have a favor to ask of you?"

Beaming at the unexpected compliment, she asked what. He explained, "Would you be so kind as to play some games with me on Saturday afternoons? I usually try to come here and shoot a few before supper. Keeps me alert and relaxed."

"Sure, you are a hot shooter yourself. I was really worried that you would run the board on me," she replied.

"Thanks, it will be good fun. Might I ask how your crack is? I noticed that you gambled that I wouldn't be able to run the board on you," Jasper asked.

"Bad, sir. I can't crack worth a darn. I just can't get much force in my drives. Jim can vouch for that," she answered.

"I suspected that might be the case after I watched your game," he acknowledged. "Say, I have a bright idea. Jim, you play too, right?" He nodded. "You know, we have enough players that we ought to start up a pool club, hold regular meetings, share tips and pointers, that sort of thing. Are you all interested?"

Everyone was indeed. "Great! I love pool; this will be fun. I'll run the paperwork by Alister tonight. What say we plan to meet about four each Saturday for an hour?" Again, this fit everyone's schedules.

"Say, Ashley, may I ask you a personal question?" Jasper asked, changing the subject for a moment.

"Willie's Hangout in Chicago," Ashley answered, figuring he wanted to know where she learned to play.

"No, I was going to ask how you did in geometry class?" Jasper chuckled. Jim, Deiter, and Lyle gave him a silly look as if to say, "What's geometry got to do with it?"

"Aced geometry. That was a very easy subject for me. Why?" she replied.

"Because, pool is all about angles and the physics of motion. You all have noticed that none of her shots was sharp, crisp, and hard. No ball flew solidly into a pocket. Rather, I noticed that her game is one of precise angles of contact and aim, with each shot placing the cue ball precisely where it needs to be for her to have a good follow up shot. That boys, is geometry in action."

"A lot of practice too, sir," Ashley admitted. "I'm so slow and hit so softly that I have to be very accurate to have any chance at all."

"Precisely so. Play to your strengths, whatever they may be," Jasper validated her. "Gosh, kids, I am really excited about this club! You've made an old man's day. Say, we had better head down to dinner. It's getting late." All walked together back to the dining room. At supper, Ashley just had to tell everyone about the new pool club. She was very pleased indeed. Gone was all her pent up anger and hostility. Shooting pool had calmed her once again.

During the next week of spell casting, Professor Thronby taught them the Skin of Stone spell. This one Amanda particularly desired to know, for she had found it highly beneficial not only in the soccer matches, but in the fights in which she had participated. That took three days for them to master fully.

However, in US History class, Professor Elaine Mac Elroy announced, "Now that we have studied about the first settlements of our country, it's time for us to take our first field trip to Jamestown, Plymouth, and the Massachusetts Bay area.

We will be going there on Thursday evening right after dinner. Boston School of Magic will be giving us sleeping quarters that night. Sorry Andy, there will be no time to tour their school." He frowned.

"On Friday, we will be taking the many guided tours, returning here on Friday night. We will travel on one of our school buses. This means that you will have no classes on Friday. The other professors know about these field trips and have adjusted their schedules accordingly. No, Miss Betts, there will be no work to make up." Several giggled at her comment. Pam relaxed at last; she had been worried that they would be missing an entire day's worth of lectures and would have to work to catch back up.

Chapter 6—First Field Trip

Thursday afternoon, both theory classes were cancelled. Lindsey went from third year to third year girl explaining what they were to take on the trip. She began with her group. "We're to wear our usual school dresses, but bring along our robes in case the weather is cold or rainy. We're to bring along at the very most five dollars spending money and nothing of great value, so no computers, please. They're worried about theft or loss, you see. We're allowed one small overnight bag with spare clothes and sundries. These will be left on the bus while we are touring and guarded by a security man. The bus leaves at six tonight, right after dinner."

Pam moaned, "No computer?" How could she live without hers? While her roommates began packing, Lindsey went from door to door, telling the other third year girls the rules. A half hour later, she began her packing as well. It was dark as the hundred third year students lined up at the main gates, awaiting the bus. Both Mac Elroy's were hosting the trip, and each went down their respective lines, checking off the names of those in line. Once they confirmed everyone was here, boarding began. As usual, they were taking the two-tiered bus, and Lindsey and her group managed to confiscate the rear seats as usual.

Andy sat next to Lindsey, who was next to Ashley. Andy lamented, "I sure wish we had the time so I could show you around my old campus."

"I know. It has to be awful going back, but not being able to visit with your old friends," Lindsey replied.

After the Mac Elroy professors boarded, four Department of Security men climbed aboard. Jimmy, their driver, was the last, having shut the baggage compartment. Slowly, the bus moved out of the parking lot and traveled up the state road 145. From there, they hit US 550 into Grand Junction, where they got on Interstate 70, heading east. For a while, everyone chatted, excited about their first trip.

Not long after that, some Black Hall students began

singing, "99 bottles of beer on the wall." Lindsey groaned. They'd have to listen to this one forever. Fortunately, they ended by 87 bottles. It was dark and boring, flying along at their incredible clip. Jimmy actually put the bus into seventh gear. He'd never gone this fast before and was excited. Not so with the students. Lindsey fell asleep, leaning on Andy. Ashley likewise leaned on Lindsey. Time flew by.

Around nine that night, the bus suddenly materialized with a popping sound in the parking lot at Boston School of Magic, waking everyone up. Professor Herbert spoke loudly. "We will be staying at their old dorm. Boys will be housed on the left, girls on the right. Their layout is very different from ours. The restrooms are at the end of each side of the hall. All students must stay in the dorm. No one is allowed to leave the dorm for any reason. We will breakfast in their dining hall promptly at six, before their students usually are up. We will reload the bus at 6:30 a.m. Don't be late. As we unload, find your bag and get into the appropriate line."

A half hour later, the two long lines marched across the rather dark campus. They could see the forms of buildings, but little else. A few Boston students stopped and watched them curiously, however.

"This place is a dump!" declared Ashley, as they entered a dorm room that held eight girls.

"Well, it's an old, unused dorm," Lindsey countered. Everyone turned in early. There wasn't even a TV set in their room or a commons room available.

At six, they headed to the main dining room, a modern cafeteria, very well equipped and quite large. In fact, it looked exactly like their own dining room. Buffet style suited everyone. Professor Elaine encouraged everyone to eat well, because lunch would not be until noon.

While they were eating, an older professor came rushing up to Andy, who was eating beside Lindsey. "Ah, here you are, Andy."

"Professor Jorgensen! Hi, great to see you. We weren't allowed to go visiting. Gang, this is Professor Jorgensen, my old archaeology professor!" Andy exclaimed excitedly.

"Andy, have you heard the latest from ArchMagNews?"

Andy hadn't. "It's Professor Jacques Flambois! He was found murdered in his campus office yesterday. The crown is missing and presumed stolen! I just had to let you know. Have to run. Great seeing you. Nice meeting you students." The older man rushed off as suddenly as he had come.

"What was that all about?" asked Lindsey.

"Professor Jacques Flambois is an underwater archaeologist. He made one of the greatest archaeological finds of the century a month ago. Diving off Cyprus, he found the Crown of Moses. He brought it back to study in his office in the Bordeaux University, France. The last thing I saw was that it was going to be put on public display this week. Man, who would want to steal a priceless, historical relic anyway? The creep!"

"What does it do?" asked Pam.

"Well, no one knows for sure, really. Biblical scholars— you know how scientific-not they are—they claim it has all sorts of God-bestowed powers. Everyone was awaiting Professor Flambois to give his first presentation to the Academy this week. Some claim that it was used by Moses to control the weather while he led his people across the Sinai, but who knows. Maybe now we will never know," Andy lamented.

"If only we had our computers," Pam griped. "Then, we could find out more information. We don't even have the news on TV."

Andy sighed, "It probably wouldn't make KMAG news. You know, the murder of a French professor in France is not of much importance over here. That's why he said it was on the ArchMagNews channel. Ah well, I guess I will have to wait until we get back to find out what's going on. Maybe by then they will have captured whoever did it." Andy tried to sound hopeful.

Lindsey wondered who would want to steal such a relic. She could only think of one person, Dominus Malefic, though she could think of no reason why he would want to go to France to steal it.

Ashley commented, "I have a really strong feeling that this is a very bad thing, but I don't know why." Pam resolved to dig into the whole thing, just as soon as she could get back to her computer.

An hour later, they climbed off the bus and began the first of five guided tours. Later, they ate outdoors at the concession stand at Williamsburg. By the time that they stopped at Mac Donald's for supper, everyone was quite tired from all the walking, though they mostly enjoyed seeing all the historical reproductions and the few actual ruins that remained. With full bellies, the students mostly slept all the way back home, as the bus drove through the early evening hours, arriving at Bradbury's just after nine that night. It was ten before everyone was back in their rooms, all too tired to do anything but head for bed.

On Saturday, Blue Hall was challenging Red Hall in a track meet. However, Andy and Pam stayed behind. Both had spent the morning together in the study hall of Yellow Hall finding out all the latest news. Pam had never heard of the ArchMagNews and was eagerly listening to the coverage. Much time was spent on interviews of various professors, who gave their speculations about this mysterious Crown of Moses. By lunchtime, both Pam and Andy realized that the facts were scant at best. After lunch, they began researching on their own, trading URLs that looked promising.

In the middle of the afternoon, Lindsey and friends returned, telling them about Blue Hall's victory. Andy and Pam had little to report. Nearly everything was mere speculation. Worse, all the Professor's lab notes were stolen along with the crown. The only hopeful detail was that the Professor had sent his preliminary findings to the Paris Archaeological Society. They had just received them and had promised to publish the document in full tomorrow on their Web page.

Sunday morning, Lindsey joined Pam and Andy for breakfast. Both had their laptops with them and were viewing their bookmarked Web pages. "Yes! It's here." Eagerly, all three scanned the five-page document. Much of the first pages contained details of precisely where Professor Flambois had found the relic. Another two pages contained the methods he used to clean the relic. On the last page, finally he began discussing what he had learned of power that the Crown of Moses held. "Certainly, its primary function is to control the weather in an area. I don't believe it can do so on a global scale, however. This power is activated by placing the crown upon one's head. During the ensuing weeks, I will be systematically analyzing the crown further, documenting every power that it possesses. Expect another formal presentation in about a month."

"Well, it sounds like this crown can just cast our usual magical Control Weather spell," Pam declared. "We will learn that one in our fifth year. I looked it up."

"Well, for a time there, I thought that Dominus might be behind this," Lindsey admitted. "Now I can see that was a silly notion. After all, if a fifth year can cast this spell, then there is no need for him to go after this crown. May be it was some art thieves after all."

"It certainly looks that way," Andy agreed.

Just then, Amanda Messaged them.

Come quick to the commons. Dominus in going to be on TV!

A.

Lindsey relayed the message, and they packed up their computers and headed to the commons. All their friends were now there, though many were still wiping the sleep from their eyes. Indeed, about half of Yellow Hall gathered around the giant screen.

The usual political campaign theme music played, and then the cameras showed a typical political stage setting. A large banner across the back said, "Dominus Malefic for President." Lindsey recognized the single man standing at the central podium—Dominus himself.

"Wizards and witches, ladies and gentlemen. I am Wizard Dominus Malefic, perhaps the most powerful wizard in our wonderful US of A. I have decided that our country needs new leadership, leadership that can rise to the real problems of our magnificent country. I have therefore given this careful consideration. Today, I'm proud to announce to every citizen of this fair country that I, Dominus Malefic, am now a candidate for the President of the United States."

The camera panned to a large crowd of supporters who

began yelling, cheering, and clapping loudly, while he graciously accepted their show of support. At last, he motioned for calm so that he could continue.

"I have already published my Manifesto. However, some have misunderstood that plain English, pushing forth the utter and outright lie that I personally hate and despise those who by birth are unable to use magical energies." He leaned forward, as if making contact with the audience, "I want to set the record straight. I do not loath and hate normal human beings! After all, how stupid do these pundits believe I am? Look, between you and me, where would we all be if we had no chefs, no waiters, no automobile repairmen, no farmers, no bankers, no bakers, or no manufacturers? Not even I could survive long without these people. No indeed, everyone has their proper place in this world."

"I firmly believe that my place is in the White House, to lead our fantastic country for the next four years down the proper road. To be elected, I need the support not only of those few in the magical communities but also all you normal citizens. I don't care what the color of your skin might be nor do I care what accent you may have. We are all Americans!"

"Over the coming months, I will come before you as I am this fine Sunday morning and outline my position on all the major issues facing our country in these trying times. For security reasons, the day and time of these broadcasts will not be published until close to the air date. You understand that many wish to kill me as I run for the highest office and honor my country can bestow upon me. I promise you that I will present a totally clear position on each issue."

"Indeed, if you have issues that you wish me to specifically address, there is an email address scrolling at the bottom of your screen. Let me know your concerns, and I will do my best to address them in the coming broadcasts."

"I will say this now. I'm financing my campaign totally with my own funds. Please do not try to send me any campaign contributions! They'll be returned. I want the world to know that I am not nor will ever be swayed by any political action group, religious group, or those who seek to gain special favors by making large financial contributions to my campaign. For the first time in centuries, you can elect a President who is completely free of such underhanded influences! This is the guarantee that I make to you."

"I need your support and vote thirteen months from now at the polls, as we all elect our next President of the United States. I hope during the coming months to prove to every one of you that I am by far the best candidate to lead our glorious country for the next four years. Until my next broadcast, this is Dominus Malefic wishing each and every American a prosperous and happy fall."

Again, the crowd responded, right on cue, as if it had been carefully arranged. For several minutes, the camera showed the enthusiastic crowd, many waving American flags. Showers of red, white, and blue balloons fell from the ceiling, adding to the overall atmosphere.

At last, the image switched back to the usual KMAG announcer, Hugo, who continued to smile, flashing his very white teeth. "Well, there you have it. Dominus Malefic is now officially in the Presidential race, along with President Lucius Dollington and Senator Missy Snow of Massachusetts. I must say, this surprise announcement has taken this veteran political watcher completely by surprise."

"However, after the short commercial break, I have four political analysts lined up, who will give us their views on this most incredible and startling announcement." His image faded, replaced by an inane jingle advertising a breakfast cereal.

"Convicted criminals cannot hold public office!" declared Pam loudly.

Someone replied, "Yes, but if he gets elected, he can do any darn thing he desires." Now a loud round of discussion began among the students, most believing that it would be illegal for him even to run for President.

A bit later, Hugo returned with the latest news, before launching into the comments of the four political analysts. "Hurricane Emily, the season's fifth hurricane is now a category 3 storm, barreling along north of Cuba. It is expected to make landfall on Tuesday somewhere along the south Texas coast. Residents there are boarding up their windows. KMAG will have full video coverage of these advanced preparations later this morning. Now, I have with me in the studio four well respected gentlemen." He began introducing the pundits.

Lindsey and her friends had enough of this and decided their time would be better spent on with their homework. A few minutes later, they gathered in the study hall. An hour later, Jim came in looking for Ashley. "Hey, come take a short break, Ashley. I have something that is really cool to show you."

Ashley's cheeks felt warm, though she didn't know why. She left her pile of books and followed him outside the dorm. "What is it?" she asked, as he slid his arm around her waist, leading her toward the Formal Gardens.

"Listen," he said as they walked to the far edge of the gardens, closest to the outer protective wall.

"What is that noise?" she asked, now hearing the strangest sounds she'd ever heard.

"Elk. The elk herds are coming down from the high country for the winter. Snow gets deep way up there," he pointed. "So each fall, the elk and deer herds migrate to the lower elevations, like they are doing right now. The elk make the most incredible noises when they are moving to the lower elevations. Isn't this a really fantastic sound?"

"I've never heard anything like it! I wish we could see them," she replied.

"That's easy." Jim cast a levitate spell on both and they rose up high into the air until they could see a herd of at least twenty-five animals. Ashley watched totally fascinated, never having seen anything like this before, for she was, after all, a city girl.

Sometime later, Jim walked her back, his arm again around her waist and shoulder. "Thanks for showing me that, Jim. It was just, well, incredible."

"I thought my little hot shot would appreciate hearing it. Very few people ever get a chance to hear them. You are now one of them," Jim smiled, giving her a little hug as he opened the door for her. Back in the study hall, she related what she'd heard.

Later in the afternoon, Lindsey and Ashley went out to

the gardens to practice their spells. After going through the ones that they had learned so far, Ashley asked, "Lindsey, would you help me try to learn some more in our special way?"

"Sure, thing. Honestly, we have our homework done for Monday, so why not?" Lindsey replied. "Let's see, we are up to Grade 2 spells now. After our last attempts, I think I can tell rapidly if you will be able to do one or not. Plus, Professor Dogs has been teaching me to recognize spells rapidly so I think that will help us. Let's go down the list, okay?"

"Okay, gosh, I hope I can learn to do a few more like you do, Lindsey." Methodically, Lindsey had Ashley going through each of their Grade 2 spells. Somehow, as Ashley tried to cast each non-verbally and without her wand, Lindsey could tell instantly whether it would be fruitful to work further on a given spell. She could sense the potential buildup of the magical energies and the actual amount.

"Okay, Read Another's Thoughts looks promising, as does Invisibility and Levitate," Lindsey noted. "I think we can get those three. Let's give them a try." An hour later, Ashley was extremely happy with the results. She could now cast all three just like Lindsey. With these three spells, she had a terrific knack.

Next, Lindsey had Ashley methodically go through all their Grade 3 spells, while she carefully observed the magical signs. Out of all these, she saw the potential of three more. Near suppertime, Ashley had mastered them, Listen from a Distance, See from a Distance, and Dispel Magic.

As the two girls walked back to the dining room for supper, Ashley observed, "You know, the ones that I'm able to do our special way—they seem to be the kind of spells that a Diviner ought to know well. Strange or maybe not so strange. At first, I was kind of hoping that I might be able to produce a Ball of Fire this way, but now that I think about it, if I could, I might just use it when I get really angry and hurt someone, violating the Four Cardinal Rules of Magic Use."

"I think you might be right, Ashley. At least the spells seem to be going that way. Should we keep your successes our secret or can we tell the others?"

"Please, I get enough stares as it is, Lindsey. Let's keep

this between ourselves." Lindsey could not refuse her. After all, she knew very well how much that staring actually hurt. She'd lived with that for twelve years.

Every student eagerly awaited Professor Thronby's spell casting class on Monday afternoon. The light drizzle that began to fall didn't affect their sprits in the slightest. This was morph week! Yes, they had diligently studied the theory of altering one's body into another's form. Finally, they would learn how to Morph Oneself into Another or Morph Another into Another. Indeed, Lindsey approached this with some hesitation, for this was the spell that Dominus had used on himself to impersonate her during her first year when he had tried to steal the Rod of the Apocalypse. Of course, there was two versions of the Morph, the spell version and the potion version. Dominus had used the potion version, which required a sample of the target DNA. While the spell version had a short, finite duration, the potion version lasted indefinitely as long as the target DNA person remained alive.

Pam was more excited than usual because this was a most intriguing spell for a Sleuth not only to know how it was done but actually to be able to use it on themselves. No, Pam had no intentions of appearing as one of the Death Stalkers so she could infiltrate the organization of Dominus. Rather, its mastery would allow her keen, firsthand insights into the spell, which she knew many nefarious men used to aid them in commission of crimes.

The first day of their attempts, only Pam succeeded in changing herself into Amanda. "Whoa! Look, there are *two* Amandas!" exclaimed Deiter, who had been surreptitiously eyeing the others to see if they were being any more successful than he was. Everyone looked at the Amandas.

"Hey, I'm me," Amanda said.

"No, I'm me," the other Amanda said.

The class roared with laughter at this seeming paradox. Pam cancelled her spell, and for the first time, the whole class applauded her. Her face heated up like an oven, however. "Very well done, Miss Betts!" Professor Arthur complimented her. "Usually, the first student is finally successful the second day. Well done indeed."

First thing on Tuesday, suddenly two Lindsey's appeared in the classroom. Again, Deiter didn't miss the change. He was having quite a lot of trouble with these spells. "Look, Ashley must have done it. She's another Lindsey!" Again, the whole class stopped to stare at the two identical Lindseys.

Lyle commented, "Well, you can tell which one is the real Lindsey." Half the class asked him how? "Oh, that's easy. That one is Ashley. See, that one doesn't know what to do with arms."

This was in fact true. Ashley had no idea what to do with the two dangling appendages attached to her shoulders. She still had her wand between her right toes, her arms dangling at her sides. Her face turned beet red. Normally, Ashley would have become violently angry and attacked Lyle. However, this time she was highly embarrassed. She felt very strange with these arms at her sides. Unable to find any outlet, she could only cry, which only added to her misery. That half of the class giggled, especially many of the Black Hall girls, led by Peaches, only added to her grief.

Anger instantly flashed upon Professor Thronby's face. "That will do!" He instantly cancelled Ashley's spell, allowing her to return to her normal form. "So you all think that it's funny, a joke, to see someone wrestling with unfamiliar bodies. Well, I believe that it's time that everyone gets a chance to experience what Miss Stokes has to deal with every hour of every day! Well, not everyone. I see that Lindsey, Pam, Amanda, Kathy, Emilio, Andy, and Audrey understand." Some of his immediate anger subsided. "You eight carry on with your casting attempts. The rest of you, it's time to gain some understanding of Miss Stokes!" He waved his wand and cast a group Morph spell. Pam's eyes opened wide! She didn't know that it was possible for one spell to impact a whole group of people!

Suddenly, there were twenty-two more Ashley's in the room! Almost at once, shrieks and cries of shock and surprise echoed around the room, as the eight stared in disbelief at the sudden appearance of the Ashley's. "Now then, all you new Ashley's you are to continue trying to cast your Morph spells as best you can!" Professor Thornby barked unsympathetically at them. Of course, all their wands had fallen on the floor during their physical alterations.

As the stark reality set in on the students, many began crying. Peaches attempted to pick up her wand with her teeth but fell onto the floor. Vainly, she tried to get back up and had a devil of a time doing so. Slowly fear crept into many of these students as well. They felt completely helpless.

Having gotten over the shock of what had happened, the eight continued to work on their spells. "I got it!" exclaimed Lindsey, who now looked identical to Ashley, although her wand also fell to the floor during the change.

"Cool, Lindsey! You did it!" Ashley now forgot about her misery and gave her partner well deserved praise for having succeeded at last. Professor Arthur nodded at both girls, and Lindsey cancelled her spell, returning to her normal form, retrieving her wand.

"Thanks, I think I got the hang of it, Ashley. Let's do this some more!"

"Hey, look at me," exclaimed Amanda, who was now a duplicate of Pam.

"Way cool!" Emilio complimented her, as did Kathy.

"How about this?" said Kathy, who now looked like Emilio. It was break through time for the eight, as they finally figured out the spell. For ten minutes, various Kathy's, Emilio's, Pam's, Amanda's, Audrey's, Lindsey's, Andy's, and new Ashley's began appearing and disappearing. All eight were now ecstatic with their successes.

As the period ended, Deiter, who looked like Ashley, came over to Ashley. "Ashley, I'm truly sorry that I made fun of you. Please accept my apology. Oh, I am Deiter Cross, really."

She looked at the image of herself, but detected he was sincere, and she replied, "Accepted Deiter. Thanks." Instantly, Deiter changed back into his normal form, surprising himself, as well as Ashley.

Professor Arthur smiled. Peaches, who had finally gotten back on her feet, cheeks wet from crying, also came over to Ashley. "I'm Peaches. I, I never realized how difficult it is to be you. I'm sorry I laughed at you. I promise I won't ever do it again, Ashley."

"Okay," Ashley could think of nothing else to say to her. Again, magic flashed as the spell cancelled, and she returned to her own form. As she stood there looking again at her arms and body, she instantly threw her arms around Ashley, giving her a big hug.

She whispered, "If you ever need anything, just ask me." Ashley flushed, but accepted her.

During the next five minutes, another twenty Ashley's came up to her and apologized to her. Each time, after she accepted it, the spell cancelled itself, and the person returned to their normal form.

"I hope you have all learned a valuable lesson here today," Professor Thornby addressed them as the period ended. "Next time you encounter someone who is somehow different than you are, before you tease them and make fun of them, walk a mile in their shoes and then see if you still feel like taunting them. Personally, I have the highest respect for Miss Stokes and what she has thus far accomplished. Practice your spells. I expect the rest of you to have this one down tomorrow."

On their way to their next class, Pam said to Ashley, "God that was an embarrassing class! I thought you handled it very well. I know I could not have! I'd of been a complete basket case, Ashley. You have more guts than I do, that's for sure."

"I was so humiliated at first, Pam. I couldn't even lash out, but then it felt rather good to see them experiencing what it is to be me. Is it possible that they understand me better now? Will they actually stop hounding me so?"

"I think so," Amanda sounded a hopeful note. "Some were more than a little shocked by the experience. I think you have earned their respect today, rather the opposite of what Dominus is doing by trying to split us all apart." Ashley took heart with this conclusion.

By the end of the week, the whole class had both of the spells down well. Ashley also discovered that she now did have the respect of her classmates. Actually, too much so, for many continually asked if she needed help with this and that. She couldn't get angry with them over this, knowing that they genuinely wanted to assist her if she needed it.

The steady drizzle continued to fall all week as well, making the grounds very soaked. The track meet between Black Hall and Blue Hall was a soggy mess, with Black Hall winning, thought their times were poor. Only a few loyal supporters witnessed the meet.

Andy took time to check up on the latest news. Not a word was heard about the murder of the French professor, however. Hurricane Emily was the major news. "Freakish!" Andy explained to the others gathered in the study hall. "It's been stalled out over the Caribbean Sea all week. It is defying all hurricane predictions."

"What's it supposed to do?" asked Lindsey, who had never given hurricanes much attention. After all, there were no hurricanes in Colorado.

Andy typed in a CNN URL and showed everyone what normal hurricane tracks looked like, adding, "See, Emily is just stalled there, a hundred miles off the south Texas coast. Weird."

"Is that why we have been getting drizzle all week?" asked Audrey, who also had little knowledge of hurricanes. Tornadoes—now those she knew about, having once actually seen one.

"According to the weather man on KMAG, yes. Here, I'll show you." He clicked on another web site that showed the overall radar images. "See how the storm's pushing rain far inland?"

"I'm glad we're not in south Texas," Emilio stated, "I bet they are completely drenched after a week of rain. Say, can anyone tell me why magnesium strips burn? I thought it was a metal." Pam and Andy groaned. It was back to chemistry tutoring.

While the drizzle continued all the next week, it did not dampen Pam's spirits. Spell casting suddenly became exceedingly interesting for her especially. On Monday, they began to learn how to cast the Spying Eye, in which they created movable eye that they could extend out from them to check on what lay ahead. "Now you can know before you go!" declared Pam.

However, Professor Thornby's admonition caused a few flushes among the boys. "If anyone thinks that they can use this spell to spy on the girl's or boy's rooms, think again. Governor Alister has installed a special spell that will instantly alert him to the culprit." Emilio sighed, as one clever use of this spell was just shot down. The girls giggled at his pronouncement.

On Wednesday, it was Audrey's turn to be very excited, Plant Growth was taught. A large patch of vegetation could be caused to grow into a dense thicket bordering upon a jungle. Most would use it to form a barrier from their pursuers, forcing them to hack their way through. Not Audrey, she saw all sorts of excellent uses for this spell. Indeed, she was the first to cast this spell successfully.

Beginning on Friday, it was Lindsey's turn to become very elated with spell casting. Finally, she learned how to cast the Lesser Invulnerability spell, which her staff had been providing her. While the spell was in operation, no Grade 0 through Grade 3 spell would have any effect upon the caster. This eliminated Balls of Fire and Lightning Bolt spells. At the moment, her spell would only last around five minutes compared to the ten or more from her staff. Still, in time, as she used it and grew more experienced with it, her duration would eventually exceed that of her trusty staff. Not unexpectedly, only Lindsey managed to successfully cast this one on Friday.

The next week, they added the Prolong spell to their repertoire, which they could use to make their Grade 1 through 3 spell durations last twice as long. On Wednesday, they began to learn how to Morph into Objects. Often, as Professor Thornby explained, one could use this to hide a group of people, disguised as trees and such. The class roared with laughter, as one by one, their classmates turned into various kinds of trees and then reappeared as themselves. Finally, on Friday, they learned an Improved Fog spell, in which the fog was so dense and thick that only a very strong breeze could move it away. It blocked all sight. Considering the continual drizzle, this only added to the darkness of the day.

"It's still parked off the Texas coast," Andy reported on Saturday morning. Indeed, Hurricane Emily was now causing major flooding all over southwestern Texas and down into Mexico. Worse, the continued weeks of constant blow was hampering the oil to gas refineries along the gulf coast. Already the price of gas had begun climbing, soaring to new heights of nearly five dollars a gallon. While this was major news for the adults, none of the students paid much attention to it.

However, as Pam passed by the big screen TV on her way into the study hall, something caught her attention. The announcer, Hugo, said, "The Department of Defense is looking into this anomalous hurricane Emily. Among knowledgeable wizards, many are speculating that some form of magic is preventing the hurricane from moving. KMAG has just learned that the Department of Defense, Texas, has requested the assistance of six powerful wizards. They are being charged with casting spells to push this hurricane on its way. KMAG reporters caught up with Mage Allen Barnaby and put these questions to him. Here is his reply."

Mage Allen declared, "While we cannot say for sure if there are any magical effects in play with this hurricane, the important point is that we wizards concentrate our efforts to get Emily un-stalled. Texas has asked us to push her back out to sea, but officials have also suggested that they would be satisfied if she just went on her way inland, dissipating into a tropical storm and vanishing altogether. Of course, we will be working in close cooperation with the Department of Magical Misuse, Texas, but it is my expressed opinion that no magic is involved. After all, it is just Mother Nature at work, showing us once more how much we do not know about Nature and storms."

Pam left the commons and unloaded her things in the study hall. While the others were working on their homework, she began doing a bit of research on her own. That the Department of Defense, Magic Section, was involved, along with many powerful mages, this was more than enough to convince Pam that something was terribly wrong. She didn't believe Mother Nature could be doing what she was doing with this hurricane, and Pam intended to prove it.

Andy came in. "Hey, it's snowing outside!"

"It won't last long," Lindsey explained. "Last two years, it snowed a bit in October, but it all melted quickly. The big snows start in November. Sometimes several feet build up on out mountain out there. What I don't get is why we have to learn the names of all our Presidents? What good is that information?"

"So we know who is on our money?" ventured Kathy.

"I can see knowing the famous ones like the ones who did notable things," Ashley suggested. "Like George Washington and Abe Lincoln. I guess they want us to know Clinton as the adulterer president, but why?"

"Maybe so we know that there have been good Presidents and bad ones," Audrey added. "Sure have also been a lot of mediocre ones too. I'm terrible at memorization."

"Just bone up on Independence stuff; our trip on Thursday is to Independence Hall and the Liberty Bell," Lindsey advised. "The November trip is to see the Lincoln sights in Illinois."

Andy ducked outside and came back inside. "Hey Lindsey," he yelled. As she looked up, he tossed a small snowball at her.

"Oh, now you've gone and done it!" she exclaimed, faking an angry tone. Everyone charged outside, and a grand snowball fight began—little snow balls, however, as only a half inch was on the ground, perfect packing snow. Only Ashley didn't participate, she couldn't make snowballs easily, let alone throw them.

Instead, Jim appeared with two heavier coats. "Care for a snowflake stroll, Miss Stokes?" he said, as she watched the silly antics of her friends, who were now casting numerous Warm spells on themselves, as they headed back inside, laughing. Jim draped the coat over Ashley, put his arm around her waist, and led her off across the snow-covered ground. Large snowflakes were constantly descending upon them.

"Whatever is a snowflake stroll?" she asked.

"This," Jim said, throwing his hands up trying to catch

some of the flakes. She looked a bit baffled, though, so he admitted, "Okay, I just wanted to take some time off of my studies and be with you a while."

She blushed, and the two walked around the picturesque campus. He returned her to the study hall a while later, her cheeks pink from the cold, but her eyes were bright. Jim had given her a romantic first kiss, taking her completely by surprise. Her stomach was now butterflies; her mind racing between opposite ideas. Does he really like me? I like him. Or is he just patronizing me because I cannot even make a snow ball? Why should he like me anyway? For some time, she stared at her homework, but made no progress.

Ashley was very glad when Pam began talking, interrupting them all. "Look, this hurricane behavior is definitely not natural. I've been looking at every recorded hurricane path since they started tracking them somewhat during the middle of the last century. Not one behaved as Emily is. Some appeared to stall for a few hours or may have had little movement for a day, but none completely stopped in its tracks for weeks!"

"Further, look at these images of the jet stream," she displayed another image on her laptop so all could see.

"Isn't that what comes out the rear of jets at the airport?" Kathy asked. "I remember seeing signs warning us to stay out of the jet's stream."

"It's a high level atmospheric air flow pattern, very fast moving. It often helps drive weather patterns or at least moves the highs and lows about," Pam explained, not even bothering to sigh. Kathy really was bad at science things. Pam wanted to tell her she would be better off reading science magazines instead of the latest teen fashion mags, but thought better of it.

"See, this time of year, here is where it should be going, sweeping way down south here. Now look at the latest images of the jet stream. See, it is being forced way north of its usual location."

"So what does it all mean?" asked Emilio, trying hard to follow her. "Someone is messing with the jet stream?"

"No, I don't think that just making the jet stream stay way north is going to keep Emily from moving. I think some kind of magic is being used on the hurricane. Probably a byproduct of that interference is what is keeping the jet stream so far north," Pam presented her conclusion.

"Who'd want to do that?" asked Emilio. "The major oil companies? They are making a killing on gas prices or so Hugo keeps saying."

Pam bit her lip. Emilio was ahead of her sleuthing. "Well, perhaps, but I don't know yet, but I intend to find out."

On Monday, Professor Cho Lin began teaching them their new Illusion based spells. "Eight more days to Halloween. I have just the spell for you ornery fellows, Cause Fear. Remember, you need to be creative in the scary sights you are placing in your spell." By the end of the hours, boys and girls were shrieking in terror from some of the sights their classmates cast upon them. Still, when it was done, everyone laughed for it was nearly Halloween.

On Tuesday, she became more serious. "Today and Wednesday, we are going to learn a spell called Imaginary Monsters. If someone is pursuing you, this one is handy. When you cast this illusion, you must imagine the horrible looking creature that you want the person to think he is seeing. It will appear to be just as strong as you are, though as you get better with this spell, its strength can become many times stronger than you actually are. If you make the illusion believable, the person will truly believe that he or she is fighting this creature. Here is where you need to be careful. If the creature is fighting your opponent, he or she will suffer real physical damage as a result. It is the mind bringing into existence what it believes is happening. Do be careful with this spell, as it is not a harmless one."

By the end of the class on Wednesday, everyone in the class just *had* to have Ashley cast her spell on them so that they could see the fabulous monsters Ashley had dreamed up! Indeed, no one else's imaginary creatures looked as nasty as those that Ashley envisioned. Even Deiter gave her a compliment for the coolest, meanest looking monsters ever. Lindsey suspected the monsters were perhaps tied into the anger that Ashley often experienced, though she said nothing about her speculation.

As they climbed onto the bus on Thursday just after lunch for their field trip, the snowfall rate had increased. Already six inches covered the ground, highly unusual for this time of year. Spirits were high as they headed off to Philadelphia to visit the sights associated with the country's independence.

This would be a day trip. Because of the inclement weather, the Department of Defense had modified the bus to go even faster. Carefully, Tom entered the precise coordinates of their destination into the GeoSat Navigator System. "Okay, Jimmy, once you hit the I70, kick it into ninth gear." Jimmy let out a squeal of pure joy! This would be the fastest bus ride ever, and he was to be the driver.

Actually, Jimmy had little to do. An onboard computer, linked to the GeoSat satellite, controlled the movement of the bus in this magically altered space. Everything was automated, based upon the latitude and longitude coordinates of their location and their destination. The computer memory contained the road map of the country, and the computer really directed the bus's movement. Jimmy merely shifted it into gear and made sure that nothing unexpected happened.

The bus followed the same path it had on their previous trip to the east coast. As they drove up to Grand Junction, the roads were nicely plowed. The scenery was breathtaking. As the bus got onto I70, blinds automatically came down over the windows. Tom explained, "We will be going so fast that it is highly upsetting to some to see the countryside flash by so rapidly. Hence, the blinds. Please do not try to peek; we have limited facilities onboard to handle vomiting." Lindsey didn't like the sound of that and had no intention of peeking.

As they got going, Ashley whispered, "Lindsey, something is going to go very wrong, I know it. What should I do?"

Lindsey felt the responsibility of Floor Monitor suddenly falling on her head. "We should tell someone. I'll message Professor Elaine." She concentrated and sent Ashley's premonition to her and to Tom, the Security man. At once, she saw both of them turning their heads to stare back at Ashley and herself. Then, Tom walked back to them.

"Thanks for your warning, Miss Stokes," Tom said somewhat condescending. Ashley didn't like his tone. "Let me assure you that every precaution has been taken for your safety. This is a completely automated system, and nothing can go wrong. So please, Miss Stokes, just sit back, and enjoy the ride. In an hour we will be in Philadelphia." He returned to his front seat.

"Idiot," Ashley whispered to Lindsey.

"What's going on?" asked Amanda and Pam chimed in. Emilio added his grunt as well.

"I sensed that something is going to be terribly wrong," Ashley tried to explain her half-formed prediction.

"Like what?" Pam attempted to get more facts from Ashley.

Near tears, she replied, "I don't know, just something. I don't see anything else."

A few minutes later, Lindsey's group at the rear of the bus was anxiously awaiting some disaster to befall them. Yet, nothing happened. The motor droned at a high pitch. The gentle swaying motion of the bus tended to lull everyone to sleep. Finally, Lindsey just closed her eyes, figuring that perhaps Ashley's prediction was slightly off.

An hour later, the bus lurched, popping into normal space. The many window blinds rose up instantly. "Philadelphia," called out Tom. Everyone looked out the windows.

Panic screams filled the bus! Water began seeping in from the front door and the rear emergency door. Outside, the eerie darkness was broken only by a dim, pale blue light. Water began seeping in from around the edges of all the windows. The bus was underwater.

"Shi'!" exclaimed Jimmy, over the screaming.

"Silence!" the voice of Professor Elaine commanded above the panic-stricken students, using her Magnify Voice spell that the students had already learned this year. "Wands out. Prepare to cast your Water Breathing spell if needed. Give us a moment to figure out the best course of action to take please. Remain calm. Fear is your enemy at this time."

"Tom?" she asked in a normal tone of voice.

"We have to raise the bus. First priority. It is too heavy for a single Levitate spell. We could begin to Teleport them all out, a few at a time." Tom thought quickly. Already the water was up to Lindsey's ankles. Tom realized there was no time for Teleports, only a few could be rescued this way.

"Kids, I have an idea. If it fails, we will all cast our Water Breathing spells and swim to the surface. However, let's try my idea first. One by one, let's all cast our Levitate spells onto the bus. Perhaps if everyone joins in, we might be able to lift ourselves to the surface in time. If not, we will resort to swimming to the surface. I'll go first, each of you continue to add yours to mine; okay, here we go. Levitate: Bus!" He waved his wand, and the magic activated, but nothing was apparently happening.

Quickly, the other three Security men cast theirs, along with Professor Elaine. One by one, beginning with those at the front, each student waved their wand and said, "Levitate: Bus." Slowly, all those in front of Lindsey's group cast their spells. Then, Amanda, Emilio, Kathy, Pam, and Audrey cast theirs. The bus wavered but did not rise. The water was now up to Lindsey's knees. Lindsey cast hers, and the bus moved even more.

Holding her soaking feet up, Ashley was finally able to cast her spell, "Levitate: Bus." Neither girl trusted their skill to do it non-verbally. As Ashley's spell detonated, the bus finally began to rise upwards. Still the water level rose. Many students climbed upon the seats; worse, the water was freezing cold, and they were soaked. Many began casting Warm and Dry spells.

Ashley, at a disadvantage, could not get up. She was still trying to hold her wand above water in case she needed to cast Breath Water at the last moment. Lindsey and Emilio saw her dilemma, and together they pulled her up onto the seat. "Thanks," she whispered, white with fear and shivering from the cold. Lindsey and Emilio at once cast their Warm and Dry spells on her repeatedly until she stopped shivering.

"We are still rising," Pam noted.

"Er, so is the water," Emilio pointed out. Now their feet were once more underwater, only the last quarter of the volume within the bus remained above the rising waters.

"Get everyone up to the top deck," Elaine hollered. Sloshing through the deep, cold water to the steps was easier said than done. There were two stairs that led upwards, one up front and one at the rear. Lindsey knew that she and her group would have to go up first back here. Yet Ashley was going to have an awful time of it.

"I've got you, Ashley," she whispered and cast her Levitate spell silently on Ashley. Then, she hopped down into the water, pushing her friend towards the stairs. One by one, the others followed her. Just as soon as Ashley reached the stairs, Lindsey put her arms around her, pressing Ashley's body tightly against the steps. "Climb. I've got you," she whispered. Ashley did her best to climb up awkwardly, but the bus was tilted at a backwards angle, and she couldn't have done it without Lindsey forcing her body up against the steps.

Up above, fifty frightened faces greeted them. Deiter saw the two struggling up, and he got up and helped grab Ashley, pulling her the rest of the way up. "All right, squeeze up everyone; we got lots coming up." Lindsey was right behind Ashley, who followed Deiter, as he helped shove his friends further forward. At last, they could move no further, having met those pushing to the rear from the front, making room up there as well.

"Warm! Dry! Warm! Dry!" Deiter began casting his helpful spells onto Ashley, who was shivering and quite scared.

Lindsey began doing the same to herself, her teeth chattering from the cold. Soon the top section echoed with Warm and Dry spells. Everyone was packed in like sardines in a tin. Tom was the last to reach the safety of the upper deck.

No one could see much of anything except those packed in tightly around them. Tom called out, "Students, count off. I want to make sure that we have everyone up here." Someone began with "One."

A minute later, Emilio spoke, "One hundred."

Tom called out, "Excellent. All accounted for. The water is now up to the first level. If we do not break the surface shortly, we will begin casting our Breath Water spells. I will punch a number of holes in the roof so that we can all swim up and out."

"I can't use my feet like this! I can't cast it!" Ashley whispered to Lindsey.

Even before she could answer, Deiter spoke up, "Don't worry. I'll cast one on you for you if we have to do it. I'll hang on to you and help you get to the surface, Ashley."

"Me too," Peaches added. Ten other "me too's" followed in rapid succession, none from Lindsey's group. All were from Black Hall students. Observing this, Lindsey smiled.

"How deep were we anyway?" Pam wondered aloud. "We've been rising for quite a while. How could this foolproof system be so far off anyway? There isn't any deep water around Philadelphia." Her sleuthing mind was busily at work, keeping her attention off the frightening situation developing around her. The water now began lapping at their feet.

Up front, some Red Hall student wailed, "I'm going to die! I just know it!"

"No you are most *definitely* not going to die today," Professor Elaine said sternly. "Cast that silly notion from your head." Lindsey managed a smile, though her feet felt like they were freezing once more.

Someone noticed and said, "Hey, we are not going up anymore."

Tom's booming voice called out, "Once more, everyone recast your Levitate: Bus spells, quickly!" Well over a hundred voices barked out the spell once again, and the bus lurched upwards, a very good sign indeed.

"See Ashley, it is getting lighter outside; we must be getting near the surface," Deiter observed, trying to encourage a very frightened Ashley. She looked and saw that it was indeed becoming noticeably brighter outside.

Finally, the bus popped onto the surface of the water. It was broad daylight now, around one in the afternoon. Still the bus rose higher, until it was entirely out of the water. "Hey, the water is going down now," someone called out.

"You all stay put. I will swim down and open the front door and see if I can get the water out quickly," Tom called out. From their cramped position at the rear, Lindsey could not see anything, only use her imagination to visualize the

Security man swimming down into the cold water and forcing open the door.

Pam observed that the more the water level shrank, the higher they rose. This she pointed out to her friends, a very encouraging sign. At last, Tom spoke again. "Okay, everyone can take their original seats now please. Use as many Dry spells as you need, but let's get it warm and dry inside the bus. My men and I will see about fixing the bus."

Taking no chances, Deiter helped get Ashley safely back down the stairs. Her feet finally on the solid floor, she looked up at him and said, "Thanks, Deiter!" He smiled from ear to ear, as he returned to his seat.

"Okay we are out of immediate danger of drowning, but now what?" Emilio wondered aloud.

"Maybe they can Teleport us back home," suggested Kathy. "That's what I would do." For some time, everyone began speculating on various methods of rescue and such. Everyone knew that enough Levitate spells could keep them safely above the water, but the bus was not a boat.

"How can the bus motor even run now?" asked Emilio. That stumped everyone.

The math professor, Herbert Mac Elroy, came back to Lindsey's group. "Miss Betts, will you please come up front with me. Once again, I need your computer genius. We need a computer miracle about now." Pam grinned and followed him to the front of the bus, where the men had opened up a compartment in the floor. Normally, the students merely walked over the metal plate that covered it.

"Can you fix our computer?" he asked.

"Well, that all depends. First, I need to know why it failed in the first place. The most obvious answer is that someone entered the wrong coordinates," Pam began deducing what had happened, taking it one logical step at a time.

"Here are the coordinates that I entered. I triple checked them. I swear I entered these numbers," Professor Herbert explained, very worried that he had somehow made a mistake.

Pam looked at them and visualized a map of the US.

"Yes, the latitude and longitude seem about right. If I had my laptop, I could verify those are correct. For now, let's assume that those are the correct numbers. They cannot be off by as much as we ended up off our destination. Let me see what numbers the computer has in its memory." She typed on the tiny keyboard and the led display showed the very same numbers.

"That checks," she replied. "The computer shows the same numbers as are on your paper. That means you entered them correctly." Secretly, he breathed a huge sigh of relief.

"Okay, keep working on it Pam. Tom's men are working on the engine. We must get it going again."

"Let's see; the numbers are entered correctly, so that must mean that there is either a huge programming error or something is. . . Wait a minute; here is the readout, which tells us where the computer believes that it is. Whoa. This is strange. Professor, look at these numbers!"

"The latitude is dead on, Pam. Longitude 80 degrees west—that's not right. It's saying that we are in extreme eastern Pennsylvania, maybe by Pittsburgh. How can this be?" he replied, extremely worried.

"Well, I've not got the proper equipment to check out the computer's program to see if the error lies there. Has the computer system been worked on recently?"

Jimmy spoke up, "No, Miss Be's. I's run jus' perfec'ly for years. No one's 'ouched 'he compu'er."

"Then, let's assume the program is fine. After all, this is the same bus that took us to Massachusetts just a few weeks ago. Honestly, we are not that far from there on this trip. Maybe it's hardware related." After turning off the computer, Pam began slowly dismantling the internal components, reseating each one after she looked for signs of damage.

"Hey, what is this little thing? This doesn't belong here. Hey, it's magnetized. Ah ha! Now I know why the computer thinks we are still in Pittsburgh. This magnet has been slowly retarding the circuitry. Look, professor, now that I have removed it, let me reboot the computer, and let's see where it says we are now at is!" A couple of minutes later, Pam activated the display of green numbers.

"Gods, that puts us out in the Atlantic Ocean!" Professor Herbert gasped.

"Sabotage! Clearly, someone has sabotaged this bus. Rats, this is so tiny that I have messed up any possible fingerprints just by my removing it. Darn. I really needed my CSI kit this time. Here, you keep the evidence." She handed the tiny magnet device to her professor, who carefully put it into his pocket.

"I believe the computer will work properly now," she replied. "Only how can the bus drive us across the ocean?"

Tom, who had been eavesdropping on their conversation, chuckled, "You leave the driving to us. Thank you Miss Betts." She returned to her seat in the back, explaining to everyone how someone had sabotaged the bus. This gave the students something to chat about while the repairs were continuing.

A Red Hall student noticed that the bus was once more sinking towards the waters below. Hastily, everyone recast their Levitate spells again, breathing a sigh of relief as they all felt the bus rising once more.

This was followed by an awful grinding noise, as Jimmy tried to start the engine. On the tenth try, the familiar hum of the engine reverberated throughout the bus and the students broke into a spontaneous cheer. Tom called out, "Okay. Fasten your seatbelts. We are going to try to get moving. Do not cancel your spells until we are over ground, please."

Lindsey chuckled at that. She had no such intention, not until she could see dry land beneath the bus! A few minutes later, they hit the beach off Trenton. At last, the bus was allowed to settle onto the ground once more. A half hour later, the bus arrived at a Mac Donald's restaurant. Everyone piled off for a late lunch and to use the restrooms.

An hour later, they were on their tour of the historical sites connected with the independence of the US. While they were on their tours, Tom had inspectors going over every inch of the bus. They pronounced it fit to make the return journey, but insisted the bus be given a complete overhaul as soon as they returned.

Around six, the bus pulled into a Domino's Pizza place,

and eagerly everyone filed off the bus and headed inside. They were expected, and trays of pizzas awaited them. With full stomachs, they climbed back on board for the trip home. As Ashley stood in line to re-board the bus, Professor Elaine whispered to her, "I am sorry that I doubted your warning. Thank you for alerting us. If there is a next time, I will take your warnings very serious. Had I acted when you spoke up, we could have avoided this calamity."

"It's not your fault. I couldn't see what was not right," Ashley replied and climbed onboard. Around nine that night, they all climbed off the bus and headed for their dorms and showers. Ashley soaked in the warm waters of the large tub for over an hour. It had been the strangest day of her life. Worse, she had been more afraid than she had ever been. Worst still, she desperately needed the help of others, who had arms. Her independence had been shattered. Perhaps this factor alone was what had totally shattered her. Ashley waited in the warm waters until everyone had left, telling Lindsey that she would Message her if she needed anything.

Finally alone, she began to cry. A bit later, she struggled to dry off her foot and pressed the #1 button on her cell phone. "Mom? Hi, Ashley here. Can, can we talk?" she asked, trying hard to restrain her tears.

Lena wiped the sleep from her eyes and sat down. "Sure, tell me what's going on, dear." Slowly, Ashley told her all about their near tragedy, explaining the many details as she knew them, particularly the awful, helpless mess she couldn't handle on her own.

"Mom, I'm so worthless like this. I keep telling myself I can do everything anyone else can do, but today everyone could see that is just one big lie that I have been telling myself all my life. I'm worthless. I'm a useless cripple like they say." After uttering what she most feared, she began crying, unable to hold it back any longer.

After letting her cry for a time, Lena asked, "Ashley, let me see if I have this straight. You believe that you are a useless, worthless cripple because when the water was so deep you couldn't cast your own breathing spell, that you couldn't climb the stairs when the bus was at such a backwards angle, and that you couldn't get off the stairs at the top for the same reason?"

"Yes," she wailed. "I even had to let Deiter pull me up the last ways. It was awful, humiliating, so helpless, mom, so utterly useless."

"Every one of us needs some help from others at some time in our lives, dear. If we use your reasoning, then every one of us is a useless, worthless cripple," she explained softly.

"What?" Ashley was dumbfounded by her reply, completely unexpected.

"Look, dear, needing assistance from someone else is part of being human. We all need some at some time in our lives. Look at Lloyd. Those pipes fell on him, nearly crushing him. He was pinned. If you had not sensed it and you kids gone to his rescue, Lloyd might have perished in a ranching accident. According to your reasoning, Lloyd is therefore a totally helpless, useless cripple and should completely give up, right?"

"Mom, no. You are being silly. He's. . ." she could not finish her sentence.

"Look, arms or no arms, we all need help in our lives at some time. You have only proven to me that you are one of us—you are human. True, you needed help in a situation where your friends didn't need the same help. Big deal. One day, they will need help that only you may provide them. Besides, didn't you just tell me that you suspected something was going to go wrong and told your teacher? Isn't that providing help that they could not have gotten on their own?"

"Well, yes," she began to agree with Lena.

"Look, my dear, in your case, you need help in different ways than the others usually do. Just look at it that way. You need assistance in situations that others might not. Yet I assure you that the day will come when they need the help that you can give. This is what makes life so interesting. It would be an awfully boring world if everyone was identically the same, now wouldn't it?"

"Well, yes," Ashley had to admit.

"Besides, what I think is the really important thing is just how you handled it. I mean when you needed help getting up those steps and getting out at the top, you allowed Lindsey and Deiter to help you without getting mad or anything else. Didn't you say that Deiter was being very nice to you as well?"

"Well, yes," she continued to admit.

"Now look at that for a minute. Just how did Deiter feel after he was able to help you up?"

"I think he felt good. No, he looked very proud of himself, not as if he was superman, more as if he was happy that he could do something for me that I couldn't do. Oh!" she exclaimed, as it dawned upon her just what his point of view had been. "Oh, I see. He felt good that he could be of use helping me when I really needed help."

"There you go, dear. You see, we all need help, but different kinds and in different ways."

"Is it that the help I need is so very different than that needed by everyone else that I think it is just me? Does that even make sense?" Ashley tried to put her flash of insight into words.

"I think so, but then that is just me thinking so. What matters is how you think," Lena advised.

"I guess I'm not a totally helpless, useless cripple after all. The bus didn't actually start rising until I cast my Levitate spell. If I had not been there, they might not have been able to get the bus up out of the water," she admitted.

"Thanks, mom. I feel better now. I'd better get out of this tub. I've been in it for several hours soaking." Lena laughed and wished her good night. Ashley dried off and headed up to bed, her confusion gone, her self-respect firmly replanted.

Chapter 7—Halloween

While the topic of conversation among the other students on Friday was what had happened to the third years on their field trip, that was not the topic for the third years. Tomorrow was Halloween. While Saturday night would be the first big school dance and party, the day also marked the first time these students would be allowed a day excursion into Telluride. Lindsey had been looking forward to this for two years now, ever since she watched Jim, Tom, and Sandy depart for Telluride, along with all the older students, leaving the campus rather deserted, except for the first and second year students.

Jim had promised to show her the sights for two years now, but as the day approached, things had changed for Lindsey and Jim. Emilio had already asked Kathy to go with him. Monique had been planning to take Pam for two years, and both were very excited about the day. Henry Waldorf had asked to take Amanda, though Tom and Sandy had also promised to show both of them the sights as well. Fellow Brown Hall student, Fred Small, had asked to escort Audrey.

The twist for Lindsey was that Andy asked her to accompany him this year. Jim was in a dilemma, he wanted to take both Lindsey and Ashley, but for two different reasons. He'd long promised Lindsey and just could not bring himself to go back on his promise to her. Yet, he was drawn to Ashley, so strongly that he could never get her out of his mind.

At lunchtime, on Friday, Jim spied the two sitting together eating lunch between classes. He sighed; it was now or never. He hesitantly approached them. "Hi Ashley, Lindsey. Say, tomorrow's the big day, Telluride," he began unsure of how to best proceed. He could see no way that would not upset Lindsey, which was the last thing he wanted to do. Why were relations with girls so troublesome anyway?

"Hi Jim," Lindsey replied, as did Ashley. Lindsey saw his face and guessed what he was facing. "Say Jim, I know that you have promised to show me the sights for the last two years now, but Andy has also asked me too. He's new here, and I think I really should partner with him. Will that be acceptable to you? If not, I can tell Andy that I can't."

The relief that instantly appeared on Jim's face told her that she was precisely on the mark. "Sure thing, Lindsey. I want to ask Ashley to go with me. She's new too and needs me. Will you go with me, Ashley?"

She blushed and said that she would. Jim looked incredibly relieved, but completely uncertain just how this had all magically worked out for him. He added, "Why don't we four stick together for a while? I can show you all some cool things. That way I won't be reneging on my promise to you either, Lindsey."

"Hey, that would be great. None of us have ever been there. Thanks. I'll tell Andy."

"Great! Just great! We meet here around nine in the morning, after breakfast. See you both then!" Jim walked out of the dining room feeling a hundred pounds lighter, though he still had no idea how this had all worked out for the best.

"But I thought that Jim was sort of, well, your boyfriend," Ashley whispered to Lindsey.

"Not boyfriend boyfriend. He has always been a very good friend to me. Amanda has said that he had a crush on me for the last two years, but to tell you the truth, I like Andy just as much, though in different ways. I think we are too young to have a crush, well a real crush anyway. According to Amanda, Jim now has a real crush on you, Ashley, but then he is older than us, so I suppose that's okay."

At suppertime, Governor Alister asked all the third year students to remain in the dining room after supper. "As you know, tomorrow those of you who have turned in your parental permission slips will be allowed to visit Telluride for the day. I wish to say a few words to you about these visits."

"One, you must always be on your best behavior. Remember, you are officially representing Bradbury's when you are in the town. Two, you may begin leaving for the town at nine in the morning. Three, you must all be back on campus by five, in time for the Halloween banquet. Failure means instant detention."

"Now the means to get there is on foot. Yes, there is a

secret tunnel that many of our staff uses to walk from Telluride into the school. You will be given the password tomorrow, which, mind you, is only good for this one day. Don't go getting any idea of making secret visits to the town. Meet here in the dining room tomorrow. Now this is important, under no circumstances are you to tell anyone else of this secret entrance. If I find out that you have done so, you will not be allowed to visit Telluride for the duration of your schooling here at Bradbury's. After all, it would then not be a secret, now would it? Enjoy your outing. Oh yes, remember to dress warmly. I'm told that there are already eight inches on the ground, bit unusual for this time of year."

With that, they all headed to their rooms. Pam commented, "Well, finally we know about at least this one secret entrance. I guess we must have looked a bit foolish to the older students, when we discovered it ourselves and were so excited about it, thinking no one else knew about it."

"True," Lindsey replied, "and that might explain how Looney and Green figured out all the other secret places around here. You know, they are suddenly shown one, and they start wondering if there are more, that sort of thing." Some of the mystery of her father's exploits began unraveling.

Ashley, on the other hand, had other worries—Alister's parting words. She sent a message to Jim and waited for him in the commons. "Hi Ashley, just getting some studying done. What's up?"

"About tomorrow, Telluride. We are going to be outside a lot of the time, right? I mean we are supposed to dress up warmly. He said there are already eight inches on the ground," she replied timidly.

"Well, yes, it's cold out so we should wear warm coats and boots. Oh, I get it," Jim had a flash of intuition. "You are worried because you are going to have to be all dressed up against the cold."

"Well, yes, and particularly the boots part. Are you sure that you want to take me? I'm going to have to rely on you for so many things, my feet will be. . ." She didn't get to finish her sentence.

Jim finished it for her, "snug as a bug in a rug. Don't

fret. I'm going be your arms, so to speak. No problem. I already assumed that I would or I wouldn't have asked you out. I'm very proud to be allowed to be your guide and arms, Ashley. I won't let you down, I promise."

"You're sure about this? That I won't embarrass you or something? I mean I've never been on a date before," she admitted.

"I haven't either, Ashley. I've taken Lindsey to some of our school dances, but that's not the same thing really. We're going to be on our own, to do what we want to do all day, a real date," Jim explained.

"But why me? I mean I'm only like a half a person, really," she asked what had been bothering her for some time. "You could have just about anyone else around here. I know that Lindsey really thinks highly of you as a friend."

"Yes, I fell for Lindsey, at first. We are good friends, but she is, well I don't know. She's not feisty like you are, nor ornery like you and I are. You don't take 'noth'en from no one. I love that spirit. I think you are the coolest, greatest, prettiest, neatest girl I've ever seen. Okay, I know that I'm seventeen, and you are only fourteen, but that's now. When we are older, three years will make no difference at all."

Jim pleaded, "Honestly, I'm nuts about you, Ashley. At least give me a chance to prove myself to you. I mean I know I don't know what I'm doing. I'm not suave and cool like Tom, but he's been dating Sandy since their second year here. Oh yes, and if you ever say that about yourself ever again, why, I will chase you down and tickle you to death! Half person, bah, you are more of a person than most everyone else here!"

She flushed, but added, "You are sure I won't embarrass you?"

"It's the other way around. I'm more scared I will embarrass you, Ashley," Jim admitted. "I'm terrified I might not be *good* enough for you."

Ashley didn't know what to make of this turnabout. She was always overly concerned about making a fool of herself, embarrassing those around her. Yet, he was saying the opposite. He saw the confused look on her face and explained, "I mean I'm not like Lindsey. I can't sense when you need something like she can. I'm almost petrified I'm going to blow it with you. You know, upsetting you something awful because I didn't see something I should've seen."

"I, I never though anyone would feel that way about me," she blurted out what she was thinking. "It's always the other way around."

"I know. Let's call a truce. You don't worry about embarrassing me, and I'll try not to worry about embarrassing you. How's that?"

"I'll try, but I can't guarantee I'll be able to do it," she replied honestly.

"Me either, but let's try," Jim suggested. She agreed and they hugged before Jim headed off to his room to study. He didn't tell her that one of the reasons he did his studying in his room was that if he studied with them, he'd spend all his time staring at Ashley, getting nothing else done.

Later that night, Emilio asked Kathy whether she would mind if he wore the same costume to the Halloween party as he had the last two years. Of course, this distraction led to everyone else chatting about their costumes. Since they were going to spend the whole day in Telluride, they all decided just to wear the same ones they wore last year.

"Rats, I didn't know that we needed to wear costumes," Andy said. "I haven't got anything."

"Me either," Ashley added, suddenly having yet another thing to worry about. Her life was definitely becoming more complicated.

Amanda said coyly, "You are going with Jim, right?" She nodded. With a playful gleam in her eye, she added, "I have just the tease for Jim. I used to have one of those Indian maiden costumes, you know, as you see in the ancient western movies. It's at home, but I can have mom send it to us in time. With a few last minute alterations, you can go as an Indian maiden. That ought to tease Jim a bit." Ashley liked the idea, and Amanda Messaged her mother. Unfortunately, no one had any ideas for Andy.

The next morning, the girls ate an early breakfast so they had time to get ready for the day off campus. Lindsey helped Ashley into warm socks and her padded boots. Once they were tied, Ashley again felt helpless, and said, "I'm really nervous and a bit scared about this, Lindsey. Like this, I can do so little by myself."

"True, but Jim knows that. He's supposed to look after you. If he doesn't or messes up, just Message me, and I'll be there pronto. How's that?" Ashley nodded. "To be truthful, I've got butterflies in my stomach too. I mean I've never been on a real date either, not like this. I guess we're both scared of messing it up." Both giggled, relieving their tensions a little.

"That why I like Monique so much," Pam interjected her thoughts. "She and I get on very well together. Neither of us has to worry about anything. We just know what the other wants and needs."

Ashley timidly asked what she had wanted to know for some months. "Are you and Monique like in love or something like that?" She wanted to ask it more to the point, but thought better of it.

"I'm only fourteen, but well, maybe we are. I don't know. Certainly, no boys are interested in me—never have been. I'm the homeliest girl in the dorm! I certainly don't want to go out with the ugliest guy, just because no one else will want me," Pam admitted what she had never told another before. "Monique really cares for me, in a special way, but I don't know, really."

"Well, maybe you will look prettier when you finish growing up," Lindsey tried to sound a hopeful note. "Monique is a knock-out blonde, though." Pam grinned. She certainly was that.

They wore their fancier blouses along with jeans. Ashley looked great in her form-fitting top that Lena had made for her. Next, Lindsey helped Ashley into her heavy cloak, before donning hers. "Just ask Jim to pull the hood over your head if you get cold," she advised. Finally, the four, joined by Kathy, headed down to meet everyone else in the dining room.

"Over here, Pam," called out Monique, also covered by her heavy cloak, though her bright red lips provided good contrast. Pam grinned and joined her; the two held hands, Ashley noted. Emilio was already waiting for Kathy, and those two joined hands as well. Henry, Jim, and Andy all three walked in together and headed for Amanda, Lindsey, and Ashley.

Lindsey offered her hand to Andy, who eagerly accepted it, while Amanda put her arm around Henry, who beamed. Jim gave Ashley a hug and slipped his arm around her waist, nudging her close to him. She smiled.

Tom and Sandy appeared and took charge. The other Floor Monitors were beside them. Tom explained, "Okay, the password today is frigid. You will need it to get into the kitchen, and the passage to Telluride is just beyond the kitchen. It is a long walk through the tunnel. It comes out in Jake's Grill, so do take note of how to find it on your way back here. If you forget, ask Jake; he's a wizard. Now, if you run into any trouble, let your hall Floor Monitors know. Everyone ready? Okay, Henry, lead on. To Telluride we go, yo ho!"

Lindsey noted that the secret door to the kitchen area was open. Close to four hundred students filed through, heading for the long tunnel that she had marked on her map that her father had made years ago. Tom and Sandy walked along with Lindsey's group.

Sandy explained, "There are a lot of shops to visit, but the fellows rather hate shopping. Sometimes, we girls go shopping while the boys take in a movie. We will be arriving at the eastern edge of the main business district, so just head west. A lot of us eat lunch at Domino's. If you get lost or something, just Message us, okay? It takes about a half hour to walk the tunnel, so plan to be back at Jake's Grill by no later than 4:30 or you will have to run."

The tunnel was long and chilly, but this far underground, not overly cold. After what seemed an endless walk, they finally stepped out of a doorway in the back room of the eatery. Mostly in pairs, they walked out into the main dining area and then on out into the street.

"Wow! Look at the mountains! They are so huge and close," exclaimed Lindsey to Andy. Indeed, the third years mostly stood and looked around at the incredible snow-covered mountains. It was as if the town was part of the mountains itself. The air was cold, and it was still snowing. While the streets and sidewalks had been plowed, with the continuous snowfall, already it had begun accumulating as soon as it was plowed. Snow was mounded up against the buildings and along the curbs.

"Monique and I are going shopping first. If you want, we can all meet at Domino's for lunch," Pam suggested, as the two of them, arm in arm, strolled on down the street.

Jim added, "We are on East Colorado Street, the main drag. It's also called 145 and San Juan Skyway. Most of the interesting shops are along here. A few are on the parallel streets on either side. Summer is the main tourist season, but from about mid-November to April skiers visit too. Right now, it is the off season, so most folks you meet are the locals, who are friendly to us students, primarily because we spend our money here." They chuckled at his jest.

"There is a movie place down at the other end, but I don't know what's on," Jim continued. "Many of the older couples go there, but not to watch the movie," he alluded to other activities that they did in the dark theater. The small group began walking down the street, becoming familiar with the many shops.

Lindsey realized that on their next trip here, she ought to spend some time shopping for Christmas presents for everyone. She said to the girls, "Hey, keep an eye out for shops to visit next time. It looks like we could get some nice Christmas presents here."

A bit later, Andy spied an interesting building. "Hey, look at this, a mining museum. I have to check it out. You interested, Lindsey?" She knew that he wouldn't rest until he'd seen inside, so she accompanied him into the museum.

Slowly, the others began to drift off, following what interested them, until at last it was just Jim and Ashley walking down the street. "Well, it looks as if we are on our own," he teased.

"Not really, look there are students walking everywhere, but I know what you mean."

"Say, I have an idea of just where to take my princess," Jim suddenly said with a teasing look on his face.

Ashley turned to face him, "So now I'm your princess?"

He blushed. Ashley noticed it as well. "Sorry, but I think

of you as my princess. You are that special and precious to me. This way." He led her down a side street. A short while later he announced, "Ta da! Would you care to join me for a game or two?" They were standing in front of Sam's Pool Hall.

She gave him a slight bump with her hips. "You planned this all along, didn't you?"

Again, Jim blushed, but replied quickly, "Oh no! Caught in the act!" She giggled. He opened the door, and they went inside. Four tables lay in the center of the room. Four other locals were already shooting at two. Jim and Ashley walked up to the cashier, and Jim paid for two games. Wearing their long cloaks, Ashley looked like any other student, that is, no one could tell she had no arms. Until now, she rather liked this aspect.

They took the back table, and Jim removed her cloak and hung both on a back peg. The two walked over to the row of cue sticks in their case along one wall. "Pick your poison," Jim teased.

Normally, she'd use her feet to take one, but she pointed with her head, and Jim took hers out of the case as well as one for himself. On their way back to their table, Jim also grabbed one of the tall bar stools for her. "Sit princess, while I remove your shoes," Jim said softly. She did as he suggested, wondering how this would turn out.

By now, the other players and the shopkeeper were all staring at her. Ashley tried to ignore them as best she could. "Rack them up, Jim, you break," she suggested. He did so. The sharp cracking sound of ball hitting balls echoed in the room. A solid ball dropped into a pocket, and Jim was off and running. He quickly sunk two more balls before missing.

"Okay, princess, let's see you shoot your way out of this. I've got three," Jim teased, hoping to keep her attention off the five men watching her closely.

Ashley decided on her first shot and slid the stool into position. Next, she carried the cue over to the stool, using her teeth, since this way was quicker than trying to get it between her head and shoulder. A minute later, she lined up her shot and began her game. One by one, her stripped balls fell into the pockets, as she began running the table on him. By the time that she called out, "Eight ball, corner pocket," all five had moved in close to watch the pair, Ashley in particular.

"Darn good pool shooting young lady!" one young local man exclaimed. "No one is going to believe this! A girl with no arms just ran the table on Jim. Where'd you learn to shoot like this, if you don't mind my ask'en, ma'am?" he said with a drawl.

"Willie's in Chicago," Ashley replied.

"Best shoot'en I've seen in a long time," added Henry, the day manager for Sam, who owned the place. "Jim, you never said that you were bring'en in a pro on us," he teased. "Good to see you again, by the way."

"She's one hot shooter, that's for sure, Miss Ashley Stokes," Jim introduced her. She smiled, at least these men liked pool, she thought.

"Only if I don't have to crack," she admitted, not wanting to mislead them.

"Rack'em up again, Jim. Mind if we watch, Miss Stokes? We might learn a thing or two from you. I'm Bill, Bill Weatherby. I live here in town."

"Well, it makes me a little nervous with people staring at me, because I'm like this," she shrugged her shoulders. "If you watch the shooting, then I guess it's okay."

"Miss Stokes, I, we was all staring at you when you first came in here. I mean, we've never seen anyone like you. We kind of figured Jim here was playing some kind of joke on us. Once you started pocketing the balls, well, that's a horse of a different color. Either you are darn good at this or mighty lucky, because after each shot, the cue ball was in perfect position for the next one."

"That's the only way I can play it, sir. I don't stand a chance if I can't position the cue ball. Can't break either," she readily admitted.

"Okay, princess, guys, I want a chance this time, so Ashley, you get to break." He looked at the men and said, "Really, it's the only chance I have." Ashley chuckled, but it was true.

A bit later, she cracked, but par for her game, she did it such that she at least got one ball pocketed. After getting another sunk, she scratched, the balls were too tightly packed from her weak crack. Now Jim had a choice. "Look, if I crack them good, the odds are that either none go in or I might knock one of hers in and scratch. Worse, with the balls scattered, she'll clean me up in no time. So I'm going to follow a new strategy this time. I'm not going to crack them—just see if I can get one or two of mine in the pocket."

Ashley relied, "Grrr." He chuckled. Turn by turn, the two continued to sort of peel the onion on the mass of balls, neither cracking them open. At last, with only five balls remaining, they opened up enough. Ashley polished off the rest of hers and the eight ball.

"Hey, that was the closest game I've ever played with you, princess. I almost had you that time," Jim teased.

"Hey, mind if I have a go with you, Miss Stokes," the local called Bill asked.

By the time noon rolled around, Ashley had made five new friends and won six games in a row. Jim helped her get her socks and shoes back on as well as her cloak. Promising to return next time, they headed out and back to the main street. "Thanks, Jim. I was really nervous about being in there at first, but they did like me, didn't they?"

"Yes, my princess, they accepted you as a fellow pool shooter, actually far better than they are. I told you that you'd have fun with me. I'm starving. What would you like for lunch? Treat is on me."

"Sorry, I don't have any idea what restaurants there are. I suppose we should meet up with the others at Domino's," she replied.

"Well, there is a real restaurant, you know, where you walk in and sit down, western style. The serve a steak that is huge, but I think you're right; we should check in with the others. I owe it to Lindsey to show her and Andy around, if they need it. Come on. It's this way."

A bit later, they walked into a packed pizza place. Hundreds of students crowded into the building. The two waited in line, and eventually Jim picked up their tray with a large sausage pizza and two cokes. Since there was no room where Lindsey and Andy were sitting, they sat where they could find two seats, next to Deiter and Peaches.

Ashley felt awkward. With her warm boots on, she couldn't feed herself and was entirely dependent upon Jim. With so many others so close to them, she felt even worse because she couldn't say anything without being overheard. Jim stuck a straw into her coke and then into his, placing hers in a perfect position for her to sip it herself. The cardboard plate, he kept in front of himself. For a minute, Ashley wondered what he was doing, likewise Deiter and Peaches, who were watching them. Jim leaned over and put the point of one slice towards her mouth, and Ashley grinned and bit it off.

"Oh cool! Now that is romantic, Deiter! Just like they do when eating the first piece of wedding cakes. Come on; here, you do it for me," she slid her plate towards him. He was a bit awkward on his first try, but Peaches loved it.

"Thanks for showing us, Ashley. You are *so* romantic," Peaches complimented her. Ashley didn't know what to make of it, but since Peaches was enjoying the attention of Deiter feeding her, she relaxed and began to enjoy their company.

Peaches went on, "You know, it's usually those in Red Hall that show us all the really romantic moves, but this is super cool. Thanks. Are you two going to the movie this afternoon? Deiter is taking me after we eat."

"We don't know yet. We've been shooting pool all morning," Ashley replied.

"What? There is a pool hall here?" Deiter nearly dropped the piece he was holding for Peaches. Jim explained its location.

"Don't you *dare* go off and leave me, Deiter Cross! You promised that you would take me to the movie," Peaches scolded him. He blushed, but that was just what he was thinking. Shortly they finished up, and she led him off toward the movie theater, telling him to feed her some popcorn during the movie.

Andy and Lindsey quickly moved to take the two vacated seats. "Looks like you two have started a new craze," she teased.

"She said that it was romantic," Ashley attempted to explain, "but, well, actually, Jim, I rather am enjoying letting you feed me." She flushed.

"What next, great Indian guide?" Lindsey asked. "I'm not sure that we want to go to the movie. It seems like a big waste of time, at least to Andy and me."

"We can walk around town, and I can show you the shops. We could also try the baby ski slope. I really can hardly stand up on skis however," Jim admitted. "Don't worry Ashley. I will be falling down as many times as you, if not more. I've tried it five times now and still can't get the hang of it, but it is fun. The slope is very gentle, so you can't go fast and get hurt. If you want to give it a try, I'll treat you all," Jim suggested.

Lindsey looked at Andy, both nodded. "You are on."

After spending an hour touring the shops on the main strip, all four headed on up to Bear Creek Road. Soon, they saw the Willow Ski Lodge and the low elevation slope. A cable car system stretched high upon the mountainside. A few minutes later, the four sat on the benches beside the beginner slope. Two dozen others were already slipping, sliding, and falling some distance away.

Jim got the special boots onto Ashley's feet and helped fasten the skis. A few minutes later, all four yelled and laughed, as they tried to stay on their feet as they slowly slid down the gentle slope. A ski instructor took pity on them and gave them a few lessons, particularly Ashley. She followed his tips slavishly, trying hard to keep her balance and not fall down. The time flew by and finally they had to stop and head back. All four looked like snowmen, as the snow continued to fall.

As they walked back, Ashley commented, "That was really fun, scary for me, really scary, but fun. Thanks Jim."

"Yes, thanks a whole lot, Jim. That was really something else. I would never have tried that on my own," Lindsey admitted.

"Fun, but I'm sore. I think I fell more than the rest of you," Andy added.

Sometime later, they entered the dorm and headed to get cleaned up in time for supper. While the girls got ready, they chatted about their day. All four were extremely happy. At dinner, Kathy told them that she and Emilio had gone to the movie, but they had done more kissing than watching. "He is so handsome, isn't he?" Kathy gushed. Lindsey suspected that Pam had also been kissing, as she had traces of red lipstick on her lips, but she said nothing about it.

The dining room was all decorated in the Halloween theme, much as it had been the previous two years. Cobwebs, fake spiders, bats, skeletons, and of course many pumpkins provided the orangish glow to the room. After eating a fancy dinner, everyone raced to change into their costumes for the rock dance.

True to her word, Amanda had received her old Indian maiden costume. She carefully dressed Ashley in it, altering it slightly with her Mend spell. Still not satisfied, she ripped off the sleeves and Mended them shut. "Thanks, that looks better," Ashley commented. Finally, she slipped on a pair of soft moccasins.

"There, you can slip them on and off easily. The only thing wrong is your hair, it ought to be long and straight, but we can't do anything about that now. Have a look, Ashley. What do you think?"

She looked at her image in the full-length mirror. "Wow. It does look like the old movies. Thanks, Amanda. You saved the day."

A while later, the six girls headed down to meet their dates and dance. Jim was a bit shocked to see Ashley wearing Amanda's old costume. He wore his same pirate's outfit. "Avast there matey. I've captured me Indian princess!" He waved his plastic sword around. Ashley giggled.

Almost at once, the dance music began. Again, Lindsey experienced the strange time shift. To her, it seemed that they had only begun when Alister announced, "Last dance." A slow tune began, and the lights dimmed considerably. Andy pulled Lindsey close to him, and she rested her head on his shoulder. She glanced over to see how Ashley was faring, Jim had her close, and her head was resting on his shoulder. All was well with the world, thought Lindsey, except that time mysteriously flew by yet again.

Back in their room, Amanda gushed, "Henry kissed me! Wow. My legs almost gave way."

Kathy, who had joined them, along with Audrey, said, "Well, that is normal, I think; at least, it was the same with me when Emilio kissed me."

"I just had butterflies in my stomach, when Andy kissed me," Lindsey replied. "What does that mean?"

"I think that you liked it," Kathy concluded.

"Then, I guess I did too," Ashley volunteered. "Jim kissed me, too."

"I thought it was kind of soft and warm," Audrey added, "when Fred kissed me. I think he is very shy though. Do you think that I should take more of the lead with him?"

"Probably," Kathy concluded, "guys don't mature as rapidly as us women. I read that in my magazines."

Pam said nothing; her lips were rather red though. At last she ventured, "God, does Monique ever know how to kiss! I lost my breath, my stomach felt all funny, and my legs nearly gave out."

"Hey, it's like I've always been saying; the girls in Red Hall know about these things. Monique has promised to give us some pointers, as has Peggy West. I think we should take them up on it very soon. I know I must have an awful lot to learn," added Kathy.

Sunday, everyone got up late. Pam was up first, checking on all the latest news. The hurricane was still stationary, almost in the same position. However, there was not much else going on, except that the wizards had obviously not been successful in moving the hurricane along its path.

However, by Monday the hurricane had indeed finally changed position. It was all over the news. Emily had moved another fifty miles closer to the south Texas coastline. Way up north from the hurricane, Pam noticed that the snow was coming down far heavier than on Halloween. Whatever the wizards had done, they had only made things worse, she concluded.

In chemistry class, it was lab day, and the students, grouped into pairs, were performing experiments and learning to write them up properly. As Lindsey and Ashley were working on theirs, Ashley doing the careful measurements and Lindsey doing the actual mixing, Ashley had another one of her premonitions. "Lyle is going to get the acid on his face, an explosion I think."

Just as they looked over at Lyle and were about to Message Professor Jasper, Lyle's beaker exploded. It missed Deiter, but the acid flew onto Lyle's face. Instantly, Lindsey cast her Clean spell on Lyle. Jasper rushed to the boy and took him over to the cleaning station. Pulling the chain, a water shower washed the remainder off Lyle.

"I can't see how your face avoided taking a terrible burn," Professor Jasper said, looking at the burn holes and discoloration of his clothes.

"Ah, someone cast Clean on me right away," he muttered.

"I did, professor," Lindsey admitted. "Ashley warned me it was about to happen, but we didn't have time to tell you. Is he going to be okay?"

"Yes, excellent you two. Quick thinking. Yes, he has a few red spots, but I'm afraid your clothes have had it."

"Mend. Mend. Mend." Lyle cast spell after spell. After the tenth time, his clothes looked reasonable, though you could still see that they had been badly damaged.

As the class returned to their experiments, Deiter mouthed, "Thank you!" to both Lindsey and Ashley. Both smiled back.

In spell casting class with Professor Cho Lin, the week was spent working more and more complex illusions. First, they went outside in the snowstorm and began creating Imaginary Terrain. Suddenly, the snow-covered lawns became ponds, orchards, rolling grasslands, rocky ground, and even a swamp. Audrey had made the orchard.

However, the next spell Pam found most fascinating, the creation of a permanent Wall Illusion. The large classroom suddenly had a lowered ceiling with walls appearing where no walls were located. Cho Lin had each student try to touch these walls, only to find that their bodies could walk right through them. To keep the clutter down, Cho Lin occasionally cast her Dispel Magic to eliminate the ever-multiplying walls and ceilings.

For Pam, the Sleuth, this spell held her interest. With it,

one could hide a doorway in plain sight, for example, simply by creating a Wall Illusion over it. No one could tell that the door was there, yet the door was fully functional, and the spell was permanent! She took very careful notes on this spell and its effects. Indeed, during their many practice session later on, she examined the wall's behavior, as she cast other spells at it. In fact, she filled an entire notebook on the spell and its effects.

For Amanda, the next spell was vitally important to her, Invisible Attack. Essentially, the caster became invisible, as if they had cast the Invisibility spell, which they all knew. However, unlike their Grade 2 spell, if they attacked while being so hidden, they remained invisible to their victim! Now, Amanda could gain a better advantage in a combat situation. Deiter also loved this spell, and the two of them actually shared notes on this spell, which surprised Amanda and Lindsey as well.

The following week, Professor Cho Lin began with a very stern warning. "This week we are going to work on learning a terribly powerful spell, one that can actually kill someone: Terror Killer. Mind you, it is all an illusion, but if the person believes in the illusion, to him and his mind it is very real. If it is attacking him and if he is unfortunate to be struck by the illusion, he dies. What the victim will be seeing is that thing that he is *most* afraid of, something horrible, something that strikes utter *terror* in him."

"The trained wizard and witch will be able to tell at once that this may be a spell in operation. As with the Dispel Magic spell, if they so suspect that it is a spell, they may be able to shrug off its effect on themselves. In which case, the spell does nothing to them. Don't try this on Dominus Malefic, for example, since it would be a total waste of time."

"Now because this spell can kill, I will be very carefully monitoring the casting of this spell. Only two of you will be allowed to make the cast at one time. Hence, we will be taking all week on this spell."

The next day, Ashley screamed in terror, as Lindsey successfully cast the spell. Cho Lin cancelled it rapidly. "What did you see?" Lindsey asked, shocked at how terrified Ashley had become.

"Falling. I was at the edge of this cliff, and I was losing my balance, beginning to fall, and I couldn't reach the rope and trees to grab on to to keep from falling. It was awful," she admitted.

A little later, Lindsey screamed in terror. After Cho Lin cancelled the spell, Ashley eagerly asked her what she had seen. White faced, Lindsey replied, "Dominus. He was cutting off my body parts a bit at a time, while I stood there stunned, unable to even think. Fingers, then hands, then arms, toes legs—he kept cutting me up bit by bit! It was awful!"

Somewhat later, Deiter screamed in terror, when Peaches succeeded. After he recovered, everyone wanted to know what had so terrified him. "I was facing this enormous dog, ten feet tall; it was ripping me apart, chewing off my arms and legs. Horrible." His face was white as a sheet.

Emilio had seen himself being eaten by monstrously large spiders. Amanda had seen herself being torn apart by a grizzly bear. Audrey saw herself in a snake den with hundreds of poisonous snakes crawling all over her, biting her frequently. Andy had seen himself being buried alive and being slowly eaten by bugs, unable to get out of the ground. Pam had seen herself being attacked by thousands of giant wasps, stinging her relentlessly. Peaches saw a huge alligator ripping her head from her body.

On Wednesday, after everyone had faced their worst terror, Professor Cho Lin explained, "Now that you all have experienced the effects of this spell, the worst is over. Any time someone casts this spell on you, you will be experiencing the same images. Hence, we will now begin working on your defenses against this spell."

"Now that *is* the best news I've heard," Pam called out.

"Yes, there is defense against such a killer spell. When you start to re-experience these same effects, I want you to begin to disbelieve the images. That is your defense, disbelief. If you are successful, the spell will evaporate and will not harm you. We will spend as many class periods as needed to get every one of you prepared to nullify this spell, when used against you. That is the best defense I can teach you."

"Please note, class, that come examination time, you will *not* need to cast this spell for a pass. I will be giving you the pass this week as you successfully cast it and repel it. It is far too dangerous to put this spell into the forty-five minute race at the end of the year." Pam thought this was the best idea she'd heard yet.

When they all passed this spell, it was now the middle of November. Outside the weather was very nasty. The snow had continued unrelenting. Already three feet of snow blanketed the campus.

Chapter 8—Houston

Saturday morning, everyone gathered around the big screen TV in the commons. For the first time, Hugo appeared un-composed as he related the ongoing news. "Despite all attempts to dislodge hurricane Emily, she still has not moved! Texas and northern Mexico have taken a horrible beating, with massive flooding in nearly every city and town. Mass evacuations are now being conducted by boat. Tens of millions are being relocated to more northern cities. The President has issued quotas for all major cities. Denver is to provide shelter for three million people whose homes are under water. The Los Angeles area has a quota of eleven million refugees. This is the biggest natural disaster this country has ever seen!"

"Gas prices are approaching ten dollars a gallon, and the President has authorized the rationing of gasoline, if the price reaches eleven dollars a gallon." All the while he spoke, video of the horrible conditions in southern Texas flew by on the screen. Further north and west in New Mexico, mostly heavy snowfalls continued to cause typical winter problems. However, at this point, many ski areas praised the snow, which allowed them to open sooner than normal.

Suddenly, every student had a Message appearing before their eyes.

Please report immediately to the dining room. Governor Alister.

While they rushed the short distance to the dining room, Lindsey wondered what was going on. Pam wondered how he could send a message to six hundred students at one time. Ashley already knew that something important was about to be announced. "Wonder what this is all about?" Andy asked, as they entered the room and took their usual seats at the Yellow Hall tables.

All the professors sat at their usual places but with stern looks upon their faces. When the last stragglers entered, Governor Alister rose to speak. "Students, as you know, this storm has caused massive flooding in southern Texas. Up here, we are getting a winter wonderland. Not so down there. Our sister magic school, the Sam Houston School of Magic, is now almost entirely under water and must be evacuated. I have offered to provide sanctuary here at Bradbury's for all six hundred of their students and professors." He gave this a moment to sink in, before continuing.

"This means that today, every one of you will be doubling up, eight to a room. Your House Mothers and Fathers will be giving out the new room assignments to your Floor Monitors." At once, all five acting mothers and fathers began handing out lists to the various Floor Monitors. Soon Lindsey was also handed several pages.

"I want to make this as painless as possible. So here's how it will be done. First, the Floor Monitors will notify those students who will be moving into a different room. As soon as you know you are to move, I want you to go prepare your things. Pack them as if you were taking the bus home on June 1. Once that has been accomplished, our staff will move your furniture and then your bags for you. Those who are not relocating, you are to go and prepare your room to receive the additional four, their beds, and bags. This process must be done by this evening. The students and faculty will be arriving tomorrow. We must be ready to house them."

"Next, they will be attending classes, using the many available rooms in our halls. However, you will be mingling during meal times and on the weekends. Please extend to these students every hospitality. Remember, their school has been flooded out. Most likely, their own homes and families have been flooded too, and their families evacuated to cities across the country. Expect these students to be very upset. Please show them that we care. Thank you for your cooperation in this time of the greatest natural disaster our country has seen. I will keep you informed, as always. That is all."

Lindsey began calling out names, as did Sandy, Tom, and all the other floor monitors. A few minutes later, everyone dashed to their rooms. Lindsey was rather happy with the arrangements. Kathy and Audrey would be moving in with them, along with two other girls she only recognized: Jenny Williams and Liza Smith. All were third year students. She realized that Alister was keeping the grades together, which was why Fern had not been moved in with them.

Organized chaos then ensued as the staff went from room to room. When the men came to Lindsey's room, they quickly moved the furniture around, making room for the additions. Next, they went next door and moved the furniture in, making a tight squeeze, though still livable, but certainly a lot more cramped. The four girl's many bags suddenly appeared and in they walked. Now they all had to organize their things, chatting about the calamity all the while.

Since the commons and study hall simply could not accommodate double their numbers, Alister assigned various large rooms in the various halls to the guests. That way they would have a good place to gather and to study. However, to accommodate so many at meal times, the courtyard, which went unused during the wintertime, was converted into a second dining hall for the Houston students.

On Sunday morning, Governor Alister held a meeting for all the Floor Monitors. "After lunch, the many buses will be arriving from Houston. These children will be frightened and disoriented. They know nothing about our campus. Hence, I want each of you to meet your corresponding students, escort them to their new quarters, and get them settled in. Once that is done, every one of them will need your usual orientations, a guided walk through our tunnels to their classes, shown the bathroom facilities, the dining room, the usual. Treat them as if they were first years arriving the last week of August. However, this will have to be crammed into one afternoon and evening."

"Since this is impossible for you to do alone, that is, how can you help six hundred students learn their way to and from their new classrooms, I will be asking every student to assist one of the newcomers, showing them around the campus and walking them through their daily schedule. Professor Cho Lin has made a list of each of our students and the corresponding student that they are to show around the campus this afternoon and evening. She will give you the lists, and you are to contact those on your list, telling them who they are to escort and what they are to do. Beside each student's name is their room number. Each student will be given their class schedule by their own Houston Floor Monitors, so you will only need to make sure that these new arrivals have theirs. Questions?"

Seeing none, he ended with, "I want to personally thank each one of you Floor Monitors." Everyone received their lists from Cho Lin. Once Lindsey had hers, she headed up to inform the fifty girls on her list. This promised to be one busy day indeed.

The eight girls managed to get themselves better organized in their cramped quarters by the time that Lindsey returned. "Got your assigned students, gang. We Floor Monitors will be meeting the buses and getting them to their rooms. As the plan goes, they will be given a map of our campus and their class schedules, so we don't have to worry about that. Once I get them up here to their rooms, then you get to go introduce yourselves and take them on a tour. Pretend that they are first years, so show them the restrooms, the dining room first. Next, walk them through the tunnel system and go with them through their classes at least twice. As I understand it, you will be their buddy for the next few days."

"Does that mean we have to babysit them?" asked Kathy. "You know, be with them all the time."

"No, well maybe be available if they have questions, but on Monday, all of us will have classes, so probably it's only today and tomorrow that we have to worry about. After that, if they need you, they can find you. I think it is just so each of our guests has someone here that they can go to for help," Lindsey replied.

Just then, a Message appeared before Lindsey's eyes. She called out, "The first buses have arrived with Yellow Hall students. I'll let you know when you need to meet your buddies." Lindsey dashed out of the door and down the stairs. As she went through the commons, Sandy and Tom were already there. "Hi Lindsey, we're getting an unexpected workout," Sandy said as the three headed down to the tunnels.

They climbed up the stairs in the Admin Hall. At least, the short distance from here to the gates had been plowed, though with the continuing snow, they still left footprints. Several professors were waiting for them, as well as Governor Alister.

Lindsey watched as the students got off the bus and found their bags. As a group, she noted they looked awful, eyes downcast; some were crying; their clothes uniformly had dried mud up to their knees. "Welcome to Bradbury's," Governor Alister spoke calmly. "As I call your name, please come up here and get your map of our campus, your class schedule, and dorm room assignment. Our Floor Monitors will move your bags to your new rooms and take you there. Each one of you has been assigned one of our students to be your guide and buddy, especially for the next two days. Once you are unpacked, your buddy will come to your room and take you on an extended tour of the campus, showing you where everything is located. They will walk you through your class schedule so that on Monday you will know how to get from class to class."

He began calling out names, and the sad-looking students walked up to get their papers. Lindsey realized that this way, everyone could be sure that no student was left behind, that all were accounted for as they arrived here. After calling out around one hundred twenty names, Lindsey, Sandy, and Tom began going down the line, checking which room each now had and moving their bags to the room, using the Move Object spell. Fortunately, five other professors lent a hand with this, particularly needed, since these students were not dressed for the cold and snow.

"Okay, I'm Sandy Rains, this is Lindsey Barron, and this is Tom Whitewater. Please follow us, and we will get inside immediately. We all are using the underground, warm tunnels to get around the campus. We have a record three feet of snow on the ground already." Lindsey and Sandy led the girls, while Tom led the boys.

Once in the first tunnel, many of the girls began chatting about how warm and cool the tunnel was. Lindsey smiled, remembering her feelings when she first walked these tunnels as a first year. Ten minutes later, they led the girls onto the second floor of the girl's section of Yellow Hall. The new arrivals quickly began finding their new rooms. Sandy called out, "We'll send you your buddies in about a half hour; that will give you time to arrange your stuff a bit. Remember, if you urgently need one of us, look for a door with the large yellow star on it, those mark Lindsey's and my doors. See you in a few minutes." Hastily, the two went from room to room notifying their friends that they should begin assisting the arrivals in thirty minutes.

"Darn awkward," Ashley whispered to Lindsey. "How am I going to carry this paper which gives the name and room number of my girl?"

"Don't worry. Mine is in the same room as yours. I'll hold both of them for us," Lindsey answered helpfully. "Really, they look terrible. I think many have been crying, at least some of the girls. I didn't get a good look at the boys, though. I think that they are frightened and a bit disoriented."

The eight girls chatted until it was time. Lindsey and Ashley walked together to room 17. Lindsey knocked and the door opened. "Hi, looking for Lisa Holmes and Alicia Mendez. Your buddies are here to show you around. Please bring your map and class schedule."

A third year girl with long, curly blonde hair, whose eyes were red from crying, timidly stepped forward. "I'm Lisa."

"Hi, I'm Lindsey Barron. Got your map and schedule? Okay. Come on. I'll show you around."

A girl of Mexican descent peered out the door. She had long, thick black hair and a complexion that matched Emilio's. Her alto voice said, "I'm Alicia. I have my papers."

"Hi, I'm your buddy, Ashley Stokes, third year too. Come on. I'll show you around."

She stepped out beside Ashley. "Oh my god! What's happened to your arms? They are gone!" she said quite shocked at the sight of Ashley, who was wearing her usual form-fitting blouse, which showed no signs of ever having sleeves. Curiously, the other six roommates peered out the door at Ashley. Even Lisa turned to stare at her.

"Yep, no arms. Lost them in a car accident when I was

two. Gosh, how did your pants get so muddy?" Ashley cleverly turned the girl's attention back on to herself.

"Flood. Our whole campus ground is under nearly two feet of water! We had to wade through it to get around and to get to the bus. It's horrible! All the basements are totally under water. We had everyone working like mad for two days moving everything out of the many basements. It's just awful," Alicia replied, as they walked down the long corridor.

"We saw some video on the news, but we haven't seen any pictures of your campus. It must have been really bad there," Ashley answered. She explained about the stairs, that boys were not allowed in this section. When Ashley got to the door to the stairs, Lindsey conveniently held it open for her and Alicia. They went down to the first floor and showed them the commons and the study hall, but explained that their new commons would be in one of the other buildings, since these were too small to hold another hundred students. Next, they showed the two the dining room, which had been doubled in size by temporarily enclosing the courtyard area.

Next, they went down to the bathroom. Both girls were elated to see such elegant facilities. Alicia exclaimed, "Gosh, you are living in luxury! Ours is nowhere near this good! I can't wait to take a bath and clean all the mud off myself. Clean spells just cannot keep up with the mess."

Now the two had to split up, as the two girls from Houston had different schedules. Ashley found herself walking along with only Alicia. She explained the tunnel system and headed for the Hall of Illusion, where these new Yellow Hall Houston students would have a room there as their commons and study hall areas.

"This is almost a maze," Alicia lamented.

Ashley saw that she was near tears and asked, "What's wrong, Alicia? Am I going too fast for you?"

"No, no, I was thinking about my family. I don't know where my parents and little brother are now. The last I heard, they were being evacuated by boat, but I don't know where they are now. I'm so frightened about them, scared really."

If Ashley had arms, she would have thrown them around the girl, giving her warm support. Instead, she leaned close to Alicia, using her leg to simulate a hug. Alicia threw her arms around Ashley and clung to her tightly, sobbing into her shoulder. She wondered what she could say to her.

"At least you are warm and safe here, Alicia. Once you get yourself oriented to Bradbury's, we can see about trying to find out where your family is at, maybe get a message to them that you are safe. I bet your mother is worried sick about you too," Ashley said comforting and guessing what she should say.

Alicia stopped sobbing and pulled back to look at her face. "Really, you can help me find them? I suppose mom is terribly worried about me too. Thank you, Ashley, thank you."

"Come on; we need to get you familiar with the campus so we can then set about the real task of finding them." Alicia needed no further encouragement and followed her closely, working hard to memorize the routes. Unfortunately, numerous doors presented themselves. At first, Ashley thought that she would just let Alicia open them for her, but then thought better of that idea. She would not be seeing that Ashley was truly independent. Instead, as they approached a door, she cast her Open Door spell, non-verbally and without her wand, which was secure to her lower left leg, snug in R. B.'s fine magical sheath.

"How come all these doors are opening for us? Are they all automated?" Alicia finally asked.

"Er, no, I am opening them."

"But how? You don't have any arms or hands?"

"Spell," Ashley replied timidly.

"But your wand is strapped to your leg. How?" a suddenly very curious Alicia asked.

"Non-verbal, no wand, Open Door spell," Ashley had to admit what she was doing.

"Gosh! Incredible! Wow! I mean when I first saw you, I thought, well. . ."

"I know; here's a helpless cripple."

"Well, mostly. We don't learn non-verbal until our sixth year!"

"We don't either, but I can do only a few this way. I need my wand for most spells. Now Lindsey Barron—she can do nearly all the spells this way," Ashley desperately wanted to change the subject.

"Wait a second! Is this Lindsey *the* Lindsey Barron who fought against Dominus Malefic two years ago? The one that was on the news for days?" an incredulous Alicia asked.

"Yes, that's Lindsey. We are in room 9, just down the hall from you. She's one of your Floor Monitors, so you're welcome to come to our room and chat with her and the rest of us anytime," Ashley suggested, very glad the focus was now off herself.

After walking around for nearly two hours, running into many, many other pairs from other halls as well, Alicia finally felt that she could find her way around alone. As they returned to their rooms, Ashley said, "Why don't you take a good hot shower or bath and get yourself cleaned up properly? There's enough time before supper. I think that we are all going to go down to dinner together. You can sit with us if you like, or maybe you would prefer to sit with your roommates. Anyway, we'll get you all when it's time to eat, okay?"

Alicia spontaneously gave Ashley a big hug, "Thanks. Don't forget, we have to find my parents and brother soon."

"I haven't. I'm going to talk to Pam about how to do it. See you in a while. Remember, room 9 if you need me." Ashley finally entered her own room and sacked out on her bed.

A little later Pam returned, "Gosh, it must be really, really bad down in Texas!" The girls chatted about what they had learned from their guests.

Ashley finally explained the situation with Alicia to Pam. "I've promised to help her find her family, but I have no idea how to do that. Can you help me, Pam?"

"I reckon all the students are pretty much in the same boat, since tens of millions of Texans are being relocated all over the country," she replied. "I will begin investigating and let you know. If she asks again, tell her I'm on it." Pam booted her laptop and began searching.

Lindsey suspected the girls' morale would be renewed after a good, long, hot, soaking shower or bath. Indeed, this was the case, she found out, as they all congregated in the hall to go down to supper together. The Houston girls were now clean and their spirits higher. However, many were asking Lindsey if it was true, that she was the one that Dominus Malefic had kidnaped and who had destroyed the relic. Oh's, and ah's echoed as they all went down the halls and stairs, after she repeatedly said that she was.

Everyone was now surprised with the decor of the dining room. One-half was decorated in the colors of Bradbury, gold and brown, while the other portion was decked out in Sam Houston's colors, green and yellow. As suggested, each Houston student sat beside their buddy from Bradbury. Alicia sat beside Ashley, and timidly asked, "Do you need help eating? I mean, well, you know what I mean."

"Nope, unless there is steak. I find cutting meat rather a chore, so I eat other things. Thanks for asking. By the way, I've got our Sleuth working on finding where your family is located," she hastily changed the subject.

Governor Alister rang a bell and began, "Greetings fellow students from Sam Houston School of Magic. Welcome to Bradbury's. I am Governor Alister Broadwell, your host. We are pleased that we can be of some assistance to our fellow students in this time of the country's worst natural disaster. Let me begin by introducing Governor Able Jones of Houston." A tall, thin man rose, Lindsey thought he looked incredibly worried.

"For today and tomorrow, we both encourage you to sit with your buddies from Bradbury's. On Monday, each school will conduct their own classes, so we will not see much of each other, except passing in the halls and tunnels. However, beginning Monday night, the dining room will be divided into halves, one for each school. We both assume that you would prefer to dine with your close friends as much as possible. However, students from both schools, please feel free to dine with whomever you desire. You do not need to stay only in your section. I believe that Governor Able wishes to say a few words. Able," he replied and sat down.

"Thank you Governor Alister for everything. We of Sam Houston School of Magic are deeply in your debt. In our hour of crisis, you stepped forward to aid us. Thank you. To all you Bradbury students, I understand that you are doubling up in your rooms. I want to thank you as well for your kindness. I know that you have taken most of this day to help all our students get orientated to your campus. Again, please accept my sincere thanks."

"Houston students. I know you are terribly worried about your families. Mass evacuations are continuing on an unprecedented scale. Confusion inevitably results. Please be patient while we work out ways and means for you to locate where your families are now at and how to contact them. In the meantime, work hard on your studies. I want every one of you to pass and move on to the next grade at the end of this year. Thank you."

Alister waved his wand and the tables filled with food. Lindsey noted that there were six main dishes, one of which was a hot Mexican dish. She smiled, knowing that the cooks were doing their best to make the guests feel more at home as well. Ashley helped herself to chicken, mashed potatoes and gravy, corn, and applesauce laced with cinnamon. Of course, many now glanced her way to see just how she could possibly eat. Ashley pretended not to notice, focusing on eating and chatting with Lindsey and Alicia.

The Houston Yellow Hall Floor Monitor came around to each of her charges telling them that the big screen TVs were up and working in their new commons in the Hall of Illusions. Many cheered, for now they could watch the news. Alicia explained, "We haven't been able to get any news for a week now because all the power is off."

"Wow, thank goodness for Light spells," Ashley commented.

Later that evening in their study hall, many were discussing the awful flooding situation and the plight of the Houston students. Pam, on the other hand, was cursing up a storm. "Darn these people anyway. Do you realize that there is no real planning or organization behind these mass evacuations? People are just going any old way. It's going to be impossible for anyone to find anyone! Idiot management personnel. There doesn't seem to be any one in charge who knows what is happening! Grr."

Pam simmered down and gave up on that avenue.

However, she had uncovered a new and very interesting file on her father's secure server in the Department of Magical Misuse, Sterling. Labeled "Failed Attempts," she downloaded it and opened the document. "Bingo, just what I have been looking for the past three weeks." Her anger turned to instant curiosity.

A while later, she added, "Now this is really interesting."

Lindsey finally asked, "What is?" Pam had been talking mostly to herself all evening.

"Look. This shows that there have been seven attempts by various powerful wizards to move that hurricane. It details the precise steps that they took, such as 'apply eastern push force' or 'apply southeast force' or 'apply southwestern pull force.' It shows just what the results have been, nada. However, the hurricane just keeps coming back to about the same spot. Here, this last entry says that Governor Able Jones gave it a due south shove, but it came right back to its spot."

Becoming curious, Ashley looked at the document on Pam's screen. "You know in a way it is kind of like a pool ball."

"Huh?" said Pam, completely baffled with Ashley's statement.

"Well, the hurricane is a pool ball. The wizards are being the cue ball, hitting the hurricane ball. It should have gone off in the appropriate direction, but it doesn't. That means it is also being hit with a counter ball. It's almost like I hit it with the cue ball one way, and just as mine hits it, someone else fires a second cue ball so that it exactly counters my cue ball. Weird, isn't it?" Ashley explained.

"Oh, I see, counterforce. I wonder if I can figure out the counterforce and where it is coming from? Rats, we don't get physics until next year," Pam lamented. After a moment, Pam asked, "Ashley, can you help me diagram this as a pool ball shot, please?"

"It's easier if I just draw it," she explained and began making a sketch using a pen and her foot. "Let's do the south push one. That's the easiest to see." She drew a ball, and then added a line with an arrow indicating the wizard's push. The head of the arrow pointed south. She then added another line whose arrow was due north on the other side of the circle. "See, the two cancel each other out."

"Ashley, I could kiss you! Perfect! This is a major breakthrough!" Pam was very excited. Quickly, she drew up the seven figures, representing the seven attempts to move the hurricane, adding the two opposing forces. She stared at the seven figures.

"Hum, this makes no sense. Every time someone applied a force on the hurricane, within hours, the counterforce is also applied. Yet, it would appear that whomever is applying the counterforce is either using the same spell as the wizards are using, which makes no sense either, or the counterforce applier is moving all over the northern hemisphere to get into position to push back on it, which also makes no sense."

"Hi Pam," Monique stuck her head into the study hall; she looked a little tired. "Been a long day with our new students from Texas. What a mess. How are you holding up? Bet you are glad that you are not a Floor Monitor today."

"Hi Monique. You've had physics, right?" Pam asked.

"Sure love. What's up?" Monique replied, moving over to where Pam was sitting and putting her arm over Pam's shoulder. Pam quickly explained what she had uncovered.

"Where the devil did you find that document? I've been looking for something like that for days?" Monique asked.

"Another one of those don't ask-don't tell things, sorry," Pam replied with a sigh.

"Figured. I see the problem. Our counterforce guy must be moving all over the place and taking almost no time to do it. Perhaps using a Teleport? How's he going to push while he is in the middle of the sea? I agree, makes no sense."

"What if it was all coming from one location? I don't know, pick a spot, say here at school. Is there any way that we could work out whether that would work, and if so, figure out where that location might be? Gosh, I wish we were in physics not chemistry this year," Pam lamented again.

"Say this *is* interesting!" Monique declared, sitting down beside her girlfriend. "Let's say the counterforce location is here, due north of the hurricane. If someone tries to push it south, you only have to pull due north to counter it. If they try to push it north, you need to push it south. That's the easy part. Now, if they push it to the west, then the counter must wait until the hurricane has moved off this direct north-south line, you see. Once it is over to the west a ways, then you can apply a force from this northern spot to push back against the west original push, but you have to let it move off of being directly south of you."

"Hey, look at these figures! You are on to something. When it was moved primarily north or south, the hurricane barely moved at all. Yet, when they moved it more easterly or westerly, it moved some twenty-five to fifty miles before it got pushed back into position," Pam observed.

"Yes, but look it sort of wobbles back into position," Monique observed. "It is almost like someone waits until it is off being dead below them and then begins to push or pull it back. However, applying that much force—see, it is a vector, Pam—is going to cause the hurricane to also move north or south. So they would have to periodically apply another force to get it back on the proper path, hence the wobbles."

"I wonder if we could work out a computer model that would show us the location from where these counter forces are being applied," Pam thought aloud.

"Sure, let's begin with the basic equations," Monique began writing them out. A half hour later, Pam had enough to proceed. The two girls hugged each other and Monique headed for bed, very tired from her long day helping the Houston Red Hall girls.

Lindsey also headed to bed early, just as tired. Ashley, who had been keeping an ear open to Pam's conversation, came over to ask how it was going. "I've got the equations, so now I'm writing a simulation program to see if I can find any geographical location that fits the observed data."

"Sounds complicated," Ashley admitted, though the equations looked much like those they were studying in math class. Ashley had never seen someone actually writing a computer program before and watched fascinated as Pam rapidly typed in her coding.

Pam explained, "I'm using the C++ programming

language. It is still be most efficient way to write programs. There, now to get my booboos out." A few minutes later, she began to run her simulation. It ran and ran. Both girls began yawning. It was approaching eleven at night. Finally, with the program still running, they decided to go to bed and let the program run on its own during the night.

First thing in the morning, Pam checked her computer. "Yes!" she declared, waking the other seven up.

Lindsey and Ashley got up and came over to see, while the others went back to sleep. It was Sunday morning, after all. "Look, it worked! It's real solid along this northwest-southeast line but uncertain more on the other axis. I need a map of the US!" She opened up Map Google and entered one pair of coordinates. All three girl's jaws dropped when they saw the location on the map: Telluride!

"I'm looking at the 90% chance of correctness locations here. It appears to be an ellipse. The narrow axis is going from Telluride up to Montrose, maybe forty miles here at the narrow part of the ellipse. Now the big uncertainty is on the other axis. Let's see the two end points. Oh brother, Gunnison to the state line! Well, somewhere in that oval someone could be applying the counterforce to all the wizard's attempts to move the hurricane. I need more accurate data if I'm going to narrow this thing down any better."

"Pam, you are an absolute genius!" Lindsey praised her. "I wonder who you should tell about your discovery?"

"No one yet. It is just my speculation, and it is far too big an oval to be really useful. Let's get something to eat. Then I will see if I can somehow get more accurate data and narrow that oval down some." All three headed down to the self-serve early morning buffet.

"Well, I think you should discuss it with Professors Herbert and Jasper, just to make sure you have the equations right and that it ought to work," Ashley suggested.

"Hi Ashley," Alicia welcomed her buddy. "It's still snowing outside."

The three went through the line, as usual, Lindsey levitated the tray for Ashley, who pushed it over to sit beside her new friend, Alicia. "Hi Alicia. Pam's gotten nowhere trying to find anyone's parents. It's a real mess. I guess you will have to be patient. I'm sure that they are all right and will contact you as soon as they can."

"Thanks, I feel better after getting a good night's sleep. Honestly, none of us have been sleeping much for the last couple of weeks. It's scary when your whole world goes underwater. We kept hoping the rains would stop, and the water would go away. I have to admit I'm amazed at how well you manage to do things. It must be so hard for you."

For once, Lindsey observed that Ashley didn't get angry or antagonistic. "Well, I never really had them. I just do things in different ways, that's all. I'm on our track and soccer teams, scored two goals in our first game. I love to shoot pool. Around here, only one of our professors can take me. I just think you all make way too little use of your legs and feet."

"Say, Ashley, have you covered the Terror Killer spell yet? We did, but I almost died."

"Wow! Well, yes we did it last week ago. Our professor took the most extraordinary protections with us. Only two of us could cast it at one time, while everyone else watched," Ashley explained.

"What did you see? I mean I saw this huge gorilla with giant teeth. He began ripping my arms and legs off! That was so horrible! This week, we are supposed to work on protecting ourselves from this Terror Killer spell. Is there any real protection?" Alicia asked.

"You bet! We worked even harder on learning to guard and protect ourselves from it. I bet you by the end of the week, you won't be afraid of that spell any longer," Ashley replied.

"Thanks. Say what were you afraid of? A giant bear? It's okay if you don't want to tell me. It was the most terrifying *thing* I've ever felt," Alicia added.

"Falling. I'm terrified of being on the edge of a cliff and losing my balance. I was falling backwards off this cliff. There were ropes and tree branches, all sorts of things I could have grabbed a hold of, if I had arms and hands. I just fell over, completely helpless to do anything about it," Ashley admitted her greatest fear.

"I mean I'm not scared of animals or people. I've been

kicked out of two magic schools already for fighting. Last one I was at, well, I kicked the necromancy professor in his privates after he chided me for not trying to learn his devil spells. Falling, that always scares me."

"I understand now, Ashley. Say, if you ever need anything, just ask me, okay?" Ashley grinned and agreed.

Just then, Professor Jasper and his wife, Angel, came in for breakfast. Pam waited until they were seated before dashing over to see him. Ashley pointed him out to Alicia, "That's Professor Jasper Jones. He's the only one around here who can beat me at pool."

Shortly, Pam returned with a satisfied look on her face. "Got to run. I'm meeting with Professor Jasper in a half hour to go over my findings. See you later." She dashed off to her room.

An hour later, Jasper commented, "Brilliant exercise, Pam. Of course, we have no idea if this has anything to do with the hurricane, but it certainly opens up new doors to pursue. You need to reduce that ellipse of certainty. Here, let me give you my login and password into the NOAH database. You will get to use it later on, if and when you begin an in depth study of the earth."

Pam thanked him and headed off to find Professor Herbert Mac Elroy. Before she went any further in her analysis; she wanted to make very sure that she and Monique had the equations correct. After all, with a wrong formula, all the data in the world wouldn't help.

"What a novel approach to this problem! I do believe that you are on to something, not sure what. Yes, you and Monique have the equations right. I recognize her handwriting, terribly ornate style. Please keep us all informed on how your project progresses." Pam was really fired up now. Both her professors thought her simulation had merit. She headed for her room to tap into NOAH's database.

She found the database a bit overwhelming at first, so much data! Cross-indexing the time ranges that she needed with the hurricane's location, she began to focus in on just what she wanted: precise locations at precise times. By noon, she was running her simulation once more. Reluctantly, she headed down for lunch.

Mid-afternoon, her program finished. Eagerly, she plotted the ellipse representing 90% certainty. The more accurate data had indeed narrowed the ellipse. At the bottom edge was Telluride; the other end of the narrow axis lay only ten miles north near Ridgway. The long axis was now down to twenty miles on either side of the Telluride-Ridgway line, covering mostly mountainous terrain.

Pam gathered up all her data sheets and computer, and headed to see Professor Cho Lin. Over tea, she explained her simulation and its results to her professor, and then waited for her reaction. "Well, this is most fascinating Pam, terribly interesting theory you have developed here. The Weather Control spell doesn't work this way, so I'm at a loss as to how someone in this ellipse zone could be countering the wizard's spells. However, I will take your results and show them to Alister. Perhaps he can see something that I overlooked."

Pam thanked her and headed back to the dorm, convinced that no one would actually believe her results. "What could the Department of Defense do with it, Pam?" Amanda consoled her, when she returned sour-faced. "They could fly over the area and look, but what should they be looking for anyway? Cho Lin said the spell doesn't work that way."

"I don't know, Amanda, just that they should do something. I'm going to email this all to my father and get his opinion as well." That ended the brief discussion. Pam typed up a very lengthy email to her father and sent it.

"Hey, Dominus is going to give another speech; come on," yelled Audrey, who came to fetch everyone to the commons. They all dashed downstairs to see what he had to say this time.

"Welcome to the fourth broadcast of the Dominus for President Campaign." They had missed two others, but he'd only gone on about financing and providing for health insurance for everyone, according to their needs. The camera panned over the cheering crowd. Monique rushed in and got to Pam's side.

"Watch that crowd carefully! I've just made an incredible discovery about the crowd," she said, and then shut up as the voice of Dominus began speaking.

"Welcome wizards, witches, gentlemen, and ladies to this fourth campaign video. In case you have not heard, I, Dominus Malefic, am running for the President of the United States. The election is now barely a year away, but I feel I needed to present more of my views to you today, especially in light of the Natural Disaster befalling our country."

"Hurricane Emily is still parked off the coast of Texas. Massive flooding has occurred throughout much of southwestern Texas, particularly the southern portions. It has taken a Natural Disaster of monumental proportions to clearly demonstrate just how completely disorganized our current administration actually is. How quickly did our President order mass evacuations? Already the death toll is over five hundred people."

"At last, he's ordered the evacuation of tens of millions of people. Have you seen the TV news videos of just how organized and well executed this evacuation actually is? Horrible, disgusting, pathetic, those are just some of the adjectives I would use to describe the administration's handling. If you have a family member or relative who used to live in the evacuation zone, then you know what I mean. No one knows where those being evacuated have been taken. Tens of millions have lost contact with their loved ones who live outside the disaster area. I say it is criminal the way this has been handled by the administration."

"What about getting the hurricane un-stalled? Ah, do you know that the government has already made seven attempts to get the hurricane back on course and moving out of the area? Yes, seven. They have called upon seven of our country's greatest wizards. Yet, what has been the result of these men and their spells? Nada. Nothing. Emily is still parked where she has been for months now."

"Yet, there is one wizard who can indeed get Emily moving once more. Yes, there is just such a powerful wizard. Yet, our government has not called upon him to ask his aid. Friends, there is one wizard in our glorious country who does have the power, the skill, the ability to get Emily long gone from her current position. However, our administration thus far has refused to call upon him for his aid. What kind of criminal action is that? You know someone can end this Natural Disaster today, yet you refuse to call for his aid, to allow him to work his magic. Is that not a clear and overpowering demonstration of a criminal action? I leave that for you to decide."

"But who is this all powerful, great wizard? It is me, Dominus Malefic, who stands before you today. I can guarantee you that I can make this hurricane become a thing of the past in short order. Yet, our government, yours and mine, refuses to ask for my aid, refuses to acknowledge me. If I am elected your next President, I give you my solemn word that I will always ask those who can aid for their help in times like these."

"Please go to the polls next November 7 and cast your ballot for Dominus Malefic for the President of the United States. I leave what must be done with the criminals who now reside in the Oval Office to you, the good people of the United States. I will return with another broadcast later. Thank you all for taking the time to listen to me."

Again, the camera panned over the enthusiastic, flag-waving crowd. The commons room erupted into dozens of conversations. Monique pulled Pam into the study hall. She cancelled her shrink spell and opened up her laptop, which had now become its normal size.

"I've been doing a bit of research myself. When I first saw those pan shots of the crowd, I thought that they looked strangely familiar. I've been off hunting since then. Here, look at this shot of the crowd supporting Dominus." She rolled a one-minute video.

"Now, watch this one, taken from the 2016 Presidential election campaign." She rolled the second one-minute video.

"Hey, except for the banners, it's the same video! How can that be?" Pam asked. "Oh, he's using that old video and modifying it! There is no crowd cheering him," Pam concluded.

Monique grinned broadly. "You got it. I've been

examining his video, and I can show you how he has altered it. If you magnify it fifty times, you can see the overlaying edges of his banners. He just took the old footage and doctored it up in Adobe. He doesn't have a campaign or any crowd of supporters. It's all a figment of his imagination, designed to fool the country!"

"Way cool, Monique! Well done!" Pam gave her dear friend a big hug.

"I've already posted this on MySpace and MagMySpace, though I don't know what good it will do. People believe what they want to believe. What do you think of his speech today?" The two continued their chat for some time.

Chapter 9—Thanksgiving Time

Lindsey and her group discussed Pam's incredible findings for the rest of Sunday evening. Unfortunately, no one was able to counter Cho Lin's caution that the Weather Control spell didn't work the way Pam's simulation suggested. Monday came, and it was back to class, not only for the Bradbury students, but also for the Houston students. While they mingled at meal times, once everyone headed off to class, the two schools operated independently of each other.

In spell casting class, the tenor changed drastically from the frightening previous week. Fabricate Object was the spell for Monday, in which they created a bit of rope, a staff, a stone, a block of wood, a piece of metal, pens, hammers—useful items that were fairly small in size. This spell went well for all the students.

On Tuesday, they all met with Professor Mary Ann to learn the only divination based, Grade 4 spell, Scrying Detection. This spell, however, took a good deal of time for most to master because concentration and alertness for minute senses were required. Ashley, of course, had this spell down pat on Tuesday, but many did not succeed until Thursday.

On Friday, they went back to Professor Huan Su. "Review weeks. Class, because of the difficulty of the Grade 4 spells, we will be reviewing them for several weeks. When you feel confident, you may take the final test on the spells. In the spring term, we will be covering the balance of your Grade 4 spells, and the final test in the spring will only cover those new ones. You see, you are getting quite a break by not having to cast all these more difficult and time consuming spells in one forty-five minute period." The entire class cheered him, and he smiled. Each year, it was always the same. His class cheered when he made this same announcement.

However, at that moment, Governor Alister entered their classroom, something Lindsey had never seen him do before! Something was clearly up, and everyone instantly perked up. All ears strained to hear his whispered conversation with Huan Su. At last, Professor Huan Su spoke, "Well, it looks as if we have a slight change of plans here. Instead of a review, Governor Alister will be taking over the class for today."

"Thank you Professor Sung. It is not often that I take to the classroom to teach. However, we are in very unusual times, times that demand that we take action. As you know, we are hosting over six hundred evacuated students from Houston. That also means their families have also been evacuated and relocated to who knows where. I assure you that it is a complete mess out there. We have students who have no idea if their families are safe or where they might be. Hence, we must come to their aid."

"I have cleared this with their Governor. I'm going to teach you a very special spell, Locate Person. Once you have mastered the spell, I ask you to cast this spell for your buddy, and then for some of the second and first year students. I'm afraid that this spell is beyond their skill. It may well be beyond some of yours as well. If so, do not worry; it really is a Grade 7 spell, not normally taught even to sixth years." Many exclamations of surprise echoed around the room. Everyone sat straight up in their seats in anticipation, none more so than Pam!

"Now this spell can only be cast for someone else, to locate a person for them. It can never be used to locate someone for yourself. Further, the person you are locating must have very strong ties to the recipient of your spell, such as a family member. The spell will fail if you try to locate a slight acquaintance. Further, when the spell activates, a telepathic connection is opened between the recipient of your spell and the person they are seeking to locate. You will be able to hear the words being said by both parties, but neither will hear anything you think or say."

"Our objective is over this Thanksgiving period to get each of these Houston students back into contact with their families—to know where their families are now staying. Without this detailed information, their buses cannot be programmed to return them to their families at Christmas time. If we can't find their families, they will have no other choice but to stay here at the school during the entire holiday season. I find that to be unacceptable, so let's do our very best, shall we?" He got a chorus of "Yes!" in reply.

Sometime later, Lena said, "Hi Lindsey. My, this is a surprise, strange way of talking. A new spell, dear? Phone's out?"

"Hi mom. Yes, new spell. We are learning it so we can help the students from Houston. Their school is under water, and they are now staying at Bradbury's with us. We need to help them find their families who have also been evacuated to who knows where. That way, they can go home to their families at Christmas time. Cool spell, mom. I gotta go. Ashley just cast this one, and now I have to learn how to do it."

"That is wonderful of you children to help out those in need. I'm proud of you. Give my love to Ashley. Bye."

Ashley blushed. She'd heard the whole conversation, of course, but could not participate. "Okay, my turn," she grinned. Lindsey now began to learn how to cast it as well.

Since only half of the class had been able to cast it successfully, Alister told them that they would resume on Monday. "You have until Wednesday to learn it. On Thursday, the holiday starts. We will be spending those four days helping the hundreds from Houston. There's the bell. See you on Monday."

On their way to their next theory class, conjuration and summoning, Pam declared, "Now that is what I mean by we ought to be doing something! I think this is absolutely a terrific plan that Governor Alister has!" Many echoed her sentiments.

In their first class on Wednesday morning, Professor Herbert began the announcement that would be repeated another seven times, once in each class. "Because of the location project beginning tomorrow, there will be no homework assigned over this holiday season." Only Pam was annoyed about this. Everyone else was ecstatic over the news.

"Now we can concentrate on helping the Houston students," Lindsey declared, eager to begin.

On Thursday morning, Thanksgiving Day, Alicia and

Ashley walked over to a quiet, unused room in the Hall of Illusion. Alicia held her card and pen. The card had a spot for the address and phone number of her family. It also held her cell phone number, just in case her parents didn't have it with them when they evacuated.

"Are you ready, Alicia? You know what you have to do? You have to get their address and phone number and give them yours," she reminded the nervous girl. Alicia nodded.

Ashley then explained how the spell was going to work. Alicia got to see just how Ashley managed to cast spells, something that she had been extremely curious about, but had not dared to ask. Ashley waved her wand with her right foot and spoke the connection words. She felt the telepathic connection begin between Alicia and her mother.

She was not expecting them to converse in Spanish, however. There was no time to cast another spell, so she had to rely upon Alicia to get the information. "Muchas gracias! Muy bueno!" Alicia said to Ashley before she realized that Ashley didn't understand her.

"I'm sorry. My mother speaks Spanish. Thank you very much. Very well done on the spell. They are all safe in San Diego with my uncle. I got their address. You were right. They left in the middle of the night and had no time to get the paper with my school cell number on it. Thank you, Ashley!" She gave her a big hug.

Lindsey found Lisa, and they went to an empty room in the Hall of Conjuration, per the instructions she had. After explaining everything to Lisa again, even though her professors had already gone over the procedure with her, Lindsey cast her spell onto Lisa.

Mom! It's me, Lisa. I'm safe. We are in another school in Colorado. Are you all safe?

Lisa! It's Lisa! She's safe! Lindsey sensed that her mother was relaying the news to her other family members. *We're in Denver right now, but they are sending us on to St. Louis tomorrow. We didn't want to call until we knew where we would end up.*

I need your address so the school bus can bring me to you at Christmas vacation. Do you still have my cell number?

Why don't you give it to me again? I'll write it down. Can we call you later when we get to my cousin's? I'm not sure of their address yet.

Sure, the Governor said that if you are still in transit when it's time for the bus to leave, you should wait a day wherever you are so that I can come and join you. If not, I have to stay here all by myself. Please, I want to be with you over the holidays, mom.

They chatted a bit longer before the spell ended. "I'm supposed to write down that they are in transit and will call me with the address," Lisa said, tears in her eyes. "They are all safe. Thank you so much, Lindsey for helping us. Mom was so relieved to hear that I'm okay, and I am too. They are going to stay at one of mom's cousins in St. Louis." She held her card close to her chest all the way back to the dorm, where she handed it to her House Mother.

By the time of the Thanksgiving feast that evening, Lindsey had helped two others reach their parents. As they all headed into the dining room, Deiter came up to her and said, "I've done six already. This is the best darn thing I've done since I helped stop the Mad Bomber. How about you?" She told him she'd only gotten to three of them and thanked him for being so generous towards the Houston students.

That evening, Lindsey called her mother to chat. "We've got over four feet of snow up here," she told her mom.

"Heck that's nothing, dear. We have nearly six feet on the ground and more coming every day. Many ranchers are starting to be in big trouble. They can't get to their herds to feed them or water them. If it keeps up, many ranchers in New Mexico and Colorado are going to be in big trouble. Will your bus be able to navigate the deep snow? Lloyd hasn't been able to keep our long entrance road plowed."

"I hope so." They chatted for an hour. Lindsey longed for the long holidays. Maybe there was something she could do to help around the ranch during this crisis.

On Saturday night, KMAG reported that the Department of Defense would be trying a new approach on the hurricane to get it to move. In response to the challenge by Dominus, they had to try something, Pam concluded. She carefully noted the day that they would be trying this, December 1. This time, she would be ready and be monitoring the storm's path on Professor Jasper's NOAH account.

During the next week, she and her friends worked hard on their spell review. All were determined to take the test before December 1, so they would have one less subject these last two weeks and more time to spend on the others.

"That went well," Emilio was in good spirits, "only flubbed one spell."

"Great, Emilio," Kathy praised him. "I missed two." Indeed, they all achieved their goal, as the first approached, marking their next chance to spend the day in Telluride. The night before, the girls chatted about the coming day. They all had plans to do as much Christmas shopping in Telluride as possible.

As they went to bed that night, Ashley whispered worriedly to Lindsey, "Something bad is going to happen tomorrow—in Telluride, I think. I wish I could sense more. Maybe we shouldn't go tomorrow."

Lindsey replied, "I don't think Governor Alister would allow us to go there if there was going to be any trouble. Let's stay really alert tomorrow."

"Oh my!" exclaimed Ashley as the group stepped outside Jake's Grill onto the street. Snow was mounded high along the sides of the buildings and the curb, leaving barely enough room for single-file foot traffic! The wide streets were now so narrow that two cars could barely pass each other. In fact, in places, they couldn't see over the mound at the curb.

"This is really bad," Lindsey added.

"Wow," Jim added. "Are you going to be able to handle this, Ashley?" He was most concerned, ever since he heard of her greatest fear brought to light in spell casting class.

"Walking is awfully tricky, Jim. Can you possibly steady me, please?" she asked for his help. Lindsey saw this as a definite change in her attitude. Seldom before did she ever ask for aid.

They did some shopping, but it took ages to get from one shop to another. By noon, they finished, ending up in Domino's to warm up and eat. "Heck, Ashley, there's no way we can get over to the pool hall. The side roads are nearly impassable on foot."

"No kidding," Lindsey butted in, "I'm all for heading back early this time."

"I second that one," Monique added. Pam nodded as well. "I had no idea it was this bad out here." In fact, none of the students realized just how bad the storm had been and was continuing to be. After eating, the group slowly made their way back down the snow-covered streets.

Chapter 10—Countermoves

Dominus looked at his satellite image on his large display monitor, showing Emily's current location and swirling clouds. Satisfied that it had not moved, he turned to his trusted Death Stalkers. Five were currently present in the old house they were now using as their headquarters. William the Bold, whose left hand was missing since his ill-fated attempt at burying the Bradbury school bus in an avalanche, paced the small room, uneasy. Len Striker, Ames Selig, Ben Johnston, and Allan Hall listened carefully to their master. Like Dominus, they were in their thirties. Len, Ames, and Ben had been imprisoned along with Dominus, who had freed them a while back. Only Allan had remained free, though he had been in hiding for those dozen plus years while his master had been incarcerated.

Dominus cursed and said, "That darn Betts girl is on to us. Annoying kid doesn't know when to leave it alone. Fortunately, they don't seem to be taking her seriously, but we dare not gamble on it any further. Well take her too."

"Then, you mean to go through with it?" asked Ben, "right under their noses?"

"Yes," Dominus stated flatly.

"I still say it is too darn risky, Master," Len added. "It could backfire and bring them down on us, ruining everything."

Dominus glared at the two. Though the others held similar opinions, they dare not say anything. "If you idiots follow my plan to the letter, no one will have the slightest clue of their whereabouts. Besides, this action will meet three objectives with a single action: we get this Betts girl out of circulation, we get Sam Barron's kid under our control—she's been a royal pain to us—and we humiliate Governor Broadwell. It's perfect! As long as you do exactly as I have planned, I will have all three of them."

"Dominus," Allan decided to speak up. "This Barron kid, she has me plenty worried. You yourself said that she was able to cast all those spells, even after you cut off her hands and sewed up her mouth. It seems to me that bringing her here is just asking for trouble. If she is taking after Sam, she's going to be major trouble. How are you going to keep her from raising the dickens with us? She was more than Rubius could handle."

"Leave that to me. Remember, I want them unharmed, unmolested. I want them to suffer despair, to humiliate them utterly! No harm, no molesting them. Understood?" All nodded.

"Okay then, on the first, we will meet here in the early morning. I will keep those Department of Defense wizards befuddled, unable to move Emily. You do your part and bring me those pesky kids."

"Yes, Master," they echoed in unison. Allan had grave doubts about the wisdom of this move, but he dared not protest further.

"Good. Another month of Emily and I'll have them begging for my aid—maybe sooner, if this latest Department of Defense action fails. They may be pleading for my assistance tomorrow! Oh, yes, don't forget to bring those protein drinks, juices, and bottled water, Len. We don't want our guests to starve, now do we?" Dominus gave a long, snickering laugh, envisioning his ultimate conquest over these annoying children, who continued to interfere with his plans.

Chapter 11—The Telluride Day

A bell sounded one p.m., as the group struggled through the narrow, snow-mounded streets of Telluride. They had shrunk their many packages in both size and weight so they fitted nicely in their pockets. Carrying bulky packages was not their problem. Rather it was the narrow track between the mound of snow from the road piled at the curb and the secondary mound of snow piled against the building, leaving only this small path to travel along the sidewalks. That was their problem. That another inch had accumulated since they arrived in the morning only compounded their walking difficulties.

Reduced to walking single file, Monique led the way, followed by Pam. Andy came next, with Lindsey behind him, ready to help Ashley behind her. Jim helped Ashley with her balance while walking behind her. Amanda and Henry had fallen way behind them. He wanted to pick up something for his dad, and now they found themselves almost a block behind the others. Actually, the streets were filled with many hundreds of students, most doing their Christmas shopping, though two hundred had opted to watch the afternoon matinee at the theater.

Suddenly, Lindsey, Pam, and Ashley's rabbit's feet began jumping madly around inside their pockets, startling all three girls. "Something is very wrong," Pam exclaimed, looking around, seeing only the mounds of snow.

"Something bad is going to happen. I just know it," Ashley added. Jim continued to hold her steady with his hands around her waist.

Regretting not having her staff with her, Lindsey looked all around as well, but saw nothing out of the ordinary. Then, she heard a low whistle coming from just in front of her.

Immediately, two snow-covered men appeared from the huge mound on the street side. They had been hiding in a hollowed-out spot and had used Imaginary Terrain to make the hole invisible. One man struck Monique in the back of her

162

head, while the other man did the same to Andy. She watched both slump to the ground.

Behind her, another two men had appeared behind Jim, one slugging him in the back of his head. The other man cast a Hold spell. Lindsey, Ashley, and Pam were unable to move a muscle. At once, Lindsey began to cast her Dispel Magic spell, non-verbally and without her wand. Likewise, Ashley began to cast her Dispel Magic spell as well.

It did them no good. Before they got the spell cast, all three girls were struck on the backs of their head with a blunt object, and all three fell to the ground unconscious. An Invisibility spell now hid all them. Strong hands picked up all three girls, and the four walked on down the sidewalk. At the corner, they moved out into the street, avoiding the few cars, which crawled along the snow-packed main street. They ducked down a side street. Only when they were four blocks away did they finally use the sidewalks.

William the Bold announced, "Boss, they're back. It seems that they brought back three kids, not two. Some armless kid was in the way."

"Excellent. Beautiful. They have not yet tried to move Emily. Keep an eye on this display while I attend to our guests. Get me the instant it begins to move," Dominus ordered, a glee in his eyes.

"Yes, Boss," William began staring at the display. Dominus walked into what had been a bedroom many years ago. Now it only held a few old chairs. The men had already deposited the three girls on the chairs and were now removing their heavy cloaks.

"Make sure you get their wands," Dominus said as he entered. "What's with the third kid?"

Ames answered, "She was in the way, a helpless thing. Didn't have the heart to hit her on the head. Brought her along. She'll make a nice plaything, don't you think?"

"Well, she's a student so you darn well better find her wand. I don't know how she could possibly cast spells, though," Dominus pulled on his goatee.

"Here it is, strapped to her leg. She must use her feet somehow, Boss." The third wand joined the other two atop the pile of winter clothing in the far corner of the room.

"Tie them up. Then we'll wake them up, and I'll cast my spells to make darn sure that they do not interfere any more with my plans. Remember, they're not to be harmed or molested, except by me. The pleasure that I will take with Barron's kid will make up for her losing my Rod of the Apocalypse!"

The four men lined up behind their master, who conjured a bit of cold water, splashing it in the three girl's faces, rousing them. Uniformly, they reached for their heads, moaning in pain. Then, they saw Dominus standing before them and the four Death Stalkers behind him. All five had their wands drawn.

"Well, well, Miss Barron. We meet again. Miss Betts, pleasure to meet you at last. You really should stop meddling in my affairs. I don't know how you figured out what I was doing with the hurricane, but your infernal meddling stops now. Idiot Mind!" His wand flashed and Pam jerked.

"Hello. Do I know you? This is a nice chair. My head hurts. I did some shopping today. How are you?" Pam said very stupidly.

Dominus growled, "Oh shut up!"

"Oh what is open that needs shutting? Do you want me to shut that door? I don't see anything else that is open, sir." She pointed to the door behind the men. "What a pretty dress you are wearing, Ashley."

"Your mouth. Be quiet," Dominus said sternly. Pam smiled at him and stopped talking.

"Tell me, Miss Betts, what is one plus one?" She smiled pleasantly at him. Finally, infuriated, he said, "Answer me. What is one plus one?"

"Oh, I thought you wanted me to be quiet. Let's see, one plus one. Ah, er, quite a lot I think. I don't believe I know that one. Is it important? Perhaps we can ask Ashley or Lindsey. They may know, sir."

"Not important. You may continue to be quiet now, Miss Betts," Dominus replied, satisfied that his spell achieved its full effect. He turned to Ashley. "Who are you, girl?"

"Ashley Stokes," she replied, unwilling to say more,

horrified at what had happened to Pam. She was acting as if she knew nearly nothing!

"Well, you were just in the wrong place at the wrong time, girl. However, if you behave yourself, I will not torture you severely. You are already being tortured, it would appear. In fact, this works out even better, Ashley. You will be caring for the needs of these two."

"Now then, Barron, you have cost me dearly. I had great plans for that rod. I have spent many years planning my revenge on Sam, but alas, one of my Death Stalkers, Allan here, beat me to it. Yes, Allan was the one who killed your father. I admit I was rather upset at first, but now, I will take great pleasure in making you suffer in his place."

"Last time, you circumvented all my carefully planned spells. Yes, I admit that back then, I had no idea that you could cast your beginning spells using your arms and non-verbally. Clever of you, Barron, but not clever enough. This time I am fully prepared for you. Realize, all three of you, that I do not want to kill you outright. Where is the fun in that? No, I will consider your deaths only when you are *begging* me for it! I want you to *suffer* long and hard, Barron, long and hard. Stun!"

Wham! Lindsey again felt that overwhelming stun spell—the same one that he had hit her with when she entered the bathroom at the Nationals when she was a first year student. She couldn't move a muscle; she couldn't blink, move her arms, and only stare straight ahead at Dominus.

"Hold her arms out, please. Barron, this time you have no arms to cast your spells. Slice! Slice!" His wand activated twice, and Len and Ben let her two arms drop onto the floor, seeping blood onto the dusty floor. Ashley screamed. Ames cast a Silence spell on her. Though she yelled, no sounds came out.

Pam commented, "Oh what pretty red water! Such nice arms. Who do they belong to?"

Ashley looked at the statue of Lindsey and saw that he had cut off her arms, leaving maybe two or three inches of them left, just enough to wiggle them. She did observe that the spell also sealed up the wounds so that Lindsey wouldn't bleed to death or need heavy bandages. Ashley gagged and vomited onto the floor. Ames cast his Clean spell afterwards.

Smiling an evil, satisfied grin, Dominus continued, "Barron, that will eliminate your arms from spell casting. One spell down, two more to go for you. Len, stick that straw in her mouth. Make sure that the end is inside her lips. Good. Seal: Lips!" His wand activated once more. Lindsey felt something happening to her lips, but could not move to find out what. Ashley stared at her. Lindsey's lips had merged, forming solid flesh. She could never open her mouth again. Her lips were now permanently joined together. Well, one might be able surgically to sever the merged flesh, perhaps. Only the straw protruded. Len now realized why they had to get all the liquids—to keep her alive. She would have to suck in liquid nourishment.

"There, no more talking for you. Ashley, if you don't behave, this will happen to you as well, understood?" Now white, Ashley could only nod.

"Two down, one to go, Barron. Like last time, when I had sewn your mouth shut, you still managed to cast spells. This time, there will be no more of that. The way I figure it, you have to be able to see to cast. Hence, Blind!" His wand activated a third time. Lindsey now saw only blackness.

Ashley stared in horror. Lindsey's eyeballs turned a solid, dull, grey! "Oh what pretty grey eyes she has!" exclaimed Pam, admiring Lindsey's new eye color, unaware that Lindsey was now completely blind.

Lindsey nearly passed out from the pain of the amputations. Her lips, well they just felt funny. Now she saw only blackness. She couldn't blink or move to find out why, only enduring the pain in what was left of her arms.

"Ames, you keep an eye on her. I don't want her vomiting and drowning on her vomit. If she does, use Clean immediately, understood? I want these three unmolested and alive! Think of the many days of torture I'll have with them before they plead with me to kill them!" He roared with self-satisfied laughter. Even his men grinned, although several really hoped that Dominus would let them have some fun with them later on.

"Len, tie the other two up to their chairs for now, please. Later, we'll have some fun and watch the helpless one try to feed Barron. That ought to give us some laughs. I'll be watching the display. I've got to counter their futile attempts to move Emily." He turned and left the room. Quickly, Len tied Pam's arms tightly behind her. "Oh, this is fun. Am I not to move now?" Pam asked stupidly. Len then tied a gag in her mouth to stop her talking. Finally, he tied her securely to the chair. He stared at Ashley, now white as a sheet, wondering how to tie her up. He decided to tie her legs tightly together, finally tying her to the chair as well.

"If you stay silent, I won't gag you, miss," Len replied. He had been unwilling to knock her over the head earlier and now didn't want to gag her. Something about her pathetic appearance struck a faint chord within him. Ashley nodded, unable to think of anything to say anyway. She was in shock over what had happened to Pam and the horrible things done to Lindsey. Ashley nearly passed out, after vomiting a second time, cleaned up by Ames.

How long have I been in the dark, Lindsey wondered, when she finally regained some motor functions? She wiggled her head and tried to raise her arms to her face, but found they only reached her ears, barely. She blinked and blinked, but nothing became visible, only a complete, utter, and total darkness. She freaked out and tried to scream, but her mouth, her lips, would not open. Indeed, her lips had been fused together with only the straw protruding from her mouth. She made hideous sounds, however, causing Ames to chuckle to himself. Lindsey wiggled her legs and found that she was not tied up. She could even stand, but thought better of that, since she couldn't see anything. Thus, she did the only thing remaining to her: she cried.

Time passed, but in her total darkness, Lindsey had no idea how much, minutes, hours, days? She heard voices now.

"Ah, they must have cast their spells. Look, Emily is starting to move. Fantastic! They are trying to move it to the southeast. Perfect. That makes it a direct line from here. Okay crown, it's time to do your thing once more."

A bit later, "That's working Boss. Emily's returning to

her position. You've done it again."

"Of course, of course. We need to keep an eye on it. No telling how many times the dumb fools will continue to try this."

Now cried out, Lindsey began to think. She remembered seeing that Dominus was wearing a thin golden circlet on his head. Was that the Crown of Moses that Andy had been talking about? If so, then Dominus was using it to hold the hurricane motionless, causing all this damage!

Worse, Ashley and Pam were in as much danger as she was. Lindsey had to do something, but what? Only one thought appeared in her mind. She concentrated and sent a message.

"Oh my head!" Jim exclaimed, picking himself up off the snow covered sidewalk.

"Are you okay?" Amanda asked. "What happened? Where's Lindsey? Ashley?"

"Don't know; something hit my head; that's the last thing I remember." He looked around. Henry helped Monique to her feet; she too was rubbing her head. Andy still lay on the ground, moaning. Jim helped Andy get up.

"Where's Pam? Pam!" Monique called out loudly. No answer came.

"Ashley? Where's Ashley?" Jim asked.

Amanda exclaimed, "We were about a block behind you and saw several men suddenly appear, then you three went down, and the three girls just disappeared!"

"Darn! Darn! Double darn!" Jim cursed.

"The Pigs! Cowards! Filthy Pigs!" screamed Monique.

"I have a very bad feeling about all this," Amanda said, a horrible knot appearing in her stomach.

"What's going on?" Deiter said, as he and Peaches came up to them.

"Ashley, Lindsey, and Pam have been kidnaped!" Amanda replied. "These three got knocked out, and a bunch of men just disappeared with them."

"Darn it! Dominus! Come on! We have to rescue them!" Deiter exclaimed.

"But we don't know where they went or where they are?" Monique replied. "We ought to let Governor Alister know, and we should alert all the rest of us here in Telluride and start an extensive search. Maybe someone saw something."

"Yes, but Alister is likely to order us all back to the school. I refuse to abandon Lindsey," Andy replied. "He'll have to physically carry me back before I stop hunting for Lindsey."

"Same here," Deiter surprised them all. "I'll be darn if I am going to go back without Lindsey."

"I'll help too," Peaches added. "Lots of us will help. Why don't Deiter and I start spreading the word to every student we can find? Get a search party going?"

"Good idea. Head down to the movie first. Let Tom and Sandy know. They'll help you get in touch with everyone," Jim added. At once, Deiter and Peaches headed back downtown. "Sis, let's see if we can pick up their trail. Andy, you go on up the street the other way, getting everyone you can find to help in the search. Monique, you contact Alister, since it was your idea and then go help—no, you stay here where it happened. You be our coordinator—always here at the kidnap spot. I suspect Alister and a bunch more will be here in short order. Come on, Amanda; let's put our tracking skills to use."

"They were definitely hiding in these holes," Amanda pointed out the obvious. She concentrated to see if magic had been used. If so, she could follow the magical energies to where they might be holding the three. She assumed that the men and the three girls had disappeared by use of a Teleport spell.

A few minutes later, she cursed, "Darn, they just went invisible! If only they had teleported, then I could follow them!"

"Over here, sis. I found their trail. They went back down this way to the corner. Looks like they went out into the street," Jim explained. Amanda looked at the signs and agreed with his conclusions. In the middle of the street, both lost the trail, too many cars had passed, wiping out the trail. Both fanned out, in an attempt to pick up the trail further on, but had no success at all. These kidnappers were being very clever, particularly in not using magic, which would lead Amanda straight to them.

"Oh good god!" the voice of Governor Alister sounded behind the two walking down in the middle of the main street, occasionally dodging cars. The two headed over to the sidewalk where he stood. "Any trace?"

Jim's crestfallen face answered for him. Amanda said, "No sir. They didn't use Teleport or Magic Door to escape with them. It looks like they just went invisible and walked away with the three of them, probably carrying them. The few footprints we found were very deep, indicating they were heavier than a normal person was. We lost them out there in the middle of the street."

Amanda saw that all their magic professors were standing in a line behind Alister. Twelve Security wizards were also fanning out across the street. Hundreds of students were also walking up and down both sides of the street, engaged in an all-out search.

Monique said, "I tried to Message Pam, but got no answer. I tried to Message Lindsey, no answer. I Messaged Ashley, she replied, 'Not now.' That was all she said, sir. At least, Ashley is alive and could send a Message. So she must still have her wand with her, wherever she is."

"Er, not necessarily," Amanda whispered. "I caught those two working on non-verbal, non-wand spells in the gardens a while back. I think that Ashley might be able to cast Message that way. If she said 'not now,' something awful must be going on or she would tell us what was happening."

"Shouldn't we get all the students back to the safety of the school?" asked Professor Cho Lin.

"Yes, we ought to," added Professor Janice, glancing fearfully around, as if the evil men might attack once more.

"No!" barked Professor Mary Ann, the divination specialist, though her head and eyes darted all over the place, looking for signs. This unexpected and uncharacteristic sharp outburst took everyone by surprise. She added, "Three of their fellow students have been kidnaped. They want to do something to help. They must be allowed to help at this time."

"She's right, Cho Lin. Let them continue their search,

even though most likely they are now far from Telluride. It will do them good to search," Alister ordered. "We must think."

"Governor?" a tall Department of Security man walked up to him.

"Yes, Bill?"

"Sir, as you know, twelve of us have been watching Telluride, discretely mind you. We saw no traces of unusual magical spells," Bill replied defensively.

Cho Lin barked at him, "Bill, you were supposed to be guaranteeing the safety of our students."

"Yes, Professor Sung. They obviously knew that we were here and used norm's methods to abduct the students," he defended himself, though he knew there was going to be hefty price to pay for their failure.

"If that is what happened, then perhaps we should continue to look for clues. They may yet still be around here," Alister suggested. "Amanda and I will begin a sweep of the entire town. I suspect that we will eventually find the telltale signs of some Teleport spells. I suggest that the rest of you continue to search the old-fashioned way. Perhaps go building to building; someone might have seen something useful."

He and Amanda began walking down the street looking for the faint traces of magical spell use, particularly those left by a Teleport spell. An hour of slow walking yielded no such signs, much to their dismay. He cast his Magical Door spell, and the two stepped back to the sight of the abduction, which was the central meeting point.

All traffic had been stopped on the main street, which was now filled with nearly four hundred students, who had been looking high and low for the missing girls. Professor Cho Lin said, "Well, no sign of them. They have just vanished from Telluride."

"We found no signs of any Teleport spell, Cho Lin, though they may have driven out of town in some vehicle, but that is not too likely since so many roads are closed." Alister reported on their findings.

What happened next surprised even Governor Alister. A flash of magic appeared beside him. Two men appeared. "Able! Bill! I haven't seen you two in many, many years!" he exclaimed.

"Able Monument, Bill West?" Professor Cho Lin gasped, staring at the two Rat Pack members. Hearing the names, the other nearby professors moved close to see for themselves. Soon word reached the students, who also tried to see this famous pair of wizards, many levitating themselves so that they could get a better view.

"Greetings Alister, professors. Lindsey has asked for our aid. She is in big trouble; Dominus has her and the other two girls," Able said quietly. "She does not know where they are at, only in some room. I believe that Lindsey is unable to receive communication. She does not answer my Messages. I have been tracking her, however. She is here in Telluride."

"Well that is in agreement with what we have found. Amanda and I have found no traces of Teleport spells, which is what I would have expected they would be using," Alister replied.

"I can't get Pam to reply either," Monique interjected. "She is in big trouble! But Ashley did once reply to my Message, but said, 'Not now.'"

"It's getting dark," mused Alister, trying to ascertain what to do next.

"Hey, look at that!" Able pointed out. "A very powerful magical energy beam." While the students who overhead this craned their necks at the sky, they saw nothing except the reddening of the sun and the clouds dropping more snow. Amanda and Alister, however, saw the blinding streak of energy.

Bill finally spoke up, "If we rush them, they may kill the girls." Bill had said nothing thus far and was quiet once more. His point, however, was solidly made, being repeated over and over by the students, as they relayed the caution on down to the others milling around in the street.

"We must make use of what we have. Lindsey was able to Message me. I've heard nothing since her initial contact, however. Perhaps we should try to contact Ashley," Able suggested.

"Let me try," Monique spoke up. "After all, I got through to her before." Alister gave her the go ahead.

Monique's face turned white; her red lips stood in sharp contrast. "Oh my god! Lindsey! Pam! She can message freely now—Ashley can. She wants to know what to do. They are tied up in a room. Dominus cast some kind of spell on Pam, who is now acting awfully stupid or dumb. She can't add one and one! Lindsey, my god! He's mutilated her! Ashley said he cut off her arms first, then something with her mouth. It is somehow sealed shut and her eyes—they are all grey. She thinks Lindsey can't see!"

Hundreds of curses echoed around the street, as more voices repeated the gist of her report to those too far away to hear Monique. "Okay, then they are alive and can be mended," Able replied. "This explains why Lindsey cannot read our Messages. Ask Ashley to ask Lindsey to send Able a message about what is happening to her, please. No wait. Ask her to tell Lindsey that Able and Bill are here along with a small army. We want to rescue them, but are worried about Dominus killing them. Do they know how many are there with them, where they are located in the building, that sort of thing? We need information, Monique."

Able! Dominus has the Crown of Moses and is using it to hold Emily in place. He's causing all this disaster! Don't do anything yet. I have an idea. L.

In her darkness, Lindsey finally began to think. Either she could sit here and cry or she could do something. But what? She began to review all the spells that she knew. Nearly all depended utterly on her being able to see. However, she suddenly remembered the See from a Distance spell. While her eyes might not work, maybe this spell would work. She cast it, and, viola! She was watching Dominus hard at work staring at his big display monitor. Light glinted off the circlet of gold sitting on his head.

On a whim, she cast her Identify spell upon the crown. She was not prepared for what happened next. A voice appeared within her head. *Hello. I am the Crown of Moses. Who are you?*

Lindsey thought, *I'm Lindsey Barron. Are you talking to me?*

Of course, silly. I was hoping that you were Moses. I

belong to him, you see. I was made for him. He told me to take a nap, and I have been, until a Frenchman woke me up. He was not Moses either. The man who is wearing me now is not Moses. Do you know where Moses might be?

No, I don't. Are you holding the hurricane in place?

Yes, he tells me that we are providing much needed water to his people.

"That's not true! The rain has flooded tens of millions of people's homes, forcing them to have to evacuate their homes and flee in a panic to other cities. Five hundred have died. It's dumped many feet of snow around here, causing massive power outages, shutting down all the roads. Farmers can't get to their cattle to feed and water them. It is the biggest natural disaster our country has ever seen.

Oh no! He is misusing me!

Can't you stop it?

No, I must do as my wearer orders me. Can you wear me?

I'll, I'll have to see how I can get you away from Dominus.

Lindsey thought hard. With her spell, she could just barely see the back and head of Dominus in the next room. Even if she could figure out some way to get the crown off his head, he would just take it off her head immediately. She couldn't even hold on to it now. Her spell expired, and Lindsey was in total darkness once more, shocking her once again, sending a bit of panic through her nerves. She felt the water of her tears trickling down her cheeks, but she refused to give in to despair just yet. *What would dad do?* She thought to herself to help keep the hopelessness at bay a little longer. Of course, she had no thoughts in reply. *Well, Alister. What would he do?* She began thinking of him. She had visions of him leaping up, snatching the crown from his head, and immediately using his Magic Door to step outside, away from him.

Immediately she saw the futileness of that. She now had no arms or hands and was totally blind. She couldn't do any of those things. Worse, she couldn't leave Pam and Ashley to this horrible man. *Focus, Lindsey. You have to get that crown from Dominus somehow! Think!* She thought to herself. An idea began coming to her.

Ashley saw a Message appear before her eyes.

Can you whisper to me? L.

"Yes! They are in the next room. Ames has gone to watch them. Are you in a lot of pain?" Ashley whispered. "Pam and I are tied up, and she is gagged. He did something to her mind."

Dominus has the Crown of Moses. The crown is keeping Emily from moving. It doesn't want to continue making this disaster, but it has to do what its wearer orders. It wants me to wear it, so it can stop the hurricane. L.

"Wow. How can you see all this? How do you know about the crown?" she whispered back.

See from a Distance. Identify got the crown talking to me in my mind. I don't understand how, but it did. I wish there was some way we could get into the room with them, maybe behind them. L.

"I have an idea," she whispered. "Ames, Ames?" Their guard stepped back into the bedroom.

"We need to go to the bathroom, please, sir?" Ashley put on her most pleading, helpless, facial expression.

"Darn. Well, okay, I sure as heck don't want to clean you up." He untied Ashley and Lindsey.

"Sir, I can't get Lindsey's pants down or mine either. Could Pam come with us to do it for us?" she pleaded, looking very forlorn. He untied and removed her gag.

"Come on; the bathroom is this way. Don't say a word to Dominus as you go by him or I will smash in your pretty faces," Ames growled.

"Pam, put your arms around Lindsey and lead her, please," Ashley begged, hoping Pam still had enough mind left to handle this. Otherwise, she had no idea how to direct Lindsey, who was completely helpless and couldn't see anything.

"Why? Are we going somewhere?" Pam asked innocently.

"To the bathroom. Lindsey can't see," Ashley whispered.

"Oh. I have to go pee too. Can I go to the bathroom too?" Pam said.

"Yes, whisper Pam. We must whisper. Come on; lead Lindsey." Pam began to push Lindsey forward. Lindsey felt a huge surge of panic. She lifted her foot but had no idea where it was going or where the floor was. It was like stepping into nowhere. Further, she nearly fell over, flailing her non-existent arms wildly in the air, but only her tiny stubs wiggled.

"Oh those are *so* cute, Lindsey. Wiggle them some more," Pam whispered.

Lindsey wanted to scream, but her mouth wouldn't open. Pam at least kept her from falling. She slid one foot across the floor a few inches and then the other. At least, she had continuous contact with the floor. She moved forward bit by bit. "Keep the door open, we don't want any monkey business going on," Ames whispered.

"We are in the bathroom, immediately behind them," Ashley whispered to Lindsey. "Pam, pull down Lindsey's pants so she can go to the bathroom."

"Oh golly, Ashley, this is *so* complicated. How do I do it? Let's see. They don't pull down," Pam whispered.

"Undo her belt; then pull down the zipper, Pam," Ashley felt like screaming at her. How could Pam be this ignorant! What had Dominus done to her?

"Good, Pam. Now pull down her panties. Okay, now move her around so she can sit down. Okay, Lindsey you can sit down now," Ashley whispered.

Lindsey panicked! *How? I can't see!* She wiggled her arms to support herself. It was like falling into the unknown as she began to squat in total darkness, unable to even feel the stool. Landing hard, she hit the wooden seat and heaved a sigh of relief. A bit later, she stood up, and Pam struggled to get her pants back up.

Then, Ashley allowed Pam to assist her. Finally, Pam took her turn. While Pam was trying to figure out how the toilet worked, Ashley received a Message from Monique and gave a lengthy reply to her. That was followed shortly by another Message. Ashley sent a reply.

We are in the bathroom of an unknown building somewhere unknown. Dominus is using the crown in the next room. We are behind them. There are five Death Stalkers with him. Ames is watching us pee, and the others are around Dominus. A.

Ashley whispered to Lindsey that Able, Bill, Alister, and all the students were outside the building and that they were still in Telluride somewhere. "They are scared that if they rush the building Dominus will kill us."

This was the best news Lindsey had ever heard! She decided to risk another View from a Distance spell. Indeed, Dominus was about fifteen feet from them. His back was to them, as were the other four Death Stalkers. Only Ames was keeping an occasional eye on the three girls, but he kept glancing at the large display screen to see what was happening. Lindsey saw the path that they would have to follow to return to their bedroom. They would pass only five feet from Dominus! Lindsey had an idea.

When we start to go back and get as close as we can to Dominus's back, I want you to kick him in his privates as hard as you can. I will get the crown off his head when you do that. Tell Bill and Able to attack at that very time, while they are distracted. Even if he kills me, I'm going to make the crown get rid of the hurricane. L.

She also sent the same message to Able and Bill. Now they waited on Pam, who was having difficulty trying to figure how to fasten her fancy belt. Finally, she worked it out, but then asked how to flush the toilet. "Oh, I see, you press this silver thing." The toilet flushed, but Pam stood and watched the swirling patterns in the water as it flushed. "How pretty."

Finally, Ashley had Pam grab a hold of Lindsey's waist. Once more Lindsey began shuffling with very small steps forward. She held her breath hoping that no one would notice her spell was in force, that she was Seeing from a Distance. Ever so slowly, they drew closer to the back of the man who had mutilated her, murdered so many people, and was the cause of this Natural Disaster.

Ashley stared at the back of the man who had viciously mutilated her two friends. Hatred unlike any she had felt before seethed within her. Just as Ames backed out of the way to allow Pam to turn Lindsey to face the door to the living room, Ashley acted. She sent her Message and put every ounce of strength into her up-swinging leg, connecting directly where she aimed, the crotch of Dominus.

Instantly, he doubled over in massive pain, the crown fell off his head. Lindsey cast Move Object, the crown now sat on her head. *Get rid of that hurricane please, crown!* At the same instant, the world once more turned utterly black for Lindsey. Her spell was cancelled. She heard all manner of wild screams, terrible noises, felt the rush of freezing air on her face, and felt her body being bumped. Vainly she waved her arms to keep her balance, but fell anyway, though she had the presence of mind to cast her Gentle Fall, landing on the floor.

Able commanded, "Okay, here's the plan. They are in the room facing the street, living room. Dominus and his men are in the center. Our girls are to the back. When Ashley gives the signal, we must disintegrate the walls of the living room, giving us a clear shot at the bastards. We don't have a Dispeller with us, so let's use all the students who want to volunteer. The second they see the walls go, they are to cast Dispel Magic spells as fast as they can into the room, while we attempt to take out Dominus and his men. Don't give them the opportunity to kill our girls. Let's all cast Invisibility and move up close to the house. They are in the last house on the left of the dead end street Red Cliff Drive."

Alister added, "Perhaps we could have a number of students also cast Hold Person spells." Bill agreed, though the Security men tried to dissuade them from using the vulnerable students. Able and Bill led Alister and the professors through the streets to the lone house, set back against the snow covered mountainside. Over two hundred students, led by Jim, Andy, Deiter, Monique, Tom, and Sandy, followed closely behind, occasionally bumping into one another; all were invisible. Orders were whispered, and the throng of students took their places on either side of the building, wands at the ready.

Able, Amanda, and Alister saw the brilliant energy trace of the Crown of Moses in action, still countering the forces attempting to move the hurricane. All three knew they were exactly on target. Able whispered precise directions to Bill; both held their staves of power. Everyone waited anxiously for the signal.

The bright streak of magical energies suddenly

disappeared. Amanda knew that something had just happened inside the building. She prayed her friends were still alive. Able received the one word message from Ashley and yelled, "Now!" Four disintegration beams flew towards the ranch home. Able, Bill, Alister, and Cho Lin shot their spells. The entire front wall the living room, which was just behind that wall, suddenly was open to view to the hundreds standing outside in the steadily falling snow.

Dominus was behind a big monitor and computer system, howling in pain. Ames was pushing Lindsey to the floor. The other four Death Stalkers, who were looking at Dominus, now jerked around to stare out at the throng of people. All the students were now visible, having cast their Dispel Magic spells as well, though none could see any direct result of that just yet.

Yet, these wizards were neither stupid nor slow to react. Indeed, Dominus chose his Death Stalkers well. Len screamed, "It's the Rat Pack! Able! Bill! Get the heck out of here!"

"Holy crap! Hundreds of them!" yelled Ben, diving for cover behind the monitor. Allan instantly cast Darkness, and the entire room became black to those standing outside. The blackness lasted for only an instant as the Dispel Magic spells that the students were continually casting cancelled it.

Dominus tried to grab the crown as it rolled across the floor, having fallen off of Lindsey's head, but Pam spied it. "Oh, this is a pretty toy!" She picked it up, looking at the pretty bauble. A fog cloud appeared in the room, but it also vanished almost as soon as it appeared. That was followed by another Darkness spell, which also lasted only a second.

William the Bold stood up, ran out towards the throng, and cast a Ball of Fire at them, "Die you filthy students!" The raging flames only got two feet out of the room before it too vanished utterly.

However, Bill fired his spell directly at William the Bold. As he had said some time back to the girls, this time he was not going for a capture. What was the use in capturing them, if Dominus freed them a short while later? No, this time Bill shot spells to kill. A disintegration beam struck William the Bold squarely in his chest, leaving a gaping foot hole in his chest. The man had the strangest look on his face before his dead body fell to the floor.

A cloud of poison gas began flowing out of the room, but it evaporated three feet from the room. Blackness again darkened the room, only to have the lights return two seconds later. A disintegration beam flew outward toward Bill, who lunged to his right to dodge it. However, it too was cancelled— this time by Alister himself, whose wand activated in a brilliant discharge of energy.

Dominus did not dare stand up to grab the crown from Pam, who was ignoring everything else going on around her, just staring at the pretty bauble in her hands, admiring it. She didn't even hear Monique screaming for her to get down.

Dominus grimaced. His men were pinned down. Only Ames had clear shots. He'd backed into the other room and had the protection of the side wall. "Ames, continuous Darkness spells; we are coming to you," he ordered. At once, Ames began casting Darkness spells just as fast as he could, one immediately after the other.

Strobe lights. That was how Jim described it later to Lindsey. On, off, on, off, as if someone was continually flipping the light switch. They could see the five men racing for the door to the side room, but each image was separated from the next in a jerky sort of motion.

Bill saw Dominus leaving and shot another Disintegrate spell at him, guessing on his next position. The right half of the large monitor vanished. A shower of electrical sparks shot in all directions, adding to the confusion. However, part of his beam struck the lower right half of the man's leg. He heard a howl of pain, but Dominus slipped into the side room.

Instantly, Able, Bill, Alister, and Cho Lin dashed into the living room, Cho Lin going for the girls, while the three men headed after Dominus. "I'm here, Lindsey. It will be okay," she said, as she gently lifted the girl up and helped her regain her footing. Lindsey could not see the look of horror on Cho Lin's face, however. Perhaps it was best that she did not. Ashley did see it and began crying, releasing all of her pent up shock and grief. Pam merely continued to admire the pretty crown, completely oblivious to all that was going on around her.

"Gone," Alister said, as the three walked back into the room.

"Looks like I got a piece of him anyhow," Bill commented touching what remained of the right foot of Dominus. "How are our girls?"

"Bad, Bill," Cho Lin replied, fighting back tears. "We need to get them back to the Infirmary immediately." She still held onto Lindsey tightly.

Lindsey Messaged Alister.

The Crown of Moses. It can get rid of the hurricane. I was trying to do it when I fell. L.

"Excellent Miss Barron. Well done all of you. I believe that it is already doing just that, but I will check further. Miss Betts, may I see the crown you are holding?" he asked politely.

"It's mine! I found it lying on the floor. It is very pretty, don't you think?" she said.

"Yes, it is. Come; we need to get you back to the school," he added.

"What school? Do I go to a school?" she asked in surprise.

"You will feel better when you get back to your computer," Ashley suggested.

"Computer? Oh, those things are *so* complicated. I'm sure I don't know the first thing about them. Why do I have one anyway?" Pam asked sincerely. She then said, "I am so cold. Why doesn't someone shut that big door over there? Who are all those people outside looking at us?"

"Pam, come here and put your arm around me, please," Professor Cho Lin ordered. Pam did so. "Teleport: Bradbury's Parking Lot," she commanded. Instantly, she and the two girls vanished, leaving Ashley standing beside Alister.

"Where are your things, Ashley," he asked.

"I'll show you," she led them into the bedroom, where the floor still held traces of blood. Over in a corner were their cloaks and wands in a pile. He put her cloak back on her and inserted her wand into her leg sheath.

"We are going to search the house for clues, Alister," Able commented and sent a message to the Security Men, who entered the living room and began confiscating what remained of the equipment there, as well as removing the body of William the Bold and the foot of Dominus.

"Is this where he harmed Pam and Lindsey," Alister asked.

"Yes, sir. We were in those chairs," Ashley replied.

"Good. Are you up to telling me all that happened to you? It could be important."

"Yes, sir." Ashley began relating what had happened, from the time that she had felt a hard blow on the back of her head until now.

Alister's face was very grim, however, as he listened to the awful details. "What happened to her arms, do you know, Ashley?" he asked when she finished.

"I think Ames threw them outside in the trash, sir," she replied. "Will she be all right? Can they regrow her arms?"

"I'm sure that in time Lindsey will be just fine," Alister tried to sound optimistic. He sent Able off to search for her arms. A while later, Able returned with a sack, grim faced.

"Take them at once to Doctor Caterwall in the Infirmary. There may yet be time," Alister suggested. Able nodded and teleported away.

"Now then Ashley, I know Jim has been terribly worried about you. I think that it is high time that all of you students head back to the campus. I'm going to take you outside to him and let you all walk back. Is that all right with you?" he said kindly.

"Yes sir. There is nothing I can do here. I want to get to Lindsey soon. She is going to need my help." A minute later, she was standing beside Jim, Tom, Sandy, Deiter, Monique, and Andy.

"Jim, you are charged with getting Miss Stokes safely back to the Infirmary. She wants to be with Lindsey. To all of you students, on behalf of the entire school, I want to thank you personally for helping us rescue the three girls. You all performed admirably. Now it is time that you head back to school. Orderly, mind you."

The crowd began ambling through the snow-covered streets. It was full dark, but the snowfall was already diminishing. As they walked, Ashley began telling Jim and the others what had happened. Of course, the hundreds of other students pressed close to hear as well. An hour later, they arrived back in the central tunnel hub beneath the dorms. Instead of going to their dorm rooms, the small group headed on down to the Infirmary.

One Security man reported, "Well, it looks like Dominus was using this equipment to monitor the hurricane. There really isn't much of interest here, though. Have Bill and Able discovered anything useful in their search?"

Bill replied, "Not really. They have a good supply of liquid drinks. I suspect they intended to keep Lindsey alive for some time, continuing to torture her. Several men have been sleeping here on and off. There is nothing here that is in any way useful to track their whereabouts, though. The five teleported away from this room. All headed to the same place. I'm leery about following their trail. As you know, we have no Dispeller. This time, we were extremely lucky to have had all those students with us."

"Well, it's darn good to see both of you back in action. We've missed you two, you know. Where have you been keeping yourselves?" he asked.

"Best that you don't know. Alister knows how to contact us, if need be," Bill replied. "It's best that we depart now. I will send word to Pam's aunt. I believe that she is in the area doing some Christmas shopping. She should have some relative nearby, don't you think, Alister?"

"Yes, perhaps she should. I believe that it is best that Lindsey's parents not be told just yet. Allow Doctor Caterwall to do what he can for her first, so that we can soften the blow to her folks," Alister suggested. Bill and Able nodded and teleported away.

"Well, there seems to be nothing more I can do here, gentlemen," Alister said. "I leave the site in your able hands. If you need something, Message me." Then, he, too, teleported away.

Chapter 12—Healing

"What is this place? I don't like its smell," Pam said as she entered the Infirmary. Cho Lin very carefully walked Lindsey into the emergency room, allowing Lindsey to shuffle her feet along floor, feeling her way along. She could scarcely imagine what was going through the poor girl's mind at this point. "What does Infirmary mean anyway?" Pam finally asked.

"It is a place where the doctor heals people who are hurt, Pam."

"What are we doing here? I'm not hurt at all. I feel just fine, never better."

"Maybe, but your friend here is in a very bad way." Cho Lin tried to reply.

"Oh Lindsey is fine. She's like Ashley now. I do like the color of her eyes, reminds me of the clouds, though I don't think that I would like my lips to grow together like hers has."

"Ah doctor, little help here?" Doctor Caterwall and two nurses entered the room. The women gasped, and he flinched as he saw Lindsey for the first time.

"We are really just fine, doctor," Pam said. "I don't know why we are here. I'm hungry. I want to eat."

"Lindsey, we are going to lift you onto the exam table," he said. Lindsey, in total darkness, began to feel for the bed with her arms, only realizing they were not there. Again, a shot of panic swept over her, heightened as she felt them lifting her up onto the bed, which she could not see. Only when she felt her back touching the cool surface did she finally relax. She felt his warm fingers pressing against her lips, discovering the small hole where the straw had been.

"I'm going to insert a straw in your mouth, Lindsey. Then I want you to suck up this entire potion. Can you do that? Nod your head." She did. The nurse held the bottle and she began to drink. The brew made her stomach feel warm.

"Now then Pam, would you climb up on that table so that I can examine you?" he asked.

"I'm sorry. I'm not very good at taking exams," Pam

replied, but climbed up anyway. "Is there anything to eat around here? I'm starving."

"We'll get you something to eat shortly. First, I want to see what has been done to you. Do you remember anything that happened to you?" he asked, as he began checking her over.

"My head got hurt. I was in a room with a lot of men. I was tied up, though I don't know why. Alister stole my pretty crown. Can I have it back? Ashley made me pull down her pants and Lindsey's too. I didn't know how to flush the toilet, but she told me how. Am I being helpful?" she asked innocently.

He examined the bump on her head. "Nasty bump, Pam. No real damage there."

"Yes, but it still hurts. Why does it still hurt?" she asked.

"Here, I will give you something to drink. It will help get rid of the hurt in your head," he replied. A bit later, he handed her a cup of liquid.

"It doesn't smell good. I don't think I like it."

"Drink up. It is good for you, Pam," he pleaded with her. She continued not to drink it, making funny faces instead. Exasperated, he said commandingly, "Drink it!"

"Okay. Okay. Don't be so nasty," she replied, annoyed with him.

"Nurse, keep an eye on the two. I need to do a bit of research," he said and left the room, along with Cho Lin and his other nurse, Jean. "This is really bad. Four very, very nasty spells at work here. It's obvious that he cast the Idiot Mind on Pam; that's straightforward to cure. Lindsey, on the other hand, is a mess. I've never seen what he has done to her lips. It's as if her skin has actually fused together. Her arms, those can be handled. She still has a bit of each left, which should be enough to restore them. Her eyes, though. Grim. I have a hunch what spell was used. Give me a minute."

Doctor Caterwall grabbed several of his medical books and began rummaging through them. After a number of anxious minutes, he exclaimed, "Yes, I was correct. It was a Grade 8 spell that he used, Blind. Now that one will be routine to remedy."

"Perhaps you should do that one first. She feels panic-stricken whenever she is moved," Cho Lin suggested.

"Yes, I do see what you mean. I'll handle that one first." He headed back into the room.

"Have you got my food?" Pam asked. He ignored her.

"Lindsey, a Dispel Magic will cure your blindness. However, as we both know, Dominus is very powerful, so it may take us a number of tries to cancel his spell. Nod if you understand me." She did, feeling awfully foolish; all this time, she could have been trying to dispel it herself.

"Dispel Magic: Blindness!" Doctor Caterwall commanded, his wand activating in time. Nothing happened, unfortunately. Repeatedly, he continued to cast his spell.

"Why are you waving that stick around? It looks silly," Pam commented.

Just then, the door opened and Monique, Deiter, Ashley, Jim, Tom, Sandy, Andy, and Amanda entered, their cloaks covered with snow, their faces grim with fear and worry.

Monique rushed to Pam. "How are you doing? I was so scared for you."

"Oh I'm just fine. I can't figure out why he keeps waving that stick over Lindsey, though. He keeps doing it," she replied.

"He's trying to cast a magic spell, I expect," Monique replied.

"What's a magic? What's a spell? I can spell the word play. P-l-a-y. See?" Pam replied. Monique turned as white as the snow that was melting on her cloak.

The others stopped some distance from Lindsey and stared, shocked. While they had seen her from an extreme distance, they had not seen her close up. Her grey sightless eyes, her sealed lips, and her three-inch long arms made them gag.

Doctor Caterwall stopped and looked at the new arrivals to make sure there were not more casualties. "Ah, good that you are here. Lend a hand. Dominus has used a Grade 8 spell on her eyes, Blind. It can be handled with a Dispel Magic spell, only I'm afraid that he is one powerful wizard. I've failed to dispel it in twenty tries. Would you all be so kind and join me in casting dispels? Sooner or later one of us will be successful."

"You bet!" Andy exclaimed and started casting at once, to no avail. Soon, all them were casting away, spell after spell. After many tries, suddenly magical energies flashed and Lindsey's eyes began to change. Slowly, they returned to normal! Light! She could see light at last! Then fuzzy images appeared, which slowly formed into the shapes of her friends. She wanted to yell out her thanks, but again found she couldn't open her lips.

Just then, the door opened and Pam's aunt Wilma and Amanda's aunt Monane entered. Monane carried a sack. "We were doing some shopping in Montrose when Able Monument came to us and said that Pam and Lindsey were badly hurt and that we should come here at once. Oh, doctor, Able sent these along." He looked in the sack and left the room with them.

"Hi Aunt Wilma. Have you brought me some food? I'm starving, and no one is getting me anything to eat," Pam replied. "They keep thinking that I'm hurt, but I keep telling them that I have never felt better. Of course, the silly doctor fellow made me drink some awful smelly stuff. Do you think that I ought to have drunk it?"

"I have an apple here for you, my dear," Wilma withdrew a shiny red apple from her pocket. "Eat this. I'm sure it will hold you for a while, until I can find you something more substantial."

"Okay Aunt Wilma," Pam took a bite. "It tastes a little funny. Perhaps it is spoiled."

"No, dear. It is fresh. I just picked it today, so go ahead and eat it all gone," Wilma insisted. Pam continued to nibble on it, though she made faces indicating her displeasure with its taste.

"I want to go home now. We live in Sterling. I just remembered. Are you going to take me home with you, Aunt Wilma?" Pam asked. Monique could restrain herself no longer, and tears trickled down her cheeks.

"Finish your apple child. We can go home after a while, but first we need to feed you since you are so hungry."

"Oh, yes, that's right. I am hungry." She ate more of the

apple. Suddenly, she sat up, "I feel awfully funny, Aunt Wilma! Oh!" She fell back down on the table and fell asleep.

Monique nearly shrieked, "What happened to her?"

"She's in the process of being cured from the Idiot Mind spell. She should be just fine when she wakes up," Wilma explained. "That is one nasty spell."

"Dominus said that he wanted her to stop meddling in his affairs, just before he did that to her," Ashley explained.

"I, I should have recognized that spell," Monique blurted out.

"It's okay dear," Wilma patted her on her shoulders. "It's one thing to learn to cast it in the safety of the school and quite another to come upon your dear friend who has fallen victim to the spell. Why don't you sit by her side until she wakes up?" Monique needed no second suggestion. She sat beside Pam, smoothing out her disheveled hair, talking softly to her.

Doctor Caterwall re-entered the room, carrying a small potion. "Ah, Lindsey, are you feeling better now that you can see again?"

Lindsey nodded; her terror and fear had gone. She felt good with all of her friends around her. That Pam was going to recover was a great burden lifted from her.

"Now, it is time to begin your first surgery. I want you to suck up this potion. It will help you sleep while I work my magic on your arms. Nod if this is okay." Lindsey nodded wildly. Everyone smiled. After a few sips of the potion, Lindsey fell into a deep sleep.

"You all may wait in that room. This will take several hours. Perhaps you all want to get something to eat and clean up and then come back and wait?" he suggested. They did as he asked. Wilma and Monane said their farewells to the doctor and left as well.

In the parking lot, Wilma said, "You know that the reappearance of Able and Bill will soon be all over the news?"

"Yes, and Dominus also knows that we are back. But do you think it was wise killing William right before the eyes of hundreds of young students?" Monane replied.

"These are hard times. Best they become prepared. A

split second and it could have been all over. I missed Dominus by a tiny fraction. Well, he's now minus one foot; that should slow him down a while. Teleport!" The two women disappeared from the parking lot.

Doctor Caterwall worked feverously for over two hours on Lindsey's arms. Indeed, because they had been dumped outside in the freezing cold, they were very well preserved, so much so that he opted for a Rejoin spell instead of the lengthier Regrow spell. Still, it meant laborious surgery for him and his two nurses. For the next twelve hours after the surgery, it was imperative that she not move or lift her arms. Hence, their last action was to strap her to a lift board, securing her upper arms to the board so that she couldn't possibly try to raise them, ripping apart all the work he'd just done.

"Our other option is to keep her asleep for twelve hours," he explained to her friends who had bathed and eaten before returning to wait on the outcome of Lindsey's operation. Alister was now present as well. "I believe that it is better for the patient to regain consciousness sooner. However, she will need someone attending to her needs."

"We will!" exclaimed the group almost in unison. Andy, Jim, Tom, Sandy, Ashley, Deiter, Monique, and Amanda. In addition, Emilio, Kathy, and Audrey had joined them.

Alister gave them permission to do so. Doctor Caterwall explained, "Her lips are still fused. I have to do further research on how best to handle that one. She won't be able to talk, so it will be more difficult handling her. Are you sure you still want to help out?" Of course, they all did. "Excellent, just realize that her body has suffered a tremendous shock and blood loss as well. She can expect to be very weak for a few days. However, I expect that her arms will be back to normal within three to four days, thanks to their foresight of putting them on ice almost at once. I bet that thought never entered their minds." Everyone chuckled at his jest.

The nurses moved Lindsey's sleeping body into the recovery room, where she would remain for at least the next twelve hours. Since only one person at a time needed to sit beside the sleeping Lindsey, Deiter volunteered to be first.

Sandy arranged a schedule for the night so that no one needed to sit up longer than an hour. The nurse explained to all them, "When she is awake, encourage her to drink as much of this potion as she can. Use the straw." The rest headed back to the dorm, except Monique, who decided to sit beside the sleeping Pam for a while longer.

Ashley didn't make it past the Yellow Hall commons room. As they entered, she was mobbed by students who pleaded with her to tell them firsthand what had happened. Henry pointed out that it had stopped snowing already, so something major had happened. Once more, Ashley related what had happened with Dominus.

She had barely finished when the KMAG News broke in with a special report. Hugo was abnormally animated this evening. "Witches and wizards everywhere, such news I have. This evening marks a milestone. The surviving members of the Rat Pack have surfaced at last. After a fifteen-year absence, Able Monument and Bill West have reappeared, attacking Dominus Malefic and his Death Stalkers! Indeed, tonight the Death Stalker known as William the Bold was slain by Bill West!"

"In a bold and daring plot, Dominus kidnaped three Bradbury students on their day in Telluride, holding them hostage in an abandoned house there. Assisted by the faculty of Bradbury's School of Magic, Department of Defense men, and hundreds of concerned students, Able and Bill tracked these villains to this house and made a spectacular comeback. Disintegrating the house walls that separated them, these two Rat Pack members attacked Dominus and five of his Death Stalkers. In the huge battle, William the Bold was killed, and it appears that Bill took off the right leg of Dominus, missing him by inches as it were. So the Rat Pack is finally back!"

"In other news, the Department of Defense attempt to eliminate the hurricane has failed once more. However, shortly after their failed attempt, Emily finally turned into a tropical storm and now is gone from the Caribbean Sea. It will take days of course for south Texas to dry up, perhaps until spring for the enormous snow pack to melt further north. Yet, these residents are cheering tonight. No more rain or snow in the immediate future. It appears that the greatest Natural Disaster in US history is finally subsiding."

At this exact instant, Hugo's feed blacked out. The screen flickered and the image of Dominus Malefic appeared on the screen. He was seated at a campaign desk, posters proclaiming is candidacy lined the walls behind him. "Good evening wizards, witches, ladies, and gentlemen of the United States of America. I am Dominus Malefic. I'm taking this opportunity to come before you once again to officially notify you that I have eliminated hurricane Emily myself."

"This afternoon, I saw that once again the combined efforts of our Department of Defense men had failed to impact Emily. Even though no one in the current administration has asked for my assistance with Emily, I just couldn't stand to sit back and do nothing any longer. Too many people have suffered horrible losses. Thus, I acted on my own to deal with Emily. At this time, I would like to announce that Emily is no more than a few light rain clouds out over the Caribbean. Now I urge those of you who can, please chip in and help all those people who have been and still are so badly harmed by this natural disaster."

"When you go to the polls next November, remember what I have done tonight on my own. Elect Dominus Malefic as your next President. Thank you and good night."

Again, the TV flickered a bit and the face of Hugo reappeared. He was talking with the engineers in his studio. "Oh, we're back. Well, you just heard it. Dominus has claimed to have put an end to Emily."

The students in Yellow Hall started yelling and protesting madly. One even turned the TV off. They'd had enough of Hugo's alterations of the truth. Ashley cleverly took this opportunity of confusion to duck up the stairs to her room.

Around midnight, Pam woke up. Monique was still at her side. "Hi there sleepy head. How are you feeling?" she asked softly, trying not to disturb Lindsey who was still asleep. Andy was sitting with her and came over to see Pam as well.

She rubbed her head, "Boy, do I ever have a headache! My brains feel like scrambled eggs. Lindsey!" She suddenly remembered her friend.

"She's over there recovering. Doctor Caterwall has done his surgery on her arms. She should be back to normal in three days, he says. We all helped him get rid of her blindness, so she can see, but the doctor is still trying to figure out how to undo her lips thing. She won't be able to open her mouth or talk yet," Monique filled Pam in on Lindsey.

"Oh Monique! That was so horrible to watch! He stunned her and cut off her arms. He is the most vicious man in the world! Did he escape? My memories are really fuzzy."

"Yes, Able Monument and Bill West, the Rat Pack members—they showed up, and Bill killed William the Bold outright. We think that Bill also cut off the right lower leg of Dominus. They found his foot there in the room. He teleported out in the nick of time. We were all casting Dispel Magic spells like mad there. I think I must have shot twenty before it was done. It happened really fast, though."

"What, what did he do to me? I felt so stupid," Pam asked.

"I should have recognized it at once, stupid me. It was the Idiot Mind spell, a Grade 5 spell. You will be learning it before long. Its effects are tough to cure, though. In class, Doctor Caterwall has to heal up those that are impacted while learning the spell. Nasty one."

"I guess so. Did I say anything, well, I mean anything embarrassingly stupid?" Pam asked.

"Who cares, Pam? It's over now," Monique answered.

Pam thought for a moment. "Say was my aunt here? I seem to remember Aunt Wilma being here with me and Amanda's aunt as well."

"Yes, Able said that he ran into your aunt, who was doing some shopping not too far away and asked her to drop in on you and see how you were doing. I think that she may have cured you. I didn't get the chance to ask her. If so, I will have to get her a good thank you present, for saving you, Pam." Pam smiled.

"Why don't you try to get some sleep now, Pam?"

"I'll look after you," Andy suggested. "Monique has been at your side all night long. She ought to get some sleep too."

Pam reached for Monique's hand and squeezed it. "Thanks," she whispered. Monique leaned over, gave her a loving kiss on her forehead, and then left. Pam looked over at Lindsey and then closed her eyes as well, trying to ignore the throbbing in her head.

Lindsey stirred and tried to get up, but could not move. Panic swept through her, but Amanda, who was watching over her, came to her side. "Morning, Lindsey. It's about nine o'clock. He has your arms on the mend, only you aren't supposed to move them even a tiny bit for a while yet. So he has you strapped tightly to this plastic board thing. I am supposed to get you to drink as much of this potion as you can manage. Okay?" Lindsey found that she could nod her head, as well as wiggle her legs, so that was something.

It was awkward trying to sip the potion while lying down with her head to one side, though she managed slowly. Amanda then began to tell her the latest news. "The big news that KMAG is reporting is that the Rat Pack is back. They are making a big deal out of Able and Bill's reappearance. Emily is history. Whatever you did, it is now gone; only Dominus came on TV and claimed that he got rid of the hurricane. Gosh, I hope people don't believe that!"

Amanda went on, "We've all been sitting up with you all night, and Deiter went first." She rattled off all her friend's names. "Kathy is due to relieve me, and then Sandy will be by. Oh yes, Pam's Aunt Wilma came by along with my Aunt Monane and healed Pam fully. She's got a terrible headache today, but is sleeping again." Amanda chatted away, filling Lindsey in on all the news that she could remember. Lindsey smiled, as she continued to suck up the potion.

As Kathy came in to relieve Amanda, Doctor Caterwall appeared. "How's my patient today?" Lindsey nodded. "Ah, good amount you've drunk, good girl. I've decided that your body has undergone enough shocks for the moment. I'm going to let your arms heal up more fully before we tackle your lips. Can you endure it a little longer? I will have you sitting up around noon, if all is looking good with your arms. Okay with you?" Lindsey nodded again. "Good girl. Now I'd best check on

Pam."

He went to her side, "And how's our computer genius this fine Sunday morning?"

"Oh not feeling so genius. My head hurts something awful, like my brains were scrambled," Pam replied. "I'm starving too."

"That is to be expected, your headache. Now tell me, what is six times seven?"

"Forty-two, why?"

"Just checking. I want to make sure that you are fully healed. I have some additional tests that I would like to perform." She agreed, and he began asking other more complex questions. Finally satisfied, he said, "Okay, it looks good. I am releasing you from my care. Amanda will take you to the dining hall to get some solid food in you. I want you to take a good, long, hot bath. That will help your head. Then, you are to spend most of the afternoon just resting, preferably in your bed. No major activities today for you. Take it easy and let your head recover. Now if in the next day or two you think something is not quite right with your mind, please come see me at once, understood?" Pam nodded eager to get up.

However, as she stood, she discovered she was quite woozy, and Amanda put her arms around her, steadying her. Together, they headed for the dining room. Just as they entered the huge room, Ashley was finally able to leave the dining room.

"What a morning! I've been besieged!" Ashley lamented. When she had come down to eat, she had been mobbed by hundreds of students from the other Halls, begging her to tell them what all had happened. Many had been there casting their Dispel Magic spells, but they could not see what had happened inside. Ashley now realized that until Lindsey was fully recovered, she was the only person who could satisfy everyone's thirst for knowledge. She resigned herself to repeating the story several times. However, the Houston students then swarmed around her, and she had to retell everything many more times.

After lunch, Doctor Caterwall met with Alister in his study. "Frankly, I am stumped on how to treat Lindsey's lips. I have not yet identified the spell that Dominus used on her. I could perform crude surgery and just cut them apart, but that will leave her scared at best, needing plastic surgery. Her eyes are now perfect, and her arms are recovering nicely. She should have no lingering aftereffects with them, though it will be at least a week or more recovering fully."

"Yes, well done on her arms. We did get a break with them. I, too, am baffled over what spell Dominus used on her lips. If we at least knew the command words, we might gain a valuable clue. I suppose that we could regress her, make her relive that moment, and see if she can tell us those words," Alister conjectured.

"It's probably buried under an enormous amount of pain. Such might not be wise, making her relive it," the doctor cautioned. "Perhaps Ashley could remember."

A half hour later, having received the summons from Governor Alister, Ashley rushed to his office, worried that something dreadful had happened, though she had had no premonition about such. "Ah, good morning Miss Stokes. I asked you here to lend us a hand." She flashed a wide grin. It was a figure of speech, but also a joke between them, as she had no hands to lend.

"Neither of us can ascertain the spell that Dominus cast on Lindsey to seal her lips together. We were hoping that you might be able to remember the command words that he spoke as his wand activated. This is very important. Do you think that you can remember that?"

Ashley closed her eyes and returned to those horrible minutes. She was vomiting from the shock of seeing Lindsey's arms removed. What was it that he had said? "It was real short. Real strange. I remember being really shocked again when I heard it. Oh! I know, he said, 'Seal: Lips!' Does that help?"

"Excellent, Ashley, excellent. Now we know the command words. Perhaps that will give us some clues. Thank you. That's all." She smiled and left, wondering what kind of spell that was anyway. Whatever it was, she didn't want to learn that one! Doctor Caterwall left to go research his medical databases, while Alister did the same in the Library. Both were challenged by this unusual spell.

Since she was this close to the Infirmary, she walked next door to check up on Lindsey. Sandy was sitting with her. "Hi, how's my sister doing?" she asked. After a brief update, Sandy left her to tend to Lindsey.

Since they were alone, Ashley looked at Lindsey laying there, her arms very pink, but still immobilized. She admitted, "I was sure scared that you would end up like me, you know. That would be horrible."

It must be awful for you to see me getting my arms fixed back up when you can't get yours back. L.

"Not at all, sis. I'm perfectly happy with my body as it is. I've always been as I am. It does all that I want it to do, but you, gosh, it would be so horrible for you, since you've always had arms, if not hands." Lindsey smiled; she understood.

"You know I've suddenly become the most popular girl in school."

How come? L.

"Cause I am the only one who can tell everyone what happened to us. Pam, she just says that her mind was scrambled. Well, it actually did, and you aren't able to talk yet. Everyone wants to know all about it and have been hounding me. Even the Houston students. They got to me this morning and had me retell it all to them, five times before they all could hear. Of course, now they've all given me a new nickname: Dominus Kicker." Lindsey grinned as much as her lips would allow.

"Actually, I think that has impressed them more than Able and Bill killing William the Bold. I wonder how Dominus will get his leg or foot fixed up? I mean we're lucky to have Doctor Caterwall and the Infirmary here. Speaking of that, Alister and Doctor Caterwall had me see them a bit ago. They wanted to know what Dominus said when he did this to your lips. I think that both don't know what to do to help you yet, but I'm sure they will figure it out."

She chatted for some time, ending only when Alister and Doctor Caterwall entered. "Ah, how's our patient this early afternoon? Your color is good," the doctor said. Lindsey nodded.

"Well, Alister figured it out. Believe it or not, the spell Dominus used comes from the Packaging Industry. It's used to help shrinkwrap goods for shipping. Alister is going to fix you up pronto."

Governor Alister looked down on Lindsey and said, "This won't hurt a bit. Ready?" She nodded. "Unseal: Lips!" His wand flashed and her lips returned to normal.

"Wow! God is this better! I can open my mouth now! Thank you both for everything!" Lindsey exclaimed. "Say, what happened to the Crown of Moses, sir? I wore it long enough to ask it to get rid of the hurricane. It seemed to think that it belonged to Moses and was looking for him."

"Yes, I understand. I had a long talk with that ancient relic from the distant past last night. You see, some highly enchanted items can actually be endowed with a primitive life form. That's why it could talk to you and me a bit. Yes, it has but one master, Moses. Apparently, Moses told it to take a nap, and it has been doing just that, napping for millennia now it seems. The archaeologist who found it woke it up, and Dominus killed him when he stole the crown from him. It seems Dominus lied to it, convinced it that people were desperately in need of water, and got it to hold the hurricane in place. You told it the truth that it had suspected all along."

"Yes, but what will happen to the crown now?" Lindsey wanted to know.

"Well, we had a long talk, as I said. We both decided that it should go back napping, waiting for Moses to return to it. Between you three and me, it is back where it originally was. The world will, however, believe that I now have the Crown of Moses. I will be saying the truth, that the world in these perilous times is not trustworthy enough to have the crown available to them. Perhaps one day, when this is over, the archaeologists will have their crown back to study, but certainly not while Dominus is on the loose."

"Speaking of which, say Ashley, I've heard that you have a new nickname, Dominus Kicker." She blushed and looked at the floor. "I think that is very appropriate, my dear. I know only a handful of people in the entire world who would have the guts to kick that man where it hurts!" Both Ashley and

Lindsey began laughing. Doctor Caterwall joined them.

"Seriously, though. Both you and Pam are now very definitely on the hit list of Dominus. Twice now, you've taken an artifact from him. I have talked to the Betts family this morning. They agree, Pam must always be either here at the school or with you at your ranch. She is not to return to Sterling where it's far too dangerous for her. I also talked to R. B. He agrees and will be working to improve the defenses around your ranch and his. We all want you three to be safe when you are at home." Both Lindsey and Ashley thanked him profusely. Lindsey was more worried than ever about her parents.

Just then, Deiter came in with a large tray of food. "Hi Lindsey. Alister told me to bring food for a starving lady, when I came to relieve Sandy. Hi DK," he grinned.

"Food! I'm starving. Crap, I guess you are going to have to feed me. My arms are still tied down. Who's DK?" Lindsey suddenly realized there was no one here with those initials.

"Ashley," he grinned. "Everyone is going around calling her the Dominus Kicker now. You probably haven't heard that yet. We all think that is darn cool! What's first? I brought a burger, nuggets, and tacos."

While Ashley grinned, Lindsey decided on the burger since it was more substantial. The three began to chat, and the two adults left them alone for now. "Well, if it had not been for Ashley's kick, I couldn't have gotten the Crown of Moses from Dominus and stopped the hurricane with it."

"We heard all about it," Deiter replied. "She's becoming a legend now. I know I don't have the courage to go kicking the most powerful wizard around in his you know what's."

A bit later, he said, "The cleanup is now all over the news. Folks are going back to the flooded out areas. It is an incredible wet mess. More north, the ranchers are having a huge problem with the incredible amount of snow. Roads are blocked, power lines down, and they can't get to their cattle herds. You should see some of the snowdrifts, unbelievably huge."

He continued, "We have about four hundred of us here at Bradbury's that can cast Dig spells. I was thinking that perhaps we could organize ourselves into some relief parties and help the rancher's in southern Colorado and northern New Mexico dig out from the snow," Deiter offered his idea, hoping to get some feedback from Lindsey.

"I like that idea, only we would need some security. None of us is of age so we would need someone to chaperone us and all that. Dominus will surely be after Pam and me more than ever now. I guess we could bunk in a barn or something," Lindsey answered.

"Yes, I know there are logistic problems, but we should do something to help. After all it was a rogue wizard who caused all this," he defended his idea a bit.

"Why don't we talk to Governor Alister about your idea, Deiter? He may be able to work out the problems for us," Ashley added. "I'll go with you, if you like, when you see him."

"Great, DK!" He was very pleased. An hour later, Amanda came to relieve him, and the two set off to discuss his idea with Alister.

On Monday, while her friends took lengthy notes for her, Lindsey listened in on her classes using Hear from a Distance spell. This way, she could at least hear the lectures. However, during their first class Algebra II, Governor Alister made a school wide announcement, surprising everyone.

"Pardon my interruption. I have a proposition for third year students and above. Mr. Deiter Cross has suggested that those of you who know the Dig spell ought to put it to use helping the stranded ranchers dig themselves out of the massive snowdrifts. As he put it, 'Since a rogue wizard caused all this destruction, we ought to help set it straight.' I agree with him. This would be an excellent opportunity for you young witches and wizards to help those in need, your civic duty."

"Therefore, I've decided that we should follow through on his idea. I have instructed all your professors to wrap up this fall term by this Friday. Normally, we have one more week before the holiday break. During this week, those who volunteer to join us will spend the week helping those ranchers in southern Colorado and northern New Mexico who need assistance in digging out from this disaster."

"Already heavy equipment is moving to the hardest hit areas and will be digging out the main roads this week. There is no way that they can get to the more isolated areas. Those will be the ones that we will be primarily involved with assisting. We will be organizing into groups of twenty-five students to a work crew. Either a professor or one of the House Parents will accompany each crew. Each work crew will be led by one student who wishes to assume the responsibility of managing his crew. I have placed sign-up sheets in the dining room. Already Mr. Cross's list is full. If you wish to be a crew leader, place your name at the top of one of the blank sheets. Please, no more than twenty-five per list."

"We will hold a logistics meeting next Saturday afternoon and begin operations on Sunday. The following Saturday, we will return here briefly so that you may pack and then head home for the holidays. Those who don't know the Dig spell and those who don't wish to participate will remain here at Bradbury's during the week. Thank you professors for your cooperation and for allowing me to address your class."

Professor Herbert allowed the class to discuss this exciting news, before he got them back on track with their math review. "To make it easier for you with all the many final exams you face this week, I will allow you to schedule your math test anytime between Tuesday through Friday. I'm told that your other professors will be doing a similar thing. So today, let's review what you should now know."

Lindsey panicked. "I'm not allowed to use my arms yet, maybe not even all week. How can I possibly study, let alone take the tests?"

Doctor Caterwall replied, "Tough break, Lindsey. I don't want you lifting any book until at least Friday. By Wednesday, you should be able to use your arms for light things, such as feeding yourself, but definitely no heavy lifting, maybe not for a whole week." She sighed; she was doomed.

However, just before supper, Professor Cho Lin came by. "Lindsey, based upon your special circumstances, all your professors have decided that they already have sufficient information on which to base your grades this term. Thus, you will not need to take any of the final exams. From what the good doctor has told us, he will not even let you lift a book until the weekend. Merry Christmas and a thank you from all us professors."

Lindsey let out a cheer and huge sigh of relief! Shortly Andy and Deiter dropped by with her supper and theirs. "Hey, my list was full before it got posted," Deiter exclaimed proudly." Lindsey and all her friends had signed up at once plus many of his. Now others were begging him to scratch someone just to let them onto his list, which he politely refused. Deiter showed Lindsey the list. She smiled and ate the fish that Andy held near her head.

"We all think this is a fantastic idea you had, Deiter," she validated him, and he appreciated it, smiling from ear to ear. "At least by the time we need to go, I ought to be able to handle it. Doctor Caterwall thinks I will be able to lift things this weekend. I hope so; I don't like just lying around here."

After supper, her group joined her, allowing her to help them cram and prepare for their exams. Emilio needed everyone's help trying to work out the best order of exams. "You should take the ones that you can do best on soon and save the hardest to last so that you have more time to study," Ashley suggested. That he claimed they were all hard didn't help.

It wasn't until Tuesday that Pam's headache finally subsided and she could effectively begin preparing for her exams. True to her nature, she decided to cram all week and take all them on Friday. The cooks also took note of this unusual early end of term for most students by serving fresh, hot pizzas for supper Friday night, along with sodas, much to the cheers of the students. Lindsey was finally allowed to join them and sleep in her own room as well. Though her arms were very weak, she could hold pizza slices and was very grateful that she was at last among all her friends.

Further, the Houston students were going back to their school on Saturday, spending the week before their end of term helping their staff clean up their school. Hence, this Friday night was really a party night for everyone. Fern, however, was not in a festive mood. Only a second year student, she would not be able to go with them. However, even she was cheered up when she found out that the all the second and first year students began forming their own work crews, intending on shoveling out the campus here, mainly by hand. Currently, the only place one could walk out of doors on campus was from the mostly buried parking lot and through the main gates directly to the Admin Hall, where everyone then went down to the tunnels.

On Sunday, the Deiter Work Crew, as he named his group, boarded their usual bus. Jimmy was driving as usual. Professor Cho Lin escorted them, along with Tom from the Department of Defense and Ulysses Smythe from the Transportation Department. Ulysses was coordinating the efforts of the crew with the temporary headquarters set up in Denver.

"All aboard," called out Jimmy, and one by Lindsey and her friends along with Deiter and his friends boarded. All were wearing heavy winter parkas. Each stowed their small pack of spare clothing below in the cargo hold. Lindsey also placed her Staff of Power there as well. This time, she definitely wanted Margarete with her, though Ashley had not predicted any trouble.

"Let's ride topside where we can see the incredible piles of snow better," Amanda suggested. As the bus finally pulled out on to 145, the highway road crews were already at work. Twelve-foot drifts lined either side of the roadway. On their way down to Cortez, they had to stop three times for avalanche control demolitions. The highway department was creating controlled slides to alleviate the possibilities of a dangerous, unpredicted snow slide. End loaders scooped any snow that reached the road from these blasts. Twice they had to wait and watch these machines do their work.

By late Sunday, they finally made it to their working area, near the New Mexico border and the continental divide. Their first stop was the Longtree ranch, whose mile long entrance road was buried under ten-foot drifts. The bus, however, was not stopped by the snow, moving over the top, barely leaving tire prints behind. Leona Longtree welcomed them, "I can't thank you enough for your help, children." Indeed, they had nearly a thousand head of cattle stuck in five locations on her ranch. They couldn't reach them, and by now, they were near starvation or worse. The students were housed in her bunkhouse, while she moved her men into her basement for the few days that the students would be here.

At daybreak, the Deiter Work Crew began its work. Bundled in a heavy parka and boots, Ashley felt very vulnerable. She couldn't use her wand and was wondering how she could possibly be of any help at all. However, Deiter had already worked it out. "Based on their directions, we know roughly where the five groups of cattle were last seen. We will pick one area and fly over that ground first. As soon as we find the herd, then Ashley's job will be to stay aloft and guide us on the ground, so that we can dig a path to them. Without her guiding us, we may end up digging in circles or miss the herd completely."

An hour later, the first herd was located about a mile from the main complex. While Ashley stayed aloft, compliments of Cho Lin's spells, the twenty-four others began waving their wands, casting Dig spells. At noon, the first of the stranded herds was reached, and the rancher was finally able to bring a tractor load of hay, grain, and fresh water to the animals. By suppertime, a second herd was found and similarly rescued.

Tuesday passed similarly, and by noon on Wednesday, the last of her herds had been brought fresh hay and grain. After accepting the heartfelt thanks from the ranchers and their hands, they prepared to board the bus to head to their next stop.

Just as they began to load, a KMAG television crew pulled up, blocking their exit. A cameraman stepped out along with Jessica Alba, their field reporter. The camera lights shone brightly, as she spoke into the microphone. Lindsey thought that her makeup was a bit garish and overdone. "We are here live in the field with one of the work crews of Bradbury School of Magic students. They have been helping clear paths to stranded animals. And here is Miss Lindsey Barron, the student who was involved with the recapturing of the Crown of Moses. Miss Barron, KMAG and the world would like to ask you a few questions. We've heard all sorts of fantastical tales about what happened there that day in Telluride. It's obvious that you are neither missing arms or are blinded. So many things are exaggerated in the retelling. Can you tell KMAG what happened to the crown? The whole world wants to know? Of course, we all know that a crown could not be behind this Natural Disaster. Yet, there is a strong fascination with the magical powers of this supposed Crown of Moses."

She thrust the microphone into her face. Lindsey didn't want to be interviewed. "Well, I was! I did get the crown from Dominus. He was using it to keep Emily stationary. After I got it away from him, I asked the crown to get rid of the hurricane, and it did so. Right now, I have no idea where the crown is at," she lied about this detail, however.

"Miss Barron, we know that this is impossible. You're a mere girl; you couldn't possible have gotten such a valuable relic from Dominus. Now, how about telling the world just what did happen there? How did the Rat Pack members pick this time and place to make their reappearance? Can we count on their continued help?"

Anger rose within Lindsey, "I did so, after Ashley here kicked him." She glared at Jessica.

"Don't be ridiculous. Ashley is just a mere cripple, a Special Needs student. It was Able Monument or Bill West who took the crown from Dominus, you know that," Jessica shot back, very annoyed that this silly girl continued not to give her what she wanted to hear. Behind her, Lindsey heard the growing anger of her friends. However, no one expected what happened next.

Ashley had taken all that she could stomach. She reared back and pretended that Jessica was a soccer ball, delivering a violent kick into her privates. As she keeled over from the sudden pain and shock, twenty-three voices behind Lindsey and Ashley began laughing. Professor Cho Lin stepped in and said, "I believe that this interview is over." She waved her wand and the camera's lights went out. The disk that had been storing the recording all of this magically erased. The students, still chuckling, finished climbing on board. A minute later, the bus moved around the blocking van, heading to their next destination.

"Way to go, DK Ashley!" Deiter called out.

"That's showing her," Peaches added. "The nerve of that woman anyway. If you had not done it, we were about to blast her!" Many other voices offered up similar support for her.

Professor Cho Lin, however, looked sternly at Ashley. "I'm in trouble, aren't I?" Ashley whispered to her.

"That was not very lady-like conduct," Cho Lin said.

"Jessica wasn't being very ladylike either. In fact, she was being a prick," someone in the back of the bus yelled out, supporting Ashley.

"If you are going to punish Ashley, then you'd better punish all the rest of us," Deiter called out, "because we were all just about to let Jessica have it. Ashley just beat us to it."

"Students, I'm merely pointing out that Ashley's conduct was not altogether proper. Let this be a lesson to you all. Follow Governor Alister's advice and never talk to reporters. As you have clearly seen today, they have their own agendas. Truth is not one of them." Now everyone began cheering, and the tensions evaporated.

When they arrived back at school late Sunday night tired and exhausted, they knew that they had done something of great value for these hardest hit people. Four hundred students had worked miracles all across their area. They also heard that several other schools of magic had been following their example, sending out work crews as well.

"It's a good feeling, isn't it?" Deiter commented to Lindsey, as they walked along the freshly cleared path that Fern and crews had cleared here on their campus grounds.

"Yes, is sure is. I'm sure glad that you thought of doing it, Deiter," she replied. Indeed, Deiter was now seen as a powerful leader among Black Hall students and many others as well.

As Deiter and Peaches entered Black Hall commons, he said, "We did it, Peaches. We've put Black Hall on the map!"

"Well, we *are* the most powerful wizards and witches around, now aren't we?" she demurely replied. He chuckled; no countering that. That was the credo of Black Hall, strong and mighty.

Chapter 13—Recovery

In an old warehouse on the northern side of Denver, Dominus groaned in pain, his leg still ached. "It's working, Boss," Ames, who had broken into the Denver Municipal Hospital—magical potions section, sounded hopeful. "As I understand it, the potion will take about a week for it to fully regrow your foot."

From the wild sensations in his leg, Dominus suspected that this potion was indeed beginning to work. He changed the subject. "Okay, where do we stand now? I must compliment Len on his brilliant thinking. Making that broadcast right away was positively brilliant. Now the whole world has heard that I acted to end the hurricane. Subconsciously, they will remember it when they go to the polls."

"Yes, but I told you it was bad business mixing our operation with trying to get those girls. We should have left well enough alone for now, Boss," Len countered.

"Ames, you were supposed to be watching them. How did they get behind us anyway?" Dominus growled.

"The armless one, Boss, claims they all had to go to the bathroom. I didn't want them to go making a stinky mess in the bedroom. What harm is there in letting them use the toilet? None, I say. It was all those Rat Pack guys. Where the blazes did they come from anyway? I thought they were long dead or something," Ames countered.

"They did take out the walls," Ben added in their defense.

"Obviously," growled Dominus, "but how did that Barron kid get the crown from me? I was keeling over from that kick from the armless one, little bitch."

"Don't know Boss. I got distracted when the walls disappeared and all them kids started shooting spells at us," Ames admitted. "I know I shouldn't have taken my eyes off of them."

Dominus reviewed his memories from that afternoon. "It felt like someone used hands to lift it from my head. I swear that it didn't just fall off. That other kid, Betts, the kid of the

Magical Misuse guy, she didn't grab it from me?"

"No, Boss. She was six feet from you. Neither the Barron kid or this other one had arms, so they couldn't have done it," Ames continued to defend himself.

"You're telling me that there was someone else there, Invisible, and none of us saw or heard them?" Dominus growled even louder. "That is not possible!"

"What else could it be?" Ames whined.

"No matter. It's done. Have our contacts inside Bradbury's find out who this freak kid is. What's her story? Probably Alister has cured both the two brats, but have our contact check officially on their state," Dominus ordered.

"Aye, Boss. I'll get on it," Ames replied, thankful that Dominus had changed the subject.

"Alister has that school locked down tighter than Fort Knox," Dominus grumbled, his leg was throbbing. "Too bad that we lost our secret tunnel into their staff area. We can't easily get those brats while they are at school. Besides, making an attack there is suicide. Six hundred magic students, even though they are just learning our craft—there are too many of them. However, in time, a good many may be joining our team."

Ben heaved a sigh of relief. For days now, he feared that Dominus would be asking them to launch an assault on the magic school, seeking revenge against the Barron and Betts girls. "Want me to continue to explore ways to secretly get inside Bradbury's?"

"By all means, Ben. Eventually, we will have need of another entrance. Don't worry. Those kids are the least of my worries just now. I'll torture and kill both of them in due time. Who knows—another golden opportunity will land on our plates. Of that I am certain. No, two things have me troubled. First, how did they find our house? I thought that you followed the plan."

"We did, Boss, to the letter," Allan answered. "We waited until the kids were in a good position; we slugged them on the back of their heads; they were definitely knocked out. We went invisible again, carrying the kids with us. We walked in middle of the streets back to the house. I swear none of us used a Teleport or Magical Door. None of that which could be traced. I swear the plan worked to perfection, Boss."

"Then how was it that our house was discovered within hours, eh? Answer that one, if you can," Dominus glared at his men, while rubbing what was left of his leg.

"I swear no one could have followed our footprints, Boss," Allan answered. "I made sure that our tracks were wiped out by the traffic on the streets. Either someone already knew of our hideout or someone tracked magical traces to it. You suppose that Betts kid was on to our hideout?"

Dominus thought carefully. If Allan was right and they had left no physical prints and had not used magical means to get to the house, then someone may have had prior knowledge of their location. "That Betts kid had no idea where she was before I turned her into an idiot. She didn't know. The attack did come when I was using the crown. I believe that there are two possible explanations. One, someone tracked the crown's energies while I was using it, most likely Broadwell or Monument. Two, the Rat Pack has gotten themselves a new Diviner."

"Yes, well where the heck did those two come from? I thought Bill and Able were long gone, distant memories of the past," Len swore. "Bill's changed. He never used to go for the kill. I can't believe William's gone. He was a friend of mine. Bastard Bill! I'm going to kill him myself."

"Gotta find 'em first," Ames spat on the floor. "Where have they been for the last fifteen years or so? Hide'n out?"

"Maybe they got scared into hiding," suggested Ben. "After all, we killed Mabel, their Diviner, and later Allen got Barron for us. Probably scared them two into hiding."

"Well, they are out now, if they ever were in hiding," Dominus growled. The throbbing was not lessening in his leg, however. "We need to find out darn fast if they have a new Diviner working with them. That's our top priority item right now. Do they or don't they have a Diviner? If they do not, then I suspect Broadwell got lucky and traced the crown's energy, and it was only a coincidence that we had the three kids there with us when he attacked. Perhaps Broadwell called Bill and Able out of retirement. Then again, perhaps Broadwell called on Able to track the crown. That would work as well."

"How can we tell if they've got a Diviner, Boss?" asked Ames, more than a little worried. If they did, he might soon find himself in prison once more.

"Len, let's see the Hit List," Dominus snickered. Len unfolded and handed him the paper. Dominus scanned the lengthy list, moving the Barron girl up several lines and adding the Betts girl to the list. "Okay, James Holmes, Denver Department of Law, has been a thorn in our side for years now. Let's plan a little Christmas present for him and his family. Get all the Death Stalkers together and raid his home. Kill every one of his family. However, also call upon the Silent Ones and have two dozen of them there as well, but have them invisible and hiding. If the Rat Pack has a new Diviner, they will come to try to prevent it. Give the Silent Ones the order to do nothing unless the Rat Pack puts in an appearance. If they show up, everyone goes for the kill on the Rat Pack members. Got it?"

"Beautiful, Boss!" Len commented, with a wry smile.

"You're the man," Ames exclaimed enthusiastically.

"We got'em!" Ben smashed his fist into his hand.

"If they don't show up, I think it is safe to conclude that the Rat Pack has no Diviner or else a crappy one at best," Dominus replied. "Either way, gentlemen, we will have ourselves a very nice Christmas present!" All laughed heartily.

"Oh one more thing, Ben. Send out word to the Silent Ones here in Colorado. See if they can locate where the Barron kid lives and where the Betts kid lives, when they are not at Bradbury's. It's not likely we will get another chance to grab them from inside the school. Let's see if we can snatch them during the summertime."

"You got it, Boss," Ben replied.

"Okay, so how are the polls looking today?" Dominus changed the subject once more.

"Big jump, up to fifteen percent now," Allan answered. "Still a long way from winning the election."

"Who cares whether we win or not? That is hardly the point, Allan. How many times do I have to explain this? If we win, we probably don't stand a chance of actually taking office.

What we are after is gaining key support from a broader field of people. That's what will enable us to move into Phase 2 of the Grand Plan. How's that gold work coming?" Dominus asked Len.

"Factory reports that the first gold bar has been fully melted down and used. They are in the testing phase now. By Christmas, we should have the test results back. If there are no hitches, they plan to go into full scale production around the first of the year."

"Excellent, excellent."

"Boss, what about the Initiation? There are two verified wizards waiting to become Death Stalkers," Ben asked.

"You are sure that they are up to our standards?" Dominus replied, rubbing his leg once more, annoyed that there should be this much pain in the healing process.

"Aye, Larry Sacks is out of Bradbury's Black Hall two years now. He claims to know the Barron kid. He seems a tough one. Then there is Tim Jones; he's twenty-six now, Black Hall, Twin Cities. He has five murders to his credit; he's a proven one. We could put Sacks onto tracking the Barron and Betts kids down. He really hates the Barron kid; claims she ruined his final year in track and field and soccer. Sacks has sworn he would get revenge."

"Yes, but the Barron and Betts kids are mine! I want them alive so that I can enjoy their suffering. I want Barron to beg me to put her out of her misery! Make darn sure Sacks knows this. I swear if he kills either one, I will peal his skin off layer by layer!" Dominus fired back angrily, his temples pulsing blood.

"We could snatch those kids again on Valentine's Day, when they will be back in Telluride," Ames suggested.

"Yes, but Broadwell is likely to increase security measures or even cancel it. At least, we have a technique worked out that works. Slug them, make them invisible, and walk away. Next, time, we could perhaps use Magical Doors to get to a distant part of town, load them into a van, and drive away. We dare not keep them in Telluride again. If we use norm's transportation, they can't track us. No magical energies to trace. That worked at the Nationals a couple years ago. It should work again."

"Could we snatch them from the Nationals again, Boss?" Len asked.

"Not likely after Snide's failed attempt to Disintegrate the Barron kid last year. He paid for it though. I gave strict orders she was not to be killed, and he didn't follow them. No, I think the Nationals are out this year. They will greatly enhance their security measures; on that you can count. No, we will bide our time. Either another Telluride snatch or perhaps a summertime snatch. We'll see. We'll get to them, but right now there are more important things to handle. Let's get busy."

"Say, should we try to track down where the Crown of Moses is now being kept?" Ben asked.

"No, it's served its usefulness."

Chapter 14—Over the Holidays

"Hi mom, dad," Lindsey said cheerfully, disembarking the school bus parked in the area cleared of snow just in front of their front porch. Lloyd and Polly had been busy for days digging out an arrival spot for the bus. This was the last stop for the bus today. The Whitewater clan had arranged to be left off here as well. Arriving in good spirits, Lindsey, Ashley, Audrey, Andy, Sandy, Fern, Jim, Tom, Amanda, and Pam were greeted by their parents.

Besides Lena and Lloyd, Polly and Fred, who took the day off from work to meet with his daughter, and R. B. and Luci, the kids were also surprised to see Aunt Wilma and Aunt Monane there as well. Indeed, it was at the insistence of Wilma and Monane (Bill and Able) that from now on, all the children would be dropped off and picked up here at the same home for safety and protection reasons. There would be more adults present in case Dominus or his Death Stalkers attempted to retaliate against the girls.

After hugging their parents, they began hugging the others. "How come you're here?" Lindsey asked Pam's Aunt Wilma?" as she hugged her and whispered, "Thanks for saving us," into her ear.

"Well, the boys are off doing their car modifications, and dad is tied up with his work, so I decided to spend the holidays with my niece and sister-in-law," Wilma replied, a twinkle in her eye.

"My brood are off with my husband on a gambling trip to Reno," Aunt Monane, Amanda's aunt, added. "I keep telling them their crazy schemes will not work, but you know boys, once they get an idea in their heads, there's no stopping them. So I hitched a ride down here with Wilma to spend the holidays with my brother and my nieces and nephews." Lindsey whispered a big thank you into her ear as well, bringing a smile to her face.

Lindsey at last looked around the outside of their ranch. Huge drifts, some more than ten feet tall, dwarfed the ranch buildings. "Looks like we are not yet done with our Dig spells," she commented. Everyone laughed.

"We've saved a good deal for you children to do. We don't want you to become bored over the holidays," R. B. jested, adding to the frivolity.

"Well, come on inside before you all freeze," Lena exclaimed. "Hot cocoa is on the stove.

A few minutes later, with the horde gathered around the table—Lena had inserted extra leaves to accommodate so many people at one time—Lena said, "We have some exciting news of our own to share with everyone. First, here are the final papers. Ashley, if you sign here, you will be our daughter. Yes, it's official now. If she signs the form, Ashley is now our adopted daughter."

She let out a yell and quickly signed while everyone watched her foot in action. Lloyd captured the moment with his digital camera. The whole bunch hugged, cheered, and kissed Ashley, who had never known a moment of such happiness. She now had a family that loved her, something she had not had since she was two.

"That's not all of our surprises. Girls," Lena said with a coy smile, "come June, you will have another brother or sister added to our family. We didn't think it was possible, but I guess I'm not over the hill yet. We're going to have a baby." Now more war hoops thundered in the kitchen, as the hugs flowed freely. Both Lena and Lloyd were quite proud parents.

"On the not so good news side," R. B. added once the commotion had died down, "power's been off for the last month around here. Thank goodness for our style of homes, we are snug as bugs. Town's rather a noisy place these days with all the generators running. If the noise is too bad for you, Sandy, Andy, you are welcome to come stay with us."

The suffering of others during this disaster had been fairly well insulated from the students while they were at Bradbury's, and only now, the enormous scope was slowly becoming clear to them. A day later, Sandy and Andy both moved into the Whitewater's spare bedrooms. Neither could sleep with all the racket in the small town of Arapahoe. At least their folks were doing well; two generators had been keeping enough heat and lights going.

After eating a light lunch, the Whitewater's along with Sandy and Andy headed to their home, using the teleport station in the front room. The kids then began unpacking their things.

The first thing that Ashley unpacked was her laptop, and then checked her email, an unlikely sequence for her, Lindsey thought. It was more Pam-like. "Hey, he actually approved it!" Ashley exclaimed. Hearing her exclamation, Pam and Audrey stopped their unpacking and came into her bedroom, very curious.

"Governor Alister, he approved my request," Ashley grinned satisfied.

"Approved what?" Pam insisted; she hated not knowing the subject of conversation.

"My idea for a school newspaper. I got it when I was kicking that stupid reporter. I got tired repeating what happened to us over and over. Besides, all the parents also would like to know what is happening with their children at school as well. I though we ought to have a school newspaper, an electronic one so that no one has to buy anything. I'm now the editor. Professor Elaine Mac Elroy has volunteered to be the staff reviewer. So these next few weeks, I'm going to see if I cant get the first issue done and sent to all the students and their parents as well. Cool, eh?"

"Why didn't I think of that?" Pam exclaimed. "Brilliant, Ashley, brilliant."

"Well, I'm going to need lots of help with it. I want to have someone from each Hall send me articles about what's happening in their Halls. I'm going to ask Deiter if he wants to be the Black Hall reporter. Say Audrey, you want to be the Brown Hall reporter?"

"Sure, this sounds exciting. Can we report on anything?" Audrey asked.

"Yes, but of course as Editor, I have the final say, as does Professor Elaine. Does one of you want to be the Yellow Hall reporter? I think the Editor shouldn't be a Hall reporter."

"I'll do it," Pam volunteered.

"Great, you two. I wonder who I can ask in Blue and

Red Hall?"

"Monique might do it for Red Hall," Pam replied. Ashley began slowly typing an email to the Red Hall girl telling her about the new school paper and asking if she would be their reporter. Then, she fired off another to a likely Blue Hall student that she knew.

"I'll do a feature article this time about the Natural Disaster and our encounter with Dominus," Ashley said when she had sent her emails. "Pam, Audrey, you can write about anything else you think the students and parents might like to know. This is going to be fun!"

At supper, Fred pointed out the newest security features. "If you hear a loud voice say, 'Danger! Intruders on the ranch!' or if you hear the voice say, 'Danger! Intruders on the Whitewater ranch!' that is the new signal going off. When you hear it, you are to get your wands and prepare for an attack. If it is at the Whitewater's, you are to head for their place as fast as you can. If it is here, they will be coming here as fast as they can. The objective is to get all of us in one place to meet the attackers with all the strength we can muster."

"There will probably not be any such attacks, but after your latest experience with Dominus, we want to be prepared. Eventually, his methodical mind will concoct some kind of retaliation. Right now, we don't think that he knows where this ranch is located, though he may know about the Whitewater ranch. However, we don't believe that he considers Amanda a serious threat at this time. I don't want to alarm you unduly, just be prepared."

"Dad, did they finish the autopsy on William the Bold?" Pam asked. "I mean did they verify it was really him?"

"Yes, like any gang of thugs, Dominus marks his Death Stalkers with a tiny skull and crossbones. The body had that tattooed on his upper arm. His fingerprints check out. The hand that was severed when he tried to kill you in that avalanche matches his stump. He did not seem to be magically altered, as when Dominus masqueraded as Lindsey here. So, yes, Pam, he has been verified as the Death Stalker."

"What concerns me is that Bill West never used to spell to kill before. Evidently, he's changed," Fred added. "I can't say as I blame him thought. Dominus is freeing them faster than we can put them behind bars."

Wilma commented, "I suspect that you have put your finger on it, Fred. It certainly has not escaped his notice that every Death Stalker ever captured has escaped to continue wreaking havoc. My guess is that he wants this to end this time." Lindsey knew that Wilma was in fact Bill West, and she knew that Wilma was obliquely telling Pam and the girls just why she had totally changed his/her attack mode.

Fred explained, "The Department of Security is now sharing all known data on the Dominus and his Death Stalkers. In fact," he looked directly at Pam and winked, "our secure computer system in Sterling is now getting a weekly update on all the known information on all the known Death Stalkers. Fascinating reading. The files arrive on Friday nights, so now we are all synchronized on the latest information. I'm not sure if this will help any, but at least there is a coordinated effort to share the data."

Pam caught his hint. This was just the kind of broad information that she desired to have and to add to her growing secret files on the Death Stalkers and their supporters. That night, she browsed her father's system and found the files. A bit of programming later and Pam had made a small utility that ran on Friday nights. In essence, when these new updated documents arrived at her father's computer system, her program shunted a copy to her secure server. For the next week, she spent late night hours poring over the information at hand, reworking into the framework that she desired, a better way of laying out the exact crimes each one had committed. In addition, she began construction of lists of the alias names they sometimes used and their known hangouts and places that they frequently visited.

One thing that she couldn't help notice was the many surprise campaign visits that Dominus had already held. It seemed that he would unexpectedly show up in a major city, such as Chicago, and hold a Campaign for President Rally. How all this could be prearranged without anyone knowing and yet have supporters in attendance roused her curiosity. This had her stumped.

She also wondered about that vacant house in Telluride where Dominus had been staying. On a whim, she looked up the records of who owned the home, which was now missing a large section of one outer wall. Mac Fluide Enterprises owned it. Why should an enterprise own a rundown home in Telluride? Perhaps it was left over from the old mining days?

Lindsey and Ashley chatted late that first night. "I just can't believe my luck, Ashley! You are my sister now! I've always been alone and now I have you."

"No, I am blessed now. I have a real family and a sister too! I can't believe this has happened to me. I never, ever figured anyone would actually want me, you know. It's, it's the first time in my life that I feel like I belong somewhere, here. That's a horrible feeling, sis, to know that you don't belong anywhere at all. Scary, really."

"Well, you belong big time now, sis. Gosh, I can't believe that mom's pregnant. We'll have to help lots around here this summer. She's going to have to watch after the baby and won't be able to do all the ranching. You know I don't know anything about babies and that stuff."

"Me either, except that they are very helpless when they are little and take lots of care. I remember one foster mother who had a baby while I was there. It took nearly all of her time, so it was easy for me to slip away from her and go play pool. Oh no, Lindsey! How am I going to be able to hold our little brother or sister?" Ashley began to cry. Here was another unexpected challenge for her.

"Oh that's easy, sis. You lie on your back and use your feet. I'm sure that you can do it," Lindsey tried to sound a hopeful note. "I have an old doll around here somewhere. Tomorrow, let's look for it. Then, we can both practice changing its diapers and stuff. There might not be a lot of time for us to learn when we get back this summer."

"You think I can do it?" Ashley's tears stopped, sensing some hope for herself.

"Sure, you do everything else, don't you?" The two hugged each other.

The next morning, Amanda and Fern came over with a surprise box. Giggling, Fern said, "We wanted to celebrate you two becoming sisters, so we baked you a cake last night. Hope you like it."

The white frosting had pink lettering, which read, "Happy Sisters." "Ashley, you cut it. I'll handle the plates," Lindsey said. Both thanked the two repeatedly.

"Well, I hope mom doesn't decide to have a baby too," Pam declared. "I think that she is too old. I guess Audrey and I are just not meant to have sisters." Audrey smiled, though stuffing a large bite of cake into her mouth. "Besides, we have the best friends anyone could ever want." Audrey nodded her agreement; her mouth was stuffed.

The adults came into the dining room to sample the cake as well. Lena commented, "Good cake girls. Say, you know when the baby arrives, this might be a wonderful time for all you girls to learn how to care for babies. After all, it won't be too many more years before you start your own families."

"Mom! We are only fourteen. It's not like we are going steady or anything. Only Sandy is getting married, but she'll be eighteen then," Lindsey protested.

"Yes, yes, but four years go by so quickly, dear. Before you know it, why, you will find some handsome, loving man and the next thing you know. . ." Lena teased them. Fern blushed; the others giggled.

Christmas Eve day arrived in short order. Both houses were full of last minute activities. Lena and Polly gathered all the girls together for a large-scale cookie-making lesson. Various batters lay scattered about the Compton's kitchen, amid chatting teenagers. Just as they were about to being the baking process, a Mag Emergency Post arrived at their front door. Lloyd, who had been outside this morning handling some needed chores in the barn, saw it arrived and signed for it.

"Pam, Special Delivery for you. Marked 'Emergency.' It's from Doctor Henry Blackburn," he called out, stomping off the snow from his boots at the front entrance way. Covered in flour, Pam raced to him, followed by everyone else. She had never received such a post before and began to worry. Inside was a hastily written letter from Monique's father.

Dear Pam,

Tragedy has struck us. Our home was invaded by a young man, who has beaten Monique so severely that she is in the hospital and will need reconstructive surgery this afternoon. Before she lost consciousness, she identified her attacker, a Larry Sacks. She said that he was a recent Black Hall graduate of Bradbury's. He beat her something horribly, demanding to know where you were now living. She whispered that she finally had to tell him where you were.

However, she does not know your address only that you are down by Arapahoe. Her last words were to beg me to warn you, Pam. She also said that he bears the Death Stalker mark on his left upper arm.

Please, Pam, let your father and everyone else know that your security has been compromised. I am terribly sorry that your safety has been threatened.

I will keep you informed by Mag Mail. I feared to send you a direct Message because the magical energy line could be traced directly back to your location. I hope that the Mag Mail is still safe.

Sincerely,

Henry Blackburn, MD.

Tears streamed down Pam's face; she couldn't read it aloud to the others. Lindsey took charge and read it for everyone.

Aunt Wilma spoke up, "Pam, I will let everyone know for you. It was bound to happen, eventually. It is very difficult to remain living at an unknown location without someone working out where you are. Your father knows this."

"Yes, but Monique! I have to get to the hospital at once. I have to be there for her," Pam wailed.

"Of course you do, Pam," Polly jumped in to support her.

"I want to go with her," Lindsey added.

The other girls immediately chorused, "Me too!"

"Now wait a second, we have dozens of cookies waiting to bake. You all can't go," Lena protested. "Besides, she will be in surgery some time, I expect."

Amanda, who had just relayed the news to her family,

piped up, "Jim and Tom want to go along with you too, Pam."

Wilma took charge. "Listen, kids, let Lloyd, Monane, and me have a private word or two, please." She ushered them aside, whispering furiously. A bit later, the three returned to the shocked girls. "Okay, we've decided that the greatest immediate threat to Pam lies at the hospital. Hence, Lloyd and I will be taking Pam there. Lindsey, Ashley, Tom, Jim, and Andy you may come with us. Amanda, you, Audrey, Fern, and Sandy will remain here, along with Monane. We need enough attacking strength here, just in case they try anything while we are gone. Only Monane and I will use the Message spell. That way no one is likely to track us. Lindsey, bring your staff."

Andy, Tom, and Jim walked into the living room, having just arrived in the entrance portal that connected the two ranch homes. "Pam, this is just horrible," Tom said. "I knew that Larry had it in for Yellow Hall two years ago, but I never thought he would become a Death Stalker!"

"Okay, Monane, keep a close watch on these two ranches. Kids, let's get going," Wilma ordered. Pam felt safe with her being with them; after all, she was really Bill West of the Rat Pack. Dutifully, they stood by the two adults. Lloyd held hands with Wilma. Next, the teens grabbed hold of one of the two adults, and Lloyd and Wilma chanted their spell. In the next instant, all stepped down an inch to the floor of the waiting room of Greeley Municipal Hospital, Magical Healing Division.

Lottie and Ellie were both there, eyes red from crying. "I'm so sorry, Pam," Lottie gushed as soon as she saw Pam arrive.

"I've got to see her," Pam wailed, her tears still flowing. Lottie pointed to the nearest room. "Henry's going to do the surgery in about a half hour." While Lloyd and Wilma established a perimeter of protection, the teens walked hesitantly into the single room. Pam's tears only escalated. Indeed, none of the children was unmoved at the sight of Monique. This beautiful girl's face was a mass of bleeding, swollen bruises. Many facial bones were broken; both of her arms were lying in weird positions, obviously broken. She was semi-conscious and a thin magical healing potion was being given interveinously—not enough to heal her, but just keep her vital signs strong.

"I'm so sorry," Pam bawled at her side. Monique, in great pain and sliding in and out of consciousness, managed an eye blink. Her mouth twitched, but it was too painful to move. Pam leaned over and kissed her on her forehead in a spot that was not injured. "I'll be right here for you, Monique, I promise."

One by one, the others followed Pam's lead and gave her a supporting kiss on her forehead. Tom added, "We'll get the guy who did this to you, Monique, I swear it!" She blinked again.

"Okay, time for surgery," Doctor Henry came in with two nurses.

"Will she be all right?" Pam pleaded with him.

"Let's hope so. I never thought I would be working my magic on my own daughter though. I'll see you in the waiting room later on, Pam." An orderly entered and wheeled the bed out of the room, followed by the doctor and the nurses.

Now came the long waiting game. Ashley whispered, "Looked like both her arms were broken."

"Yes, and her face! He must have used something hard to smash it up like that," Lindsey added.

Lottie, a heavy sadness in her voice, added, "Metal pipe. I found it beside her when I returned from shopping. He smashed in the front door to get at her. What's our world coming to anyway?" She began to sob once more.

Pam spent the longest three hours she had ever endured, sitting and waiting. Finally, Henry came into the waiting room. "She's in recovery now. Give her a half hour to come out of the anesthesia, then you all can see her. The next few days are critical. With both arms in casts and her face so heavily bandaged, she will need constant tending. We really won't know what else will have to be done until the bandages come off her face a week from now. She may be facing several more surgeries, but I swear I will leave no stone unturned until she looks just like she did before that beast got a hold of her. Any word on catching him?"

Wilma replied, "Not yet, but I'm sure they will get him.

Looks like Dominus is still recruiting new Death Stalkers."

"I've got my rounds to make. Lottie, they will be bringing her into the room here in about a half hour. Give her my love for me, will you? I'll check back as soon as I can," Henry whispered to his wife.

A while later, the orderly pushed her bed back into the room. Everyone gathered around her. Indeed, both of her arms where in plaster casts, held rigidly at her sides. Except for her forehead and mouth, her whole face was entirely bandaged. "I can't see!" Monique whispered, her lips barely able to move. She tried to move her arms up to her face, but was unable.

"It's okay dear, your eyes are bandaged, and your arms are in casts," Lottie whispered. Everyone's still here."

"I feel horrible," she whispered.

"Your dad says you will be fine in about a week. I guess it is my turn to help you, Monique," Pam said. Of course, the others told her they would be here as well.

Five Security Men walked in, "Excuse me, which one of you is Mrs. Blackburn?"

Lottie identified herself. "We are from the Greeley Security Force. Your daughter's room will be under twenty-four hour guard by five of us. The Death Stalkers will not touch your daughter again, ma'am. I promise you."

Wilma and Lloyd both felt relieved. At last, the Department was doing something. She said, "Kids, let's get you home and some supper in you. We can work out a schedule so that one of you is here with Monique 24/7. Agreeable with you?"

Pam nodded. "Monique, I'm going to get some supper, then I will be right back at your side." She lowered her head close to Monique's ear and whispered, "I love you." A faint smile appeared on Monique's lips, followed by a grimace of pain from such a movement.

Wilma had them walk outside the hospital. "You are probably wondering why we did not just teleport from the room. I wanted to alert you before we arrive. It seems there has been some trouble at your home, Lindsey. Everyone is all right. I believe they have caught the person who did this. Now hold on everyone." A minute later, they arrived in Lindsey's front room, over the teleport area.

It was mid-afternoon; the smell of freshly baked cookies permeated the entire home. The teens and women had been busily baking all the many dozen cookies—ten different kinds to be precise. Someone knocked on the front door. Audrey went to open it.

"Hello. I am looking for Miss Lindsey Barron. I was told that she lived around here somewhere," the young lad asked.

Audrey saw dried blood on his winter parka. He held a staff, obviously a wizard. "Who are you?" she replied, not answering his question.

Amanda walked into the hallway to see who was at the door. She recognized Larry immediately. "Audrey, get away! That's Larry Sacks, the one who beat up Monique!" She grabbed for her wand.

"Going to do this the hard way are you, Amanda?" Larry fired off a spell from his staff. Amanda froze like a statue, her wand raised in the air uselessly. Audrey tried to close the door on him, but he gave her a shove and shot a spell at her. Magical Missiles hit her, wounding her and sending her screaming in pain, falling backwards over a chair.

"Danger! Intruders on the ranch!" The warning shout came from R. B.'s latest protective spell.

Fern, Monane, and Polly raced down the hallway. Monane shot a powerful spell at Larry, who sucked it into his staff. Polly attempted to Hold him, but he dove out of the way, firing off a Disintegrate spell back at Monane. She dove for her life, landing behind a sofa, which promptly partially disintegrated. Polly ducked back into a study, using its wall for a little protection.

For a minute, spells flew in all directions. Larry was making heavy use of the Disintegrate spell, while absorbing nearly all of Monane's spells with his staff. She did likewise with her staff. Polly shoved Amanda out of the line of fire, and at last dispelled the Hold spell that the teen was under.

Larry realized that he was out gunned. There were too many witches here for him to handle alone. Besides, he had not yet seen the object of his first quest, Lindsey Barron. Audrey's wand lay six feet from her hand. She just could not get to it without being blasted again. "All right. I want you to surrender or I will kill this girl who came to the door. She doesn't have her wand, and she is already bleeding. Drop your wands and staff, and stand where I can see you. Now! Or I will kill her!" Larry yelled his bluff, though his staff was pointing at Audrey, lying on the floor.

Monane knew that she only had to stall another few seconds. R. B. and Luci were on their way now. He had Messaged her. No one in the house expected what happened next, except for Lena.

Boom! A huge explosion thundered through the house. 20 gauge shotgun pellets splattered bits of Larry's head on the entrance door behind him. The smell of gunpowder flashed through the home. Lena, holding her shotgun with smoke still trickling from its barrel, stood steadfast at the bedroom end of the long hallway. "No one messes with my kids!" she hollered angrily.

R. B. and Luci suddenly materialized beside the body of Larry, which was slowly falling to the floor. Both were quite startled by it, nearly casting spells before they saw what little remained of his head. "Sorry we're late. I was in the bath. Lena?" he asked, looking down the hall at the very angry face of Lindsey's mother, who merely nodded.

"Check on Audrey; she's hurt," Monane called out and went to check on Amanda who was now getting to her feet. She was mostly confused and bruised where she had hit the floor when Polly had gotten her out of the line of fire.

Luci yelled, "I'll get Audrey. R. B. Check for more of them." He cautiously opened the door and then went outside.

"Wow, some shooting, Lena!" Sandy exclaimed. "Our spells weren't doing much."

"Nobody, but nobody messes with my kids! You are all my kids. Is he dead? If not, I'll give him another dose," Lena said sternly.

Polly, who went to check on the bloody body, called out, "He's dead. Chalk up one Death Stalker. Gosh, Dominus is recruiting them awfully young these days."

R. B. came back inside. "Looks like he was alone. Who is he?"

"He's the one who nearly killed Monique earlier today," Amanda explained. "Larry Sacks, the one Monique identified as the man who beat her up, forcing her to tell him where this place is at!"

Lena put her shotgun down and ran to Audrey's side. Luci was helping her take a sip from some potion bottle. "It's a healing potion," Luci explained to a worried Lena. "She'll be fine in no time."

"Thanks, Lena, mom," Audrey whispered, still rather shaken up by her close brush with death. However, the three puncture wounds were now beginning to heal themselves, and she felt very itchy in those three locations on her chest. Lena knelt down and hugged her tightly.

"Well, I'll get a hold of the Department of Defense. Have them send someone for the body," R. B. took charge. "If either of us had pigs, I'd just as soon feed what's left of him to the hogs."

"R. B.!" Luci exclaimed, annoyed with him. "Not in front of the girls!"

He smiled, but he'd already made his point. "I think something is burning in the kitchen." Indeed, the sweet aroma twinged with gunpowder now held an acrid smell of burning cookies. Polly and Lena dashed into the kitchen. By the time that they had the minor crisis under control, two Department of Defense men were standing in her front room, examining the dead body.

They took everyone's statements about what had happened. Lena was very annoyed. "Look, this kid tried to kill us. Here, you can have what's left of my sofa!" She handed him a wooden leg with a bit of the green upholstery on it. He chuckled.

"I don't doubt your story ma'am," he said. "It's not often that we pick up a Death Stalker who was killed the normal way. In fact, this might be a first. Good shot, ma'am." Lena's annoyance changed to one of self-satisfaction. Of course, she was a good shot; she had been on her own most of her life, except five wonderful years with Sam Barron and now these two and a half with Lloyd.

"Well, this wraps up the break-in and beating up in Greeley earlier today," the other man commented. "We'll remove the body. I believe that we have all that we need."

Just then, the others returned from the hospital. Tom, Jim, Andy, Wilma, Lloyd, Lindsey, Pam, and Ashley materialized in the now packed front room.

"Oh!" came startled voices of the arrivals.

"That's him! That's the one who nearly killed Monique!" Pam declared. She added, "Is he dead? What happened to his head?"

"Mom, she shot him. He was going to kill me," Audrey explained. "He hit me with a bunch of magical missiles and then was going to kill me if they didn't surrender. See the holes in my blouse? Now it's ruined."

"Are you okay," Ashley asked concerned about Audrey.

"Yes, I'm sipping this healing potion that Luci gave me."

"Dog gone it!" Tom exclaimed, putting his arm around Sandy. "We missed all the fun!"

Sandy poked him, "Fun! You call nearly getting killed fun? He was sucking up all Monane's power spells, had Polly and me pinned down, had Amanda frozen in place, and Audrey near death. I don't call that fun, Tom Whitewater!" Everyone roared.

The Security Men teleported away, taking the gruesome body with them. Lloyd went to Lena's side and held her. "What a *woman* I have here, *best* woman in the whole wide world!" Lena blushed; the girls giggled. Andy, Jim, and Tom didn't see what was funny, however.

Amanda added, "You should have seen her! I've never seen her angry like that!"

"I'm sorry, but nobody messes with my kids," Lena said once more. Everyone chuckled.

"I guess we will have to replace that sofa. Boys, cleaning time. Let's get this place cleaned up pronto," Lloyd suggested.

"As soon as you are done, you can all have some freshly baked cookies," Lena added, hoping to make them work faster. Her front room and entryway area were a mess.

"Try mine," Fern offered everyone. "They are soft

chocolate drop cookies."

"No try mine. They are gingerbread cookies," Ashley countered, helping herself to one with her toe.

"Good thing Emilio isn't here," Pam added, sampling one of hers. "He'd eat at least two of them all." All the teens laughed.

"How's Monique?" Amanda finally remembered and asked. Solemnly, Pam related what they had seen.

Sandy quickly began sketching out a chart of times. "Okay, let's work out who will take what shift." Lloyd interrupted her and got the adults to agree that always one of them would be accompanying the teens. That produced six shifts. Polly volunteered to take them as well. Pam and Audrey would take the morning shift; Lindsey and Ashley, the afternoon shift; Amanda and Andy, the early evening shift; Jim and Fern, the evening shift; Sandy and Tom volunteered to take the late night shift.

Later as they ate their meal together with the Whitewaters, Pam apologized. "I'm sorry that they now know where we are living."

"They might not know precisely yet," Wilma countered. "I suspect that Larry was given the assignment to find where Lindsey lived. I'm sure that he didn't have a chance to notify Dominus or anyone after he found out this was the place. In fact, he may not have reported in after beating it out of Monique. After all, all he got from her was a vague possible town, nothing concrete."

"I'm inclined to accept that conclusion," R. B. added. "Still, I will see what additional improvements I can invent for our security. By the way, Merry Christmas everyone. It's Christmas Eve." With all the excitement, everyone had forgotten about it.

"As soon as we get the dishes done, girls, we are invited over to the Whitewater's this evening," Lena explained, an added incentive to get the many dishes done quickly.

"But you all have to look out," Fern added hastily after looking at her younger brother, "Jim's got mistletoe hanging about the house."

Jim jumped up and said, "Now you've gone and done

it!" He chased Fern around trying to tickle her for spilling his surprise.

When Luci finally got them to stop, Ashley asked Fern, "What's that mean—the mistletoe thing?"

"If you walk under it, he gets to kiss you!" she explained, grinning at Jim. Ashley blushed.

"Yes, well, I took precautions. Since Fern and I are on the early evening shift and will miss the party. . ." He didn't finish his sentence, but held a bit of mistletoe over Ashley's head. "Ta da. Now you've got to kiss me," he declared. She gave him a fast kiss on his cheek.

"Not like that, like this," he teased and gave her a loving kiss; she blushed red. "Come on Fern. We have to get going. Monique needs us." Fern chased after him, trying to tickle him back. Polly had her hands full with those two as she took them to the hospital.

R. B. said, "You know, there is one matter remaining that we should discuss. When they took Larry's body away, they left his Staff of Power behind. It now belongs to us. I will take it back with me and see if I can find out what spells has been enchanted into it. I suspect many attacking spells. My opinion is that we should give it to one of the girls for their protection. I'll see if I can alter its enchantments to fit that person."

"Wow! That is a fantastic gift," Sandy declared.

"Consider this the price he had to pay for attempting to kill you all," added R. B. "Now who should get it?"

After a brief discussion, the adults decided that either Pam or Amanda ought to have it. Pam suggested, "While Dominus may be after me, I'm a Sleuth, not a fighter. I think that Amanda ought to have it." Since no one objected, R. B. said, "Good. I will get to work on it. Now, let's party. Is that how you kids say it?" The teens chuckled.

"Nearly so, dad," Tom answered. "Party on!"

Late that night after the party, Fred finally arrived from Sterling. After giving Pam and Polly a warm hug and kiss, he said, "Sorry I missed the party. I heard about the brutal attack on Monique and how you got him here. Good shot, Lena, by the way. I stopped by the hospital in Greeley to see how she was doing, paid my respects to the Blackburns. All three are deeply grateful that you are unharmed and have killed her assailant. Monique managed a smile, though I could tell that it hurt her some to do so. Say, have I missed all the presents being opened?"

"Thanks dad. No, we are going to open them first thing in the morning, before Audrey and I head to the hospital," Pam explained.

Christmas morning came early, primarily because the two girls needed to relieve Tom and Sandy, who were watching over Monique.

Lindsey did her usual action, moving each person's presents into a pile before them from large pile underneath the tree. Fred rose and said, "Pam, your mother and I have only gotten you one present this year. We would like you to open it first, dear."

Pam flushed, accepting the small box that her father handed her. It must be valuable, she reasoned, but in such a small box? Perhaps it was some expensive jewelry? She tore open the box, unable to contain her excitement. It held only a small paper with some writing on it.

Dearest Pam,

With all that is happening in our world and with you, we have decided that it is time for you to have this.

Mom and Dad

There was a small sketch of a staff. Fred said, "Yes, it is your own, personalized Staff of Power. Right now, it is over in R. B.'s workshop. He is performing the enchantment spells into it, totally tailored to a Sleuth's particular needs. After that run in with Dominus, we just wanted you to have some extra precautions. R. B. wants to see you later today when you get back from helping Monique." Pam could not believe what he was saying. At last, she hugged them both long and hard. Such was a very, very expensive gift indeed.

While there were many unique and wonderful presents given this season, I will mention only another one. Lloyd and Lena had one relatively heavy package to open from Ashley. She insisted that they open it together. Inside they found a music box with a couple standing on the lid. When you started the music, the couple seemed to dance around the top. The engraving in gold read: To the Best Parents in the World: Lena and Lloyd. Both adults had tears running down their cheers as they hugged their newest daughter tightly.

Suddenly, Fred's pager went off. He looked down at the scrolling message. "Darn! Not on Christmas Day! I have to go to Denver. Big trouble. Dominus again. I'll try to be back as soon as I can." He kissed Polly and Pam and took off for Denver. His departure dampened the festivities of the day. Everyone was now wondering what had happened.

A short while later, Pam and Audrey left with Lloyd to relieve Tom and Sandy, who spent the late night hours at Monique's bedside. Since it was a hospital, there wasn't any real need. It was all moral support for the injured girl. After all, she had been there for Pam and Lindsey. They found Tom and Sandy asleep in each other's arms. After waking them, wishing them a merry Christmas and telling them about Fred's sudden departure, the two left for home.

While Lloyd stood outside with the Security Men, Pam and Audrey went to Monique's bedside. Lottie was there having been up all night with her daughter. "She's supposed to start drinking all of this medicine that she can. I'll leave her to you while I get some breakfast. Thank you both for being here. I know how much it means to my daughter." Pam smiled.

Pam leaned over and kissed Monique on her forehead, about the only thing not bandaged about her face. "It's me, Pam. Audrey's here too. How are you feeling?"

"My arms and face hurt," she whispered. "At least, I can talk a little today." Pam insisted she start sipping the potion, while she explained the latest news.

"Mom said he came after you at your house, Audrey," Monique whispered slowly. "I'm so sorry. It's my fault."

"No it is not your fault, Monique. No way. It is Larry's fault entirely. He'll never hurt another person, not ever," Audrey whispered back.

Monique managed a flickering smile, though it hurt. "I heard Lena got him."

"Yes, he was threatening to kill me. She just blew his brains out with her shotgun. Mom's impressive. I was scared,"

Audrey replied. "She's like my foster mom now."

A bit later Monique whispered, "Pam, it's okay if you want to leave me after this. I mean I will now look really ugly—my face—probably scare the little kids when they see me. So it's okay if you want to find someone else."

"Now you are talking silly, Monique. I love you because of you, not what you look like. Besides, your dad has said that you will probably be just fine. Maybe there won't even be any scars," Pam sounded a hopeful note and squeezed Monique's fingers gently.

"I can't even cry," Monique moaned. "I'm so helpless like this."

"We know, that's why we are here, to be your eyes, ears, and hands. It should only be six more days; that's what your dad said," Audrey answered.

"Hey kids, listen to the news. It's big," Lloyd called in and turned up the KMAG news.

"I'm Tammy Yong filling in for Hugo who has the day off. We are covering the breaking story of a bombing in a subdivision of Denver. The home of the head of the Colorado Department of Law, Denver branch, James Holmes, has been the target of another Death Stalker attack."

"You are seeing live footage taken an hour ago as flames from the explosion burned their home to the ground. Firefighters were able to save the neighboring houses. Eyewitnesses have told authorities that a half dozen Death Stalkers arrived here around seven this morning. After a short battle, they set off a massive bomb, which nearly leveled the home, setting it on fire. Neighboring homes suffered many broken windows from the blast."

"Authorities are being pulled in from all over the state to help track down those responsible for this carnage. According to acting Law spokesperson Kathy Jakes, James Holmes, his wife, and two daughters perished in the blast. Their bodies were found around their Christmas tree in the living room, evidently opening their presents when this tragedy struck them."

Lloyd turned it down and left the girls to chat. He didn't want the girls to hear the wild speculation over who would be the successor and lead the Department of Law here in Colorado. Indeed, Lloyd had spotted Fred Betts among the people in the background, behind Kathy Jakes. Lloyd, like many others, feared that the next head of the Department of Law might be a Dominus supporter. If that happened, well he didn't want to think what would be the result, too horrible to imagine.

It was well known that within the Department of Law in Colorado, Dominus had several sleepers, waiting to be activated. If traditional promotions were followed and the next head of the department came from within, there was some chance that one of Dominus's secret supporters might now lead the Department of Law. However, since this was a State of Colorado position, the governor would appoint the replacement.

At suppertime, Fred finally came home in time to join everyone for Christmas dinner. "What an awful day this was. I can talk about it now. The decision's been made by the governor. He has appointed Kathy Jakes to take over as head of the Department of Law. She's a good choice we all feel, because she hates Dominus. However, she picked Casper, the Head of the High Plains Department of Magical Misuse to replace her position. She and Casper have worked on a fair number of cases in the past, and I think she trusts him."

"Anyhow, turns out that impacts me," Fred concluded.

"How dear?" asked Polly.

"You are looking at the new Head of the High Planes Department of Magical Misuse."

Exclamations of surprise and congratulations filled the room. Fred continued, "However, I will still be located in Sterling. I said I can run it all from there just as well. I will be overseeing not only Sterling, but also the Greeley, Fort Collins, Boulder, Colorado Springs, and Pueblo departments. Only the Grand Junction and Denver Departments of Magical Misuse will not be under my direct control."

For Pam's benefit only, he added, "I will be adding another server to my collection in Sterling. They did agree to move it from Boulder, where the previous man ran the High Planes department. So I don't get confused, I'm keeping the same passwords. Darn computers, I have a devil of a time trying to remember all those passwords." He winked at Pam, knowing that she would soon be a frequent, but sly, visitor on his expanded sites.

The day after Christmas, R. B. took Amanda into his workshop to work on her new Staff of Power. "Now then, little daughter, we must choose the spells that your staff will be able to cast."

"I want to be a Tracker, dad, not a fighter. Maybe we should give the staff to Jim or Tom," Amanda suggested.

"A Staff of Power does not have to have just attacking spells, little one. First, I have enchanted it to be able to cast the usual Continuous Light, Dispel Magic, and the Impervious Protection spells. That last one is the one that Lindsey's casts, which makes you virtually immure to all spells below Grade 4. I have added one of your favorite spells, Skin of Stone, which you make use of in your soccer games. It will Teleport as well, but promise me that you will not try that one until you learn to cast that one yourself. A goof on that one and you may be killed."

Amanda promised, remembering that Lindsey had told her that both Governor Alister and Professor Cho Lin had given Lindsey the same warning. He continued, "As a Tracker, you must never be fooled. While you may be able to learn this spell later on, I have added See True to your staff. With it you always will be able to see things exactly as they really are. If you could have cast this in your first year, you would have been able to see that the not-Lindsey, as you called her, was actually Dominus. Even invisible things will be quite plain to you. However, the spell will only last eight minutes."

"Wow! Now that is a useful spell, dad!" Amanda began to appreciate her staff even more. It was not turning out to be an attacking weapon, as she had feared.

"I have added one of my own most powerful spells, a Grade 9 spell in fact, one few know: Sixth Sense, which is the spell that is in your lucky rabbit's feet. Mind you, the spell only lasts some fifteen minutes, but during that time, you will just know when something is about to happen, giving you time to react ahead of time."

"Now then, we must put in one offensive spell at least. I tried to get it to accept a Hold Person spell, but it failed. Would Paralyze be an acceptable attacking spell for you?"

"Sure, if it isn't permanent."

"No, it only lasts a few hours before it wears off." He waved his wand and shot the spell into the Staff of Power. It took. "Okay, we have one final action that must be done, little daughter. We must give your staff a name. What would you like to call it?"

Amanda thought for a moment. Lindsey's was called Margarete. "How about Little Wolf," she said. R. B. smiled and cast that name onto the staff and then finally ended his rather complex enchant spell. He then cast his Make Permanent spell on the Staff. That spell also took.

"Now we must see if Little Wolf will accept you, Amanda. Here, take a firm hold of the staff and introduce yourself as the new owner of the staff."

Amanda picked it up and held it firmly in her left hand. "Hi, Little Wolf. I am Amanda Whitewater. I'm your new owner." At first, Amanda felt nothing. Then, suddenly, magical energies shot from the staff through her arm and into her body.

R. B. was smiling, so Amanda relaxed. It must be okay, she thought. "Okay, go sit the staff over by the door and come back here." She did as ordered. "Now say 'Come to me Little Wolf.'" Amanda did as her father instructed. Her staff flew into her left hand.

"Way cool, pop! Super!" she exclaimed. "Thank you!"

He smiled, and added, "Now go to your room and cast say about ten Light spells into it. Its command word for spell absorption is Absorb It. If you say to Little Wolf, 'Charges,' it will tell you something like 10 out of 25. It is a good rule of thumb to keep Little Wolf always about half charged, so you have room to absorb spells."

"Okay, it's like Lindsey's staff then. Say, how do I know how many charges a spell will need in order for Little Wolf to cast it?"

"A general rule is the Grade of the spell is the number of charges the staff needs to either cast it or are available for it to

234

absorb it. Beware. Dominus often casts Grade 6 through Grade 8 spells. The Sixth Sense spell needs nine charges to cast, so it bleeds off excess charges rapidly. Now go play with Little Wolf, little daughter." Amanda dashed off to her room to charge up and experiment with her new Staff of Power.

Pam received a Message from R. B. Hastily, she told her friends that R. B. wanted to see her, and she dashed for the teleport station by their front door. A moment later, she stepped into the front hall of the Whitewater's. R. B. was there waiting for her. "Good afternoon, Pam. This way to my workshop. We have work to do. Mind you, I have never known a Sleuth before, so I'm depending upon you to help me decided what spells to attempt to infuse into your personal staff."

The two chatted for a while, R. B. jotting down the agreed upon spells. At last, he began the tedious work of enchanting the staff. He put the Continuous Light spell into it, followed by Dispel Magic, Impervious Protection, Teleport, See from a Distance, and See True. All took properly. For her attack spells, he installed Hold Person and Disintegrate. However, the Disintegrate she would be using for many other purposes than killing someone. Like Amanda, Pam had no heart in killing or harming others. Pam chose the name Alf for her Staff of Power.

R. B. gave her some instructions and sent her off to join Amanda, figuring the two girls could work together getting familiar with their highly valuable staves. This inventor had been studying the children and their skills and weaknesses, conferring with Monane several times as well. He knew that the path chosen by Lindsey, Amanda, and Pam led to danger and confrontations with very evil men and women. They had to be protected. Hence, he had been working behind the scenes to procure staves for Pam and Amanda. That Larry's fell into his lap was a bonus, saving him a significant amount of money.

Still, he faced the most difficult challenge of his invention career, from his point of view anyway. It was Ashley. There was no doubt that she was on the path of a Diviner. R. B. well knew what had happened to the Rat Pack's Diviner, Mabel. Indeed, Monane told him all the gory details of her murder. R. B. knew that if Ashley pursued the career that she seemed destined to follow, she would become a prime target for men like Dominus. Hence, the problem that R. B. had been working on since Halloween was how to design a Staff of Power that Ashley could use.

Unlike wands that needed precise motions unique to each spell for them to activate, a Staff of Power did not; only the spoken word was required, assuming the staff contained sufficient charges to cast that spell. His lengthy career and research yielded nothing that would be able to provide Ashley the kind of protection he wanted her to have at her disposal except a Staff of Power. Yet, without the arms and hands to hold the staff, it was pointless.

In late November, R. B. began a series of experiments using his own Staff of Power. Indeed, Luci thought he had gone nuts when he stood outside in the snowstorm, half buried in the giant drifts, casting magical missiles at snowballs. Yet, it had proven extremely educational. He discovered the basic fact that the staff only needed some physical contact with him in order to accept his orders and launch the spells he commanded. Armed with this data, R. B. paid a visit on the Compton's.

Given the go ahead from Lloyd and Lena, R. B. had set to work. Most staves were between five and six feet long. While this was acceptable for the other girls, who were still growing and had arms with which to manage the tall staves, a staff this long would not work for Ashley. For her, the staff shouldn't exceed three feet. Yet if the staff was going to hold sufficient magical charges and still be that small, the wood would have to be absolutely the finest quality, strong and not easily broken. Early December, R. B. acquired a number of exotic wood samples from the dense rain forests of Brazil.

After much experimentation in his workshop, the black teakwood offered the best promise for his need. The morning after Christmas, it had arrived. With Pam and Amanda off learning and working with their new staves, R. B. began the enchantment of his new experimental model. As his first enchantment spell began, preparing the beautiful piece of teak for holding the spells that he had selected, R. B. realized that this was going to be an exceptional staff indeed, perhaps the finest he had ever made. Next, he began the second phase of its construction, the imbedding of the spells that the staff could cast.

He put in Continual Light. This was always the first spell he bequeathed He'd done it so many times that he could readily sense how well the staff would turn out, based solely on how it accepted this particular spell. Next, he installed the usual Dispel Magic, the Impervious to Spells, and Teleport spells. They were accepted extremely readily. "Incredible!" he muttered to himself.

Given Ashley's situation, he installed the Fly spell next, giving her a means of escape. Next, he enchanted the staff with the See True spell, since this would aid her unique skills, just as it would for Pam and Amanda. Ashley was a feisty child, who took nothing from others. He smiled, recalling them telling him about Ashley actually kicking Dominus in his privates. Yes, Ashley's staff ought to have some strong attacking spells.

The staff readily accepted the Lightning Bolt, Magical Missiles, and Ball of Fire spells. Yet, still the staff could hold more, impressing even R. B. He rummaged through the standard books of Grade spells. Then, he hit on the right one. He added Terror Killer. Only now did he sense that the staff had reached its capacity.

All that was needed now was to enchant the name for the staff, bind everything together, and then have it accept Ashley as its owner. He sent a Message to Ashley to come over right away. Around four, Ashley stepped into the front room of the Whitewater's, wondering what R. B. wanted of her. He'd never asked to see her alone before. "Ah, there you are, Ashley. Come with me. I have a little something for you as well." She followed him into his workshop.

"Your father and I have joined forces to make you your very own Staff of Power, uniquely suited to your needs, Ashley."

Annoyed, she replied, "You know I can't hold a staff like Lindsey does. Why are you teasing me with this?"

"I'm not teasing you. You don't need to hold a staff in

arms and hands to operate one. It must merely be somehow attached to you. In your case, I have made this harness affair, rather similar to your leg harness for your wand. The staff is quite short, barely three and a half feet long. It will fit on your back with its top sticking up slightly over your head."

"You're kidding me?"

"Nope. Yours is an exceptional piece of wood, from Brazil. Teak. Very strong, very dense, holds enchantments better than any staff I have ever made."

"Wow. Incredible. Thank you, Mr. Whitewater! I've never even dreamed I could have a Staff of Power. I've rather steeled myself, knowing there are some things I really won't be able to do. I mean everyone has some things they can't do. Will it work for me?"

"Of that, I am sure. Now I figured that you would like some attacking spells in yours." She grinned—that she would. Quickly, he listed off the spells that her new staff could cast for her. Her eyes opened wider and wider, until she was in total awe of the staff. "Now, then, Ashley, all that remains is for you to give your staff its name and then bind it to you. What would you like to call yours?"

Ashley thought for a moment and said, "Zappo! Because that's what it can do, zap bad people."

"Zappo it is." He cast the name into the staff and finished off the last of his binding spells of enchantment. Next, he inserted it onto the leather harness that would hold it to her back. For the first time of its use, he needed to strap it onto Ashley's back for her, adjusting the straps just right. At last, he commanded, "Bind." Ashley felt a surge of magical energies flowing from Zappo through her entire body.

"It sort of tickles me all over," she giggled.

"There, Zappo has accepted you and will work for you alone. Now then, you see it can't come out of the harness unless you unstrap it, say for polishing and cleaning. The command words of 'Zappo: To Me' will cause the staff to come to you and for the harness to automatically fasten itself on to your back as it is now. 'Zappo: Off Me' will cause it to unfasten itself and lie on the nearest object, like a table or bed. Go ahead and try it."

She did so, watching in utter amazement as the staff and harness unfastened itself and flew to his workshop bench. Again nearly awe struck, she watched as Zappo came to her; its harness fastening automatically.

"Now then, this staff is superb, holding thirty charges, far more than normal." He explained its use and then sent her off to join Pam and Amanda, who were still in Amanda's room experimenting with theirs.

"Look at what Lloyd and R. B. just gave me!" Ashley exclaimed, as she entered Amanda's room.

"Holy cow! You've got one too!" exclaimed Pam.

"I never thought you'd be able to use a staff, Ashley. This is utterly incredible," exclaimed a wide-eyed Amanda.

"I know! I didn't see how I could ever be able to use a staff like Lindsey and you two. Now I can, only R. B. said I needed to have you two work with me to get the hang of it. It comes off easily. Watch this! Zappo: Off Me!" The harness undid itself and her staff flew and landed on Amanda's bed. "Zappo: To Me!" At once, the staff and harness flew to her back, and the straps fastened themselves.

"Now I can be a real witch, too!" Ashley said gleefully.

"But you already are a real witch, Ashley," Pam didactically replied.

"I know, I mean, like you, with a staff and all," she corrected herself.

Pam and Amanda had their staves charged and were experimenting with them, so they began putting Ashley through the hoops with her staff. However, suppertime loomed close, and they agreed to work on it more after supper. Ashley dashed home to show everyone else her greatest possession yet.

After supper, she and the girls bundled up and went outside. Even though it was dark, Ashley practiced casting lightning bolts at the snowdrifts, throwing in a few balls of fire as well. Later inside once more, she also discovered that she could easily sit down while still wearing her staff, quite unlike the other larger staves. Ashley now realized that she could wear her staff nearly anywhere, and it would be always at the ready.

Shortly the entire Whitewater clan dropped over, Jim wanted to take photos of Ashley and her staff, as well as Amanda, Pam, and Lindsey. In truth, everyone really wanted to see the girl's new staves.

On Friday, Ashley and Pam watched as Doctor Blackburn removed the bandages from Monique's face. Already, he had cut off the casts. Her arms were stiff and sore, but otherwise fully healed. Pam held her breath, likewise Monique. Pam remembered how her dear friend looked before she underwent surgery. Her facial bones were smashed in several places. Pam prayed that Monique would be fine now.

She wasn't. Her face was a mass of discoloration; black and blue marks covered most of her face. The left side of her face appeared slightly different from her right side. Monique nearly fainted when her dad finally held a mirror for her to see her face. Bawling that she wished she had died, Monique felt life slipping away from her. She looked incredibly ugly.

"Dear, your face is still healing. In a month, all the swelling, the discoloration, will have gone. It's a miracle that you look as well as you do, though I know that you don't think so just yet. Please, give your face time to finish healing. Considering how crushed your left cheekbones were, it is not surprising to see one side slightly larger than the other. In a month, we will do another minor surgery and get the two sides back in balance. Then, Monique, you will look mostly as you did before."

"Dad, how can I face anyone looking like this?" she wailed. Her dad looked crestfallen and didn't really have a good answer for her.

Ashley did. "Here Monique, you can pin this photo of what your face looked like before surgery to your chest. Then, anyone who sees you can see the before and after. Honestly, Monique, it doesn't look very bad. I mean there's swelling and black and blue stuff, but other than that, not bad at all."

"I, I looked like that?" she stared at the photo of herself just before surgery for the first time. Until this moment, she'd not seen what she had looked like after the savage beating. "Oh my god! Dad? This is me?"

"Yes, dear. Pretty awful."

"I guess it really is a miracle, dad. Thanks." She stopped crying, but continued to stare at the photo and then her face in the mirror.

"Just no makeup for a month, dear. I know that's going to be hard, but your skin has undergone a horrible trauma, so give it time to heal, please. We do not want it to become infected."

"Not even lipstick?" Monique protested. "But all Red Hall girls wear red. I will look like a freak or something."

"When the swelling on your bottom lip goes down, okay on that, but nothing more," her father conceded. Monique felt that she had won a small battle however. "Now then, you can go home today." That was the best news she'd heard yet.

A few minutes later, with all her personal items gathered, the Security Men, her father, Lloyd with the two girls, all teleported to the Blackburn home in Greeley. The Security Men took up positions outside the home, where they would patrol for the next week, just in case of more trouble.

"Oh Monique, you look awful," exclaimed Ellie when she saw her older sister for the first time.

Monique held back tears and showed her little sister the before photo. Ellie gasped and said, "I'm sorry, really you look so much better."

Once settled, Pam and Ashley just had to show Monique their new Staves of Power. This greatly interested Monique, who for the first time since the beating, completely forgot about herself. Even Ellie forgot to pester her older sister.

"Gosh Ashley, yours is like a mini-staff, but it has more power than the regular ones. R. B. really knows his magic!" Monique exclaimed. "Those must cost at least ten to twenty thousand dollars or more." As far as Ashley was concerned, hers was priceless, unique, and completely suited for her needs.

Sunday morning, the empty bus arrived to take them back to school. Naturally, the three girls had to show Jimmy their new staves. He was definitely impressed, as expected. After piling their many bags into the cargo hold, Jimmy climbed aboard and the slow trip began.

Later, as they walked across the campus, the students

could not help but notice that the staff had been busy while they were gone. Neat paths had been shoveled through the huge mound of snow. One could finally walk outside between the buildings, though few would do so, since the tunnels were warmer, and one did not have to wear heavy winter coats.

Pam's first action, after stowing her things, was to go look for Monique. She was quite worried about how she would be, emotionally, that is. Certainly, many would stare aghast at her face. If nothing else, she intended to provide moral support.

Ashley, on the other hand, set to work getting out the first issue of the Bradbury school newspaper. She had already gotten several articles from the student reporters for the other halls and she had written several feature articles herself, including a complete description of what had happened to Monique. By suppertime, she was finally satisfied at the total layout and sent it to Professor Cho Lin to get her okay. Ashley's plan was to have it ready to email to all the students by Monday, the first day of classes this spring term. However, she had not yet worked out how to get it more broadly distributed to their parents, for example. Pam had suggested that it be put on the Bradbury's main web page. If that were to be, Ashley would need the services of Pam or Monique, since she knew nothing about making web pages.

In the early evening, Ashley had permission to publish. Cho Lin only made a few suggestions. "Just say that Larry Sacks was killed in the combat, not that Lena shot him. Why? This does not then give the Death Stalkers useful information about Lena—that she is capable of shooting them. If they are alerted that she likely will use a shotgun against them and if they try something again, they will be gunning for her at once." After she finished making the changes, she Messaged both Pam and Monique, meeting them in the Yellow Hall study hall.

"I don't know how to thank you, Ashley," Monique said sincerely. "Everyone keeps asking me what awful thing happened to me. I find it very hard to talk about it. Your article explains it all very well. Now they can read it, and I won't have to keep retelling it, reliving it, so to speak."

Ashley was absolutely amazed how rapidly the two

computer experts got the entire issue online, ready to be read by anyone browsing the school's web site. She was even more amazed at how easily she could now email this first edition of the Bradbury Student News to all six hundred students. "See, you select 'all students,' 'select the edition,' hit 'send.' Viola. Nothing to it," Monique proudly demonstrated. That evening, six hundred students got some very interesting reading material. Some of the articles were:

What Really Happened that Day in Telluride, by Miss Ashley Stokes Compton

Larry Sacks Turns Death Stalker—Attacks Miss Monique Blackburn,

by Miss Ashley Stokes Compton

Students Rally to Help Victims of Emily, by Mister Deiter Cross

Yellow Hall Accomplishments, by Miss Amanda Whitewater

Red Hall Accomplishments, by Miss Monique Blackburn

Black Hall Achievements, by Mister Deiter Cross

Brown Hall Accomplishments, by Miss Audrey Lemon

Blue Hall Accomplishments, by Miss Julia Harms

Also proving most helpful, Pam set up a special email address for anyone to leave comments and suggestions to the editor. This way, Ashley's personal email would not get flooded with the newspaper-oriented emails. This proved a very wise move. By Monday morning, the whole school had read the newspaper and had sent Ashley over a hundred email comments. Most were highly supportive of her efforts. Indeed, as they walked to Monday's first class, they overheard many talking about the key articles.

Chapter 15—Back to Studies, Well, Not Quite

The first day back, all the professors must have been conspiring with each other. In every class, a mountain of homework was assigned, over the groans of the students. "Look, gang, there really isn't much else to do right now," Pam tried to console everyone who had gathered in their study hall that night. "We've got so much snow outside that we can only walk on the nicely dug paths. Besides, it's cold outside."

"But I could play pool," Ashley lamented. Pam ignored her.

"I'm going to have a rough time in Dispeller Theory class," Lindsey pointed out to no one in particular. "I have just gotten barely able to identify a spell from all the words, excepting the last word. Now Professor Dogs is making me identify them from only the wand motions! That's next to impossible."

"Well, Professor Mary Ann is making me make real divinations now," Ashley replied. "How am I supposed to do that? They just come to me whenever."

"Governor Alister is making me track all sorts of impossible spells," Amanda added, just as hopeless sounding as her friends.

"Well, I'm getting to do some real sleuthing," Pam pointed out. "Professor Cho Lin has given me a homework project in which I have to solve something that actually happened. At least that will be interesting, though quite time consuming, I might add. I have to get a real result for her."

"I guess I got it made," Emilio joked. "I get to go on a real desert survival field trip this spring!"

"Yes, but Emilio, he's going to make you survive on what you find out there in the desert. No Twinkies for you, no jerky sticks, no Oreo's. Probably no water canteens either," Pam dutifully pointed out. His smile turned sour, as he realized she was probably correct.

"Now you see why I am really lucky to have taken the Study Hall and not an elective!" Kathy pointed out. "I had hoped to take Potion Making next year. I want to become a healer or nurse or maybe even a doctor, but I am likely to flunk chemistry. He said that you needed to do well in chemistry in order to take potion making. I thought I would be good at potion making because I'm good at cooking, following the recipes and all that. Now I just don't know. Chemistry is so awfully hard."

"Kathy, every science course you've taken has been hard," Pam pointed out. "Why should chemistry be any different? I don't see why you can't do well in potion making. After all, you're not going to be trying to invent some new potion, just mixing things."

"I'd rather do some excavation of a Civil War site than write a paper on it," Andy complained, sliding his computer aside. "Honestly, it's a big conspiracy; they are all assigning tons of homework."

"I think that the spells we are going to be learning are really hard ones," Audrey threw in her thoughts. "Besides, I hate those necromancy spells. I don't see how you can put up with Professor Dogs, Lindsey."

"Well, he's all right on the Dispeller theory so far. He's not given me much ill-will over my hating his dark arts," Lindsey admitted.

"Bet that doesn't last too long," Emilio commented. "Ah well, who wants to check over my algebra?"

"Oh, give it here," declared Pam, putting aside her work. Lindsey examined Kathy's math assignment. Before long, the group exchanged numerous assignments among themselves, checking each other's work. They all found it hard to get back into the swing of homework; their minds were still on their long break.

Late Thursday afternoon, Ashley sat in the darkened room of Professor Mary Ann, ready for more of her Diviner Theory. "Now it's time we put some of the things we've learned into practice, Ashley," Mary Ann said, after verifying that no one was eavesdropping on them. "Sit back and relax. Let the visions come to you."

"Real ones? You mean I am supposed to have a real vision—right now?" Ashley asked, rather startled. "But I don't have control over when I have them; they just come to me."

"Yes, yes, we know that. A good Diviner must be able to sit back and control when the visions come to her as well. Now sit back and focus. Let your mind expand. Let your awareness extend outward. Notice anyone sending out thoughts of needing help. Today, we are just shot gunning it, picking up anything you can. Later, we will focus on specific people. Today, just pick up anything you can."

Ashley sat back, but her stomach growled. Her thoughts drifted to supper just an hour away. *It never comes at my beck and call, not when I want it to, the visions. Ah, well. Outward? Heck, I can't get past my stomach. Relax, Ashley.* She tried to calm her mind as her professor wanted. *Premonitions don't come when I want them too. They just come.*

Suddenly, she saw an image in her mind: a woman lay in a semi-darkened room, bleeding and unconscious. Badly beaten, the woman's arms lay in strange positions, perhaps broken. Ah, her wand lay off to her left. A name flashed in her mind, Ashley spoke. "A woman, Millicent Prague—I never heard of her—she's been badly beaten, is bleeding badly, and is unconscious. I think maybe her arms are broken. I see her wand."

"What?" shrieked Professor Mary Ann, suddenly becoming quite frightened and terribly worried at the same time. Ashley jerked her body alert. The shriek unnerved her. "She's my dearest friend. What is going on? Where is she? Tell me everything you've seen?" Ashley repeated all that she had seen in her premonition.

"Never mind. Let me check for myself," a very upset Mary Ann interrupted her. A few seconds later, she looked white as a sheet. "You may be right, Ashley. I cannot contact her. She is not answering my Message, and I too believe I see her in dire peril. We must get to her at once. Wait here, I must get Arthur." Poor Mary Ann was so upset, disoriented, and scared that she ran over to her husband's office in the Hall of Alteration, instead of simply Messaging him! A few minutes later, Arthur led his out of breath, but still unnerved wife, back into her office.

"Ashley, Mary Ann says that you had a vision of her friend Millicent?" he asked calmly.

"Yes, Professor, I did. I think that she is badly wounded or something. She's bleeding and her arms are funny. I think she may be unconscious, sir," Ashley replied.

"I'm afraid that Mary Ann was horribly mistreated by Dominus Malefic many years ago. The trauma is still within her, especially when someone close to her is hurt. You are not just making this up, are you Ashley?"

A surge of anger nearly exploded from Ashley's four foot six frame. Arthur did not miss this and hastily added. "No, I see you are not. Tell me, can you recall anything about the location where she is lying? From what Mary Ann tells me, it is not her home. We need to find her somehow before it is too late."

"I don't know. I've said all that I could see, a darkened room somewhere, like a warehouse maybe," Ashley answered, struggling to suppress that surge of hostility inside her.

Just then, Cho Lin, accompanied by Amanda, knocked on Mary Ann's door. "Arthur, take Amanda. She can track for you. Alister's off on some urgent business elsewhere. No one knows where. You might also take Lindsey for extra protection," she added.

"Right, sir. Girls, go get your staves immediately. Lindsey too," Arthur ordered. "We'll get some healing potions packed and meet you here as soon as you can get your things." He nodded to Cho Lin, who waved her wand and stepped through a magical door, leaving them to their rescue mission.

As the two girls headed down the stairs to the tunnels, intent on racing back to their dorm room, Amanda suddenly halted. "Silly us. We should also make a magical door; come on. I'll do it." She waved her wand and spoke, "Door: To My Dorm Room." Magical energies flashed and a door appeared. Amanda opened it, and the two stepped through it, arriving before the door to their bedroom.

Another magical doorway appeared just as hers vanished. "Got your Message. What's up?" Lindsey asked, as the three entered their room. While the three grabbed their staves and put on winter coats, Ashley explained what she had seen in her premonition. "Gosh. Alister took off somewhere else? I wonder what emergency he has to handle?" she asked. Ashley and Amanda shook their heads, having no idea. Lindsey created another magical door, and the three stepped through it, arriving back at the office of Professor Mary Ann.

"We're ready. Mary Ann has three healing potions packed. I see all three of you have your staves, excellent. Now then, Amanda, it is up to you. We must find Millicent. How do we proceed?" Arthur asked.

"The simplest way is for you to Message her. I can follow the magical line of energy, only you will have to sort of teleport us along the route," Amanda replied. *If only we were fourth year students and knew how to teleport, so many things would be so much easier!*

Mary Ann concentrated, though she was still extremely pale and upset, waved her wand, and sent a Message to her friend. Amanda likewise stayed sharp, looking intently for the faint lines of magical energy. "Ah, there it goes, straight that way. At least we know the precise direction, just not how far," she explained.

"Okay, that's the general direction of Denver, where she lives," Arthur commented. "I believe that we will gamble first on her still being somewhere within that city of several million people. I'll take us there first, and then we'll check again. If I'm wrong, we'll try a series of hops. Mary Ann, you put your arm around Ashley, I'll hold onto you. Lindsey, Amanda, you hold onto each other and to my other hand. I think it best, dear, if we arrive Invisible to others. We'll attract far less attention this way. Everyone ready?"

He satisfied himself that the students and his wife were all set, and then he cast his Mass Invisibility spell followed by his Teleport without the possibility of error spell. Considering the huge size of Denver, Arthur chose his destination point to be the far southern suburbs, where their arrival would attract even less attention. It would not do to apparate right on a busy street corner in the downtown section, where the skyscrapers threatened to touch the sky. A moment later, the small group touched the sidewalk on Eastside Drive. Huge snow piles lined either sided of the sidewalk. Street crews had not yet begun to use the end loaders to remove the mounds, but they had gotten the streets and sidewalks cleared, at least for single-file walking.

"Oh dear," Amanda exclaimed startled. "There's so much magical energy around here! So many spells have been cast. I don't know if I can tell anymore!"

"Give it your best try, Amanda. I'll Message her myself," Arthur replied. "Watch for the newest line from me," he suggested. He waved his wand and sent another Message to Millicent. Amanda watched diligently. The only thing that saved her from defeat, considering the thousands of magical energy trails streaking through the skies around Denver, was that the one she wanted came from Arthur at her side.

"There, I see it. That way. Northeast. At least a mile or more," she called out. Fortunately, no one was outside walking down Eastside Drive to hear her voice and see no physical body speaking. "Now what?"

"Why don't we just try flying and see if Amanda can follow that line?" suggested Ashley, eager to try her staff's spell. It seemed something that she could do. Ashley didn't like being teleported, preferring to move under her own volition.

"Good idea, except if we are invisible, how can we see Amanda to follow her?" asked Mary Ann.

"Well, we will have to become visible, no other option," Arthur replied. "Besides, many in Denver choose to fly to and from work; it's faster and safer than driving. Fewer accidents. Only do not go high because airplanes may run into you." He cancelled his Invisibility spell, and all cast their Fly spells. Amanda then took the lead, slowly following the single faint line of magical energy among the thousands that she saw all around her. Arthur and Lindsey flew on either side of Amanda, intent on protecting their Tracker. Mary Ann, eyes darting in all directions, and Ashley flew behind the three.

Below them, they could see the various enormous mountains of snow, which had been moved from the heart of Denver to the outskirts. Twenty crews were still working on the massive snow removal project as the growing twilight descended on the sprawling city of millions. Streetlights cast eerie shadows below them. Ashley noted that the bustling air traffic of other wizards and witches heading home from work had now died down. Her stomach growled; it was five thirty and past her usual dinnertime. Below her, the golden arch of the fast food restaurant beckoned her, but she remembered that she had not brought her purse with her. With a sigh, Ashley banished the idea of getting a quick bite.

Amanda's concentration was intense. Never before had she attempted to follow one thin line amongst so many. Vast numbers of magical spells, more than a few Teleport spells as well as Fly spells, had been recently cast. She had to go slowly, focusing all her attention on the one faint trace, blocking out all other thoughts from her mind. At last, she saw the trace enter a darkened building below her. "There, that place. It goes inside there," she pointed and began to hover in place. Now her stomach growled; Amanda felt utterly drained. She felt weak, weaker than she'd ever felt before. Slowly, she descended to the ground before she fainted. As her feet made contact, the world began to spin and turn black. She had passed out, exhausted from the intense strain.

"Ashley, Lindsey, look after Amanda," Arthur ordered. "We will go inside and see if we can find Millicent. Best hide yourselves with an Invisibility spell. Message us if trouble comes."

"Aye Professor Arthur," Ashley replied, Lindsey was already at Amanda's side, propping her up, holding her head in her lap. "Sis, you had better cast the spell. My staff is nearly out of charges, and with these boots on, I can't use my wand."

"Okay, my staff is nearly out too. I'll cast spells to recharge both our staves. Invisible: Ashley. Invisible: Amanda. Invisible: me." Lindsey then cast a number of spells while Ashley commanded Zappo to absorb them. Then, she did the same to her own staff. "Have you got anything to eat on you? I'm starving, but I bet Amanda is really starving."

"Er, no, and I didn't think to bring my purse. The arch is not far from here, but no money. How about you?" she replied, fearing the worse.

"Me either. Ah well. Look, Amanda's coming around."

"I'm so weak. I think I overdid it with the tracking," Amanda whispered.

"Lie still. We are outside and invisible. Professors Arthur and Mary Ann are inside," Lindsey replied.

"I'm, I'm so cold! Can we go inside too," Amanda whispered. Lindsey felt her body shivering like mad and decided that either she would have to cast many Warm spells on Amanda or they should at least get inside out of the freezing cold. She canceled her Invisibility spells and helped a very weak Amanda to her feet. Draping one arm over the shoulders of Ashley and the other over Lindsey's, Amanda slowly moved toward the door. Lindsey carried both of their staves in her free hand.

"Darn, need a third hand," she joked, as she tried to open the door, but the two staves got in her way. Ashley wanted to help, but with heavy snow boots on her feet, she was even more helpless. At last, Amanda managed to turn the knob, and the three entered. It was an abandoned warehouse. At least no one was present but themselves at this late hour.

"Over here," Arthur called out. They had several Light spells activated and were working on their friend, Millicent. The three moved close to see how badly Millicent had been injured. "We've got the bleeding stopped and a bit of healing potion in her. I think she is stabilized enough to hazard moving her. Her arms are in bad shape. She's been severely beaten and stabbed. If we had not gotten to her when we did, I'm afraid that she'd likely died. Thanks, Ashley, Amanda."

"Arthur, we dare not give her more healing potion. With her arms like this, they would heal this way turning her into a cripple at best. We have to get her to an emergency room. But where? Where will it be safe?"

"I know, dear. Denver Municipal is close, but I don't think that would be a wise choice. Whoever did this to her likely lives around here and might sneak into the hospital to finish her off. We need a safe place."

"How about Doctor Blackburn?" Lindsey suggested. "He's on our side—what with Monique getting so badly beaten. I'm sure his hospital can be made safe. We did it when Monique was there."

"Ah, excellent idea, Lindsey. I don't know the man. Could you possibly Message him? Tell him the gravity of the situation. Millicent's life is at stake here," Arthur replied.

Ashley sat down beside the injured woman. Mary Ann was crying to herself, though her eyes and head darted around the huge empty space, as if the culprits might reappear at any instant. In fact, Ashley thought that she was even more fearful than ever before. "Will she make it?" she whispered.

"Think so, if we get her to a hospital soon," Mary Ann's voice replied, distantly and softly. Ashley got the distinct impression that the professor's attention was elsewhere and not here in time either. She wondered if Mary Ann was remembering what had happened to her so many years ago. It was a good hunch. Nevertheless, as Ashley sat there, she began to see just how helpless and useless she actually was when someone was injured. She could do nearly nothing to help poor Millicent. Perhaps if someone removed her boots, she might do a little dabbing of the blood on Millicent's face, but hardly more. Perhaps if I can learn to teleport, she thought, but sighed. Not even that would make up for her lack of arms. Her years of suppressing her longing for what she did not have slowly began unraveling in her mind.

"He said bring her at once. He'll be waiting for us in the emergency room," Lindsey interrupted the silence.

"How can we move her?" Mary Ann asked. "Her arms— we might do more damage, Arthur."

"I've thought about that. Wall of force." He waved his wand and conjured one. "Like this," he said. The small group watched as he slid the invisible barrier underneath her body, though she groaned slightly as he pushed it under her body, moving it a bit. "Okay, everyone, feel around for the wall and let's see if we can lift her up. Gently now." Amanda, Lindsey, Mary Ann, and Arthur fumbled for a time, but managed to get their fingers under its edge. Ashley stood aside, the other two girl's staves resting against her body. No one saw a tear form and then drip down her cheek. She felt useless, a mere coat rack, or staff rack as it were.

Next, everyone managed to grab a hold of each other, Mary Ann's left hand held onto Ashley, who gripped the two staves tightly between her legs. Arthur waved his wand and transported them all to the emergency room at Greeley General.

"Ah, here you are. You caught me just as I was heading home. Orderlies, gently, gently, get her up on the cart. Yes, good. You can cancel your force wall now, sir," a tired looking Doctor Blackburn said.

"Professor Arthur Thornby. My wife, Professor/Diviner Mary Ann," Arthur introduced himself.

"Good to meet Monique's teachers at last. She's spoken highly of both of you. Hi Lindsey, Ashley, Amanda. Good to see you as well. The patient's name and what happened to her?"

"Millicent Prague, a Class Two Diviner," Mary Ann replied. "We don't know how she was injured, but I suspect she was attacked by Death Stalkers not long ago in an abandoned warehouse in Denver. We must speak with her when she regains consciousness. It could be terribly important."

"Okay, why don't you wait in the recovery room? Nurse, show them, will you please? I've work to do." Doctor Blackburn hastily followed the Gurney down the hall into the surgery room. A matronly nurse led the five to the recovery room, where the girls had spent considerable time with Monique over the holidays.

Amanda collapsed on the couch, nearly unconscious. "I see we need to get some food in her fast or the good doctor will have another patient," Arthur noted. "Here, Lindsey," he handed her a twenty. "You know where to get some food, I take it. Please, take Ashley with you and find us something to eat. Probably protein for Amanda would be best, not lots of sweets," he advised.

"Thanks, we know the way," Lindsey replied. "We spent quite a lot of time here with Monique." She helped Ashley remove her heavy parka, and then the two dashed off down the hall on their quest for dinner.

"I'm sorry, professor; I'm so weak. It's never happened like this before," Amanda whispered from the couch.

"It's all right. We pushed you rather hard this evening. I

was going to ask Alister to lend a hand, but for some reason, he's not answering my Messages. Strange. It's not like him. Ah well, he probably has more important things to attend. You'll be fine as soon as we get some warm food in you, Amanda." She smiled, but noticed that Mary Ann was still pacing around the room, looking for enemies in every corner, her body shaking as if in terror. He noticed Amanda noticing his wife and added, "This attack on her Diviner friend is terribly reminiscent of what happened to her some twenty years ago. Rather unsettled her." Amanda nodded that she understood, but felt sorry for Mary Ann, and wondered what awful thing had actually happened to her. Dominus must surely have been involved.

Twenty minutes later, the two girls returned, Lindsey's arms were piled with sandwiches and drinks. Ashley, who had used a levitation spell on a tray, pushed the tray of drinks along in front of her chest. "We're back. Will someone please take off my boots so I can feed myself?" Ashley asked, slightly embarrassed once more by her situation. Arthur assisted her, while Lindsey began feeding a chicken sandwich to Amanda, who was now so weak that she couldn't sit up by herself.

However, everyone was far hungrier than this first round of food. A half hour later, Ashley led Arthur to the many vending machines so that he could buy yet another round. As the two walked along the nearly deserted hallways, he said, "Ashley, I want to thank you for finding out that my wife's dear friend was in trouble. If it had not been for you, Millicent would have perished. Thank you."

Ashley smiled, appreciating his kind words, though her mind was now racing down an entirely different path. *How have I been able to think that I was fine without arms all these years? I'm darn near useless!* It was all that she could do to avoid crying as they walked up to the vending machines. "Oh, you get big bills changed over there at that machine," she pointed out to Arthur, as he stared at the machine's instructions.

A minute later, he returned with a stack of ones. "What would you like, Ashley?" he asked kindly.

Darn, I cannot even operate a stupid vending machine

myself! After a pause to regain her thoughts, she replied, "The chicken nuggets basket, please. Amanda ought to have more nuggets as well. I think my sister would like the roast beef."

"Thanks, I really don't know what you girls prefer. Mary Ann and I have not been blessed with children as yet, though not for the want of trying," he offered her a small insight into their home life.

"Golly, wow," Ashley came up to the present for a minute. "I mean maybe it isn't too late. Lena and Lloyd are expecting in June, so Lindsey and I will have a little brother or sister soon." She began to see Arthur and Mary Ann in a different light. They, too, had physical problems of some kind. No children yet and they were in their early forties, but then maybe she was too old now. *Darn it, Ashley, stop wallowing. Vending machines were not made for armless people. You could operate it, only it would take a little doing. I got to pull myself together here.* She took a deep breath, hoping that would clear her mind. It didn't.

Sometime later, Doctor Blackburn appeared, "Good news. She will recover completely. One arm was merely dislocated, though the other one had a compound fracture. She has a nasty concussion and will have a headache for some days. We've given her a blood transfusion to make up for the rather large amount of loss she suffered. I will say this, another hour and you would have had a corpse on your hands. Missed the key artery in her neck, fortunately. Good timing. They will be bringing her into this room in a few minutes. You are welcome to stand guard and wait until she regains consciousness. I'll check in first thing in the morning, and there will be a wizard guard on duty outside the door here twenty-four/seven."

"Thanks, Doctor Blackburn," Mary Ann heaved a big sigh of relief. "Thank you, I owe you a big one." He smiled and accepted her gratitude, though he did not say anything. In these times, he knew that the good guys had to stick together or Dominus would gain control. After he left, Mary Ann suggested, "Perhaps Arthur, you should take the girls back to the school? It may be some time before she is able to tell us what happened."

"No, it's okay, Professor," Lindsey hastily interrupted. "We want to stay—at least until we find out what happened."

"Curiosity," Mary Ann mused to herself. "Teens abound in curiosity." She relented, and the five moved their chairs around the bed, as the two orderlies wheeled the unconscious Millicent into the room and gently lifted her on to the bed. Mary Ann fussed with her friend's covers for a bit, making them look perfect. Then, they merely sat in silence, waiting.

An hour later, Millicent came to at last. A frightened, scared look flashed on Millicent's face, as she struggled to figure out where she was at and how she was doing. "It's okay now, Milli, we got to you in time. You are in Greeley General and Doctor Blackburn has fixed you up. We've a wizard on guard just outside for your protection. He says you will make a full recovery."

Millicent sighed and used her left arm to feel her face and head. "My head hurts too, neck and arm. Oh, it's in a cast, broken."

"Yes, but it will heal. He said if we had delayed even an hour more, you would not have made it."

"How? How did? Did you divine it, Mary Ann?" a somewhat confused Millicent tried to ask.

"My student, Ashley Stokes Compton. It was her divination. She told me about your dire situation. Another of our students, Amanda Whitewater, a budding Tracker, led us to you. Are you able to tell us what happened to you?" Mary Ann finally asked the question that all five wanted to know.

"I thought I was a goner. Dominus. It was Dominus and three of his vile henchmen. They came to my house in Denver and abducted me—took me to this empty, filthy warehouse."

"What did Dominus want anyway? Why you, Milli?"

"He insisted that I divine something for him. I refused, but they hit me over my head and broke my arm. I tried to get free and my other arm was horribly damaged as well. I had to divine for him; I tried not to, but I had to."

"What did he want divined?" Mary Ann asked.

"Weird thing. He wanted to know what Alister did with the Crown of Moses. I was in so much pain that I had to do it, though I didn't want to. I finally saw what he wanted to know, had to tell him."

"That's okay. But what did you tell him? It might be important," Arthur's soft, understanding voice asked.

"Only that he put it back where it came from, nothing more. That seemed to satisfy Dominus. He turned to leave, and said, 'Kill her.' That's when the tall one slashed my neck. I couldn't move either arm to protect myself. I felt so helpless lying there, unable to put my hands on the wound to stop it or even to cast a spell to do something about it, to summon help, nothing. Such an awful, horrible feeling, you know, helpless, so utterly helpless! I drifted into unconsciousness after that, figuring I was dying."

Millicent suddenly duplicated something Mary Ann had said minutes ago. "Wait, you say one of your students divined what was happening to me?"

Mary Ann motioned Ashley to move in closer so Millicent could see her better. Ashley answered, "Yes, I had a premonition about you, though I didn't even know you. I told Professor Mary Ann about it, and we all came to your rescue."

"Oh dear, you, you have no arms! You know what I mean then, what I felt like," Milli replied quite startled by the appearance of Ashley.

"Yes, I use my feet, where you all use your arms," she said defensively, though the usual antagonism and anger failed to materialize in her as it normally would have even a year ago.

"I know what I was going to say," Millicent's train of thought flittered about. "No, I should tell you thank you for saving my life, Miss Ashley. Thank you, thank you."

Ashley smiled, accepting her thanks. Yet, again, Millicent's thoughts drifted. "Oh yes, Mary Ann, do you realize that, if she did that with me, then she must be at least a Class 2 or higher!"

"Excuse us," Lindsey interrupted. "Can someone tell Amanda and me what that means, Class 2?"

Mary Ann answered her. "Yes, well Diviners are not all the same. We have classes, which relate to our skills. A Class 0 Diviner is much like the norm's fortune tellers, mostly faking it, but occasionally glimpsing something vague in someone's future. A Class 1 Diviner is able to foretell futures with some certainty, but only with people with whom they are quite familiar. A Class 2 Diviner, which Milli is, is able to see futures and pasts of others, though not with complete accuracy or clarity, necessarily. A Class 3, which is my level, is a Class 2 who has the skills to teach others how to properly divine. Class 3's is sort of off to the side, really. A Class 4 is able to concentrate and notice the past or future of anyone. Further, they can also predict with good certainty the path another will be following. There are very, very few Class 4 Diviners. The last true Class 4 Diviner was Mabel Pruit of the Rat Pack, whom the Death Stalkers murdered. Hasn't been another one since then."

She continued, putting Milli's comment into proper context. "Since Ashley was able to pick up on what had just happened to Millicent, someone whom she did not even know existed, and accurately so, this could only be done by a true Class 2 Diviner, or higher. That I did not notice my dear friend's plight and Ashley did is also puzzling, suggesting that Ashley may have far more Diviner capacity that I do. We will continue her training and see what comes of it. Honestly, many of us have been saying all along that if Dominus is to ever be captured again, they will need a Class 4 Diviner to do it. Yet, there is not one Class 4 Diviner in the world right now, not that any of us know of, that is."

Lindsey and Amanda now understood more about the art of Divination than they had before. Their opinion of Ashley rose even higher. However, Arthur decided that it was best that the girls be returned to Bradbury's before it got too late. After Ashley accepted a weak hug from Millicent, the four returned to their school. Arthur landed them outside the main gates and opened the gates for them. Though it was now nearly eight at night, they scooted down the tunnels to their dorm, seeing no one. Arthur returned to Greeley.

Chapter 16—Now Back to Studies, Well. . .

"Well, tell us all about it!" Pam exclaimed as they walked into their room. Kathy was also sitting on Pam's bed waiting to hear the news as well. Amanda merely laid down and fell asleep. Lindsey began to relate their exciting evening, beginning with Ashley's premonition. Of course, Pam made Ashley tell her all about that before allowing Lindsey to continue their story.

A half hour later, she finished up. Pam's reply was thoughtful. "Two things stick out in my mind as vitally important points, Lindsey. First, why could none of you contact Alister? It's not like him to suddenly cancel Amanda's class and just disappear. Two, why does Dominus want to know what Alister did with the Crown of Moses? Cause more hurricanes?" No one had any answers.

"Well, you three did great," Pam complimented her friends.

"Yes, just swell! Good going!" Kathy added her praise to them. "I had best get down to the study hall. Emilio and I are going to need more help with our math and chemistry tonight. Pam, please, please lend us a hand," she begged, batting her eyes rapidly.

Pam grinned. "Okay, besides, I'm supposed to meet Monique tonight too. She's going to have her next round of surgery here in two days, and she is getting worried about it."

A bit later, Lindsey joined Pam and friends in the study hall. Ashley wanted to take a bath and did not join them. Actually, she wanted time alone. Her mind was still going in circles over her own disabilities.

After correcting many goofs in the two's papers, Pam spied Andy and went to have a word with him. Andy commented, "Hi Pam, boy Lindsey, Ashley, and Amanda sure had an interesting evening. Dominus just keeps on committing crimes, doesn't he? I wish someone would put a stop to him."

"Well, yes, Andy, but I wanted to ask you something. Just where did that archaeology professor discover the Crown of Moses anyway? This might be important. I'm following a hunch," Pam admitted, when he looked at her in a rather funny way.

"Ah, well," he stalled, unwilling to admit that he had forgotten the complete details. "Oh yes, off the coast of Cyprus, yes. Now I remember, off the coast that is closest to Syria. Why? Is that important now that the crown is safe somewhere?"

"Maybe yes, maybe no. I just don't know, Andy. You know that no one has been able to contact Alister since early this morning. He's simply vanished."

"Yes, I heard it from Kathy. Amanda's special elective class was cancelled. Glad mine wasn't. You ought to take archaeology too, Pam. I think you might like it," he suggested.

Pam wrinkled her nose up, "No thanks. I have enough trouble dealing with those that are alive. Let the dead rest in peace. Thanks, I'd better get back."

He added, "Honestly, how would Emilio and Kathy ever pass anything without your help? You've a kind heart, Pam." Andy and Pam walked back into the study hall.

There, Andy put his arm around Lindsey and whispered something in her ear; she blushed, but excused herself. The two walked out into the relatively quiet commons, where they could chat.

Ashley filled the tub with hot water and managed to add her favorite salt scents. At last, she slipped into the tub to relax. Leaning her back against the side, she let her body soak, as she closed her eyes. "Why do I have to be so darn different than everyone else anyway? What did I do to deserve this?" she muttered aloud, shrugging her limbless shoulders. Years of suppressing her deepest feelings had somehow been undone today. She felt raw, cutting emotions that she had thought were long gone. Only they were not long gone, just deeply buried.

Slowly her body began to slide down further into the water. She tried to use her arms to pull herself back up, but they did not work. A feeling of panic struck her as she tried even harder to make her arms pull her up back out of the ever so slowly rising waters. She knew that she was helpless and would soon drown. The sky was getting light now; dawn was coming. She could see the deep blue waters lapping at her ankles; her feet were no longer visible, but she could feel the heavy chains holding her arms and legs firmly to the stone here at the edge of the warm, blue waters. She sighed, knowing that she was about to drown as the tide rose higher, maybe by noon, she guessed.

Suddenly Ashley screamed and did nearly fall under the water. "It's Alister! He's about to die!" She climbed out of the tub and fumbled for her towel. "Darn it; this will take me forever to dry off. Wand, where are you?" She looked around, shuffling things about with her feet, until she found it under her clean clothes. Picking it up, she waved it and began sending messages.

Lindsey! Help me. Bathroom. Alister! He's going to die unless we get to him! Help! A.

The message fluttered between her and Andy, as she was telling him about Millicent. "Oh gods. I've got to go help Ashley, Andy. She's had another premonition or something. She is saying Alister is in danger."

"Hey, I'll get some others. I'm not letting you go off this time by yourself," Andy exclaimed.

Pam and Amanda came rushing out of the study hall. "Ashley? Did you?" Amanda started to say very worriedly. From the terrified look on Lindsey's face, both knew that she had also gotten Ashley's panic-stricken Message. All three raced down the steps to the bathroom.

"Help me. I have to get dried off and into clothes. It's Alister! He's going to die, drown, if we don't get to him in the next couple of hours!" Ashley nearly screamed at her three friends. With the three working together, Ashley was dried off and clothed in less than three minutes. No sooner had they climbed the stairs than professors Delius Dogs, Cho Lin, and Huan Su Sung came racing into their study hall.

"Ashley, what's this all about?" demanded Cho Lin, unable to ascertain whether this was a prank, a foolish hunch, or a real premonition.

"I had another premonition, like I had this afternoon, with Millicent. It's Alister. He's chained to a rock, and the water is rising. If we don't get to him soon, he'll drown. I just know it!" Ashley wailed, unable to say it any other way. Her whole body was shaking.

"I wish Mary Ann were here," Cho Lin said softly. "I'm not so good with this divination stuff. I don't know if she's telling the truth or not."

Delius spoke up in his deep, harsh voice, "Cho Lin, she is telling you what she knows, what she has seen. Rather ask whether this is what is really happening with Alister—that is the key question. I have no doubt that Ashley is telling you what she has somehow seen. She is neither fibbing nor teasing us, but she believes this is what is happening. It is up to us to determine how best to deal with her premonition."

Huan Su scratched his head, "Well, it would begin to fit other observed facts. No one has been able to contact him all day. If he were chained up, he would not be able to use his wand to reply to the many messages sent to him today."

"All right. We ought to organize a search party or a rescue party then," Cho Lin replied. "But where do we look for him? He could be anywhere in the world."

"I, I, ah, might have an idea," Pam timidly spoke up; the adults stared at her. Since they only looked at her sternly, she took that as a sign to continue. "Ashley and Lindsey said that Dominus tortured Millicent to get her to divine what Alister did with the Crown of Moses. According to them, Millicent was forced to tell Dominus that Alister put the crown back where it was found. According to Andy, the archaeologist found it in the waters off Cyprus, where it is closest to Syria. Logic would suggest that is where Dominus is now searching for the crown again." She finished, a satisfied look on her face, convinced she'd just worked out another puzzle.

Monique just walked in to the commons, coming to visit Pam as planned. Seeing the three professors there chatting seriously with her friends, she decided to listen in and heard Pam's recital of her theory.

"Again," Huan Su said softly, "that would seem to fit with Ashley's premonition. It would be dawn about now that far to the east of us. What's this?" He stopped talking and stared at a magical, long distance viewing eye that had slipped into the room. He waved his wand and dispelled the eavesdropping spell. A moment later, Deiter Cross, looking a bit annoyed, slipped into commons to see firsthand what was going on. Huan Su gave him a cold stare, but he ignored it.

"Okay, we should put together a rescue party," Cho Lin decided. "We will need Trackers and ways of handling combat with Death Stalkers. I bet he has an army of them nearby."

"Dear, you know that you cannot go and leave the school," Huan Su replied. "You are in command of the school when Alister is gone. Delius and I will handle this."

"I'll Track for you," Amanda declared. "I'm a bit tired from finding Millicent, but I've recovered enough. Besides, my staff may be useful sucking up Death Stalker spells."

"I'm nearly a Dispeller already. I'll come too," Lindsey announced.

"You'll need me, in case I get any more premonitions," Ashley added, "and besides my staff can suck up more spells than theirs."

"Hey, I'm coming too," Andy added. "I'm not letting Lindsey out of my sight this time."

"Count me in too, Professor Delius. You need someone from Black Hall represented," Deiter interjected, his face just as stern as Delius's countenance.

"I'll go too, just in case you need more clues unraveled," Pam suggested.

"Me too, where Pam goes, I go as well," Monique added. "I represent Red Hall."

Jim, who had come to say goodnight to Ashley, but had not heard all of what was going on, piped up, "Where Ashley goes, so go I."

Lindsey added, "Professor Delius, I can see if I can get Able and Bill to join us. I'm sure that they would do anything to help out Alister."

All three professors, who were about to protest all their students becoming involved in this deadly mission, turned to stare at Lindsey. "What? You? You know Able Monument and Bill West, the Rat Pack wizards?" asked an incredulous Delius.

"Er, yes sir. Amanda, Ashley, Pam, and I do. They've told us that anytime we need help that we are to call on them," Lindsey answered, not wanting to divulge any more data than necessary. Deiter's face had a look that said, "I thought so!" Or perhaps it meant, "I was right all along!"

Cho Lin looked at Delius, who looked at her. He replied, "Lindsey, would you please contact the Rat Pack for us. Tell them that this might be a wild goose chase, but then again it might mean Alister's life. We must act within a half hour. If they can come, meet us at the Bradbury front gates in thirty minutes."

"Yes, professor," Lindsey answered. She concentrated and sent the message.

"Well, go on; do it," Delius demanded.

"I just did. Able is replying." They saw a message appear before Lindsey's eyes, vanishing in a puff of blue smoke once she read it. "Able says they will be there in twenty minutes, but bring as many staves as possible."

"Wise man," Cho Lin smiled. "More staves, more spells absorbed. They lack their Dispeller, so staves will have to do. Huan, dear, you take my Staff of Power with you." He smiled. "Okay, that will give you five staves and two Trackers and one fledgling Diviner and one Sleuth. If you all can't find Alister, I don't know what else we could do. As headmistress, I charge you two with the complete safety of these students. If anything happens to them, you two will be held fully responsible."

"Yes, dear, that is the official school policy. You've followed it to the letter. Now, let's all get our things ready. It could well be a long night. Meet at the front gates as soon as you can get ready. Let's move it kids," Huan Su replied. Hastily, they all headed up the stairs to get their things, while Monique and Deiter ran to their Halls to get what they thought they should need.

"Are you going to be able to do more tracking?" Lindsey asked Amanda, while they hastily stuffed a few things into a pack and donned their winter garb once more.

"I have to," Amanda sighed, "I'm tired but I ate a ton and slept a bit, so maybe it will be okay. Besides, Able will be with us. I'm sure glad you found out what is happening with

Alister, Ashley. Golly, if you had not discovered it, why, he might be dead. Looks like Cho Lin takes over the school when he is gone. I didn't know that."

"I figured she might be the one," Pam broke in. "There have been enough clues these past two years. Let me get you bundled up, Ashley." Pam, having stuffed her computer into her backpack, moved to help her friend, who was standing looking forlornly at her parka and boots sitting on her bed, unable to get either on by herself. As Pam helped her get her boots on, she could not help but notice water in Ashley's eyes, but she had the good sense not to say anything to her about it. Pam suspected what must be going through Ashley's mind right now, and it wasn't Alister.

Bundled against the cold at last, Ashley managed to speak briefly, "Thanks, Pam." She flashed a smile, but her face became a stone almost at once.

"Why are you taking your computer anyway?" asked Amanda, now ready herself.

"I am going to try to make the tracking easier for you and Able. I'm also bringing along these portable angle finders. Actually, surveyors use them, but I've been experimenting with other uses. I hope to get the chance to try them out tonight, if Able is willing," Pam explained, though neither Lindsey nor Amanda and any idea what she had just told them.

As they headed down the stairs, Lindsey commented, "Deiter was pretty cool with his Scrying Eye spell, you know, butting in on us to see what was going on."

"He doesn't want to be left out of the action," Ashley replied without even thinking about it. All three gave her a surprised glance, Ashley shrugged her shoulders, concentrating on not falling down the stairs, bundled up as she was.

Outside, Lindsey exclaimed, "What the heck are we walking for? Silly us! Door: Main Gate!" A shimmering door appeared before her and the four stepped through, arriving at the main gates. Deiter was already there waiting for them.

"Hi you all! I'm ready for action," he replied full of energy and excitement. This was his first real action trip. That he might be helping to save the school's Governor played only a minor role in his thoughts.

"Cool spell. Too bad Huan and Delius spied your eye," Pam complimented him. He grinned, as Monique appeared, bundled up against the cold as well. She wore her crimson parka, and her face was covered with a very soft, fluffy material.

"My face skin is extremely sensitive to the cold. Gosh, I hope I get back to normal soon," she explained. Pam already knew Monique had this new problem, but Saturday her father would be arriving to perform more surgery on her face, and Pam hoped that would then get Monique back to normal. Just then, Huan Su appeared, carrying his wife's Staff of Power. Delius, Jim, and Andy were right behind him, and Huan Su opened the gates. The party stepped outside into the parking lot. Able and Bill were not yet here, so they had no choice but to wait.

Delius asked, "Ashley, any further word on Alister? Any more premonitions?"

"No sir, just an overwhelming feeling of helplessness, but I can't tell if that's his or mine," she replied honestly, but softly.

Lindsey, Pam, and Amanda shot Ashley a glance; all three wondered why Ashley now felt so helpless. Something must be going on with her, but now was not the time to chat about it. Jim misinterpreted her statement.

He replied, "You are the most un-helpless helpless person I know, princess." It was a tease, and she managed a brief smile.

Delius missed her meaning completely. "It makes sense—if he is chained to a rock with the tide rising and no way of escape, a hopeless situation and no way to contact anyone. Have hope, Ashley; we are about to be on our way to rescue him. I suspect that we will get to him in plenty of time."

A poof of magical energies announced the arrival of Able and Bill, who made their entrance with staves in hand. "Evening professors, children. So Alister has gotten himself into a jam, has he?" Able spoke for them.

Delius replied, "Yes, according to Ashley's premonition,

he is chained to a rock with the rising tide intent upon drowning him. Yet, she believes that dawn is rising there. Ideas on how to find him?"

"Yes, I do," Pam unexpectedly spoke up; all eyes turned to her. "Triangulation. I've been studying a bit about your Tracking thing, and I have a suggestion that may get us to his exact location fairly rapidly."

Able chuckled, "All right, Pam, out with it."

Hastily, Pam pulled out her two Marshal Angles. "Surveyors use these. You sight through here and line it up with the precise direction that the magical energies are heading. Next, you read off the angle down here. I plot that line on my computer. Next, we pick two other very different, nearly perpendicular locations to that line and repeat it. That will give me three lines. Where they intersect, that's where Alister will be located. Here, I'll set them up and both you and Amanda send him a Message, observe the energy line, and line up the Marshal Angles."

"Clever idea," Delius complimented her. "Go ahead. Give it a try, Able, Amanda. It can't hurt and might work. If he's halfway around the world, it will be a lengthy, tedious process to follow that energy line all the way to him." Pam set up one for Able first and then the other for Amanda. Able waved her wand and sent him a Message. She then strained to see the faint line arcing from her position toward his. After a bit of fiddling, she had hers lined up. Meantime, Amanda followed suit, but took longer to get the Marshal Angle device properly aligned.

Pam read off the angles, ninety-three degrees and ninety-three, both had the same reading. Her computer was in hibernation mode, and quickly her global positioning system appeared. She had already marked the observation site here at the school. She entered the angle and watched a line streak across the world map.

As everyone gathered around to catch a peek at her monitor, she explained, "See, he lies somewhere along this line. Now to minimize the error, we need to pick a spot where the line may be closer to perpendicular to this one, say up here somewhere in England or down here in Egypt. Ideas?"

"Let's try Cairo first," Able suggested. "Great pyramids, you all know that landmark. We shouldn't get lost or separated on that teleport."

Pam hastily stuffed her laptop back into her magically enhanced pack, while the adults conferred on their Teleport spells. Once Huan Su was satisfied that everyone was properly accounted for and in physical contact with one of the four adults, he gave the go ahead.

Four spells energized within seconds of each other, and presto, the small group found themselves standing next to the great pyramids in Egypt. It was very early morning here and the view, spectacular. While the kids stared at the view, Pam hastily set up her two Marshal Angles. Amanda and Able once more sent Alister a Message, carefully aligning the machine to point in the precise direction that the magical energies had taken. It was about forty-five degrees east of north this time.

Once more Pam activated her computer. She had to find their current location first, which took a couple of minutes, since she was not entirely sure just where these pyramids were located. Soon, the GPS unit in her computer registered her new precise location. Finally, she was able to enter the angle and plot the second line.

"Wow, Ashley and Pam were right!" Andy exclaimed. "They intersect at the edge of Cyprus. Cool!"

"It lends even more credence to Ashley's divinations and fits what Millicent told Dominus," Delius added. "I don't think that we need a third observation. Let's all teleport to that edge of Cyprus, and then let our Trackers follow the energy lines to him."

Hastily, Pam packed up her two measuring devices and her laptop. The adults once more conversed about their exact destination. Only Able had ever been there before. This promised to be a tricky hop. At last, Able decided that the only way this would work would be for him to take the other adults there so that they could have a solid idea where to arrive.

"Okay, listen up, kids. Able is going to first teleport us adults there and then back again. This way, the rest of us will have a good idea where we are going. While we are gone, Jim you are in charge of the students. Stay right here and stay out of mischief. We will only be gone a couple of minutes."

"Yes professor," Jim replied. Monique looked a bit miffed; she was just as old as Jim was, and didn't see why Jim should be in charge and not her.

The four adults disappeared. Pam whispered to Monique, "It's a guy thing. Delius is a guy. If Cho Lin were here, you'd be the one in charge." All the girls chuckled.

"Say, while we are waiting, why don't we use our Door spells and get to the top of the pyramid. I bet the morning view is incredible," Jim suggested.

"He said to wait right here," Lindsey countered, unwilling to disobey Professor Delius.

"She's right. There you go trying to get us all into trouble, Jim," Monique scolded him.

Jim laughed, "Just teasing you. You are all much too serious! But then again, I bet it would be spectacular from up there."

The four adults reappeared, Jim's term of being in charge was entirely too short for his liking. Once more, everyone got into their positions, holding on to each other. Again, the four Teleport spells activated, and the group found themselves on a hillside amid a grove of low trees.

"Okay, Trackers, what's next?" Delius asked.

Amanda volunteered, "Before when I had to find Millicent, we flew in the sky as I followed the energy line. Is that how it's done, Able?"

"Yes, dear, that would seem to be the most appropriate at this time. It shouldn't be too far from here. Everyone cast your Fly spells and fall in behind Amanda and me." Shortly, the whole group took to the air, flying east by north. They passed over two small villages; Lindsey could see several people in the streets moving about. No one took much notice of the small group, however.

The smell of the sea was in the air. Sea gulls swooped beside them. The group now flew over the Mediterranean Sea a bit, as they headed for the eastern most point of the island. Then, more hills appeared below them. A half-hour into their flight, they approached their destination. They halted, landed to be more precise, on the top of a hill. Below them, the rocky coast thrust itself into the depths of the sea. It was a small cove area, not easily accessed from the hilltop without use of magical spells.

Alister lay down there somewhere, though from here, he could not be seen. However, what did get their attention were two things. First, far out to sea, they could see a stationary ship, bobbing in the waves. Second, in the cove immediately south of this cove were a dozen men standing around a bonfire. Even from this distance, Bill was able to spot several known Death Stalkers among them.

Bill commented, "If we go down to the cove below after Alister, I'm afraid we will be spotted from that ship out there. Those are certainly Death Stalkers down there. We need a plan of action."

Delius took charge, "We need to keep some of us up here to keep an eye on the Death Stalkers below. I think they'll need to come up here to get down to where Alister must be. That rocky promontory likely blocks them from coming along the coastline directly. I'll stay up here on guard. Perhaps some others should stay here too. The rest, you go find Alister, but when you do, set some on guard duty. I suspect you may be attacked from that ship out there. I'll keep Lindsey up here with me. The rest of you, go find Alister."

"Sounds like a good plan to me," Bill replied, "Let's get going. Either Fly down there or Gentle Fall. Action." While Lindsey wanted to go with the rest of them, she dare not counter Delius's orders. She watched her friends disappear over the cliff side; most chose to Fly down.

"Okay, let's setup a perimeter of observation," Delius ordered. "I used to be in the Army, you know. You stay here. Message me if you see any action down there. I'm going to explore around here and see if there is anything that we can use to our advantage should the Death Stalkers come after us." Lindsey nodded, and Delius moved away from her. She noticed that he moved very silently and made use of all available cover. This was a side of her most disliked professor that she hadn't seen before. Lindsey hated the Dark Arts, Delius's specialty. Yet she admired how stealthily he moved, how he took charge at once.

A couple minutes later, Lindsey spied the men below her conferring. Something was up. Just as she was about to Message Delius, he appeared behind her, startling her; he moved completely silently. She whispered, "Something's up down there. I think they must know that we're here to rescue Alister."

"Darn, I didn't think all fifteen of them would come charging up the hill towards us!" Delius cursed softly. "Two of us can't hope to hold off fifteen Death Stalkers. We need some help. Did you know that there is a graveyard not more than a thousand feet from here?" Lindsey shook her head no.

"Ah, here come our reinforcements." Lindsey turned to look where he was pointing. There marching out of the graveyard were a dozen zombie-like corpses and twenty skeletal men, if indeed they were men. "A bit of necromancy coming to our aid. They are already dead, so it's better to have the already-dead fight for us rather than us, don't you think?" Clearly, Delius was trying to make a point that necromancy had its useful aspects. However, Lindsey's skin crawled.

Below their position, the first of the men were already halfway up the hill. She saw several others casting and figured that they were either about to Fly up or to use a magical Door to step up to the hilltop. Delius ordered his newly acquired minions out in front, and they began moving awkwardly down the hill. Suddenly, chaos erupted on the hillside as men, skeletons, and zombies collided. Magical spells flew fast and furiously.

Two men stepped out of their magical doors ten feet in front of the two. Delius sent one flying backwards down the hill by casting a heavy Push spell, effectively taking that one out of the combat for a moment. Lindsey recognized him, the Stalker known as Len. The other one shot a spell towards the two, but Lindsey recognized it at once, a Ball of Fire. She commanded Margarete to Suck It, giving Delius time to counter-spell him. She also recognized this one. He was called Ames.

Lindsey and Delius were as close to the cliff side as cover would permit. The Death Stalkers would have to take the hilltop in front of them. Three more men appeared. Lindsey recognized only one, the man called Ben. She shot a Ball of Fire back at the four men. All four reacted instantly, dodging out of the perimeter of the detonation. Delius shot a Disintegrate beam at Ames, but he missed, as Ames dove out of the blast range of the flames.

This confusion gave the two a second chance to get off another spell before they would have to defend. Lindsey shot a mass of Webs over two of the men, who couldn't effectively dodge both the flames and the sticky webs. Both became entangled. However, shortly afterwards, another man came up over the hill's edge and shot a Dispel Magic on the webs, freeing the pair.

Ames countered and shot a Disintegrate beam back at Delius, but missed, hitting the solid rock in front of him. The spell removed a good part of the cover behind which Delius was hiding. Delius's said, "Ah, more help comes!" Lindsey heard a fluttering sound and hazarded a glance behind her. She saw thousands of bats flying as a large mass. They flew over the two and began attacking the numerous men who now had arrived on the top of the hill. Lindsey watched as the men flailed their arms to keep the bats off them. Three attempted to dispel the magic of Delius, two failed, but the third finally succeeded. Lindsey watched, as the bats left as suddenly as they had come.

At this point, fourteen men had crested the hill and were making for the two. Lindsey's ordered her staff to absorb spells as rapidly as she could. Delius commented, "Well, we've held them off as long as we dare. Time to split." He cast one last spell, creating a Death Fog that seeped towards the oncoming men. He rested his hand on her shoulder and teleported the two down to join the others, arriving near Jim, Deiter, and Ashley.

Delius commanded, "Kids, I will watch our rear. Lindsey, help Ashley keep us from being attacked, please. Do not look behind us." His voice sounded intensely cold, perhaps even evil, Lindsey thought, but did as he asked.

"Can you absorb for a minute? I need to discharge Zappo a bit," Ashley asked her sister. She began sending lightning bolts out to the ship as fast as Zappo could cast them.

"Okay, that's better."

Huan Su reached the rocky shoreline first. The blue waters of the sea lapped onto the rocky shore. Boulders, some large as a person, lined the edge of the island at this tiny cove, making walking nearly impossible. One by one, the others landed nearby, most choosing to land on one of the larger rocks. As Ashley landed, she spread her feet far apart and hoped that somehow she could keep her balance.

"Further this way," Amanda called out, "just a few feet more." The terrain was so rough that one could not walk along the water's edge, not without feet getting wedged between the stones.

"Veritable boulder field," Jim commented, as he struggled to get onto the same rock as Ashley. He put his arm around her waist to steady her and felt her perceptibly relax somewhat. He knew that for once he had guessed right.

"Jim, Ashley, Deiter, you stay here," Huan Su ordered. Keep an eye out for anyone trying to get here from along the shoreline and keep an eye on that ship out there. It seems to be anchored there, strange place to anchor."

"Aye, aye," Jim said teasingly, as though Professor Huan Su was a pirate captain. Ashley gave him a slight nudge implying he shouldn't be making fun. "We should sit, Ashley." He helped her sit down and joined her. Together, they could see both the coastline to the south and the white vessel bobbing on the undulating currents about a half mile off shore.

Deiter wanted to protest, but thought better of it. He asked, "Do you think that ship has anything to do with this? Could Dominus be on it? Didn't they find that crown on the sea floor? Maybe Dominus is out there diving for it right now."

They heard Able's voice call out, "Alister, we're here. We'll have you rescued in short order."

Indeed, they all reached him about the same time. He was attached to the largest boulder in the area. Already the sea was lapping at his upper chest, cold, clear, blue waters at this time of year. His face was blue-white with the cold; already hypothermia has set in, and he didn't recognize anyone nor could he speak.

"Amanda, Monique, Pam, Andy, continuous Warm spells on his body. Huan Su, Bill, what do you make of his bonds?" Able asked.

"It's like someone has made the rock form around his wrists. Ah, I have it," Huan Su declared. "Have you figured it out, Pam?" Even now Huan Su continued with the student's education.

"Yes sir. He was probably knocked out. They made mud chains over his wrists and stuck both ends to this rock. The spell Mud to Rock was used to turn it into stone. We need to reverse those spells, sir," Pam answered. Monique grinned; her Pam was right again. She knew those spells and knew Pam would be learning them next year.

A moment later and Alister's hands were free, Warm spells continuously cast began slowly raising his internal body temperature. "The real problem is how to free his ankles," Bill noted. They were under four feet of water.

"Andy, Monique, you two are the strongest; see if you can hold him up out of the water as much as possible," Able suggested. "The problem is that we can't cast the spell under water. While we can indeed breathe water, while doing so, we can't speak the command words. We can't lower the water to get to his ankle restraints."

"Crack the stone; that seems to be the only way," Bill commented thinking hard and fast.

Ashley, Jim, and Deiter could hear the others talking about Alister. While they wanted to help, all three knew that there was really nothing that they could do that the others were not doing. Just then, Deiter saw a flash of light from the ship. "What's that? There on the ship." All three stared.

"Kind of like light flashing off of something reflective, maybe glass or a mirror or a shiny piece of metal?" Ashley offered. "Oh no! Someone is watching us through binoculars!" She'd just had another premonition. "They are going to attack us from out there!"

The three got to their feet, but it took both boys to help Ashley up. Standing on a curved boulder top was not an easy task for her. Suddenly, the sounds of a combat reached their ears from above, followed shortly by a Message from Lindsey, saying the Death Stalker men were storming the hill.

Not long after that, the three saw a streak of lightning arcing their way from the ship. "Zappo: Absorb!" Ashley shrieked. At the very last instant, the lightning bolt and its magical energies entered her staff.

Undaunted, Deiter shot a lightning bolt back towards the ship. Jim followed suit, seconds after Deiter's spell arced towards the ship. Both hit the ship. Bits of the ship flew in many directions, but from this distance, they could not see much else result. "Jim, keep them pinned down with more lightning bolts; you too, Ashley. I'm going to go see who is there shooting at us," Deiter ordered. Jim shot another bolt towards the ship, but this time someone cancelled it. Ashley was about to do the same, when she sensed another one coming their way and again had Zappo absorb it.

Deiter's magical eye appeared and rapidly began flying out across the water towards the distant ship. A swarm of bats flew past them and on up the hillside behind them. Jim tried another bolt, because there were few other spells that would reach such a distance.

"Darn it; the fighting has begun," Bill commented. "Andy, Haun Su, keep us covered. We are going underwater and try to crack the rock holding his legs. Come on, Able; we have very little time before they will descend upon us." Both Bill and Able picked up a heavy boulder and dove into the waters, each heading for a foot clamp made from the stone. It was hard for them to pound underwater, but the two kept at it, knowing they just had to crack the stone that encircled Alister's ankles pinning him to the rock. Both men now sported gills and at least didn't have to surface for air. Repeatedly, they pounded on the rock loops around his legs.

Unfortunately, they got nowhere. At last, Huan Su tried a different spell. "Be as Moses, Part the Waters!" His wand activated, and the waters all around the base of the rock moved out to sea, the path of least resistance, leaving Bill and Able floundering like two fish out of water. Hastily, both cancelled their water breathing spells. Simultaneously, Monique and Huan Su cast their Rock to Mud spells—one on each of Alister's leg bindings. Bill and Able laughed and freed his legs at once.

"What a pair of idiots, we make, Bill," exclaimed Able as they helped lift the semiconscious body of Alister up onto the top of the huge stone boulder.

"We are all idiots," Huan Su replied. "I don't think that any of us has encountered anything quite like this before. I needed to think it out."

"Glad you could think!" Bill commented. "I'm going to Delius. The Death Stalkers are coming down now. I can see them from here. You all teleport Alister back to Cairo. I'll bring the others along at once."

Bill shot a Disintegrate beam up towards the top of the hill, causing six men to suddenly duck for their lives, giving him time to make a door to step to the side of Delius. He was just in time to hear Delius trigger his spell, "Death to you all!" Lindsey, who was absorbing another bolt from the ship, heard his words however. A chill went up her spine, though she dare not look behind her. Bill saw another six men attempt to dodge his spell. Two younger men, whom Bill didn't know, stopped in their tracks and slumped to the ground, dead.

Bill saw his chance, shot another Disintegrate beam, and struck the Death Stalker called Allen Hall in the head. Allen was trying to get out of the way of the Death spell and now had a three-inch hole through his brain. He stared into space as his body fell over the cliff, dead. Delius called out, "Two to one; I lead."

"Force wall now!" Bill called out. Indeed, other Death Stalkers had now caused a whole section of the cliff side to collapse down on top of them. Bill saw that there was no time to get the protection up to deflect the falling rocks. Instead, he grabbed Delius and pulled them back onto the four students. As soon as he felt his body touching everyone, Bill called out, "Teleport: Cairo!" At that instant half of the cliff side landed on the boulders on which they had been standing, but the group was now back in Cairo, more specifically, near the Great Pyramids.

Deiter began screaming, holding his head and frothing at his mouth. The other group had Alister on the ground and were warming him and drying him off. Huan Su raced over to Deiter, as Delius shot a Dispel Magic on to his student of Black Hall. "What's happened to him?"

Jim answered, "Don't know. He was using his magical Scrying Eye to spy on those on the ship and then we landed here."

"Crap! We teleported him while he was observing through the eye! He's seen things he should never have seen!" Delius angrily explained.

"Well, at least he is alive. I had no other choice. Another second delay and we would all be buried under tons of cliff," Bill defended his hasty move.

"True, true, brilliant move, Bill. Saved our butts. Let's get them both back to Doctor Caterwall pronto," Delius ordered. A minute later, the group appeared at the main gates of Bradbury's School of Magic. It was ten p.m., as they roused Doctor Caterwall.

Everyone helped get the two onto the emergency tables while the doctor and the nurses came running into the room. "You found him. How badly injured is he?" he asked.

"Hypothermia at least," Huan Su suggested, "maybe other things. He was in the cold ocean for several hours at least. His feet are very cold indeed. Deiter was looking through a magical eye when Bill had to do an emergency teleport. He has extra-dimensional shock."

At once, the good doctor set to work. Bill took Pam aside, "Pam, for your records, I eliminated the Death Stalker who went by the name of Allen Hall. He was one of those that Dominus broke out of prison. Also, talk to Delius; he managed to kill two of the newer recruits. Perhaps he can give you a good description of them." She nodded and knew what Bill meant by telling her this. Pam was fully documenting everything about these Death Stalkers, storing the information on her private, secure server.

To the others, Bill said, "Well, Able and I need to get going. Give Alister our regards when he recovers. Amanda, Lindsey, keep us posted. Good night all; it's been fun." He winked at Pam, while Able smiled at Amanda. The two walked out of the Infirmary to the main gates and then teleported home. Both of their morph spells were about to wear off, hence their hasty exit.

No sooner than the two had left the emergency room when Cho Lin entered. Huan Su had Messaged her, but she knew that they had arrived anyway. Since she was now in charge of the school; the Alert spells had already notified her of their coming. "How is he? Deiter? What's happened to him? Huan Su?" Her voice more than screamed, how dare you allow a student to get hurt.

Carefully, Haun Su and Delius explained what had happened. The others watched the ministering of the doctor and nurses. Alister was wrapped with many heating blankets. Nothing could be done for him until he warmed up more. Now he turned his attention onto Deiter, who Lindsey thought looked like an insane person. He forced some potion down the boy's throat, thought only a little actually made it into his system; most joined the frothing coming from his mouth. Deiter was quite delirious. Doctor Caterwall persisted and soon had more potion into the boy's system. Slowly the convulsions and writhing subsided, as did the frothing.

"There, now he will be in a restful sleep. When he wakes, he'll have a headache, but will be fine otherwise. It's Alister who worries me. His body is old and has taken quite a shock. I don't know if he will make it."

"What can we all do?" asked Lindsey, extremely worried about Governor Alister. She, as nearly everyone else here, had become quite fond of the middle aged man.

"Glad you asked. I could use all of you at this point. We need to start rubbing and massaging his feet and legs in particular. If you don't mind lending your hands? Perhaps if you would work in shifts? It will be a bit tiring, but as soon as we can get his circulation going better, I can administer potions that will greatly speed the healing process."

Ashley felt heavy emotional pangs once more, as she watched Jim and Monique begin to rub and massage Alister's feet. "Hey, why don't you and Lindsey start in on his arms and wrists, use your feet, dear, you can do it," Doctor Caterwall suggested. Ashley faked a smile, but did as he suggested. Amanda quickly slid a stool over for Ashley to sit on so that she could get her feet to work. Amanda also removed the heavy snow boots for her friend. At last, Ashley began to try to mimic the motions that Lindsey was trying on his other wrist. Soon, she was doing a passable job of massaging his wrist where it had been imprisoned in the rock cuff.

After a while, Jim commented, "Well, I know one job that I don't want, massage therapist! My arms are giving out." Monique smiled; hers were too. Andy and Pam spelled the two. Suddenly, Alister moaned and pulled his arm out from under Ashley's feet.

"Good, good. Here, Alister, drink this," Doctor Caterwall said softly, forcing some grey looking potion into his mouth. Slowly, Alister began to drink the liquid. It smelled awful, Ashley thought, as she got a good whiff of its peculiar smell. Lindsey curled up her nose and backed away.

Chapter 17—Explanations, then Studies, Finally

"He will sleep until the morning," Doctor Caterwall pronounced, as Alister finished sipping his potion. Indeed, color was returning to the rescued man's face, and his breathing seemed normal. Deiter, too, was now sound asleep. "I'll notify you when they awake in the morning. I'm sure that you'll want to see them both."

That satisfied everyone, though Lindsey would have preferred to sit beside them, just to make sure. Since tomorrow was weekend time, everyone agreed. En mass, the group left the Infirmary. "Well, that was awfully scary," Monique admitted to Pam, as they held each other as they walked back down the dimly lighted tunnel to the dorms.

"Yes, I prefer to Sleuth and not fight. We nearly got killed, if it hadn't been for Bill West," Pam replied.

Jim, whose arm was tightly around Ashley's waist, holding her snugly against his body, added, "No kidding? That's as close to death as I care to come. I don't know what I would have done if my dear Ashley here would have gotten hurt."

"But we had to rescue him, Jim," Ashley corrected him. "If we hadn't acted, Governor Alister would be dead. I can see I'm not ever going to be worth much out there, you know, fighting battles and all that. I'm just mostly useless," she lamented, her deep emotions swelled within her once more, as she recalled how she could only barely stand on the boulder by the sea.

"No you are not, sister," Lindsey countered. "Look, Ashley, if you hadn't had your premonition, we wouldn't have known Alister was near death nor where he was at. Without your skills, well, you know what I mean. You're not useless. You're more vital than you even suspect."

"She's right, you know," Andy butted in. "None of us can even remotely glimpse the things that just come to you! I mean I know a lot about archaeology, but nothing about this Divination thing. I think what you have is incredibly valuable, Ashley, incredibly."

"Yeh, well you got arms and I don't. Jim had to hold on to me to keep me from falling off that boulder. Some witch I am—can't even stand on a rock," Ashley retorted. "Besides, I couldn't do a darn thing actually to rescue Alister, now could I?"

"But you kept the rest of us alive by absorbing countless lightning bolts coming from that ship," Jim countered.

Amanda, who had been silent, spoke up, "Ashley, think of us all as a team. Just like track, we all have our strengths and weaknesses. When we all work together, we are stronger than anyone of us would be working alone. That's the edge we have over Dominus and his gang of cutthroats. Andy's right; none of us has your skills and gift. Without it, we're the ones who are useless. Think about that a bit. We'd have been sitting around moaning over how useless we were to help Alister, if you had not given us the warning and direction."

Ashley seemed to relax a bit; at least, Jim felt the tension easing from her body. As they reached the stairs, they had to separate. Jim wheeled her around and stole a good night kiss. Ashley blushed, but allowed it. Not to be out done, Andy gave Lindsey a kiss as well.

While they were thus distracted, Monique gave Pam a kiss. Pam blushed and returned her affections. Monique then headed for Red Hall, as Pam opened the door to head upstairs. Amanda followed, with Lindsey and Ashley, with slightly pinkish cheeks, right on her heels.

"No more premonitions tonight, please," teased Amanda as the four headed to take a quick shower before bed.

"Let me shower before you have another one," Lindsey added.

"Oh, I see someone is in trouble, so we'd better get going," Ashley teased them back. Pam chuckled, but her thoughts lay elsewhere at the moment. Ashley added seriously, "I was just taking a bath when it came. I think maybe because of the way I was in the tub was rather like the way you found him was how it came to me." She used her foot to adjust the hot water steaming from showerhead to her liking. A bit later, Lindsey, who was using the stall next to her, leaned over and washed her back.

That's when she noticed the tense muscles in Ashley's back. Amanda, dead tired, as well as Pam, had showered, and already left them. The two were alone. "You're so tense, sis. Is something wrong?" Lindsey asked.

"God, that feels so good! Do you mind doing it a bit longer?" Ashley replied, not answering the painful question. After all, it was her problem, not Lindsey's, and besides, no one could do anything about it anyway. "Ah, like that." Maybe Lindsey would forget what she'd asked.

A few minutes later, the two turned off the water and began drying off. Lindsey noted that Ashley obviously didn't want to talk about what was troubling her and decided to let it be. She'd talk about it when she was ready, Lindsey figured. Once back in their room, the two turned in, since only the nightlight was now on. Amanda was already sound asleep; likewise, Pam.

The next morning, when Lindsey lent Ashley a hand getting dressed quickly so they could all visit the two patients before breakfast, Lindsey saw that Ashley's pillow was rather wet. Her eyes looked a little red as well. Had she been crying during the night? Lindsey decided not to inquire with Amanda and Pam still in the room. All four headed down to the Infirmary together.

"Come in, have a bite," Professor Cho Lin beckoned. Indeed, the faculty was here, and the four were the last of the students to arrive. Jim and Andy moved to the sides of Ashley and Lindsey respectively, offering them seats politely.

"I didn't know I was making this much trouble," Governor Alister spoke up. Lindsey thought that his voice sounded strong. He'd recovered a good deal from his near-death experience rather well. However, she also detected a note of uncertainty in his voice that she'd never heard before. His smile tried to dissuade others, but how could that horrid experience not have unsettled him?

Doctor Caterwall entered, pushing a large cart filled with more breakfast items, and the newer arrivals helped themselves. "Well, perhaps we should begin at the beginning," Professor Mary Ann began the meeting. "It begins with Ashley and me; we were having our afternoon lesson. I'm afraid that I pushed her rather hard, and she did have a premonition. It was my dear friend, Millicent Prague. You've met her, Alister, a Class 2 Diviner. We've just come from the hospital. She finally regained consciousness." First, she explained in detail how Ashley's visions had warned them and how Amanda found where she was lying in the warehouse.

"I'm afraid that she, too, may never fully recover from her ordeal," Mary Ann explained. Alister and Arthur both nodded, and Lindsey suspected that something similarly traumatic had happened to Mary Ann, leaving her so fearful and flighty. "I'll spare the details; students are present, Alister. It was Dominus and his Death Stalkers. They kidnaped her, took her to the warehouse, and forced her to do a divination for him. He wanted to know what you did with the Crown of Moses. She told him that she saw you putting a crown back where it came from. Through with her, he ordered a Death Stalker to finish her off. He slit her throat, but missed the main artery; we barely got to her in time. Another hour and she wouldn't have made it. Alister, she's under guard now, but when she is released, I was hoping that I could bring her to stay a while with me, until she recovers."

"Yes, of course, Professor, of course. Ah, now it begins to make some sense. I figured something like that must have happened. Pray, how did you find me? I believed that my time had finally come," Alister replied.

"My doing again, sir," Ashley spoke up. "I was taking a hot bath when I got back. I think maybe it was because I was sliding helplessly into the tub that somehow put me into contact with you. I saw you were going to be drowned and raised the alarm again, only Mary Ann and Arthur were still in Greeley."

"Yes, Huan Su and I took charge right away," Delius interrupted Ashley, figuring she had said her piece. He explained how they had organized a rescue party, but Pam interrupted him to explain her latest invention to assist Amanda and Able in triangulating the magical energies. Delius interrupted her to add that they had asked the girls if they could get a hold of Able and Bill to lend a hand.

"Yes, Pam's invention worked," Amanda interrupted Delius, insisting that Pam get due credit. Besides, she thought Alister, her Tracker teacher, might be interested in it. Indeed, she was right. Alister had Pam and Amanda explain fully how it worked.

"I'm sorry, Amanda, that your training isn't done. It's my fault that you got so utterly worn out finding Millicent. I will address that shortcoming in our future sessions." He winked at her, and she felt a bit of relief. Perhaps Tracking would not be so utterly exhausting in the future.

"Yes, well, we landed on Cyprus, as both Trackers agreed on your location," Delius continued. He explained what had then happened. Soon, he was relating the combat that they had had with the Death Stalkers, both those on land and those out in the ship off shore.

"Yes, I saw him, Dominus!" Deiter, who had been listening silently from his nearby bed, interrupted Delius. "I used my long distance magical scrying eye to spy on those on the ship who were casting spells at us on shore. While Ashley and Lindsey were having their staves absorb the spells, I was trying to have a look-see at whom our attackers actually were. One was the female stalker, Nadia van Nye. I didn't recognize the other one, though. Dominus was also there. He wasn't at first. He must have been diving, because he had gills when he climbed on board the ship. Then, he too began casting spells at us. It was he who gave some kind of signal, just before the side of the hill came tumbling down on us, and we were teleported. . ." His voice trailed away.

Lindsey knew that he was now seeing again whatever it was that had so terrified him, when they had teleported him while his magical eye was still active. Yet, as she looked at the boy, it was not the fear and insanity that she saw in his eyes. No, it was something else, something quite different. He didn't say any more, but he did look at Pam and Monique strangely.

"Bill's quick thinking and action saved us all," Delius finally ended their tale. "Honestly, I don't know how these girls are in a position to contact the Rat Pack. It should be one of us professors, Alister. Perhaps you should rethink that decision. We all know that you can contact Bill and Able when you chose. What if this should happen again?" Lindsey saw that Delius really hated that she and her friends knew something critical that he did not.

Alister, however, only grunted. "Well, I owe all of you my life. Thank you. It began mid-morning. You see, Dominus, once again, made use of his powerful spell, Restricted Wish. That spell has caused the forces of good more darn trouble! Nearly did me in this time." He looked aside at Lindsey and Amanda, "That's the spell that gave the Rat Pack immense trouble in capturing him. It took them several years of effort finally to get around that spell of his. Anyway, that spell forced me, suddenly and without being able to tell anyone, to teleport to Cyprus midmorning yesterday."

"I knew that I was in trouble the instant that I felt his spell contacting me, but I was utterly helpless to do anything about it." He looked at Ashley as he said this. She gave him an understanding look, a look that no one else present, save perhaps Lindsey, could.

"They had me surrounded, twelve of them, wands pointed at me, as I arrived. They took my wand and imprisoned me on the rock where you found me. Dominus told me that it would take nearly twelve hours for death finally to take me. He gloated in the suffering and despair that he knew I would experience. I've never felt so helpless in my life. I could do nothing. I could not send a Message for help, though I saw a few of yours before I passed out from the bone chilling cold. He did let me know that he had recovered the crown from the seabed where I had left it, however. His gloating was short lived, as he soon discovered I had planted a fake crown there in the sea. He tried to get the real location out of me, but by then I was unconscious for the most part."

"What I cannot figure out is why Dominus would want the Crown of Moses back?" Cho Lin said thoughtfully. "I've given this a good deal of my attention, while everyone was off playing hero. Look, his hurricane plot was exposed. If he attempts to bring on more bad weather, everyone will know it is he who is controlling the weather. I can't see what possible

Vic Broquard

use he could have for the Crown at this time."

"Ego maybe," suggested her husband. Huan Su added, "Perhaps he wanted it back just so that he has it. Or maybe to show up Alister or even to kill him."

"Well, if he wanted Alister dead, why go to all that trouble of chaining him to a rock and wait twelve hours for the tide to drown him?" Delius replied. "One Disintegrate spell to his head and Alister is eliminated."

"You don't know him well enough, Professor Delius," Lindsey ventured to comment, "not like we do." She was referring to her imprisonment her first year when Dominus masqueraded as her. "He would never do a quick kill, not to Alister."

"She's right, Delius. Dominus and his ego has to drag out our torture as long as possible. I'm afraid that Miss Barron and I have made it to the top of his hit list. If he ever gets a hold of Miss Barron, you can count on his delaying her death as long as possible. He is very sadistic in nature towards his enemies," Governor Alister pronounced.

"Again, I thank you all for saving my life. Together, we are stronger than Dominus and his henchmen. Never lose sight of that. I am deeply in all of your debt. Now, if the good doctor will release me, we ought to get back to our normal duties."

"Yes, yes, both of you may return to your duties, only I wish both of you to take it easy for the rest of today. If you have any lingering symptoms, please come to me at once," Doctor Caterwall ordered. "Oh yes, Monique, your father will be arriving this evening. You are to meet him here around six." Monique nodded. The meeting was over, and one by one, they filed out heading to the dorms.

Pam and Monique were the last to go. Something told Pam that Alister wanted a word with her in private. "Ah, Miss Betts. Please come see me tomorrow. I have a bit of spell research that might interest you." Pam smiled. Monique squeezed her hand as if to say, "Way to go hot shot."

"Sir, what did you do with the Crown of Moses?" Pam ventured to ask what her attention was solidly upon for some time now.

Alister chuckled at some private jest, before he said jovially, "The Crown of Moses is now upon its rightful owner." Pam squirreled up her nose and tilted her head, not grasping what he was saying. Then, she realized that he had given her another puzzle to solve. He was not about to openly say what he had done with the real crown.

Walking arm in arm back to their dorms, Monique asked, "Pam, so what did he mean by that wise crack about the Crown of Moses? Where did he put it?"

"He wants me to figure it out. I think he thinks the fewer who know, the better."

"Okay, let me know when you work it out. Oh yes, thanks for coming with me tonight. I know that dad's going to do more surgery on me, probably on Sunday. God, I don't know what I'd do without you, Pam!" Their hands tightened in each other's.

Chapter 18—At Sea

"They got away again!" Ben Johnston reported in to Dominus, who was eating his supper on deck. He had just returned from the rocky hillside, where the Death Stalkers had been removing the collapsed hillside looking for the bodies, as Dominus had ordered. Ben feared that Dominus would have his head for somehow allowing this rag-tag group of teachers and students to escape, especially with Alister Broadwell.

Instead of the expected wrath, Ben saw a smile on the face of his master. Dominus grinned, while Nadia massaged his legs, and he ate another date. "No matter. I've found what I came for, Ben." Several other Death Stalkers arrived on deck, stepping out of their Magical Doors. All expected to face the bile of Dominus, since every one had escaped, while three of their own had died.

"I, I don't understand, Master. They escaped. Allan is dead and two new ones as well," Ben replied perplexed. The other Death Stalkers grimaced. They too did not understand this unexpected jovial mood of their master.

"That's why I'm the leader, and you are my followers. My plan worked to perfection," Dominus replied.

"But Master, the crown is a fake! Millicent lied to us," Ben added.

"She did not lie, Ben. She spoke what she could see. Alister is a crafty opponent. He knows quite well that his actions can be revealed by a Class 2 Diviner. She told us what he wanted any Diviner to be able to tell us about what he did with the crown. You still don't get it, do you?"

Ben hung his head low. He certainly did not. Dominus explained, "I don't want that crown back, silly. I would not dare use it again. They would be on to us the very minute I used it to control the weather."

"Then why come here after it? Why did you torture Millicent? Why kill her?" Ben asked, more confused than ever. "We lost three good men today." He was somewhat annoyed now. Allan had been a friend of his.

"One. We taught Alister a lesson in humility that he will never, ever forget! Two. Did you not notice the Rat Pack came to his rescue? Of course, they again used a bunch of students to help them. Three. Bill has indeed changed."

"Yah, I noticed that. Twice now he has killed, not captured."

"Precisely. Bill has changed. Fifteen years ago, Bill would never have killed our men. He always chose to capture them, not kill them. Twice now, Bill has spelled to kill. Indeed, we are looking at a changed man! We must use that to our advantage. He must be a very angry man now. That point we must use to his demise. I needed proof that Bill has changed. Today, I got that conformation. We will adjust our plans accordingly." Ben nodded. This he could understand.

Dominus was not done lecturing his men. "Did you notice that the Rat Pack came to his rescue? Do you not find that keenly interesting?"

"Well, now that you mention it, I suppose so."

"Long have we suspected that Alister could somehow contact the Rat Pack. Today, I eliminated that avenue of communication. Alister needs his wand to cast his spells. Chained to the rock as he was, there was no way that he could contact the Rat Pack. Yet, right on time, the Rat Pack arrived. Most interesting, is it not? Someone else, probably connected with Bradbury's, knows how to get a hold of the Rat Pack. We must discover who that person is!"

"Yes, and kill them," Ben added.

"Maybe, but if we know who, I'll make good use of them first!" He laughed a snickering laugh, and his men joined in with him. All had visions of using this unknown person to lure the dreaded Rat Pack survivors to their deaths.

Dominus stopped laughing as suddenly as he began. His face tightened up as anger flooded his muscles. "Four. This is the most important piece of data of all. While I suspected this from the attack on us in Telluride, now I know it for a fact."

"What Master?" asked Ben, unable to fathom what was so critical. Everything seemed to fit. What could possibly be left that was so vital?

"How did any of them know that we had Alister and that he needed rescuing or even where he was located? We are in Cyprus, of all the places on earth, mind you. Yet, here they all come to his rescue. How can this be? How did they know we had Alister, that I was killing him, and that he was here on Cyprus? Answer that one."

"I, I, I can't Master," Ben admitted.

"That's why I'm the leader. I can. There is a powerful Diviner somewhere on the campus of Bradbury's, that's what. Only a powerful Diviner could have discovered all that information in so short a time, like less than twelve hours from start to finish. It can't be that sniveling Thornby woman. A darn Diviner got us last time. I swear this time I will not let another Diviner get to us!" He smashed his fist into the side of the cabin so violently that the wood gave way leaving a hole in the wall.

"Our number one priority must be to find out who this new powerful Diviner is and then eliminate him or her somehow. Men, it is the Diviner or us. Only a Diviner can stand in our way to World Domination. There isn't a Dispeller alive to threaten us. Bill has given way to anger. No, the only obstacle standing between my goal, our goal," he hastily added, "and total defeat is this new Diviner. Somehow, someway, we must find out who that is."

"Gentlemen, Nadia, let us dine and put our heads together. We have a very serious problem to solve and solve quickly," Dominus suggested, a sneer on his lips. "Do we have anyone on the inside now? Shame Larry Sacks graduated."

Chapter 19—Avalanches, an Operation, and Studies

Everyone spent Saturday studying, all except Monique and Pam. Monique fretted away in her room, dreading another operation. Already she had suffered the utter humiliation of having to be seen with her face looking so awful. She couldn't even wear her red lipstick. Now, she was facing going under the knife once more.

While Pam sat in the study hall with the others and occasionally answered her friends' homework questions, Pam was not doing homework. Rather she was working on two projects. First, she updated her triply secure server with all the latest information on the Death Stalkers, noting carefully the death of Allen Hall, and the other two, whom she still had not identified. She logged the details of the attempted murder and torture of Millicent and Alister.

That accomplished, she focused her mind on the riddle that Alister had given her. Where had he placed the real Crown of Moses? Just after lunch, Pam had a satisfied look on her face. "I'm off to see Alister, gang. I don't know what spell research project he has for me, but it ought to be interesting. Cya later."

"Have fun," Ashley replied.

"Ah, Miss Betts, right on time. Tea?" Governor Alister met her in his office. He looked much better now she thought, back to his old lovable self.

"Please. It's in the Natural History Museum, Cairo Egypt." Pam smiled cleverly.

"My, my, that was indeed quick. I must be slipping in my old age," he replied pouring her a cup. "Irish Breakfast, though it is afternoon. Correct."

"They have a complete life-sized statue of Moses there, along with several exhibits depicting his life back then. I suspect you used a Permanent Illusion to disguise it, because the images on the Net don't look at all like the real one." She accepted the offered cup, though she would have preferred a Coke-Classic.

"Sir, I've been thinking. There really isn't any logical reason for Dominus to want to get that crown back, is there? I mean, if the weather suddenly goes weird again, we all will know he is at it again. So why go to all the trouble that he has to secure it?"

"Miss Betts, I've thought about that for hours before you all came to rescue me. I've thought about it since. You and I see eye to eye. He can't possibly have wanted it so that he can use it again. While he might want it back just because he had it, I think that is too feeble an excuse, considering it is Dominus. No, Miss Betts, we must look deeper. That whole affair must have had some entirely different purpose for him, though I've yet to figure out what. Put your Sleuthing mind on that one, please."

"Now then, I have a spell research project for you to work on, though I know you are years from ever being able to cast the spell. Our Achilles heel is his incessant use of the Restricted Wish spell. Please research that spell fully. We must find a way to counteract that spell. I know Sam Barron worked on that one. It gave the entire Rat Pack a most difficult time trying to apprehend Dominus. They only succeeded when Sam managed to get Dominus tricked into casting it. We know that he can only cast that powerful spell once per day at the very most. Sam tricked him into using it; only then could Bill capture him."

"I know that this spell is way over your head, but give it a go, please. I'm hoping against hope that you, with your fresh mind, can see something that I have overlooked. I have notified the Librarian that you have full and complete access to our stacks. If we have it here, it is yours to examine. Carte blanche." Pam's eyes opened wide. This was a fabulous offer.

"Yes, sir. I will get right on it," she gushed.

"Well, don't forsake your studies, Miss Betts. I've been over and over it for years now and found nothing. So do it in your spare time. Keep me posted."

"I will sir! Thank you!" Pam left and headed to the Library. At least, she could read the spell book that described the Restricted Wish spell. Then, she could make plans for further research.

The Librarian Lillian Angel Jones smiled. She'd just received Alister's message and put a stamp onto Pam's library card. "There you go, dear. You have total access. Just be careful. There are spells in the stacks that can cause you a great deal of difficulty, if not kill you." Pam promised that she would stay out of trouble and headed into the stacks. She'd never been in here before—no student had, as far as she could tell. Using the data Alister had written on an index card, she found the ancient volume.

She sat down on one of the small tables and found the spell. She read.

The Restricted Wish is a most powerful Grade 7 spell, yet it is one of the more difficult spells to master. Rightly so, declared Wizard Heberfuss Beaker, when he included it in this particular grade level in his 1899 revision of the grade spells.

Pam skipped over the narrative a bit.

It fulfills the wish in a very literal way. For example, the caster says, "I wish for a small bag of gold to appear on my table." The spell may place the bag there one hundred years in the past, one hundred years in the future, or maybe even in the present, since time was not made part of the wish. Further, the bag might be one quarter of an inch in diameter or perhaps five inches, for what is meant by a small bag? Of the gold, it may well be in a fine powder form, since nothing specific was stated. Further, wishing for riches, wishing for major changes in the reality of the world will simply not be fulfilled, as this is a 'restricted' wish.

Duration of the effect of the wish is also limited, depending upon the magnitude of the reality change that the spell is to cause. Obviously, attempts to make large changes in the way things are in the present will result in tiny durations, if at all. The rule of thumb is to keep the alterations of reality minimal so that the spell's effect lasts for a long period.

She skipped on down the page to the bold-faced caution.

Each casting of the spell causes an unnatural aging of the

caster; his or her body ages one year. Casting Restricted Wish fifty times ages you fifty years!

She thought to herself, "Well, we can get rid of Dominus if we can get him to use the spell fifty times." That was followed by her tally of known times that he had cast it—two that she knew about recently. Pam sighed.

As she got up to put the volume back, she noticed a Scrying Eye floating just behind her, watching her every move. She found it a bit unnerving and cast her Dispel Magic spell on it. "Ouch," she heard the familiar voice of Deiter Cross reacting from outside of the stacks. Grinning, she put the book back, grabbed her notes, and walked out to the main section. Deiter was sitting in the last booth before the entrance to the stacks.

"Spying on me, Deiter?" Pam whispered a bit annoyed with him.

"Can we talk somewhere?" he whispered back. Since she was heading back to the dorms, she agreed, and the two entered the nearly deserted cafeteria. "I've heard that you have a total pass into the stacks. You can study any volume in our entire library, completely unsupervised, right?"

"How did you," she began quite flustered. She had only had this new privilege for a short time. How had he known? Yet, she really didn't care about that, so she changed her question mid-question. "Why were you scrying on me?"

"I asked you first. It's important," he countered, unwilling to let his question remain unanswered.

Pam gave in, since his face told her that she would not get an answer from him first. "Yes, as you know, Alister has given me a special research project, a long term one. Now answer my question," she replied huffily.

"I thought so. I was trying to see if it was true—that you had total access to our stacks. Pam, can I get you to do a little research for me? It will benefit us all next year when we learn the Teleport spell." Pam stared into his eyes. He didn't flinch. He was serious and not conning her, she decided.

"Well, that depends. I've got an awful lot of work to do myself." However, curiosity got the better of Pam. She just had to know what Deiter was so interested in discovering. "What do you want researched?"

Deiter glanced around the room. Satisfied that no one was listening in on their conversation, he explained, "The Teleport spell. I had my Scrying Eye working when Bill used Teleport to take us from Cyprus to Cairo. Pam, I *saw* things! Wild, weird, strange things. Extra-dimensional things. I swear that I saw them! That's what drove me temporarily crazy. I don't remember just how I acted, but it must have been strange indeed. I want to know about them—what are they, all about them. Caterwall won't tell me anything about them; neither will Alister, though at least he doesn't say I was imagining them. Please, Pam, please? I'll do anything for you to thank you, anything." His face flushed, as he began to imagine some things that Pam might request in payment.

Pam's imagination ran wild. Here was something that she didn't know about, not in the least. Well, that was to be expected, she told herself; after all, Teleport was next year's study. Yet, she knew that Deiter had seen something that he was not supposed to see and, more than anything else, that pricked her curiosity. "Okay, I'll see what I can find, only don't rush me. I have this project for Alister, which is very important, plus all my own to do too. I'll let you know when I find out something concrete. How's that?"

"Thank you! Thank you! Pam, you are the greatest," he lavished praise on her. She thought he was going a bit overboard on it, though. "I've got to get going. Pool time with the professor and Ashley. I owe you. I won't forget it, Pam." He got up and left, heading for the stairs to the stadium complex. Pam went on up to her room. Soon, she would be heading to meet Monique and her father, and she wanted to clean up first.

Pam was missed in study hall. Kathy whined, "We have this paper to do for chemistry class. I don't understand these two laws that we are supposed to do the paper on: Boyle's Law and Charles' Law. I can't even see most gasses. How am I supposed to know if they are true, let alone write a paper showing how these laws may be at work in our everyday world? Besides, whatever have they to do with potion making? That's what I want to do, study making potions next year."

"Say, can I listen in on the answer?" Emilio added quickly. He saw a way to learn what he didn't know without having to ask similar questions.

Andy tried to explain—Lindsey was grateful since she was already checking over the punctuation of everyone else's English papers. "Look, suppose you put your teapot on the stove and turn on the stove. The stove heats everything up, right?" They nodded. "How do you know when the water is boiling?"

"It whistles silly," Kathy replied.

"Exactly, when the air inside heats up, it expands, doesn't it? If you boil water in a pan, the gas can expand outward filling the room with the steam, the water vapors. Gas expands when it is heated or it tries to do so. In the teapot, it can't expand much or the metal pot explodes. It goes out the little opening as fast as it can; hence, it whistles. Also, the pressure goes up inside the pot because the expanding gasses can't expand as fast as they would like. Pressure cookers won't let any of that air pressure out, so the pressure increases many fold, cooking the food far faster than normal. Car engines work on the same principles. The gas is ignited by the spark plugs; the gas is really hot, but it is forced to stay in the cylinder. Hence, the pressure goes up. The pressure then pushes hard against the top of the cylinder, which is the piston head, forcing it to move. That's how cars get their power. Similarly, if you shrink the volume of the gas much smaller, the pressure goes up. Or if you expand the volume, the pressure goes down. That's how our fireballs work. When they go off, the pressure at the detonation point is huge, naturally, since there are no walls, no metal containers to hold it like in a car engine, so it expands outward to some thirty feet. Poof."

"Oh, I think I see," Kathy tried to see if she was following him. "When I blow into a balloon, I am putting the air inside under a lot of pressure, so the balloon then expands to a large volume. Is that right?"

"Yes, you've got it. See if you can figure out other ways these work around your kitchen and house," Andy suggested. Kathy thanked him and began writing away, making sure that she got all his ideas jotted down so she could refer to them.

"Hum, so that means the higher an airplane goes, the lower the pressure because there is a larger immediate volume for the air to occupy, the higher you go," Emilio noted.

"Well, yes, the air is less dense up there, but you can look at it that way. There is a larger volume of space for the air to occupy the higher you go," Andy thought about this one a bit, wondering if gravity played a role.

"Okay, I think I have a handle on that one, but the next stuff that we covered makes no sense at all," Kathy added. "What's it mean, find the mole weight of water? Moles live under the ground. They dig up yards. Dad had a bunch of moles in our yard, and they made a horrible mess of it until he got rid of them."

Ashley choked, trying not to break out into an outright laugh. Lindsey paused in her work to smile. Andy couldn't believe what he had just heard. Hence, Ashley tried to explain this one to Kathy. "I think that you have the wrong definition of a mole. You are talking about the animal that lives underground. Professor Jasper is talking about something different. What's the formula for water?"

"Oh, really? That might explain why I am so confused. I know that one, H_2O. Two hydrogen atoms and one oxygen atom," Kathy said proudly, confident that she at least knew that answer.

"Yes, now what is the atomic weight of two hydrogen atoms and one oxygen atom?" Ashley asked.

"One plus one plus, er, ah, sixteen I think," Kathy fumbled around. "Eighteen total."

"Good. So when we mix ingredients in chemistry, we use moles, which means that atomic weight measured in grams. One mole of water would be eighteen grams of water. See, it's pretty easy to figure."

"Oh! Oh! Now it is starting to make sense," Kathy replied. "Thanks!"

"I think you had better re-read this week's chapter, Kathy," Ashley suggested. Kathy smiled, knowing that she had to do just that. Otherwise, none of the assignment made any sense at all to her.

Andy changed the topic. "Sure wish our history tours had not been cancelled because of the hurricane. I was starting to enjoy traveling about the country seeing the historic sites.

My sister said that she also got to go visit the Alamo, Gettysburg, Custer State Park to see the buffalos, and even ride a bit on the old Oregon Trail. I guess the Alamo is out— probably still flooded out."

"As long as we don't get sabotaged," Ashley added. "I wonder if we will get to visit any more of them? They do sound interesting. I like getting away from all the studying for a day or so."

"Oh!" Kathy exclaimed. She was reading the pages she was supposed to have learned at the start of the week. "I just realized that I can solve these equations using the math that I learned last week in math class! How convenient. I wonder if Professor Herbert and Professor Jasper know that their things overlap so nicely?"

"They probably arranged it that way," Andy suggested. That reminded him that he still had twenty math problems to do. Hastily, he set to work on those. Indeed, they all were back into the study groove once more. Things had finally gotten back to normal at Bradbury's.

At six, Pam walked with Monique to the Infirmary to meet with her father. While Monique was being examined carefully by her father, Pam sat quietly nearby, her computer on her lap. "Ah, healing very nicely, dear. Only a small follow up surgery is needed. I want to get this raised area carved down a little so your face is symmetrical again. Nothing huge. The bandage will be small. Shall we get started tonight? It will only take an hour. I can stick around tomorrow to make sure all goes well." Monique agreed. Pam gave her an encouraging hug, and Monique followed her father into the next room to prepare.

An hour later, Monique was brought back out of the surgery room. Doctor Caterwall had assisted her father. All had gone well. Monique had only been given a local anesthetic and was chatting with her dad when they came into the waiting room. She had a large bandage on the left side of her face, but she looked calm otherwise. "Dad wants me to spend the night here, just in case," she explained. "I'm doing fine this time, Pam. Why don't you head back to the dorms? I'll come see you in the morning around breakfast time. Dad says I can now wear all the lipstick I want. That's a relief anyway."

Pam thought that Monique was in good spirits. They hugged, and she returned to her room, relieved that all had gone well this time.

Sunday afternoon, Governor Alister made a campus wide announcement. "May I have your attention? The Colorado Avalanche Patrol has come today. They are going to be causing some controlled, small avalanches of the snow pack on our mountain. The idea is to create several smaller ones so that we are not hit with a big one, which may well wipe out our entire school. As you know, the snow pack is huge this year. I tried to have them do it during the Christmas break, but they had to concentrate on the major highways. Now it's our turn."

"Will all those students who can cast a Force Wall, please bundle up and report to me in the Formal Gardens? We will be erecting barrier walls all around the western side of our outer walls to deflect any impending small avalanches. Please, do not Levitate into the skies over Bradbury's. They will be firing their 105mm canon into yonder mountain snow packs. I don't want one of you being hit by flying artillery shells. Meet me in the Gardens in fifteen minutes please. Thank you. That is all."

"Now this is different," Pam commented as she began putting on her warm clothes.

"Well, I'm going to help too," Ashley insisted. "Lindsey, don't tie my right boot. I will slip my foot out and cast with it. I guess I'll also have to cast a lot of Warm spells too." Lindsey did as she asked, though she smiled, glad that her sister was coming too.

A bit later, hundreds of students gathered around the gardens. Once more, Alister used the voice magnification spell to coordinate them. Each of the professors took a portion of the students and organized their spell casting efforts. Soon, hundreds of force walls were erected along the western edge of the outer stone walls. The snow pack was two-thirds up to the top of the walls, however. Lindsey estimated that the snow depth there must be at least ten feet.

"Boom!" The loud sound of the canon firing its shell from the parking lot over the top of the school echoed in the winter wonderland. Shortly afterwards, the shell exploded far up the side of the mountain. Lindsey watched intently, as did hundreds of others. Small at first, the snow began to slide down the slope. Rapidly, it gathered momentum and more snow. Before long, it was a full-fledged avalanche, thundering down the mountainside. Not long after that, it slammed into the force walls and was deflected off to the north, missing the school walls.

Ten more shots were fired in total. Each one caused a small avalanche in its wake. When the last one finally ended, a white wall some twenty feet tall, dwarfing the outer stone wall lay just beyond their wall. It was an incredible sight to see. Many took pictures of it with their cell phones, including Lindsey and Pam.

As they walked back inside, Deiter commented to Lindsey, "I can see the wisdom in this controlled avalanche making. Do you realize what might have happened to our school and us if Nature had unleashed an avalanche using all that snow pack? We'd be wiped out, buried under tons of snow. Incredible."

January was filled with more spell casting classes. Lindsey surmised that there would be more history class trips once the weather warmed up and spring began. Hence, the professors chose this time to pour on the workload, knowing that their student's time would become more limited in a couple of months. This made the workload more bearable.

Unfortunately, their next spell teacher was Professor Janice, whose specialty was charm and enchantment spells. Her bright red lips and covert attitude had not changed. Lindsey remembered the awful times she had had with Professor Janice during her first year here and was not enthusiastic about having her teach these new spells. Pam had blackmailed Professor Janice into leaving Lindsey alone. As they all walked into her first class, Professor Janice gave both girls a long, cold stare.

"We are going to be learning some very difficult spells during these next weeks. Pay attention. Proper wand activation is essential! If you goof these spells, you may cause harm to yourself, and we wouldn't want that, now would we? Open your books to page twenty-five. This week we will spend on one of the easier ones from Grade 4, Bestow an Emotion. With this spell, you can impart into another person any emotion from blind courage, fear, anger, antagonism, warm friendship, tranquility, even utter hopelessness. However, some of you already carry around your own hate and hopelessness, so those might not be such a big deal." She stared at Lindsey and Pam, but soon her eyes floated over Ashley, who chose not to meet her stare.

Ashley did realize that this was the calming spell that Tom had cast upon her just before their track and soccer games. Hence, she concluded this spell was worth knowing well. It was useful.

What an emotional roller coaster week this was. Strong, acute emotions flew about the room. It was easy to stir up hatred in others, especially with Pam and Lindsey towards Professor Janice. All too easily, antagonism appeared in Deiter, Lyle, and Ashley, though such was far more difficult to raise in Emilio and Kathy.

On Friday, both Pam and Lindsey finally realized something about this spell. If a person was normally inclined towards a particular emotion in life, it was easy to exaggerate such, making it temporarily acute. However, if the person rarely displayed that emotion in life, their spells only brought such an emotion on in the mildest form. They both found this an interesting aspect of the spell.

Even PE proved challenging. On Monday Betsy announced to the girls, "The State of Colorado had mandated that in order to get your high school diploma, you must be able to swim ten laps non-stop, make a normal a dive into the pool, and be able to run one mile in at least eight minutes. This is part of your fitness program, mandated by the Presidential Council on Physical Fitness. Neither are Bradbury rules. A fit girl is a healthy girl, as I always say. This is a fine time to accomplish all three goals, so that you will not have to worry about them in future years. We've been swimming for several weeks now, so let's get everyone through the ten laps this week. I know some of you have also been practicing your diving. Hence, next week we will knock that requirement off the list. The third week, we will be running laps in the underground stadium. This way, the boys will not be watching, and you can do what you have to do to pass the state requirement. Okay, everyone into the pool."

"Ten laps?" moaned Ashley. Lindsey grimaced. Ten laps was nothing she couldn't do right now, but for Ashley—now that was a problem.

"Should I say something to Betsy for you Ashley?" Lindsey asked sympathetically.

Again, the raw emotions that had been brought to the surface recently came swelling over her. With all her might, she fought back tears, made all the harder because of the catch in her throat as she tried to answer her sister, "No, I'll try it first."

As they got in the water, Kathy and Amanda prepared to do their ten laps right now. "I don't know if I can do ten laps," Pam whispered.

"Sure you can," Kathy encouraged her. "Just swim along side of me, and we'll get done together." Pam jumped in beside her, and as Betsy blew her whistle, they began their ten laps.

Ashley carefully slid into the water, rolled over onto her back, and began slowly kicking her way along. By the time she had gone some twenty feet, Amanda and several other girls had already reached the other end and were heading back towards her. Cleverly, Ashley had stayed on the other side of the pool so she would not be continuously in the other's way.

What's the matter with me anyway? Last year I would have been angrily insisting that I could do this. I wouldn't take no for an answer. Now I am crying like a baby, but in the water, no one can tell. I'm in grief. I should be fighting but I can't. What's the matter with me? Ashley had no answer for herself. She just kept paddling along.

She heard the cheers from Kathy, Amanda, Lindsey, and Pam. They had just completed their ten laps, though they had to lift an exhausted Pam out of the pool with a Levitate spell. Pam lay on the side gasping for breath; this had been more effort than she had ever done in a pool. *Oh great. I am on my third lap,* she thought to herself. *Maybe my legs will just give out and I can drown.* She kicked harder. *What am I thinking? I should be angrily fighting to get this done!*

The bell sounded, time for lunch. Everyone dashed out as usual, but not Ashley. She doggedly continued to paddle along. Lindsey came over and knelt down. "Are you going to keep going until you get ten laps, Ashley?"

Ashley wanted to cry, but managed to grunt, "Yeh."

"Okay. I will stay here with you and spot for you. I'll be your twin until you get done," Lindsey insisted. She knew the pool rules: no solo swimming ever.

Betsy came over. Her mind was in turmoil as well. Ashley was a Special Needs student. If she merely wrote that notation on her report to the state, Ashley could receive a pass on this PE requirement. Betsy regretted not having mentioned this to the young girl before now. Indeed, she had been giving Ashley no special treatment or favoritism this school year. She had many reasons for doing so, though now, she began to doubt them all. "What lap is she on?" she whispered softly to Lindsey.

"Five, I think," Lindsey answered back.

"Okay, if she gets into trouble, you get her out fast. I will get you two some lunch and bring it here. At this rate, you won't have time to get it yourself." Betsy dashed off to the cafeteria. About a half hour later, she returned with three sack lunches. Quietly, she ate hers and gave Lindsey the other two. Lindsey thanked her and proceeded to munch on hers, all the while keeping watch on Ashley.

The bell sounded for their next class, still Ashley was not done with her laps. Betsy's next class came, and she had to instruct them. However, she wrote out an excuse slip and passed it to Lindsey. "Here, give this to your next professor; it will excuse your absence. Let me know when she finishes. She is the most determined girl I have ever known, Lindsey."

"I know," Lindsey replied, unable to think of anything else to say. Her heart ached for Ashley. However, intellectually, she knew that Ashley was going to succeed no matter what. She just had to.

Fifteen minutes later, Ashley finally touched the end of

the pool; her ten laps were done. Her legs were so exhausted that Lindsey had to cast a Levitate spell to get her out of the water. "Thanks, I don't think I could get out on my own, Lindsey. I made it. Can I just lie here a while?" She fought back tears. Lindsey laid the sack lunch beside her and allowed her private time. Eventually, Ashley began devouring the lunch, an action Lindsey thought was a very good sign.

Betsy, who had observed all this, wisely kept her distance until Ashley had finished eating, and Lindsey at last helped her to her feet. Now she bounced over to the girls. "Well done, Miss Stokes-Compton. Well done indeed. You are the most amazing young woman I've known. You have your state pass on swimming ten laps. Now both of you, go hit the showers. Lindsey has a pass to get you into your next class without any repercussions. Again, Ashley, that was an incredible show of fortitude and determinism. Well done." She heaped praise on the young girl. Still, Ashley fought hard to keep from bawling and managed a smile, though she dared not say a word. With Lindsey supporting her, she headed to the showers. She had chlorine in all her sinuses.

A few minutes later, the two headed off to their spell casting class. Ashley still wasn't talking, so Lindsey continued not to pry. They walked along in silence. Of course, when they walked in, everyone looked at them. Lindsey mouthed, "She passed. Ten laps." Pam and the others nodded and smiled. Pam even gave Ashley a thumbs up sign of victory.

Ashley continued to say nothing about the swim that day, and Lindsey continued to hold back bringing it up. The next day in PE class, Betsy began their diving lessons. However, once she had most of the girls going to it, she came over to Ashley, who was still standing at the side of the pool, trying to get up the nerve to attempt a dive.

"If there is one thing I can tell about a new diver, Ashley, it's when they are scared. You look positively petrified. Am I right?" Betsy spoke softly so that others could not hear her.

Ashley was in a different mood today. Indeed, fear was a very different emotion. "Yes, scared stiff of diving. I can jump in feet first, no problem with that, but to dive headfirst?

I, I, I can't bring myself to do it! What if I head down like a rock and hit the bottom of the pool? I don't have any arms to redirect myself up like the others, and I can't figure out any way to compensate for that."

"I've an idea, Ashley. Come with me." Betsy led her to the deepest end, where the water was over ten feet deep. Lindsey tagged along, unwilling to let Ashley face this alone, though she didn't know what she could really do about it.

"Ashley, you have one thing going for you that none of the other girls have. You are much lighter than they are, no arms. This is a benefit. You will come to the surface more quickly than they will. Here in this depth, there is absolutely no way that you will hit the bottom from a standing dive, no matter whether you have arms or not. A person simply can't get up enough momentum to carry themselves to the bottom from a simple dive from the side. They would have to use their arms to continue to pull themselves downward if they wanted to reach the bottom. Do you follow me?"

"Are you sure?" she asked timidly.

"Absolutely. Now I want you to try it. I am going to have Lindsey dive to the bottom and wait there for you. I want you to make your normal dive and just relax. See how far down you actually go. If I am wrong, Lindsey will keep you from hitting the bottom. I want you to see just how far you really do go down before the water forces you back up. Take a deep breath and let it out. Take another one. Good. Let it out. Now you have extra oxygen in your system. Take another breath, hold it, and dive head first." She resisted the temptation to give Ashley a little push. Good thing that she did.

Ashley saw Lindsey at the bottom holding her breath. She knew that she could not hold it long, so she had to try. She leaned over and did a head first dive, trusting Lindsey and Betsy. Down she went. To her amazement, she only got within a few feet of her sister before she began to rise back up. She was able to bend her back into an arch to help speed it along. Soon she was kicking her way straight up to the surface and rose nearly to her waist above the water before settling back down, treading water. Rolling over, she paddled back to the edge. Lindsey swooped up beside her, a grin on her face.

Since getting out of the pool here was next to impossible, Betsy merely Levitated her up and out. Lindsey joined them. "See, you did it. You have your pass on diving now, Ashley," Betsy said cheerily.

"You are right. I got nowhere near the bottom," Ashley giggled; her fear had been left in the waters.

"Now if you choose to dive from the high dive there, that's nearly twenty-five feet up, then you could hit the bottom if you don't arc your back and reverse course," Betsy explained. "Although the water out there is some twenty feet deep where the divers land, you might be able to touch the bottom if you tried."

Several girls were indeed going off the high dive. Peaches was a life-long swimmer. Ashley watched as she took a long run and jumped onto the end of the board. Peaches rose high into the air and did a back flip before pulling out, hitting the water in a perfect dive. Ashley watched as Peaches slid down deep into the pool and then gracefully rose to the surface, her arms pulling her up in strong strokes. "Fantastic, Peaches," Ashley called out, as Peaches swam close to them and climbed out onto the side.

"It's fun, but you have to watch it carefully. One summer, I hit the water broadside once and cracked three ribs," Peaches replied.

"You are really good. How come Bradbury's doesn't have a swimming or diving team?" Ashley asked.

Betsy replied, though Peaches listened in as well, "We'd love to, but we've never had enough good swimmers to field one team, much less go to the National Swimming and Diving Competitions. Peaches is the best diver I've seen in years, but no one else is anywhere as good as she. There aren't enough good swimmers coming to Bradbury's. Now at Florida State, it's another story. Their boys and girls swimming teams always go to the Nationals."

"Hey, Ashley, watch this next dive; it's for you," Peaches called out. She was the only one using the high dive and soon several others stopped to watch as well. After a bit of climbing, she reached the top. Ashley saw her do just as Betsy had had her do, take several deep breaths before beginning. Peaches raced to the end of the board, leaped high, landed on the very edge of the board. The upswing took her high into the air. Ashley watched as Peaches had her whole body extended doing two and a half back flips before her feet hit the water perpendicular to its surface. She sunk down until her feet touched the bottom, before she pushed off to the surface, and swam over to Ashley. "How's that one?"

"Incredible, you landed the way I prefer to land, feet first," Ashley commented. "I didn't know you could land feet first."

"On some free style jumps, you can land feet first. The main thing about diving is to always, always make sure that you are far enough out from the board so you don't hit it with your body while flipping. I goofed that one once too, hit the board, and broke my arm. God did that ever hurt!"

Not only Ashley, but also many others gained a higher respect for this Black Hall girl this day. Indeed, Ashley continued to chat with Peaches about diving, as they all walked back to the dining room for lunch.

The second week of spell casting with Professor Janice turned out to be even more interesting than the previous one. When they entered the classroom on Monday, three animal cages were sitting in three corners of the room. One held a ferocious Colorado mountain lion. Another held a growling timber wolf, while the third had tiny, close spaced bars with three sidewinder rattlesnakes inside.

"Gosh, whatever are we supposed to do with these wild animals?" Kathy gushed as they all took their seats. Everyone was staring at the animals. Hating snakes with a passion, Emilio moved as far from the snake cage as he could.

Professor Janice made her grand entrance as usual, displaying more than normal delight. "Today, some of you may get injured if you do not follow my instructions to the letter." Lindsey realized that Professor Janice once more was taking enormous pleasure in their discomfort.

"Today, we are going to learn to Charm Animals, wild, vicious animals, and poisonous animals at that. This is a skill that I insist all of you learn perfectly. After all, who knows when you might run into a grizzly bear or a wolf? If you will recall, we had a pack of wolves break into our own dining room not long ago. If you remember, all of you ran like scared chickens back to your dorm rooms."

Lindsey remembered that day vividly. Run? They were ordered to do so by Governor Alister. "Today, we are going to learn how to deal with wild animals and not by killing them. Open your books to page thirty-four. We have lots of work to do this week. Pay particular attention to the proper wand motions for this spell."

"I sure hope she doesn't let them out of their cages!" whispered Kathy. Pam echoed her sentiments, though she doubted very much that Professor Janice would be allowed to do just that. It would be too dangerous to have a wolf or lion running around the campus, she thought.

By Wednesday, Deiter, Lyle, and Peaches were the first students to master the spell, charming all three to their will. By the end of Friday, Emilio finally had overcome his terror of the snakes and had managed to charm the three rattlesnakes, much to his delight.

However, on Thursday, Andy taught Pam something. He had finally gotten all three charmed. True, Professor Janice did not let any of them out of their cages. "Hey, Pam. Here's a trick you can do. When you get the charm going, cast Understand Languages." He winked at her, but did not say more. Pam gave him a strange look, but did as he suggested. Lindsey watched her and saw that she was now speaking in a strange way, more like growls to her ears. Pam had an incredible look on her face, however.

"Wow, you can kind of talk to them! How did you figure this out?" she asked Andy.

"Just a hunch. They are not much on conversation, but the wolf and lion are definitely hungry and do not like being in a cage. Guess that's pretty obvious anyway," he replied. Pam jotted down this variation in her computer notepad. Useful tip, she thought.

The next two weeks were spent creating massive Confusion in Others, Charming Fires to Hypnotize Others, creating an Enhanced Weapon, which had a better chance of striking its target, and Cause Confusion in Others. Indeed, the latter spell wreaked havoc within the classroom, when one by one, the students mastered the spell, causing their classmates to be quite confused. All the while, Professor Janice's red lips smiled, thoroughly enjoying watching the students bungle their way through this spell. Lindsey was now more convinced than ever that Professor Janice was a sadist at heart.

Yet this was nothing as the pleasure Professor Janice had the following week. She taught them to Cause Others to Fumble. Soon the entire classroom became an overlapping zone of fumble spells. The students dropped their wands, books, or tripped. All manner of fumbles occurred, much like an ancient Charlie Chaplin old black and white movie. Soon, in spite of their own fumbling, everyone was roaring with laughter, so much so that it only added to their difficulties. Lyle tried to sit down and missed his chair, landing solidly on the floor. Instead of becoming angry, he roared with mirth even harder. All the while, Professor Janice seemed particularly to enjoy the day.

With that spell mastered, a much more subdued spell was taught: how to turn any mirror into a scrying device with which to read another's surface thoughts. Lindsey purposely "forgot" to remove her anti-scrying pin and ring this day. No way was she going to allow another to read her thoughts.

The week before Valentine's Day, Professor Janice explained. "Today, we are going to learn our last enchantment spell, Create Cottage. With this spell, you can create a very secure, highly inhabitable dwelling. The look and design is of your own choosing. Once the cottage comes into existence, it will last only for about twelve hours for you. However, when you get as proficient as I am with this spell, the dwelling will remain for an entire day. First, we will go over the wand motions, for these are extremely intricate indeed, the most complex of any Grade 4 spell. The command words are also very lengthy and your cottage is being defined by the words you speak."

She spent the entire class period going over the motions and the words, much to everyone's dismay. All wanted to get outside and get trying. Pam's comment was echoed my many,

"For once, she's teaching us something highly useful!"

As they met outside on Friday to continue their practice session, Pam discussed her recent findings with her friends. "I spent all last night in the Library. Guess what I found out? This is the spell they used to build all of our unusual buildings here on campus. Once they were made, some very powerful wizard had to then cast the Make Permanent spell on each building. Now I know why our buildings look the way they do. I wonder who decided what each one was supposed to look like?" Everyone gasped as they realized what Pam had discovered about their school.

"Impressive! Good job," Lindsey complimented Pam, who grinned broadly.

Valentine's Day came and went, without mishap. True, the older students again got to spend the day in Telluride. This time, thirty Security Guards were patrolling the streets, protecting the students. While the boys dutifully allowed their girlfriends to dictate their activities for the day trip, Ashley insisted on spending the morning playing pool with Jim. In the afternoon the movie theater was packed with students, few actually watched the film, naturally.

What was interesting was Pam's excursion. She and Monique walked over to the house in which Dominus had held Pam and the others captive. Pam wanted to see what was so special about this house that a large corporation would want to retain ownership of it. "It's nothing but a run-down house, now badly in need of repair," Monique pointed out. Indeed, the destroyed walls still had not been repaired.

"No one has been in here since we were rescued," Pam concluded. "Look at the dirt and trash on the floor, still there. It must be abandoned. This doesn't make sense, Monique. Why would a big corporation hold on to this dilapidated house? Not even repairing it? Honestly, I bet the city council will be soon condemning it and tearing it down."

"Who did you say owned it?"

"Mac Fluide Enterprises," Pam replied.

"Never heard of them. I'll see if I can find out more about them," Monique declared. "Movie time?" Pam grinned, the two headed to the theater.

That evening the dance was held. The girls dressed up for the affair and thoroughly enjoyed themselves. As the four finally entered their room, the strong flagrance of the many flowers only added to their day. Indeed, Andy, Jim, Monique, and Henry had all sent them bouquets. Of course, Pam sent Monique twelve long stemmed roses as well.

The day of romance ended when Pam pointed out that next week they would be getting their new necromancy based spells from Delius Dogs. That sobered them all up at once.

On Monday, they entered the Hall of Necromancy, more than a little anxious. Delius, dressed in his black robes, paced the floor around his classroom. "I know that some of you do not like the dark arts. However, let me point out that because of the dark arts, there are two less Death Stalkers walking the land." He was referring, of course, to the men he had slain during the rescue of Alister.

"How effective do you believe that you would be at attacking and defending against a Death Stalker if you were deathly ill, eh?" Many made comments to the effect that they would not be.

"Of course you wouldn't. One of the spells we are about to learn is to Cause Disease in another person." Half of the class gasped. Lindsey protested at once. She would never want to cause another person to become quite ill. Even Pam quailed at that thought. Deiter, on the other hand, thought this could be a useful way to lessen a Death Stalker's skill.

"However, class, we are not going to go around making each other deadly ill. Heavens no. Poor Doctor Caterwall is ill equipped to handle a hundred sick children. If I did that, Alister would fire me." Lindsey giggled certain that he would do just that. Maybe they were only going to pretend to cast this spell, she hoped.

"No, in as much as it is possible, I believe that any good wizard or witch must be able to undo what they have caused. While it is not always possible to do so, as in the case of a Disintegrate spell, with disease, it is possible. Hence, as you learn to Cause Disease in another person, you will also be learning how to Cure Disease as well. For each disease that you cause here in class, I expect that you will also be curing that disease. Bad marks will be awarded to the person who fails to cure what they cause. Is that understood?"

While everyone nodded perfunctorily, Lindsey wondered what the effect of a bad mark actually was. Delius did not say and did she have the stomach to ask.

By the end of the week, the classroom was filled with all manner of stenches from rotting flesh, abscessed sores, and the like. Students looked like and felt like they were on death's door from the awful diseases their classmates had caused their bodies to contract. Yet, one by one, each disease was shortly thereafter cured. Only Lyle failed once to be able to cure what he had caused. Lindsey watched to see the effects of the bad marks he received, but other than a sound scolding by Delius, she saw no other ill effects.

"Well, I think that is it a very good thing that we have learned to cure diseases," Kathy proclaimed during Friday night's study hall session. Pam could only agree with her. "While I don't intend to go around making people sick, now at least I can cure and help them."

The next week proved quite different. Suck Life Force was the spell for the next five days. Deiter excelled at this spell. Lindsey did try it, however, but once she observed the visible impact the spell had on her partner, Ashley, she vomited and refused to do it again. For the few hours of the spell's duration, Ashley felt horribly weak, just sat around like a zombie, and could not cast a spell more difficult that Grade 0. At least, all the students successfully cast this spell one time. Many, like Lindsey and Ashley, decided never to do that spell again. Its effects could not be removed by a Dispel Magic spell, only time or bed rest allowed the person to recover.

Deiter did his best to try to convince Lindsey that this would be a useful spell against Death Stalkers. "Look, if they are attacking you, trying to kill you, wouldn't it make sense to cast this one, to weaken them allowing you to capture them?" He added that last for her sake. He would follow Bill's lead and just kill outright the Death Stalker, but he figured Lindsey would want no part in actually killing someone. He was right.

By Friday, Deiter had convinced many at least to

practice this spell, just in case they ran into a Death Stalker who was attacking them. He felt that he had gotten at least a dozen students over their hurdles with this spell and took some pride in having done so. Even Lindsey had agreed to practice it more. Deiter also realized that there was a huge gulf between himself and Lindsey. She was a Dispeller, not an Eliminator, while he greatly desired to be just like Bill West, a powerful Eliminator. Nevertheless, Deiter had very strong feelings for Lindsey and Ashley and Pam and Amanda. He wanted them to be able to protect themselves better from Death Stalker attacks—hence, his personal pride when he finally got all four to continue working with the spell.

During these weeks, in PE class, Pam ran into another hurdle, the mile run. When she finished her first try, she thought that she was dying, so awful her body felt. Fourteen minutes was way over the eight minutes that she needed to pass. Of course, Amanda, Lindsey, and Ashley passed on their first attempt, with Amanda coming in with a time of 5:30, Lindsey only seconds behind her and Ashley, a half minute later.

Kathy fared little better, her first attempt fell well short at thirteen minutes. "I hate running!" she declared. "I want to look pretty, not run my feet off!"

Ashley felt sympathy for the two. She had more experience than any other at facing enormous physical hurdles. "Look, if I can do it, so can both of you. Now all you need to do is keep at it. Each day, we will have a go at it. I will run with you both. The important thing is not to overdo it, as you did today. We just go at a speed you can handle, that's all. Bit by bit your bodies will get better and better at running longer distances. Soon you will be able to do it in the eight minutes. Trust me. I know you can do it."

Pam and Kathy had little other choice than to trust Ashley. Indeed, each PE class, Ashley jogged alongside of the two. Since they were both about equally unskilled and unfit in running longer distances, Ashley correctly had them slow way down at the start, finding a pace that they could endure for the whole mile.

"Well, I am not dying," Pam commented after the first

day. "Going slower, I can at least do it without killing myself."

"Me too, I don't feel so horrible," Kathy added.

For the next few weeks, Ashley kept at it with Lindsey joining them as well. Over half the class still had not met the passing standard; this Betsy fully expected. While the boys routinely mostly passed on their first try, every class of girls she had taught did not. In fact, it was rare to have any pass on their first attempts as had Lindsey and her friends. Although she had not told her students, this mile run was the most challenging of all the PE tests that they had to pass for their diplomas.

After working on running for three weeks, Pam and Kathy, with Ashley and Lindsey at their sides, crossed the finish line. Betsy punched her stopwatch and announced, "Pam, Kathy, you've passed, just under eight minutes. Good going." Both girls were elated.

"Thank you Ashley! I never, ever thought I would be able to do this. I was resigned to not getting my diploma," Pam confided. Suddenly, she had a revelation about Ashley. Many things were incredibly difficult for her to accomplish, yet, given time and practice, the young girl had worked out ways to succeed. In a flash, Pam now understood Ashley far better than ever before. She was eternally grateful for all the assistance, help, and encouragement that Ashley had given her, in effect, getting her through it. Now she realized that Ashley had no one to do the same for her when she had a difficult time mastering something. She had to do it all by herself. Pam marveled at just how much self-determination and self-drive her dear friend actually had within her.

Things began improving for Kathy and her chemistry class as well. In study hall one night, she let out a shriek, disturbing everyone. "Finally, I've learned something useful! Now I know why milk is homogenized! Now things are making sense to me. Perhaps this chemistry stuff is useful after all."

"What do you mean?" Lindsey asked.

"Well, milk has a lot of fat globules in it. They take and break down those large globules into very tiny ones. Now the fat globules take a very long time to join back together, longer than the jug stays full," she explained. "If milk isn't homogenized, then very quickly those globules combine and float to the surface, where it's called cream."

"Oh, so that's why our milk tastes so different," Lindsey replied.

"I wondered why ours does taste different," Ashley added. "Ours comes straight from the cows."

"Yes, and if we don't drink it quickly, cream forms on top. That's why we milk each day, just what we can use in a day or so," Lindsey added.

"Right, but they also add a lot of Vitamin D to it too, since we don't get much sunshine in the winter time," Kathy added. Pam smiled; finally, Kathy was finding chemistry useful.

Chapter 20—Of Trips and Sports

When March came, they discovered that the many field trips to visit historic places in the country had been rescheduled. The heavy snows had forced postponement of a number of them during the late fall. Professor Elaine announced, "During March, we are going to try to catch up on all our US field trips. Come April, many of you will become active in sports again. In May, besides all the final exams, Yellow Hall will again be competing at the Nationals. Hence, if we are going to take our trips, they must be made in March."

"Beginning this Friday, our trips are on once more. Each Friday, we will visit another famous site. I have cleared this with your other professors, and they have agreed to adjust their assignments and due dates accordingly. Hence, you will not return overloaded with work to get done furiously, but that does mean you will have to work even harder during the week nights."

First, the class visited the Alamo. While everywhere remnants of the massive flooding from the fall were evident, they had an educational trip there. An excursion to Gettysburg and the battlefield came next. Custer Park in South Dakota followed, allowing them to see buffalo and to get an education on the many historical uses these massive herds had played in historical times. Their last field trip was even more unusual.

They spent a day traveling the old Oregon Trail that the early pioneers followed out west. A historical troupe gave one-day excursions. Essentially, the bus unloaded all the students at the embarkation point. Groups of six climbed into one of the many Conestoga wagons. Their guides, dressed in period costumes, then drove them along this portion of the restored trail for the day. At four, they halted and helped prepare a replica evening meal that these early settlers may have eaten. After supper, they climbed back onto their bus to head home. All had a feeling for what the early settlers had to endure to travel thousands of miles across the country.

During March, in spell casting class, it was all review.

The objective was to get everyone ready to pass their final exam on their Grade 4 spells before the hectic times of April arrived. Indeed, by the first week in April, everyone had finished the test. One subject down, the rest remained. At first, Pam thought this was a very practical idea, to get this subject completely finished so they would all have more time to get their work done in the remaining subjects. However, a week later, she felt badly that she was not getting to learn more new spells. On the other hand, no one else shared her dismay.

On April 1, the group was studying in the study hall their dorm. Jim came in and spied Ashley, who was sitting off to one side. She needed more room to work with her feet. Jim came up to her and said, "Ashley, I just came to warn you that someone has let those rattlesnakes of Professor Janice's loose in Yellow Hall. I thought I saw one come in here. Have you seen it?" He looked quite serious indeed. Ashley jumped up and began looking around her feet for the dangerous reptile.

The second that she reacted, Jim called out, "April Fool!"

"Why you rascal! I nearly peed my pants! Now you've gone and done it!" she called out playfully, as everyone suddenly realized what Jim had done. She jumped up and began to chase after him, trying either to give him a swift kick in his rear or to bump into him. For a minute, the two dashed about the study hall, Jim, careful to keep the tables between him and Ashley, all the while laughing. At last, she faked one direction, went the other, and banged in to him. He gave her a quick kiss and ducked out the door.

"Honestly, that's my brother!" declared Amanda, totally annoyed with Jim's behavior.

"Oh that's okay, Amanda. He got me good. I wasn't expecting it," Ashley chuckled, finally getting back to her seat. Amanda noted that she continued to smile for some time after that, and she calmed down about Jim's joke. Lindsey realized that these two were quite the playful pair.

April again brought the track meets and the soccer matches back to the forefront. With the incredible volume of snow, the playing field was soggier and muddier far later in time than it had been in previous years. Tom had cleverly arranged their last soccer match for the end of April, figuring they would have a dry field by then. Their first track meet would be a week earlier, but the track itself was always in good shape, once the snow had been removed. The other teams began their matches earlier. Black Hall took on Blue Hall the first Saturday in April. It was one giant mud puddle, with patches of snow still covering portions of the field. Lindsey found the game more humorous than a serious match, as everyone slipped and fell constantly in the mud. Black Hall won, but every player was caked in mud as the final bell sounded.

With Nationals coming up the first weekend in May, Tom had his runners out for practice sessions every Saturday morning in April. "Gang, we always got beaten because we had to run so many races in one day. So my plan is to run four races each Saturday to get us better used to what we are going to face in May." He had to explain how the Nationals worked to Ashley and Andy, however.

"We start out with sixteen teams, sixteen schools. Eight races later, the field is down to eight teams. We've raced once, you see. Next, four more races eliminate half of these, and we will have raced a second time. Now the four winners race again and this is our third race of the day. Then, at night, the losers race again for third place. After that, the winners race for first place, that's our fourth race of the day." None of this would be a problem for Andy, who only had a very short sprint to do. For Ashley, it would also not be much of a problem, she only had to cover a quarter of a mile each race. No, the long distance racers took the brunt of the exertion.

Tom also had another idea in mind. He wanted the inexperienced Ashley to become more comfortable running the races. His plan was for her to get in four or five races before the Nationals came. That way she might be more comfortable with the whole thing.

Phillip Royston assembled his Black Hall track team for the big race against Yellow Hall. "We have them beat this year! That idiot Tom has had them all out there racing this morning. I watched them; they ran the equivalent of at least three races already. When they take the field in a couple of minutes, they are going to be completely pooped out. This time, Black Hall will show them that we are better and faster than they are!" His team members cheered, and they all headed out onto the field, certain of a track victory over Yellow Hall.

Andy lost the short distance sprint seconds after the meet began. However, Fern flew down the finish line, taking the mile race from Black Hall. Even though this was their effectively fourth race of the day, the twenty mile racers pretended this was their last Nationals race. Amanda crossed the finish line a hundred feet ahead of Phillip, ensuring an undefeated track record for Yellow Hall this year. Tom was very pleased with the outcome, but Phillip was not.

Their soccer match, normally played on dry grass, took place in the incredibly muddy field. As with the previous games, it was kick, slip, fall, and slide in the mud for one and all. However, unlike the nastiness of Black Hall, the Brown Hall players were out for fun. Even though the game was trying, everyone had a good time, including Ashley, who fell more frequently than anyone else. Under these conditions, she was not remotely upset by her performance. No, she was beginning to get worried about the Nationals, little more than a week away.

Midway through April, Emilio became very excited. He was going on a desert survival field trip with Professor Jasper Jones and his wife, Lillian Angel. For the weekend, they were going to be camping in the Great Sand Dunes National Park in southern Colorado. He'd never been there and was quite pleased to get to go on a camping trip.

None knew that the Librarian Lillian Angel or the professor were so into primitive camping. Pam saw her librarian in a new light now. Since Emilio had no real camping gear, Jasper loaned him what he would need, and Friday night after supper, he proudly showed everyone his borrowed sleeping bag, backpack, and gear. "Be careful you don't run into snakes," Pam cautioned him.

"Have fun and take along a bag of Oreo's," Lindsey suggested, knowing his penchant for snacks.

"Right here," he gaily produced a large bag from inside his pack. "Soda's too," he added. The girls laughed; some desert survival trip. Undaunted, he headed off to join the professor, who was leaving at seven p.m. "Cya Sunday suppertime."

"Bet he doesn't come back that cheery," Amanda teased.

He returned tired, dirty, and a bit sore, but looked very happy. He'd discovered some rugged hills nearby and had brought back numerous rocks for further study. He also had taken over a hundred photographs with his cell phone and promised to show them to everyone as soon as he got them organized.

The third week in April also brought Lindsey her greatest Dispeller challenge yet. Delius explained, "On Saturday morning, you are to report to the Hall of Necromancy, main lecture hall. We will engage in a mass mock battle to test your skills. I need to see just where we are at in your training." Lindsey agreed, though she had no idea what he meant. On Saturday morning, she walked into the large lecture hall. She'd never had a class in this large room and was unfamiliar with it.

At first, she thought that perhaps she had made a mistake. Deiter Cross was there along with Lyle, Peaches, and eight other Black Hall students, including Phillip Royster and Henry Freeze. Professor Delius walked in right on time, "Ah, I see everyone is here. Lindsey, we are going to have a mock battle. The scenario is that you have run into a group of ten Death Stalkers. You have your staff, and they have their wands. They are out to get you. Your task is to stay alive. When you decide that you need to absorb a particular spell, point your staff in the direction of the spell caster and say 'Absorb' and I will note it down. I'm the referee in this mock battle."

"Now you Black Hall students, your task is to kill Miss Barron here. However, you are not, I repeat *not*, to use any spells above Grade 4 on her. She only knows spells through Grade 4. Her test is only on these beginning spells at this time. Is that understood, Phillip, Henry?" Both nodded, though Lindsey saw them both grinning. She steeled herself. This was going to be an awful challenge, but she was not about to give them any satisfaction seeing her flinch from it.

"Now when you cast, you must not, I repeat must *not*,

say the final command word. No spells are going to be actually cast or absorbed in here. I don't want any of you to get hurt, and I don't want my lecture hall incinerated in a ball of fire. I don't want sticky webs all over the seats. Do not actually cast any spells. I will be noting down what spells each of you cast and at what time. Is this understood? Remember, your objective is to eliminate Lindsey, if you can. Honestly, at ten to one odds, you should not find this too difficult a challenge."

"Now then, for the benefit of my Black Hall students, who have never been associated with a Dispeller, I need to explain what Miss Barron will be doing." He winked at Lindsey, though she had no idea what he had in mind. Her thoughts were all on trying to figure out how she could stay alive against ten of them.

"A Dispeller's job is to absorb or counter various spells so that the others in her party can survive and achieve their goal. Do not expect that she will be trying to absorb every spell that you cast. Expect that she will have some defensive spells up at the start. Realistically, you would not know in advance what protections she might have or choose to use during the battle. It is up to you to try and work those out for yourselves and then counter them if you can."

"Further, she has a Staff of Power, which can shoot spells for her. You would not know what those might be. Again, she is free to use them at any time as well. One caution, though all Staves of Power had the ability to Teleport their owner, Lindsey is forbidden from using that spell, it is above her grade level. I know that this is a bit unrealistic. Yet, she will not be using that spell. Finally, no physical contact please. We are not here to beat up Lindsey; rather this is a test of her spell recognition abilities and her quick thinking reactions to spells coming at her. Any questions?"

"Oh yes, if one of you shoots a Dispel Magic, I will adjudicate what its effect is and notify the party involved what, if anything, is gone."

"Professor, what about distances?" asked Phillip.

"Assume the distance is exactly what you see in here. She will begin at the entrance door. You ten begin against the far windows in any grouping that you desire. Oh yes, one more thing. This whole exercise is being recorded for future study and reference by both Miss Barron and me. With eleven of you acting at once, I may not be able to keep up with your pace of action. Hence, I am recording it so I can review it and make sure that I missed nothing. By the way, in case you are interested, I am told that this exercise has not been conducted here at Bradbury's for fifteen years. All of you should feel quite honored at the chance to participate in this exercise."

"Professor, what about time limits? How long do we have to get her?" Henry asked, snickering at Lindsey.

"Actual combats are really quite short, are they not, Miss Barron?" Professor Delius nodded toward her. "When we were rescuing Alister, we came under an extensive attack both from land and sea. How long did it last, would you say, Miss Barron?"

Lindsey had no idea but made a wild guess. "Maybe five minutes or so. Not very long; it went very quickly."

"Eight minutes to be very precise from start to finish, which left three Death Stalkers quite dead. Your time limit is five minutes. If Miss Barron can fend all ten of you off for that long, you may presume that her associates will have either killed or captured you by that time."

Henry gave him a dirty look, but Deiter nodded and said, "Yes, it went incredibly fast, honestly it did!" Delius smiled. Deiter had performed very well, gaining valuable information during the attack, verifying that Dominus was present on the ship and controlling the Death Stalkers.

"Remember, the Dispeller is not particularly out to slay you, only to protect those around her who are after your hide. Are we ready?" Everyone took their places.

At the entrance door, Delius asked her what defensive spells she would have cast upon herself. Lindsey replied with the two she usually cast, the Skin of Stone and the Major Invulnerability staff spell. "I usually insist my party members also have these cast upon themselves as well, sir."

Delius duly noted them on his clipboard. He pressed a record button and called out, "Start." At once, the action began. Just as she suspected, Henry and Phillip immediately tried to order the others to go to certain places and tried to order them to cast certain spells, all of which only created an initial confusion among her attackers, slowing them down. Instead of having ten spells shot at her at one time, they were coming at her quite staggered.

Two shot Magical Missiles, which she ignored completely. She absorbed the Sticky Web spell that Deiter cleverly shot at her. She had a moment and cast Invisibility on herself at which point, the inside lights went out, startling everyone. Lindsey moved carefully from her original location, trying not to bang into too many chairs. The others made a considerable noise. Delius called out, "You cannot see her now."

"Dispel Magic!" shouted Phillip. The lights came back on as three volleys of Balls of Fire landed where she had been located. Again, she ignored these. She had an idea now.

"Darkness," she called out. Delius turned out the lights once more, and Lindsey moved her location once more. Peaches cancelled this one, while Deiter shot more webs to the location where Lindsey had been. She was not there as the lights came back on. Phillip shot a cloud of poisonous gas her way; this she absorbed. A Forget and an Acid Arrow came at her; again, she ignored these, continuing to move about, while the others had now fanned out around the opposite side of the room.

Someone shot a Hold Person spell at her, while another sent a Flaming Arrow at her. Again, she ignored these. Deiter tried to cast the Phantasmal Killing spell at her, knowing how terrified they had all been in class when they learned this one. Again, she ignored it because her protective barrier countered it. Phillip tried a different approach; he shot Grabbing Tentacles at her, attempting to bind her up. This she absorbed because it potentially could interfere with her unseen companions.

Henry got wise and decided to shoot a Dense Fog spell covering her area, making it impossible for her and her party to see anything. This she Dispelled. Phillip tried to drop an Ice Wall on top of her, so she absorbed this one to avoid having her companions harmed. Since the others were now getting a bit too close to her, she shot another Darkness spell and immediately cast the new improved Invisibility spell they had learned this year. Using this darkness time, she maneuvered close to the right hand wall, where she knew Phillip and Henry were located.

While several others hastily cast their Dispel Magic spells to undo the darkness, she shot her web spell over the area where Henry and Phillip were located. Instantly, Delius called out, Henry and Phillip are out of the action. They are entrapped in sticky webs. The lights came back on, and they saw Lindsey was now standing close to the two sixth year students. At once, she cast Darkness, and hastily vacated that location; the lights turned back on as Peaches cast her Dispel Magic, which undid Lindsey's Darkness, but left the two boys still tied up in the sticky webs.

"Mirror Images, please," Lindsey signaled Delius.

"You now see five Lindseys. If you attack her, please identify which one by number," Delius called out.

"Brilliant. I should have thought of that one myself!" exclaimed Deiter. "Dispel Magic, Lindsey's area. Mirror Images: myself," he called out.

"You see only one Lindsey, but you see five Deiters," Delius reported.

Again, a large number of Magical Missile spells and Acid Arrow spells came at her, which she ignored. Lyle and another two headed to help Phillip and Henry, casting five Dispel Magic spells before the two became free once more. Deiter cast a series of Dispel Magic spells on Lindsey.

"Lindsey your skin feels normal; your globe is gone."

Hastily, she recast her globe and then her stone skin spells. Just in time, Deiter began shooting Magical Missiles at her again, and she barely got her protections back up in time.

"Time's up," called out Professor Delius.

"But sir, I've just now figured out how we can kill Lindsey," Deiter protested. Phillip and Henry looked very, very upset. This had not played out at all well, nothing like they had imagined.

"Well done, Miss Barron. You managed to survive five minutes against these ten." Lindsey felt a surge of pride. Somehow, she had done it. "Would you like to share some observations with us, Miss Barron?"

She was on the spot. "Er, do you mean point out what they ought to have done? I'm not sure what you are asking."

"Okay, before you answer that, Mister Cross, you just said that you figured out how to kill Miss Barron. Would you like to elaborate?"

"She's got good defensive spells on her. I just figured out how to get rid of them. Now all we have to do is to coordinate our efforts, work together. Have half of us cast Dispel Magic spells, while the other half cast Magical Missiles or other damage causing spells right after the Dispels go, that way she doesn't have time to recast her defensive spells," Deiter observed.

"Excellent, excellent observation, Mister Cross. Precisely so. She is particularly vulnerable to the spell sets you have to work with *only* when her two protective spells are gone," Delius replied. "Is that so, Miss Barron?"

"Yes, I got very worried at that point and barely got them back. I goofed there. I ought to have gotten the Invulnerability spell back up first, not the Skin of Stone, sir. Honestly, I thought you all would have wiped me out in less than a minute, but you acted just like the Death Stalkers that I have faced. They never act together. They all run about just as you all did, never working together as a team," Lindsey stated what she felt was the case.

"Precisely said," Delius acknowledged her.

"Well, this was the most fun that I have had in a long time," Peaches volunteered. "I learned more in these five minutes about *real* use of spells than I have in a whole year of school! Please, we ought to have more of these mock attack sessions!"

"Hey, I'm with her!" Lyle added. "I actually had to think about what to do and that slowed me way, way down!"

"Professor, don't you think that we ought to be getting some training in attacking and defending," Deiter added. "Since the Death Stalkers are running wild out there, isn't it in our best interests to get more practical, hands on type of training like this session? I mean, it took me five minutes to figure out how to get to Lindsey. Five minutes! In the real world, I might not last five minutes, if others were not Dispelling for me." Many agreed with him; a chorus of 'yeh's' went up. Delius smiled.

"I will bring this up with Governor Alister. Yes, I would prefer that everyone undergo similar training, now that Dominus is running wild around the country. While it is too late to do anything about it this term, maybe I can convince him to do more of this next school year." His comment brought a loud round of "yes's" from his students.

Phillip raised an objection, "Professor, it was not a real fight. Honestly, the Death Stalkers aren't going to be limited to puny Grade 4 spells! They are going to be using Disintegrate spells, like I would be using, to say nothing of all the other Grade 5 and 6 spells."

"Yes, yes, that is very true, Phillip. However, this was only a test of Miss Barron's skill in handling up to Grade 4 spells. Assuming she continues her Dispeller training here, we will be working on spells that she does not yet know how to cast. She's only finishing Dispeller Theory I, Phillip. After all, how many of you would have been able to pick and choose just the correct spells to absorb out of all those that you all cast at her? In my opinion, she chose to absorb the correct ones, ones that would have caused problems for her companions. You see, a Dispeller has but split seconds to make that call. She has to determine correctly what spell is about to come her way, decide to absorb it with her staff, and then get the command to the staff in time for it to activate. With ten of you going at it simultaneously, this is quite a chore."

"Yet, Phillip is correct. The Dispeller will always be facing the casting of spells of which they are not familiar. Decisions must be made about those as well, all in a split second, but that is covered in Dispeller Theory II."

"Wait a minute," Deiter exclaimed. "You mean that a Dispeller, who doesn't know what spell is being cast at them, can somehow know that they could ignore it or need to absorb it?"

"Yes, Mister Cross, indeed, yes. There are many clues that are broadcast as the spell is being cast. The Dispeller has but tiny fractions of a second in which to observe those clues and make a rational decision to act or not to act. In Dispeller Theory I, Miss Barron has learned to recognize what spell is coming by both its beginning words and by the wand motion accompanying the spell. It grieves me that none of you ten thought to cast a Silence spell over Miss Barron so that she could not hear you speak your command words. Then, she would have been forced to rely solely upon your wand motions. Had I been among you, that would have been the first spell that I cast, knowing that I was facing a Dispeller, that is."

Deiter nodded; he was learning key information today. Yet, Peaches said what many of these Black Hall students had just come to realize, "Golly, being a Dispeller is incredibly hard! I thought that they were just glorified users of Dispel Magic, that is, until today. I can't identify a single spell until I have heard all the words, and, by then, the spell has been cast! I'd never be able to identify anything just by watching wand motions. However can she do it?"

"I've been drilling her an hour every day for the last seven months; she'd better be able to do it," Professor Delius teased her, while answering Peaches query. "By the way, Henry, Phillip, I hope that you two have learned a valuable lesson here today. Had this been a real combat, both of you would very likely have been slain by Bill West, assuming that you were Death Stalkers. Once she had you entangled, he would have finished you off with a Disintegrate spell. I saw him do just that during the last battle, blasted a hole clean through the heart of Allen Hall." Both boys looked very antagonistic, Lindsey thought.

"It's not just a nice, fun game that Dominus is playing out there. People are being killed or badly wounded. Professor Mary Ann's Diviner friend nearly lost her life to the Death Stalkers. As you also know, Monique of Red Hall was horribly disfigured and nearly killed by one of our ex-Black Hall students. I helped train Larry Sacks, but he has brought more shame on Bradbury's Black Hall than anyone in over a score of years. Yes, we Black Hall's pride ourselves on our importance, our strength, our logic, our might, but we don't go around bashing in the faces of pretty young girls and trying to murder innocent women and children like Larry did. Had he not been eliminated, I would have asked Governor Alister for a short leave of absence so that I could go bring Larry to justice myself! Larry disgraced not only me but every last one of you Black Hall students."

"Yeh, but what if Dominus is right? What if it *is* time that the strong and powerful rule the world instead of the wimps?" growled Phillip. "Everyone knows the politically correct crowd has nearly brought the world to ruin with their do-good drivel. The so-called Democratic platform of doling everything out free to those who won't work for a living and take it from those of us who are strong to give to the weak has made the US a second-class country. It didn't work in Sweden; it didn't work in Canada; yet the idiots who have been running the US haven't a clue. Maybe it *is* time for a change."

"Maybe it is time for a change, Phillip. I won't argue that point with you, because I agree with your analysis. However, Dominus is not the desired change. He has only his own self-interests at heart; he cares nothing for his minions, the Death Stalkers. They are just his henchmen, there to do his bidding, to be discarded when they are no longer useful. Mark my words, if Dominus gains control of this country, the US will plummet into a "third world" status overnight. The world saw just such a leader over a century ago; Herr Hitler was his name, leading his 'superior men' to world domination, but in reality, he led them to their complete destruction. Perhaps that would be a good assignment for all Black Hall students, now that I think about it. Thank you Phillip, you've given me an idea for the best educational assignment ever." Phillip growled even more.

Lindsey didn't need extra-sensory perceptions to read Phillip's mind. If ever there was a student leaning towards full support of Dominus Malefic, it was Phillip. Every counter-word of Professor Delius cut into him. Anger and antagonism seethed in his mind; his reddish face, an open book.

"Now then, would anyone like to watch the video of our exercise today?" Delius asked. Nearly everyone did, only Phillip stormed out of the room. Deiter took a seat beside Lindsey, while Peaches sat quietly on her other side.

"I was slow to throw back counter-spells," Lindsey admitted. "I ought to have given you more troublesome spells at first, you know, stalled for time. I was just too nervous. Honestly, I was a little frightened of making a complete fool of myself in front of all of you."

"I know. I could tell you were nervous, Lindsey," Deiter replied. "I didn't say anything because that might have only made things worse for you, but I didn't hold back, though. I just didn't catch on until the time was up. Another minute and I'd have had you." He grinned.

Lindsey smiled, "I know. I almost panicked there. I put the wrong spell up first."

"You are correct, Miss Barron, you ought to have given them more spells to counter, especially at the beginning," Delius broke in, as he sat behind them. "I admit, the next time we do this, I need a better way to handle Invisibility spells. Turning the lights out just didn't work at all well and got confused with Darkness spells. Ah, here we go."

Right away, everyone began to see all their bumblings and fumblings. Not one student failed to make comments about what they goofed up, did wrong, failed to do, didn't even think of during those five minutes. Professor Delius merely smiled for the five minutes of the video playback. He did not need to critique any of the participants, for each was seeing quite clearly their own mistakes. Yet he also saw just how valuable this mock battle session was from an educational point of view. He certainly wanted his Black Hall students fully equipped to deal with the harsh, real world out there when they graduated, and he saw this as a valuable tool to that end. Nothing would stop him from getting just such a program installed in their curriculum next term.

A half hour later, Deiter, Lindsey, and Peaches walked through the tunnels together, heading for their rooms. "I don't trust Phillip any longer," Deiter commented. "Did you see the way he reacted to Professor Delius?"

"Yeh, well he didn't even stick around to watch our pathetic performance either," Peaches added.

"I'm going to keep my eyes on him," Deiter stated flatly. "He might even be feeding Dominus information on us students. I wouldn't put it past him."

"Yes, but what would Dominus want to know about us?" Lindsey asked naively. "We are just high school students." Neither had an answer to her question.

Chapter 21—The Tip

Around nine o'clock, Jake and Milo had left their dorm room, which they shared with Phillip and Henry to visit the Library. Henry was working on his latest paper, and Phillip was messing around with his computer. Something attracted Henry's attention. At first, he couldn't figure out what, and then he realized it was Phillip. Phillip hated computers and was rarely on his. Yet, there he was typing away, two-fingered style.

Quietly, Henry got up and moved behind Phillip to see what he was so keenly working on; it was an email. More than just an email, the receiver was Dominus! Henry suddenly was all eyes. He read over Phillip's shoulder.

In answer to your query, it was the third year student Ashley Stokes who divined that Millicent Prague was near death, and a bit later, I'm told, she also raised the alarm about Alister being in a life and death situation. She is a pathetic case, no arms, barely able to cast any spells at all. Stupid girl thinks she can run and is on Yellow Hall's track team. You can meet her at the Nationals in a week if you like. I wouldn't bother with her; she's a hopeless, pathetic cripple.

I just wanted to let you know that I support your Manifesto. Clearly, it is time for the strong finally to lead this country. I hope to be part of the strong leaders one day very soon.

Sincerely,

Phillip Royster

"You can't send that!" Henry butted in.

"Why the heck not? Everyone knows it was that Ashley bitch who did the divination, not Professor Mary Ann. It's common knowledge around here," Phillip countered, anger rising in his voice. "Besides, how dare you read my email? If you tell anyone about this, I swear I'll tell Dominus and ask him to have the Death Stalkers kill your whole family!"

Henry, who had been friendly with Phillip for the past six years, was taken aback. He didn't know quite how to respond. "But Phillip, haven't we been friends? What's gotten in to you? It's me, Henry Freeze. We're buddies."

"Yeh, well, whose side are you on anyway? After that fiasco with Dogs, I'm not so sure anymore. Just don't say nothing, and nothing will happen," he growled and hit the Send button. Henry backed away quietly, highly disturbed, but what could he do? Phillip had already hit the Send button; nothing could stop the email, not now anyway.

Henry went back to his papers, but only fiddled with them. For some reason, his stomach felt rather funny, almost nauseous. He decided to go down to the cafeteria and get something for it. "Back in a while. Upset stomach. Want anything from the vending machines, Phil?"

"No, I'm heading to the showers." Henry ducked out of his dorm room and headed for the dining room, where the vending machines lined one wall, supplying late night snacks. However, when he got there, he felt even less like eating. He popped two quarters in and retrieved the steaming cup of coffee. He sat down in the deserted room.

"What the heck do I do now? Darn Phillip anyway! Well, he probably didn't tell Dominus anything that he didn't know already. We all know Stokes was the diviner behind Alister's rescue. If I tell, would Phillip actually follow on through with his threat? Surely not. But what if he did? Perhaps I should just keep my mouth shut. I don't like them anyway; she is always hanging around Lindsey's crowd. Fools with fools."

Henry's stomach felt even worse with the coffee in it. "Maybe I just ought to sleep on it. Tomorrow's another day. It's not like Dominus is going to come to Bradbury's after the helpless kid anyway." With that rationalization, he headed back to his room and went to bed far earlier than normal, nursing his stomach. Henry slept ill that night, tossing and turning. Twice he awoke in a cold sweat. He felt like he was burning up and then freezing. Around four in the morning, he decided that he must be sick, but to go to the Infirmary at this hour required waking up a Hall Monitor and having them take him there. No student was allowed on the grounds after midnight. He dosed off again. At six, he awoke again, sweating profusely, and decided to go to the doctor now that it was light and safe to do so. He hastily put on some clothes and headed down the stairs to the tunnel.

"Doctor, I don't feel well at all, couldn't sleep right, chills and fevers maybe. Am I sick or something?" he said, having roused Doctor Caterwall. He was sitting in the Emergency room while the sleepy-eyed doctor began examining him. After taking his vital signs, peering down his throat and into his ears, the doctor muttered.

"Is it bad?" asked Henry, sensing that maybe he really was quite ill.

"No, no fever. I'd say you have a bad case of stress. Your nerves are a bit frayed. How are your studies going? Having trouble with them? Spell casting going all right?" he probed for more information. He knew he hit something because Henry's face suddenly flushed.

"Ah, yeh, stress, must be it. What do I take for it? Got a pill for me?" Henry asked, relieved that he was not truly coming down with some illness.

Doctor Caterwall chuckled, "My boy, I wish I had a pill that would relieve stress. If I truly had such a magic pill, why, I could retire a millionaire. No, my dear boy, I'd recommend rest. I will write out an excused absence from classes today for you. I want you to go back to bed and just take it easy. Get some sleep. Come see me tomorrow if you still feel bad." He punched a few keystrokes in his PDA and hit send. "There, the notice is sent. You won't have to go to classes today. Now go back to bed, Henry." Henry thanked him and left.

Somewhat relieved, he returned to his room. Phillip, Jake, and Milo were dressing. "Hey, where have you been? You are up early," asked Jake.

"Thought I was sick. Chills and fevers all night. Caterwall excused me from classes; told me to spend the day in bed. Hey, take good notes for me, will you Jake."

"Sure thing. Glad you are not sick. We all might catch it," he teased. The three joked a bit and left, leaving Henry alone in his room. Henry noticed that now he did feel a bit better and decided to try to get more sleep.

Around ten, he awoke again in chills with beads of sweat soaking his tee shirt. He got out of bed, and his eyes rested on Phillip's laptop. His stomach gave a lurch as his eyes rested upon it. "Darn, it's Phillip!" He dressed and decided to take a walk; perhaps that would ease his discomfort.

Sometime later, his strolls through the empty tunnels led him to the Admin Building. Governor Alister was just coming down the steps. He could not avoid him. "Morning Henry. Shouldn't you be in classes? Oh, yes, I remember now. Caterwall said you were not feeling good. Is there something you wish to tell me?"

"Er, no, I was taking a walk; woke up with the chills again," Henry replied half-truthfully. His stomach felt like it was turning upside down.

Alister looked straight into his eyes and asked, "Is there something that you should tell me, Henry?" Henry's face turned beet red. No matter how he replied, he knew his goose was cooked.

"Black Hall students are strong and powerful." The words of his mentor, Delius Dogs echoed in his mind. He sighed. *I might as well tell the truth and be done with it.*

"It's about Phillip, Phillip Royster. I caught him sending an email to Dominus Malefic last night. He told him that it was the pathetic girl Ashley Stokes who divined that you were in dire peril and raised the alarm."

"Ah, interesting. Is that all he wrote Dominus?" Alister probed, though he did not raise his voice or give any visible reaction, good or bad.

"He said she was on the Yellow Hall track team and that he could meet her at the Nationals in a week, if he wanted. He said that he supports that infernal Manifesto, that's all. Oh, he told me that if I told anyone, he would ask Dominus to send his Death Stalkers to kill my whole family."

"Ah, that would be enough to give anyone stress," Alister replied. "How do you feel now?"

Henry suddenly realized that he felt light as a feather. The gnawing ache in his stomach was gone, replaced by hunger. "Better, sir. Please, I don't want him trying to get my family killed."

"Oh, I'm sure that Dominus has far more important things to do than go after your parents. I shouldn't worry about that. Phillip has betrayed Black Hall and all of us. I'll keep your name out of it. Now why don't you run along and get something to eat, and if you feel better, catch your afternoon classes." Henry smiled and agreed, walking back down the tunnel to the dining room.

During the ten-minute period between classes, Alister met with Herbert Mac Elroy in his math classroom. "Did he confess?" Herbert whispered.

"Yes, came clean. Your filter has worked perfectly, Herbert. I'm going to get Phillip now; we need to use this opportunity to examine his computer, though. Monique or Pam? Which would be better to use?"

"Probably Pam. Monique has been having a hard time with her recovery. Besides, Pam is a Sleuth anyway," Herbert replied. The next class of the students began entering the room. Alister smiled and left.

At noon, a Security man and a gentleman from the Department of Law sat quietly at the side of Governor Alister's office, awaiting the student. Phillip knocked and entered, having received the message from Alister. "Come in, Phillip. Have a seat. Please hand your wand over to the Security man," he spoke softly and kindly.

Phillip's anger surged to a boil; although he had no idea why he was being summoned, the presence of the two officials suggested that he was in a good deal of trouble. He weighed his options. Giving up his wand meant the end of any magic use and thus means of escape. Yet, he couldn't teleport out of the school. Alister had too many protections guarding the campus. He was Black Hall trained and was not about to give up without a fight. He hedged his bets and drew his wand from his pocket, but held on to it instead, taking a seat before Alister's big desk. Carefully, he slid his hand holding his wand down beside his pant leg, hiding it from the view of the Security man and Alister. "What's this all about? A wizard does not hand over his wand without an explanation."

"Very well then, Phillip. Our campus email filters have been monitoring your repeated communications with Dominus Malefic. Until the latest email, I have been inclined to overlook them as youthful folly. Your latest one disturbs me greatly. Dominus has been attempting to kill Diviners, recently. Yet you divulged the name of the young girl who correctly divined that I was about to die at the hands of Dominus."

"But everyone knows that," Phillip protested. At least Henry had not squealed on him. Darn computers anyway, he thought to himself.

"While around the campus it is widely known, it is not, until now, widely known out there. Your actions have put Miss Ashley Stokes-Compton in the gravest of perils, son. If any harm comes to her via Dominus and the Death Stalkers, I'm afraid the Department of Law will be charging you with conspiracy to commit murder. As it stands, you have given me no choice but to expel you from Bradbury's and turn you over to the Department of Law to face such charges as they deem appropriate. If Miss Stokes is murdered, I'm afraid that you will likely face capital murder charges yourself."

Phillip saw no way out of this mess, except to act. This dumb Security man was not going to get him, not a Black Hall student, but he would have to plan his choice of spells carefully. He needed to distract them a bit longer. "How is telling Dominus about the hopeless cripple a crime anyway?" While Alister patiently explained the ramifications, Phillip worked out his sequence. "Darkness." The room became instantly black. Phillip dived across the room, far from the chair he was in and cast his Magical Door spell. Just as he stepped through his door, he heard the Security man casting a Hold spell, but it was aimed at the chair on which he had been sitting. He grinned. Alister canceled the darkness, just in time to see Phillip step through his door, leaving his office.

"Darn, I thought you said he would come quietly," he growled.

"I thought he would; perhaps I was just hoping that he would," Alister replied. "Locate: Phillip Royster." His wand activated. "He is heading for the stone barrier wall in the Formal Gardens."

At once, the Security man cast a Door spell and took up the chase. The Law man said, "Well, I will add attempted escape to his charges. It doesn't look good for him, Governor. I assume that you will be taking extra precautions with this young girl? As you know, the Department of Security is now stretched incredibly thin."

"Yes, William, I will see to it. I will also forward along to your office all the accumulated emails that Phillip has sent to Dominus. Perhaps you will find other things that he has reported that impact other of your ongoing investigations."

"Thanks, perhaps. I wonder what his motives are? Why support the worst criminal this world has ever seen? Anyway, we will give him a thorough examination. Perhaps he has been Charmed by Dominus to do his bidding." William replied, sounding a hopeful note.

"It seems that many are indeed doing just as he has, I am afraid. I'm not a politician, so the why I leave up to you. Yes, if he has been charmed into doing this, then I will re-instate him, once the charm has been removed."

William grinned, "Cagey as ever, Governor. Okay, I will be on my way. I should perhaps lend Sam a hand recapturing Phillip. Good day." He bowed and left.

Alister used his Door spell to step into the penthouse of Black Hall, where he talked with the Black Hall housefather. "Here is his computer, as requested. I searched his things, but found nothing other than his books and personal items. I have collected them and will be mailing them to the Department of Law, sir."

"Thank you. Grim business this is." Alister took the computer and headed back to his office.

Outside, Phillip made a dash to the outer wall. He knew that he only had seconds to make good his escape. "Alister thinks he can keep students in and protected from the outside world. Idiot. Morph Me into a Butterfly." His wand activated, and a monarch flapped into the spring sky, fluttering away. The insect saw the Security man racing towards the formal gardens. Hastily, the monarch flew up and over the wall.

Phillip could not resist the opportunity to taunt the stupid Security man. He canceled his spell and allowed the man to see him waving at him from the other side of the wall. Just as the glimmer of recognition appeared in the Security man's eyes, Phillip's wand activated once more. He vanished from view, appearing on the main street of Telluride.

"Now what the devil do I do?" he said to himself as he walked along the street. Quickly, he surveyed his situation. He had fifty cents in his school pants, and he was still wearing his school blazer, which identified him as a Bradbury student, especially here in Telluride. He could not go home. By now, his parents would have been alerted, but he doubted that they would aid him anyway. The fools, they disliked Dominus.

"I'll show them. I'll show everyone!" He ducked into a side street and hid behind a dumpster, which was still encased in snow from the winter's deluge. He waited patiently, while being invisible. Finally, he spied another young man about his size. His wand activated, and the fellow froze mid-step. Phillip dragged him behind the dumpster, changed into his clothes, and took his wallet. "Ah, thirty-three bucks, good." A few minutes later, he stepped out on the street and headed for Sam's, where there was a kiosk with email computers.

A dollar later, he'd sent his email message to Dominus. He bought a few sandwiches and some sodas and left. On the street again, he discretely went invisible and headed to the abandoned house where Dominus had held the three girls captive. Once inside, he went upstairs and laid down on the floor, biding his time. He cast a few protection and alerting spells, then ate his snacks. Either Dominus would send someone for him by nightfall or he would be off on his own. "So what if I don't have that stupid diploma; it's just a piece of paper. I've already learned all that they are going to teach me anyway. Besides, I get out of having to take the stupid tests in a few weeks. World, here comes the next greatest wizard, Phillip Royster. I hope you are ready for me." He toasted himself with his can of soda.

An hour later, his magical alarm sounded. He got up, hoping it was Dominus. "Royster, we know you are up there. Surrender and you won't get hurt. We have the place surrounded." He glanced out the window to see several blue uniformed Security men guarding the house near the exposed front room.

Phillip waved his wand and called out, "Teleport: Denver. Guess I will have to find another way to join up with him." The Security men dashed into the room, wands at the ready, but they only found his litter and a half eaten sandwich. Phillip was gone this time.

"Thank you for coming, Miss Betts, Miss Stokes-Compton. I've some unfortunate news to tell everyone, but I wanted you two to hear it first," Governor Alister spoke softly to the two girls who had answered his summons just after supper. He had waited until they had eaten to call them into his office.

"It seems we have misjudged one of our Black Hall students. Phillip Royster has been sending information to Dominus via emails. Unfortunately, he just sent one that identifies you, Ashley, as the diviner who sounded the alarm that I was in extreme danger."

"Oh," Ashley replied, uncertain what this might actually mean. "Is Dominus after me because I sensed you were in trouble?"

"I'm afraid that might be so. You see, it was Mabel Pruit, the Diviner, who was primarily responsible for his capture last time. I think he may be worried that you might be somehow after him, though this is pure speculation on my part. I will be increasing the security around the school, so I'm sure that you have nothing to fear from him while you are here. I will let your parents and the Whitewater's know as well. I understand that R. B. has already increased the security around your home, so you will be safe there."

"Okay," she replied, thinking nothing more about it.

"I will have to make a school-wide announcement about it shortly. While I am doing that, Miss Betts, on my desk you will find Phillip's computer. I wish you to go over its contents with a fine-tooth comb. Find out all that you can about his nefarious activities. Document them fully. I will need to send a copy to the Department of Law. Also, as you know, Herbert's email monitoring program is working perfectly. We've been intercepting a number of Phillip's emails to Dominus. This one got red flagged. I expelled him today and turned him over to the Department of Law, but the wily student managed to escape them."

"Wow, sure Governor. I'll get right on it," Pam said

eagerly. Here was a new sleuthing opportunity dropped right into her lap. Ashley headed back to join her friends, while Alister began the school-wide announcement about Phillip Royster.

"Gosh Ashley," Lindsey exclaimed highly agitated. "Now Dominus knows about you! We'll have to be extra careful, because he's probably going to be after you too. I hope he doesn't try anything at our ranch."

"Alister said R. B. is working on more defenses," Ashley replied, rather unconcerned. After all, why would Dominus really want to bother with her? She was just a mostly helpless, pathetic excuse for a witch.

Chapter 22—Preparations

Pam walked into Governor Alister's office, computer in one arm, a pile of illustrations in the other. "Ah, do I detect that I am about to be the recipient of a presentation?" he said with a wry grin as she entered.

"Aye, sir. I've finished my analysis of Phillip's computer and his emails." Pam explained all that she had done. "Now for my findings." She unfolded her first exhibit. "On the left are samples from six emails reputedly coming from Dominus, at least Phillip thought so. On the right are samples prepared for me by Monique, excerpts from some of the more recent speeches of Dominus for president. First, notice the ones on the right, those of Dominus. Notice his choice of words, his style—you can tell that he is literate." She paused briefly so Alister could skim over them.

"Now notice the emails Phillip received. I've underlined key sentences, like 'No way, kid. Gotta find out who tipped 'em off to the fact that Broadwell was being killed.' See, it's crude, street talk. Uneducated might be a better way of putting it." Alister nodded his agreement and pulled on his short beard, in thought.

"I was able to obtain a few court transcriptions made during the trials of the Death Stalkers who were captured by the Rat Pack. On this exhibit, I have put up four short transcriptions on the right, with Phillip's received emails on the left. If you will note my highlighted sections, there is a close similarity with the manner of speaking to the Death Stalker known as Ben Johnston. My conclusion is that Ben was sending these emails for Dominus. Phillip thought he was talking with Dominus, when in fact it was only one of his henchmen."

"Positively brilliant, once again, Miss Betts. Well done indeed. I do see the similarity. Striking, once it is pointed out. What put you on to this?" he asked, most curious about her thought process.

"If I were Dominus, why on earth would I be personally

exchanging emails with a) someone I did not know, b) a mere high school kid, c) with someone who could well be an agent of the FBI out to find me, and d) knowing as any literate computer user knows that emails can be traced back to the sender and their location discovered, that is, where their computer ties into the Net. However, Ben, probably under orders from Dominus, has changed servers three times now during the course of these emails. Cagey fellow. Probably the Department of Law will not be able to find him because he's likely changed it again."

"Ah, I see, it does make sense. Thank you for a job well done. I will relay your findings to the Department of Law. By the way, Phillip was traced to that old house in Telluride where you three were being held. He was there for a few hours until they closed in on him. Unfortunately, he again gave them the slip. Perhaps, we have trained him too well," Alister admitted.

A couple days later, Audrey hurried into the Yellow Hall study room; she had to find Lindsey and Ashley. She was very worried. "Ah, there you all are. Say, you know how I can sometimes sense things," Audrey began, trying to be as clear as she possibly could. Both nodded.

"Well, I just sensed that you all should *not* go to the Nationals this year. Something bad is going to happen there! I just know it! Please don't go," she begged them.

"We have to go, but let's go tell this to Alister. He will know what to do," Lindsey declared. All three headed to his office. Lindsey had Audrey explain her feelings, what she sensed. Unlike the concrete premonitions that Ashley had, Audrey's were more like keen intuitions to keep herself alive, to avoid danger. Still Alister took her seriously and agreed to check on things and ask for additional security, satisfying them for now.

As the first Saturday in May drew closer, Ashley became more and more nervous. She began to realize that she would be running before a large audience, and everyone, absolutely everyone, would be staring at her. That alone was enough to frighten anyone, a bad case of stage fright. She took to taking long, hot baths late at night, hoping they would help calm her fears. On Thursday night, as she slipped into the warm waters around ten, suddenly she saw images of the stadium flashing by in her mind. Like a slow motion picture, they came frame by frame. There they all were. They had won the championship. Victorious, they all assembled to receive their huge trophy. A huge, violent, yellow explosion detonated in front of them. She saw fragments of her dear friend's body parts flying in all directions. Then all went black, cold, lifeless black. She shrieked so loudly that someone heard her from the commons.

A minute later Lindsey, Amanda, Pam, and Kathy came running into the bathroom, certain that something terrible had happened to Ashley. They found her naked in the tub, shaking violently, unable to speak, not even recognizing them! "Ashley, Ashley! What's wrong? What's happened?" Lindsey fairly screamed at her sister. Ashley only vaguely responded, as if she could not even see that it was Lindsey standing over her.

"We have to get her out and dried off, some clothes on her, and then get her to the Infirmary," Pam declared. "Something happened. I don't see anything in the room; the water is not boiling or anything like that."

"Maybe she is having another one of her divinations," suggested Amanda, as she and Lindsey lifted her out of the tub, trying not to get themselves soaked. It was a bit difficult until Pam had the good sense to cast a Levitate spell on Ashley. While three of them dried her off, Pam sent a message to Doctor Caterwall, Governor Alister, and to Professor Mary Ann, just in case Ashley was indeed having some kind of divination problem.

While they hurriedly dressed her, Pam received word from Alister to take her to the Infirmary and that Mary Ann would join them there. Lindsey was so upset that Pam took charge as soon as Ashley had some clothes covering her body. "Door: Infirmary. Come on; let's get her there pronto," Pam directed. Lindsey obeyed without hesitation. Seconds later, the five stepped into the Infirmary's emergency room. Doctor Caterwall came running in, still buttoning his shirt. He had been about to retire for the night, when the call came.

Alister and Mary Ann appeared shortly afterwards.

While Doctor Caterwall examined Ashley, Lindsey told the other two what little they knew. She'd been taking a bath, and they heard her scream and found her delirious.

"She's in shock—seen something would be my guess. I can find nothing physically wrong with her. Perhaps this is your province, professor?" he suggested.

After her eyes darted about the entire room, as though verifying that no enemy was present, Mary Ann waved her wand and cast a spell that none of the girls knew. Almost at once, she, too, shrieked, though not as loud as Ashley had. Mary Ann had the good sense to cast a second spell, again, one none yet knew. Now everyone began seeing the images that were repeating over and over in Ashley's mind.

Waving her wand, Mary Ann called out, "Premonition: Cease." The images swirling through Ashley's mind vanished as rapidly as they had come. She looked around herself, totally disoriented.

"How? Where? What? We're all going to be blown up!" she shrieked.

"There, there, Ashley. You are quite safe. You are in the Infirmary. It was only a premonition of what may be. Take deep breaths. Yes, that's a good girl," Mary Ann said softly, but commandingly. White as a bed sheet, Ashley's complexion reflected what she had seen, but just as ghastly were the faces of Amanda, Lindsey, Pam, and Kathy. They'd witnessed her vision of their bodies being blown into small bits, grim.

"We can't go to the Nationals," Ashley tried to explain, but faltered.

Alister said soothingly, "Of course, we can now. Thanks to you, Miss Stokes-Compton, we are now forewarned and will take the necessary measures to prevent what you saw from happening."

"Yes, yes, dear child. This is exactly what a Diviner does. She spots the likely things that are to come into being so that others may change them for the better," Mary Ann explained to her young student.

"Is, is, is this the kind of things that Ashley has been seeing, I mean in the past," asked Lindsey.

"Yes, this is often what we Diviners foresee, disasters

before they happen," Mary Ann answered.

Lindsey threw her arms around her sister, hugging her tightly. "Ashley, I had no idea how awful your visions were." Slowly the color returned to the faces of the girls.

"Will we be able to learn that spell, the one that allowed us all to see what she was seeing?" asked Pam, finally recovered sufficiently to ask what had made her most curious, the use of a new spell.

"Mind See is an advanced spell, a divination spell. Perhaps in your sixth year you may be able to learn it," Mary Ann replied. "Certainly, Ashley is highly likely to be able to learn that one, since she is already a Diviner. Premonition: Cease is also in the province of us Diviners, though Ashley has not yet learned that one. We have been working on her gaining control over her visions this term. We have much more to learn." She smiled at Ashley in a motherly way.

Pam asked Alister, "Sir, do you suppose that this is a direct result of Phillip's email to Dominus?"

Alister thought for a moment. "While it would appear so, I wouldn't want to so state. After all, attempts on Lindsey's life were made at the last two Nationals. This could be just a continuation of those attempts to get at her. Yet, coming on the heels of his email, it does look highly incriminating, I admit. I will pass it along to the Department of Law. Now, I must look into various ways of preventing that explosion from happening. I am responsible for your safety at the Nationals. Trust me, Ashley, I will not let that explosion or any harm come to you or your fellow students while at the Nationals. I give you my solemn promise on that. Now, if you will excuse me, I have many Messages to deliver. Again, thank you, Miss Stokes-Compton for your incredible perceptiveness and premonition." He bowed and left them.

"Well, she is free to return to the dorms," Doctor Caterwall suggested, quite relieved that his services were not needed. The others left the Infirmary, choosing to walk back to the dorm, breathing in some cool night air. Mary Ann followed them to their dorm to make sure her student made it back safely.

As they were walking, Mary Ann said, "Well, Ashley, as

you can see, you need Diviner Theory II and III yet."

Ashley giggled for the first time. "No kidding!" she jested. Lindsey smiled too.

The next day, Ashley's dire prediction was all over the school. It seems that everyone had heard about it. Tom even held a meeting of the whole track team to discuss it. However, Lindsey repeated what Alister had promised, and everyone agreed to go anyway. After all, if Alister couldn't protect them, then they were doomed anyway, Tom thought.

During the next two days leading up to the team's Friday night departure for Des Moines and the national track meet, Ashley cast Emotion: Calm on herself continually. She just could not deal with the raw emotions flying through her body when the spell ceased. The moment she was not under the spell's effect, her mind raced away on her own armless body or else the explosion that was going to blast her pathetic body into unrecognizable bits. Though she wouldn't admit it, the former gave her more trouble than the latter.

"It's going to be televised," Pam encouraged her friends as they were packing for the trip. "Everyone in Yellow Hall will be watching on the big screen. I know Alister will prevent you from being hurt. Good luck. If Ashley's premonition is right, you all are going to take first place!"

Lindsey grinned, hiding her concerns and worries. "I'll believe that when I see it, Pam. Honestly though, this year I think we have our best chance at winning it, right Amanda?"

"We've the fastest twenty-milers, and we've trained long and hard at running four races in one day. If we don't, I sure don't know what else we could do about it," the Apache replied truthfully.

Meanwhile, Alister held a secret meeting in his office. Professors Cho Lin, Huan Su, and Delius, paced the room, along with the PE coaches Hank and Betsy. In addition, Bill West and Able Monument stood quietly in one corner. Alister addressed them, "Well, the fools running the Nationals have given me their assurances that nothing is out of the ordinary. They've swept for explosive devices and found none. I'm afraid, however, that they're not taking this seriously enough. Not even an idiot would plant a bomb there way before the

Nationals begin at the giant stadium."

"Well, you have to protect them," Cho Lin argued. "Besides you've given them your word that nothing like Ashley's vision would occur."

"Contingency plans?" Able Monument asked quietly from the sidelines.

"Speculations first. I have given this considerable thought, though I admit I cannot read the mind of Dominus. My best guess is that one of two scenarios is in play. The first one is the elimination of Miss Stokes-Compton herself. The second one is the elimination of all there, that is, Miss Whitewater, Miss Barron, and Miss Stokes-Compton. Thus, there are two scenarios at play here. If the goal is to get Ashley, she could be attacked at any time, particularly during the races, where she would be a lone target, prime for an attack. If the goal is to get them all, then the only time that he could guarantee that they would all be close together and at one location is the winner's circle, when the trophies are handed out, assuming that they win a trophy. There could be other possibilities, but I think that these two are the most likely. Does anyone disagree with my analysis?" None did.

"But how can we protect her while she races?" asked Hank. "You know that magic is not allowed on the runners."

"I have pleaded my case to the Officials and gotten a ruling in our favor. We will be allowed to place an 'In the Event of' spell on them, subject to the scrutiny of the Officials, who must be allowed to verify the spells," Alister answered.

"Well, that's something to work with then," Able Monument stated flatly. "Cast that spell on all the team members. Normally, I would have a Teleport spell activate in such a case. However, most of the team don't yet know that spell. Surely, you're not going to have Teleport be the contingency spell."

"No, I had considered that, but rejected it for the younger students. Further, if it is an explosion that occurs, there wouldn't be time for them to step through a magical door or to climb the rope into the extra-dimensional space. I could place the Skin of Stone on them as the contingency spell. Yet, would such a spell protect them from an explosion? I don't have the answer to that one. You see, I don't have all the answers," Alister freely admitted.

"Then what?" Cho Lin protested. "We should just cancel going to the Nationals. I don't see any way we can guarantee their safety." Huan Su and Delius agreed with her. Able and Bill said nothing. From long experience, they knew Alister had not said all that was on his mind.

"If it is an explosion that we must defend against, I have an idea. The three older boys could be completely protected with a Teleport contingency spell that I can cast upon them prior to heading to the winner's circle. If an explosion does occur, they can be instantly teleported back to our parking lot," Alister explained.

Naturally, everyone waited for his suggestion for the six younger ones. "I checked the rules. There is nothing in the rules one way or the other about who goes up there to accept the trophy. Suppose that six of you, with contingency spells in full force, morph into the six younger students and pretend to be them, accepting the trophy. If the explosion does come, you all would be teleported to the safety of our parking lot, along with the boys. I would then be free to bring the others back with me later on, though; of course, they would also be morphed into yourselves and as such would not be harmed, bothered, or questioned."

"Devious, Alister, you have the most devious mind that I know," Delius grinned. "I love it! Count me in!" Smiles uniformly broke out on all faces.

"Who will agree to become Miss Stokes-Compton," Bill asked. "One of us is going to have an awful time of it. She's had years to adjust to her situation. One of us will have but seconds."

"Yes, that is so, Bill. It will take some guts to be 'Ashley.' You will be very likely unable to cast any spells until the spell is canceled and you return to your normal form. Volunteers?" Alister asked, hoping that he would not have to appoint someone.

"She's Yellow Hall. It is my responsibility," Cho Lin spoke up. "It should be me. I will talk with her about it, and perhaps we can get in a practice session beforehand."

"Dear, what won't you do to get out into the field!" her husband teased her.

"Well, Huan Su, this time I won't be left behind," she retorted playfully. "But if it happens, you are going to have to look out for me. Alister's right, I'll be the most helpless Ashley imaginable. Honestly, I don't know how she does it."

"Thank you, professor," Alister replied, visibly relieved. "Now my plan is once substituting us for the team, we throw up a series of connected invisible force walls between us and the explosion site, based upon Ashley's images. Now about how to protect Ashley while she is racing, should option one be the plan of Dominus. Ideas? We can't put magical spells on her while she is running, except perhaps some form of contingency situation."

Hank spoke up, "Well, last year, someone fired a Disintegration beam at the team. Will the officials allow us to protect her from such spells, perhaps put a full protection on her?"

"I certainly hope so," Alister answered up.

"Bill and I can morph into small flies and stay fairly close to her," Able suggested. "Perhaps the rest of you can take sections of the crowd and keep them under constant observation. Alert us of anything unusual or suspicious."

"Thanks, I believe that will work. Will you be traveling there with us?" he asked.

"No, if we make any appearance per se at the Nationals, the media will be all over us, detracting from the plan and our effectiveness. We will arrive there shortly after you get there. Even better, we will pretend to be relatives of them. Let's see. Say I will be what's her name, oh yes, Monane Tumble," Able suggested. "Bill, why don't you pretend that you are that aunt of Pam Betts? Everyone knows those two old biddies are buddies, going everywhere together. That way, our appearance will be disguised totally. No one will suspect the Rat Pack members are with you."

"Devious, devious! A man after my heart," Delius complimented him. "Brilliant even. You are giving Alister a run for his devious money. I have only one question, Alister. After the kids finish the last race, when we morph into them, and they, into us, where are we going to perform these spells?"

"If they take either second or first place, we can duck into our locker room. We have at least ten minutes while the fourth and third place trophies are presented, if I remember right," Alister answered.

He continued, "Okay, then I thank you all for sticking out your necks to help me protect our students. We have two hours before the bus leaves to make our final preparations. Able, we ought to be arriving there at ten tonight. Give us at least thirty minutes to get settled in and a room prepared for you. Message me upon your arrival and I will come meet you." With that, Alister ended the meeting.

"Pack for me dear," Cho Lin told Huan Su. "I need to be with Ashley for a time. I think that this is going to be the hardest thing that I ever tried to do." He smiled and gave her a loving kiss.

"Why do we need to meet tonight here in your office?" Ashley asked. She'd gotten Cho Lin's message and rushed over to see what she wanted.

"Dear, Alister has a plan to protect you students from the foreseen explosion. Once safely on the bus, he will explain the entire plan in full details. For now, I can tell you this much. When the team goes to pick up the trophy, all of you will be safely elsewhere. Others will be taking your places, Morph spells. I will be pretending to be you, Ashley."

"But I don't want you to get blown to bits either," Ashley wailed.

"Emotion: Calm." Cho Lin reactivated the spell that she saw just wear off Ashley. "There, that's better." Ashley was quiet once more. "None of us will be blown to bits. We all will have all sorts of protective spells on us at that time. Even if there is an explosion of such magnitude as you saw in your vision, none of us will be harmed in the slightest. However, Ashley, if I am to be morphed into you, I need some help from you right now. I don't know how to get along without any arms. As Alister said, I won't be able to cast any spells while I am in your form, but the help I need is in just, well you know, doing normal things."

"Okay, what do I do?" she asked.

Cho Lin carefully cast her spell, waving her wand perfectly. Magical energy flashed. Ashley watched Cho Lin's wand fall to the floor. Standing before her was another her. Cho Lin reached for her wand before she realized she had no arms. She nearly fell over and would have lost her balance had Ashley not immediately bumped into her, stabilizing her. "God, this is so *utterly* different, so, well I don't know *how* you manage it!" Cho Lin exclaimed. "Thanks, I almost fell over there."

Ashley quickly sized up the situation; the calm spell was working wonders for her just now. "Honestly, I have the most trouble of all trying to maintain my balance. Usually standing still is okay, unless you are on a boulder." She remembered her awful time on the large rock while rescuing Alister. "Walking and going up and down steps—well you have to be very alert."

Cho Lin replied, "Well, I don't think that there will be any stairs with which to deal, well maybe not."

"Try walking about your office, in and around objects," Ashley suggested. Cho Lin did as she asked, but more than once caught herself trying to use her arms for balance and nearly falling as a result. "Slow and easy does it," Ashley suggested.

"Ah, that works. I have to keep my full attention on what I am doing, don't I?"

Ashley grinned. The two chatted and experimented for close to an hour before Cho Lin sent Ashley off to finish her packing. After she was gone, Cho Lin hazard doing a little more, she managed to get the office door open, having stuck her foot in it as Ashley was leaving. Now she began to wander the halls and classrooms of the Hall of Illusion. "God, this is the most challenging thing that I have ever attempted," she said to herself.

"I suspected so," Huan Su surprised her, entering with both of their backpacks ready to go. So startled was Cho Lin that she nearly fell over, flailing wildly with her non-existent arms. Huan Su caught her just in time to keep her from falling over a desk. "More practice, dear?" he suggested. She laughed, and they continued to practice until it was time to go.

All of Yellow Hall stood in the commons yelling and

cheering their track team. More than a few wondered if this would be the last time that they would see them alive. The sendoff was loud and boisterous, meant to instill a sense of victory in the nine track members. Had Ashley not been under the calm spell again, she would have felt sick. Now, however, she sensed just how much her fellow classmates were behind their team. A sense of pride surged in her, drowning out all other feelings and emotions. This gave her something to ponder. She had never felt this emotion before.

When they began their short walk to the main gates, many students from the other halls lined the sides of the sidewalk, cheering them on and making almost as much fuss as their Yellow Hall mates. Deiter caught Lindsey's attention. "Go get 'em, Lindsey! Bring home the trophy to Bradbury's! Go get 'em, Ashley. You can do it!" Ashley blushed from the unexpected attention. Even the Black Hall students were rooting for her; thus, pride in herself and what she was attempting surged even stronger. Frankly, she did not know what to make of it.

Once on the bus, Tom exclaimed, "Gang, what a sendoff! That's the best sendoff ever, at least that I can recall. Everyone is behind us. Super cool! We can't fail this time."

"As long as we stick to the game plan," Jake teased him, recalling how their careful plans went awry last year at the meet.

As the bus began rolling, Governor Alister walked back to the group. "May I have your full and undivided attention?" A pin could be heard dropping in the next instant. "We have worked out some careful plans to protect you at the meet. First, Bill and Able, the Rat Pack, will be joining us, once we reach Des Moines. They will be masquerading as Monane Tumble and Pam's Aunt Wilma Weltsi. While you are actually racing, those two will be small insects following close beside you, protecting you from any interference. The rest of us will be watching the stands and the crowd for anything unusual. If someone attempts to shoot a spell at you while you are running, we will deal with it so that you are not harmed."

"However, that was not Ashley's premonition. Once the racing is over and before the team is called out to accept your trophy, we all will be morphing ourselves into the six younger students. Jake, Tom, Jim: I will be casting an In the Event of contingency spells on you. If there is an explosion, you will be instantly teleported back to our parking lot and not injured. We professors and the Rat Pack will have all manner of protection spells on us and will attempt to deal with the bombing. Meanwhile, the six younger ones will be safely on the sidelines far from the action, morphed into us professors! If trouble comes, no one will bother you, and I will teleport you all to safety as soon as possible."

"Hey, I like that, but what about Tom, Jake, and I coming back to help rescue the others?" Jim asked.

"No, no, under no circumstances are you to return. Shortly after you three arrive back, the other six will join you. If the explosion occurs, the stadium will be filled with chaos. I can't protect anyone in such madness. Do not return period! Trust in your teachers, Jim." He sighed. He so wanted to be the protector of his Ashley, but saw what Alister meant. If there was an explosion, in the panic and confusion, he would never be able to find anyone, let alone Ashley.

"What I am telling you now, you are not to repeat to another until this is over. Now I want you all to settle back and put your attention on winning this track meet. That's your job; bring home the trophy. Leave the protection to us adults," Alister reminded them of their true goal.

They arrived on time and without incident. The giant parking lot at the huge stadium in Des Moines was nearly empty. Only the sixteen school buses were parked near the player's entrance. However, a dozen Security men were on hand to greet them. Amanda commented that she felt like the President, as they escorted the group safely inside, their eyes constantly surveying the empty lot, as if Dominus may suddenly make a surprise appearance.

Quickly, Alister conferred with the manager, who led them personally to their assigned rooms. More security men paced the long hallways, guarding all the sixteen different teams. "We are in this block of rooms. Monane and Wilma will be along shortly. I am putting them next to Ashley and Lindsey. Amanda and Fern, you two have the room next to them. Emilio, Andy, you are next to the Whitewaters, and Tom and Jim, you're next. Jake, you share with me. The other professors will be in the next set of rooms."

"It's getting late, so I suggest that you quickly unpack and get a good night's sleep. Big day tomorrow. Hank will be by in a few minutes with the details of your first race. Do your best, team; that's all any of us can ask of you; do your best." Alister attempted to take some of the growing pressure off the nine.

Lindsey opened the door to let Ashley inside. Cho Lin observed the two carefully. She was still in awe over how Ashley managed. Lindsey took Ashley's pack off her, and the two began settling in, unpacking their spare clothes and their track outfits.

"Oh, this *is* nice," Ashley commented, as they were led into the adjoining hotel complex for the visiting teams.

"Sure is," Lindsey replied. "Usually, there are two of us to a room. Guess you bunk with me, sis."

By the time that they were finished, Hank knocked on the door. "We're up at nine in the morning. If we win the first meet, then we will not be up again until one. If we win that, we race again at three. If you make it for the final race, that's at five. Get some sleep, ladies." Hank teased and continued to make his rounds with the news.

As Lindsey and Ashley crawled into the crisp sheets, Ashley asked, "Is that a good schedule?"

"Yes, as good as can be hoped for anyway. Our first year, we lost and had to race again at four, right after racing at three. Now that was awful. If we keep winning, we have two hours to recover a bit. Night sis," Lindsey whispered.

Ashley stared off into the darkness of their room. While she expected to be deathly nervous about the morning and even more terrified of the explosion of her vision, she found herself reflecting on the strange emotions she felt as they were leaving. So many were cheering her on. They were rooting for her and her teammates. Pride, she had felt the emotion of self-pride, not undeserved pride, but true pride; they were going to race against the best high school athletes in the country. She was a part of that elite group. This emotion was new to her and held her attention.

Chapter 23—The Nationals

"Wake up sleepy head. Time to get breakfast," Lindsey gently woke her sister.

"Morning? So soon?" Ashley got up, and Lindsey helped her get into her track outfit. "Rats, I forgot about eating. If I wear my running shoes, I can't eat."

"Not a problem, sis. We are bringing along our track shoes. They don't want us wearing spikes into their dining room; mars up their floor. Just wear your usual ones, so you can take them off. I'll levitate your tray as usual. We'll probably get to see a lot of the students from the other schools, though. Just ignore them like I always did." Lindsey chatted away as they left their room, joining the rest of the group, heading to the dining room.

"Hi, Monane, Wilma. I'm so glad you came with us," Ashley said to the two older women, who joined in behind them. She and Lindsey thought it was funny that they were pretending to be themselves, but after all, very few actually knew that they were Bill and Able.

The dining room was filled with the other schools and their faculty. More than a few eyes glanced at Ashley. Rumors of an armless girl athlete began circulating among the other schools, though it would not be until noon when everyone would know about Ashley. Hence, she had a pleasant breakfast. Once finished, Hank took them all on a tour of the track, allowing them to familiarize themselves with the racetrack. From Ashley's viewpoint, it seemed to be an identical surface to the Bradbury track.

"Normally, we get to watch the other races from the stands," Tom explained.

"Not today, son," Governor Alister broke in, "Hank will scout for you. I don't want to have you all together in a group for any length of time. Security reasons. We'll rest up in the safety of our rooms until time for our races."

Regretfully, Tom and the others followed Alister back into their room. A minute later, Tom went door to door, "The races are on channel 6! Watch the other racers, please."

Dutifully, Lindsey turned on the TV and switched to channel 6. A live feed was being broadcast in-house. She wondered if Pam were watching. If the feed went national, maybe it would be on the sports channel, Ashley suggested.

At 8:45, Tom had them get their track shoes on, and the group headed for the warm-up area. Lindsey noticed that the other professors were now standing guard, watching those around them, paying them no attention. Dutifully they warmed up.

"Now I am getting butterflies," Ashley admitted to Lindsey.

"So am I," Lindsey replied. "Perfectly normal. If you didn't, why, I'd think you were weird!"

"Hey, I'm a bit nervous too," Fern admitted.

"So are we all, good sign," Amanda answered her little sister. "Even Jim and Tom are a bit nervous, only they won't admit it." All the girls giggled.

"Okay, we are up against the Twin Cities. I've noticed that those tough schools that we raced against last year all graduated their older runners. LA has already lost! We can do it this year. I know we can. Let's take the Twin Cities out of the running." The team gave a cheer in unison and headed for their positions.

"Just block the announcer out of your mind, Ashley," Lindsey advised. "Concentrate on doing your normal running. Ignore absolutely everything else. That's the only way I can face this." Ashley managed a grin, forced. However, her sister had arms.

Shortly after the gun sounded, Andy returned to the sidelines victorious in his first heat. "Go get them, Ashley and Lindsey!" he yelled enthusiastically. The milers were up next. Carefully, Lindsey adjusted the carrying pouch and baton for Ashley. Her team members moved on down the track, getting into their positions. Then the gun sounded the start of her race.

Actually, here in the morning, four teams raced simultaneously on the quad tracks. To avoid confusions, each pair ran in the opposite direction. Ashley sprinted down the track, forcing herself to become oblivious to the tall boy from the Twin Cities who was running next to her. She didn't even see that she was slightly ahead of him, as Jake came up to her, matching her speed and gently took the baton from her.

Lindsey was there waiting for her, and she slowly jogged down from her race. "You did perfectly, Ashley," Lindsey complimented her.

"Ashley? Ashley Stokes?" the voice of the boy who had just raced against her called out from her right side.

Both girls turned to see who was talking to her. "Jim? Jim Nottingham?" Ashley said questioningly.

"Yep, it's me. Gosh, good to see you again. I never knew you were a runner! You beat me. So you are at Bradbury's?"

"Yes, oh, Jim this is my sister, Lindsey Barron. I'm now officially her sister. I got adopted," she tried to explain, but gave up. "Jim was often looking out for me when I was at TC last year."

The three headed back to the sidelines, chatting away. Jim wanted to know how she liked Bradbury's and if it was true that she had gotten kicked out of TC. Ashley rather enjoyed chatting with her old friend, and Lindsey listened fascinated, hearing some things about her sister that she hadn't known.

Their chatting was momentarily halted as everyone watched the finish of the mile relay. Fern crossed the line five steps ahead of the TC girl, clinching the race for Bradbury. Now Lindsey had to get ready for her first long run of the day.

"Ten laps," Tom reminded her. "Watch for Amanda's signal at the halfway around point. We just need to win the race, not set new course records. Save some for the last race," he teased. However, he was also thinking of how Lindsey had unilaterally broken with their plans last year, going all out to win one race to keep them in the running for the next match.

Lindsey bolted off at the sound of the starting gun. At once, she found her well-practiced pace. She followed her own advice and paid no attention to anything except running her own race at her own Apache-style pace. Amanda gave her a thumbs up sign after a half mile, though she knew she was dead on without the signal. Her long hair floating behind her,

Lindsey again realized how wonderful she felt on these long distance runs. A sense of total freedom filled her as she flew around the track. She handed off easily to Jim and took her cooling down jog, finally stopping beside Ashley, who was still chatting with her friend Jim from TC.

She listened in to their chatting, while watching how Jim was doing. Already, she had opened up a lead, Jim was only adding to it. Tom, monitoring the stopwatch, joined her. "Right on pace. Here, you get the watch. I have to get into position now." Lindsey took over the timing.

Jim, now fully a hundred yards ahead of his TC opponent, handed off to Tom, who continued their constant pace. Lindsey marveled at just how well the four runners could find, keep, and maintain the same pace. Jim's time was only a second faster than hers was. Later on, after Tom handed off to Amanda, his time was only two seconds faster than Lindsey's was. Their lead had swelled to nearly four hundred feet now. When Amanda crossed the finish line, over five minutes later, they had beaten the TC team by closer to five hundred feet, hardly a race at all. However, their all-important total time was sitting at 118:35, a good slow race, leaving them in the best condition for their next race.

Her friend Jim commented to Ashley, "Skunked! Say, can I join you at the banquet feast tonight, Ashley? It's been great seeing you again. I've missed you at TC."

"Okay, if things work out, sure Jim. Say hi to the old gang for me, will you?" He agreed, and Alister, complimenting the team on its first victory, ushered them into the changing room and then on to their hotel rooms, completely ignoring the many reporters who were trying to get an interview with the team, especially Ashley, the armless runner who was now causing quite a stir.

"We play the winner of this heat, so pay attention," Tom counseled them as they turned on their TV's to watch the next race.

"Which one? There are two heats going on," asked Lindsey.

"Atlanta versus Chicago," he replied.

"Hey, that's Fred, there on the Chicago team," Lindsey

noted. She explained how Fred had been friendly to her the last two years she had raced in the Nationals. "He's a really kind hearted fellow. I wish he were going to Bradbury's," she admitted. Ashley giggled, but kept her eyes on Fred, who was doing rather well in his race. However, Atlanta had the older runners, while Chicago had lost many of its older runners and the new additions were in their first Nationals.

"Atlanta looks tough," Tom said. "He'd called a conference after that game. They had two hours to develop a strategy to beat them. "Long legs, older boys, tough combination to beat."

"Yes, but their twenty-milers can be beat," Jim pointed out. "They constantly keep adjusting their speed, which has to cost them plenty in such a long race. I say, we keep to our game plan, Tom. Give them continuous just under six minute miles the whole way."

"Yes, but what if they begin to take a commanding lead?" asked Lindsey. "We cannot afford to leave all the catching up to Amanda. She'll have nothing for the rest of the day."

"Okay, okay. You win. Play it by feel. Just don't get goaded into breaking your pace. If you need to pick it up, then stay consistent with it. Let's not play their game of speed up and slow downs. That's a sure way to lose."

At noon, they headed to the dining room for lunch. Thankfully, all reporters and cameras were outlawed from the room, giving the racers some measure of privacy. All the key races were ahead of them. Tom had his team dining slightly early, so that they would not be running on full stomachs. While they were eating, Hank procured various energy drinks and high energy bars for their afternoon recovery periods. They would not be dining until close to six, if all went their way. With the potential for three complete races this afternoon, getting just the right nourishment into each person was critical, though the students barely realized such. That was the province of the coach. While they didn't know it, this was Hank's unique skill—the ability to sense just what each person would need and when. He carefully acquired every item on his lengthy list.

Finally, it was time for their one o'clock race against the Atlanta School of Magic. They fielded nine older boys, all at least six feet tall, thin and lanky, excellent runners. Andy promptly lost his sprint race. Meanwhile, word had spread about Bradbury's armless runner. Ashley's tall opponent, standing well over a foot taller than she, tried taunting her, hoping to unsettle his opponent.

"What's your problem?" Ashley replied in a tone of annoyance with a hint of antagonism. She then put him completely out of her mind. This was easy to do because Lindsey stepped between them, adjusting her waistband and the baton. Lindsey didn't move until they were getting set to start.

As the gun sounded, the tall fellow called out, "Bet you cannot even run!" It annoyed Ashley a bit, and she stumbled out of the starting block. She recovered and put him out of her mind completely, concentrating on just running down the track as fast as she could go. When Jake finally took the baton from her, she noticed that the long legged boy was already a little ahead of them.

When Lindsey joined her as she jogged to cool down a bit, Ashley complained, "It's hard to race against him. Look at his legs! He's got a giant stride compared to mine!"

"Well, we all just do the best we can. There is no way you could ever catch him, at least not on such a short run as this. Maybe over a longer run you could, if he tires out. Let's see how the others do." Ashley only now realized that she was the shortest person on their track team.

Jake held on, barely, his opponent gaining a few feet on him before he passed off to the slowest runner, Emilio. Lindsey wondered if Emilio would rise to the occasion and go the extra bit. He did, fresh from his camping trip, Emilio felt better, happier, than he ever had in his life. That Kathy had given him numerous kisses also helped is self-esteem. He kept his opponent from gaining any extra ground, before passing off to Fern. Now it was up to the Apache girl to either win or lose the race. She was about ten feet behind as she began her blaze down the track.

Fern, who had been watching the other runners from

Atlanta carefully, realized that they poured it on as they took the baton, fading out as they approached the next person. She took advantage of this by only maintaining her opponent's pace. As the finish line loomed ahead, only then did she pour it on, imagining Tom was at her side and that she just had to beat him. The look of utter dismay on the tall lad's face as she blazed past him right at the finish line was classic. Dumbfounded! Worse, he had let a young Apache girl beat him. He cursed and swore as he left the field.

Now it was Lindsey's turn to face these older, taller boys. Everything rode on this race, as it always did. She wondered why the point system was as it was. Even if one team won the sprint and the mile relay, that only gave them fifteen points, the twenty mile relay gave twenty. The disparity seem weird to her just now.

Her opponent tried to leave her in the distance right from the starting line. She refused to yield her pace. After all, there were five miles to do, not a few feet. Amanda gave her the thumbs up sign halfway around the track, and she knew she was on her pace. Now she just continued, enjoying herself once more. God, I love to run, she thought to herself.

When a mile remained of her portion of the race, she finally peeked at her competitor. He had been speeding up and slowing down the whole time. Although he still led her by ten feet, she could see that he was tiring rapidly and decided just to continue as she was a little longer. She could always increase her pace towards the end. Perhaps the boy would have nothing left.

She avoided the obvious desire to catch him until they rounded the bend. Only a half mile remained. Already, she had begun to close the gap, so she ever so slightly increased her pace, just enough so that they were dead even as she handed off to Jim, who was smiling. He had already noticed her subtle moves. Tom had alerted him, via the stopwatch.

Lindsey took her cool down period and then joined Fern and Ashley on the sidelines, waiting for her turn with the stopwatch. Jim followed Lindsey's lead perfectly, maintaining their usual pace until the very end. As he handed off to Tom, both teams were still tied. Likewise, Tom resisted the growing temptation to show off and followed Lindsey's strategy to the letter. When he handed off to Amanda, both teams were still tied. More importantly, they were right on their usual, normal pace. They were not tired or exhausted, perfectly setup for their next race, if they won this one.

Amanda knew that she was facing Atlanta's best runner. He also knew that he was facing Bradbury's best, although why it should be a young girl completely eluded him. Both runners knew that everything rested on them. The outcome would be decided by themselves only. One team would be finished, while the other would advance to the semifinals.

He chose to pour it on right from the handoff, counting on both putting some distance between him and this pretentious girl, and then maintaining the lead. Amanda watched him attempt a four-minute mile and nearly laughed. True, he quickly moved way ahead of her, but this she ignored.

Three minutes later, his hard fought lead had dwindled to nothing. Amanda was still on her usual pace, only now right beside him. As they came down the final stretch, the tall sixth year runner watched her long, black hair fly past him. He tried to keep her pace, but knew it was all over. Amanda sailed past the finish line, having only had to increase her pace slightly. She, too, was still in the best possible shape after finishing this race. They had raced their way into the semifinals for the third year in a row. Amanda felt a surge of pride. She would return home with another trophy for her school.

Now the TV cameras and reporters thronged about the Bradbury team. Alister and the adults kept Ashley completely hidden from view, waiting for Amanda to cool down. Just as soon as she was, they all headed to their rooms once more. Hastily, Hank handed out the drinks and appropriate energy bars. Ashley found herself gobbling hers. Why was she so hungry?

"Rest up, gang. We are up again at three. It's either New Orleans or St. Louis that we will be facing. Watch them both carefully. I doubt they will make the same mistakes as Atlanta did."

At three in the afternoon, only four teams remained: New Orleans with its young runners, St. Louis, Orange County, and Bradbury. While Bradbury raced against St. Louis, Orange County raced against New Orleans. Hank decided to monitor the other race closely, regretting that he did not have a way to record the other race. Thus, he would have to observe them and give whatever advice he could to Tom, should they be in the finals.

"Hey, little armless girl, you must be good if you got this far," a tall boy from St. Louis with a deep bass voice spoke to his competitor as they lined up on the starting block. Lindsey, as before, adjusted Ashley's baton perfectly.

Ashley felt obligated to answer since he was being polite. "I try my best," she replied. The big boy grinned. He knew that he could easily take her or so he thought.

Shortly after Andy at last won his sprint, the miler's began their race. Ashley raced down the track using her normal Apache pace. After all, she had spent much of the summer trying to keep pace with the others. What she had not realized yet, was that all this long distance running had strengthened her endurance. Although this was now the third race of the day, she barely felt the exertion, being nearly as fresh as she had at the start.

The St. Louis team was suffering from exhaustion at this point. When Ashley handed off to Jake, she gave him a commanding lead, much to the shock and dismay of those on the St. Louis team. Now, everyone began to take note of her, and Alister has a hard time keeping the various reporters away from her. She had become the object of their desires. Someone just had to get an exclusive interview with this amazing young woman.

A few minutes later, Fern easily beat their runner, and the Bradbury team took a commanding lead. Lindsey also observed how tired the St. Louis longer distance runners were. She too only had to maintain her usual pace, giving Jim a significant lead when she handed off. By the time that Amanda crossed the finish line, she was a quarter of the track ahead of her opponent. She had not deviated from her pace in the slightest.

As she joined her teammates, all were jumping and cheering. They had made it to the last race for first place!

Reporters thronged around them, held at bay only by the physical bodies of the many adults, who promptly escorted the team back into their rooms. While they all continued to cheer each other, Hank again went around doling out drinks and bars, working very diligently to match what he sensed each body now needed. He paid the most attention to the four long distance runners, naturally.

Finally, he sat down with them to coach them on their next and final race. "It's us against a very, very good Orange County team. Their runners are all at least fifth years, maybe sixth. They are good, and I've not spotted any flaws. You are going to have to race your very best if you hope to beat them."

"Hey, we are in the best shape yet. Look at our three times," Tom pointed out. "118:35, 117:40, 118:45. We are being very consistent. We have all four of us in about the same shape at this point in the race, unlike last year when Lindsey and Jim had been forced to use all they had and were both spent for the last race. I know we can do it, I just know it!" Tom's enthusiasm was catching.

"Okay, listen up everyone," Alister broke in. "When we go out this time, they will be doing a formal introduction of the players for both sides. If someone is going to attack you, this would be an ideal time. Each of you will be in the spotlight for a short period. We will be on our highest alert. You all stay alert as well."

Until now, Ashley and the others had forgotten all about the impending calamity that Ashley had foreseen. Suddenly, it all came back to her. "However, I don't anticipate any trouble," Alister added. Just as quickly, her fears evaporated. No, the explosion came during the trophy presentations. Time enough to become scared then, she thought to herself, just keep from falling down or doing something stupid.

A fanfare sounded, time for the two top teams to march onto the field. Indeed, this was spotlight time for each team member. The nine stood facing their opposing nine from Orange County School of Magic. One by one, their names were called out, and each had to step forward a foot to thunderous applause.

Lindsey smiled as she stepped forward, but her eyes swept down the line of her opponents. All were fifth or sixth year boys, all tall and thin, and every one of them looked the part of a runner. She knew that they faced stiff competition. Lindsey only hoped that they had run enough during the winter season to be up to the challenge. In southern California, they had the advantage of good running weather all year round. For an instant, she thought this was not fair.

Ashley stepped forward, very conscious that thousands of eyes stared at her. The enthusiastic applause was deafening. She'd experienced nothing like this in her life. That emotion of self-pride grew even more within her, confusing her even more. She was being acknowledged for herself, for her being on this team. Ashley just did not know what to make of this at all. She spied all nine of her opponents staring at her, and several even didn't try to mask their stares. Normally, this would have driven her attention back in on herself, but her newfound pride forced it back out nearly as fast.

The team gathered for a last minute word from Tom. "Stiff competition, but we can do it. Let's show them what we have. You all are the greatest!" This was Tom's pep talk. Then the final meet began.

Less than a minute later, a dejected Andy was finished for the day, beaten badly by the fast Orange County sprinter. "I prefer being a goal keeper," he grinned at Lindsey, who was helping get Ashley ready. Both girls giggled; they knew what he meant.

As Ashley got ready, she looked up at her opponent. "Gosh, you are tall," she exclaimed.

"Yeh, I know, six-ten. I play basketball mostly," he replied.

"Can't, no arms," Ashley joked. "Play pool though." He gave her a grin, though she knew that he didn't believe that last. Then, the gun sounded and they were off. "Concentrate, Ashley," she thought. She ran as fast as she could safely run. Soon, she saw Jake getting up to speed, and then felt him grab the baton from her. Just as she began to slow down, she lost her concentration for an instant and stumbled.

Ashley knew that she was about to take a nasty fall,

right here before thousands. The tiny fly buzzing along with her, waved its tiny wand, held in its tiny foot. Monane cast a slight Levitation spell, keeping Ashley from falling, releasing her the second she had her footing back. "Thanks," Ashley whispered into the air, hoping that the fly heard her. She jogged to the sidelines, where Lindsey was waiting for her.

"Good race, sis," Lindsey exclaimed.

"Yes, but I ended up miles behind him. He is really tall, and I'm really short, not a fair race," Ashley complained. Jake was having his own problems; his competitor was also taller than he was and with a correspondingly larger stride. He too lost more ground. Emilio then did his best, but their slowest runner lost even more ground.

Poor Fern now had a real dilemma, as she took the baton from Emilio. With a quarter mile to go, she was about two hundred feet behind. Many would have given up and coasted to the finish line; the race was over. Not Fern, she decided that this guy wasn't going to cross that line before her, and she gave it everything she had, stretching her legs into the longest stride she could muster.

What Fern did not know, nor did anyone outside of the Orange County team, was that they had switched the order of mile runners. Abe, who was now running and normally led off the mile relay, had twisted an ankle in the last race. Barely able to run, they decided to put him last, hoping to gain a large enough lead that Abe could somehow hold on to it or perhaps have Bradbury's last runner just give up.

Fern flew down the track at the fastest pace she'd ever set for herself. She closed the gap so rapidly that she began to wonder what was happening. The limp of her opponent gave it away; he was running on a sore leg! Emboldened further, Fern pushed herself to her limits and flew across the line one stride ahead of him.

The crowd went wild over this surprising comeback, yelling and cheering. Fern, however, turned to see how her opponent was doing, not well at all. He could now barely walk. She moved to his side and offered him her shoulder. "Hey, lean on me. I'll take some of the weight off your leg. Which way?"

"Thanks. I have to sit down fast before I fall down. Make for our coach there. I knew I shouldn't have run," the tall boy said, grimacing from the pain.

"You had to or forfeit your team's chance to race at all," Fern said what she knew he had thought.

Although fighting a stabbing pain in his leg, he flashed her a grin. "Dead on."

"I'd of done the same thing," she answered, as the coach and several other team members took over for her.

"Thanks, miss," their coach acknowledged Fern, who turned to return to her teammates.

"Way to go Fern! You did it! Congratulations! Whoopee!" were among the various comments thrown her way, as everyone patted her on her back. Now Lindsey took up her starting position. She knew that, while Fern's great race was terrific, what mattered was the twenty-mile relay and its twenty points.

Almost at once, her opponent began pulling out in front of her. Lindsey refused to yield her pace to him just yet. Amanda signaled her that she was on her pace at the half-mile point, and Lindsey guessed that he must be trying for a five minute mile. This being his fourth race of the day, she strongly suspected that he could not maintain that pace. Indeed, two miles later, still on her original six-minute mile pace, she began to make up lost ground; he was slowing down. Encouraged, she continued until Amanda signaled her this was her final half mile. Now, Lindsey decided to see just what she had left. Had all her summer long distance running paid off? She poured it on, straining herself to the limits.

After she handed off to Jim, Tom called out, "Amazing, Lindsey, 5:30 last mile for you!" Indeed, she had given Jim a slight lead over his opponent. Lindsey wished that she could tell Jim to keep to the plan. It was working perfectly, but there was no way that she could. She jogged to cool down and then took her position beside Ashley.

Jim knew this was his time to shine. Though it was his fourth race, he was prepared. Still, he knew that he would be deep trouble if he intentionally deviated from the grand plan. Lindsey would never forgive him. Against the adrenaline surge he felt, he kept his usual six-minute mile pace. However, he kept telling himself, "Wait for the last mile. Then, I'll show them what an Apache can do!" Amanda gave him the thumbs up sign, which helped him considerably, as he was slowly edging up in speed. Finally, racing settled him down, and he just ran, as he always loved to do out there on the High Plains.

Amanda gave him the full speed signal, and Jim kicked into high gear. He flew down the track, giving Tom a challenge in getting up to speed with him. He had opened up their lead to a hundred feet now. When he finally cooled down and joined Lindsey, who had the stopwatch, she called out, "Super Jim! 5:10! Incredible."

Hank joined them, bubbling with excitement. "You kids realize you are on course to set a new first place speed record? There's been faster track records, of course, but that was set in one of the first elimination races. First place race is the fourth in the day; speeds always slow way down. Incredible!"

"Yahoo!" exclaimed Jim. "I'd better take up Amanda's position so she can get into her take off position. I'll tell her!" He jogged across to Amanda's location on the other side of the track. Amanda's arms punched skyward. Lindsey knew that she was reacting to their times.

At last, Tom passed off to Amanda; he'd maintained their slight lead, even though his opponent had kept pace with him the whole five miles. As he jogged to Lindsey, she reported, "5:09! You beat Jim and me! Good going!" He punched his arms into the air. Across the field, Jim gave the thumbs up sign to his older sister. She too was right on her pace, a six-minute mile. Jim was proud of the way his sister looked as she flew down the track, her long, black hair flying out behind her. "What a sister!" he exclaimed to himself.

"Go Amanda go!" screamed Pam at the top of her voice. She and nearly everyone else in Yellow Hall were yelling and cheering in front of the big screen TV. She and Monique had been watching their races all day. "They are going to do it! I just know it! Look at her fly!"

"Go! Go! Go!" Monique added to the noise in the commons. All the other four commons were also filled with cheering students. Bradbury's was going to be on the map for sure now!

She was up against the best Orange County long distance runner. Tired and exhausted though he was, he was just as determined to beat this Apache girl. He forced himself to keep her pace, mile after mile. As they entered their last mile, the toll of running four long races in one day began to take a heavy toll on him. In spite of his best efforts, he began to fall behind her.

When Lindsey gave her the signal that this was her last half mile, Amanda really kicked into high gear, giving her final sprint all that she had. At the end, the race for first place turned into a no contest. Amanda crossed the line a hundred feet in front of the gasping runner. They had done it! Bradbury's School of Magic had finally taken first place at the Nationals! Lindsey could scarcely believe her run time, 5:04! She'd beaten both her brothers. 116:23 was their winning time, a new track record for the first place race!

The overhead monitor kept flashing 116:23 along with "New Record." The crowd yelled, cheered, stomped, and whistled. Amanda jogged to cool down, punching the air above her in victory. As soon as she neared her teammates, they swarmed around her. Everyone was yelling, "We did it! Super run, Amanda!"

The announcer called for the Bradbury team to take a bow for the audience. As they all stepped forward, the noise was even louder. Back in the Yellow Hall commons, it was mass pandemonium; everyone including Pam was yelling loud enough to be heard in Des Moines. Then, suddenly, Pam realized that the predicted time for the explosion was nearly upon them. Using her voice magnification spell, she yelled, "Quiet! The predicted explosion is about to happen!" Exultation gave way to an instant silence; everyone edged and maneuvered to try to see the big screen. What was happening now?

As the noise finally died down, Alister rushed his group into their private locker room. Huan Su and Delius cast their lock spells on both doors so that no one could enter and interrupt them. "Stick to my plan. Do not deviate," Alister warned them. Alister, Monane, Wilma, and the professors, went down the line of students, casting their spells upon them. First, Tom, Jim, and Jake received their In the Event of an Explosion: Teleport to Bradbury's School of Magic's Parking Lot. Each also received a Skin of Stone spell. All three then went to stand near the door.

Hank had cleverly brought everyone's wands into the locker room. He retrieved them from his hidden bag in an unused locker, handing each to their owner. The boys now felt a whole lot better about this.

Quickly, each adult was paired with the student with whom they were going to exchange identities. Cho Lin cast her Polymorph Self into Another spell on Ashley, who suddenly looked exactly like Cho Lin. Hank handed her Cho Lin's wand, and she tried to pick it up with her foot before realizing she had to hold it in her hand. "I, I can't use it like this," Ashley wailed.

"Hopefully, you won't have to," Cho Lin replied. She then cast a Skin of Stone on Ashley-Cho Lin. "Okay, here I go." She took a deep breath and cast her spell on herself. A flash of magic, and Cho Lin-Ashley appeared before Ashley-Cho Lin. Her wand dropped to the floor. "Can you please put my wand in my pocket?" she asked.

Ashley-Cho Lin tried to pick it up with her foot before catching herself. Awkwardly, she picked it up with her hand and put it where Cho Lin-Ashley could get to it, when she returned to her normal self. Huan Su then cast a Skin of Stone on his wife.

Monane changed into Amanda, and Amanda-Monane moved back out of the way with a Skin of Stone on her. Wilma-Lindsey cast the same spell on herself and on Lindsey-Wilma. Betsy-Fern did likewise for Fern-Betsy. Huan Su-Emilio fixed up Emilio-Huan Su, as did Delius-Andy for Andy-Delius.

"Hey, they are making the second place presentation now," called out Hank.

"Okay, Hank, as soon as we leave, you throw up an invisible wall of force just in front of the students here. If the explosion occurs, get them all teleported to the Bradbury parking lot immediately. Do not, I repeat, do not wait for us," Alister ordered him in very stern words. "If trouble occurs, get them out of here immediately. Understood," he looked at the seven faces. Hank promised and opened the door.

"Remember to throw up your wall of force, once we get into our positions," Alister said his last order.

"Oh and remember to act like you just won the trophy," Tom added, waving to the stands nearby. Already they had begun clapping for them. Alister allowed Tom, waving at the crowd, to lead his team into the stadium. As Huan Su-Emilio passed him, he whispered, "Alister, the Orange County team is way too close. If there is an explosion, they will be hurt as well."

Alister whispered, "Throw your wall out in front of them instead; give them a fighting chance." Now Alister, too, began waving at the crowd. As Delius-Andy passed by Alister, Alister cast his See True spell on him. As he moved to follow the line of students, Alister also cast it covertly on Huan Su-Emilio and then himself. Alister left nothing to chance. Three of them would be able to see through any disguises that might appear.

Alister noted that the presentation ceremonies were taking place at the same spot that they had been for the last few years. They were at one end of the huge stadium. Herbert Musk would be making the formal presentation. This was the man who refused to give Alister's warning much credence, though allowed him some extra leeway for his student's safety.

The huge first place trophy was on a small cart now in the center of the arena. Herbert began slowly pushing it their way. A microphone hung down in front of where they were lined up. Herbert's presentation would be heard around the world. When the cart was about a hundred feet from them, the crowd yelling and cheering, Alister saw that the man walking towards them was not Herbert Musk. Rather, it was Phillip Royster! He'd used the same Morph Self into Another spell, taking Herbert's place! Delius and Huan Su also saw the same thing, whispering it to the others standing beside them.

Although he continued to wave to the crowd, fear crept into Tom's very fiber. All along, he hoped that Ashley's premonition was somehow wrong. He wanted nothing to mar the sweet victory for which he'd worked so long and hard.

Now, it seemed Ashley might be right. What was Phillip doing here, pretending to be the master of ceremonies?

As Phillip-Herbert drew a bit close, Alister called out to him. "Phillip, don't do this! It's not too late to turn back." Phillip-Herbert flinched. Alister had seen through his disguise!

Phillip was at a turning point in his life. Again, he was asked to make a decision for himself. Unfortunately for him, he now considered that there was no going back for himself. He was now committed to Dominus. He glared at Alister and continued to roll the gleaming trophy towards the line of students. When he reached them, he stood beneath the microphone. He began, "Ladies and gentlemen, it is time to give these first place runners their due. . ." He got no further words spoken, however.

The trophy suddenly detonated in a blinding explosion! The last anyone ever saw of Phillip-Herbert was the look of total shock and surprise on his face. (Alister later explained that Phillip had been used and discarded and did not know he was carrying a bomb with him.) The massive explosion hit the walls of force and shot upwards to the roof as well as sideways, before deflecting off the additional wall Huan Su-Emilio had placed before the Orange County team. Magical energies flashed, Tom, Jim, and Jake disappeared instantly.

At that same moment, secondary explosions ripped along in the shape of a large rectangle surrounding the floor on which the line of students and Alister were standing. The many explosions were timed to go off at the same instant with the big one hiding the smaller ones. As they tried to brace themselves from the concussion of the explosion, the floor beneath them gave way, and they and the floor of the stadium began falling rapidly downwards into the basement.

Cho Lin-Ashley flailed her non-existent arms wildly in a desperate attempt to maintain some form of balance. She fell hard onto the collapsing floor. All were momentarily stunned as their bodies hit the floor, which hit the concrete basement floor of the stadium. Not even Alister had anticipated this event!

Ashley-Cho Lin shrieked in panic as her eyes saw the very explosion she had seen in her premonition! The massive shock wave and flames raced towards where they were standing. All stood frozen to the spot, unable to react that fast. Thankfully, the wall of force deflected and forced the flames, heat, and concussion shockwave up and over them.

Hank recovered and got everyone holding to each other and to his left hand. "Teleport: Bradbury's Parking Lot!" he screamed, amid the deafening noise. Again, magical energies flashed, and the shocked students and coach arrived at their parking lot, standing beside equally shocked three boys!

Hastily, he canceled all their spells and opened the main gates. "Kids, race to your dorm. Stay there!" They needed no further encouragement and began running to their dorm, completely forgetting about making magical doors to speed their progress. Hank messaged professors Blake, Arthur, and Jerry, who had just witnessed the explosion on the TV. Seconds later, they appeared beside him at the main gates. Hank looked terrified and worried about his wife, Betsy.

"What do we do now?" he asked. Jerry had been left in charge of the school and Hank had to defer to him.

Wearing masks to filter out the acrid fumes of pulverized concrete and burning debris, Ten Death Stalkers slowly inspected their handiwork from the nearby hallway. The dust obliterated vision for a minute so that neither party could see the other, which gave Alister time to recover his senses. "Cancel morph spells!" he called out. Cho Lin unfortunately could not; she was mostly unconscious.

As the dust began to settle, the Death Stalkers saw Cho Lin-Ashley lying on the remains of the floor. "Get the armless one, top priority. Find the one called Lindsey, if you can. Kill the rest," one voice ordered. Three men moved carefully over the debris to get to Cho Lin-Ashley, while the others took up defensive positions, looking for the others.

Alister knew that he had time for only one spell, before they would be madly blasting away with spells. With no Dispellers, not even staves of power to help counter spells, his faculty were in dire peril. He heard the others moaning and groaning, coming to their senses. "Wall of Force," he commanded, placing the barrier between the oncoming men and Cho Lin-Ashley.

Huan Su-Emilio came too and struggled to his feet. "Get her to the school!" Alister ordered. He was very willing to oblige. Monane saw the glimmer of the force field and shot another behind it, just in case. Then, she helped Wilma to her feet.

"Do we go after them?" Wilma asked Alister, though coughing like mad from the dust.

"Teleport home at once," he ordered. He saw that the three Death Stalkers were now at the barrier wall, looking in at the small group. None was a student, except for Cho Lin-Ashley. Shock filled their faces.

"Where did the students go?" one asked.

"Quick, upstairs, they must have changed places!" Seven Death Stalkers retreated, heading for the stairs, shortly followed by the other three. Alister watched as the last of his faculty vanished, leaving only himself behind. He sent a Message to Hank, and as soon as he received the reply, he too returned to Bradbury's.

Meanwhile inside the stadium, chaos, death, and destruction escalated. The roof above where the explosion went off collapsed down on all those in this area. Many were trampled as they tried to escape, panic-stricken. Hundreds were badly burned by the explosion. Soon the very air within the enclosed stadium became nearly un-breathable. Toxic odors filled the open space, only adding to the frenzy.

Undaunted, the many television crews continued to pan the scene of destruction, while their reporters continued their wild explanations. At last, the acrid smoke even curtailed their heroic attempts to report the news, forcing them to join the massive throng trying to get out of the place. MagNews had a field day.

As the students headed to the dorms, Jim put his arm securely around Ashley. "I won't ever let anything bad happen to you, princess. I love you." Right now, she needed that and leaned her head onto his shoulders, glad to have someone on which to lean. The images in her mind were quite frightening. None was unaffected by what they had just seen. Tom was white as a sheet, as they all entered the hushed silence of

Yellow Hall's commons. Literally, everyone was glued to the horrifying images on the screen. More than a few were sobbing to themselves.

"We're back; we're safe," Tom announced. Like a bolt of lightning, heads turned to connect a face with the voice.

"Tom!" shrieked Sandy. "You are alive!" She pushed and shoved her way through the throng to grab hold of him, kissing him madly, nearly crushing him in her grip.

"All safe and sound," Jake added.

"But we just saw you all standing there getting blown up," the tear-filled face of Audrey called out, unable to connect their presence with the horrifying images she'd just seen.

"The professors took our place," Jim tried to explain.

"What? All of our professors have been blown to bits?" someone else called out.

"They are probably safe," Jim tried to calm things down. "Alister had our escape all planned beforehand. I'm sure they will all be back here safely in a couple minutes.

By now, Pam, Monique, Kathy, and Audrey had made their way to their friends. Pam's eyes were red from crying. She just threw her arms around Lindsey and held on tightly. Soon, half of Yellow Hall tried to hug them as well. News spread rapidly, and many others from the four remaining halls tried to squeeze in to see the track team for themselves, if not call out congratulations to them.

The horrible images continued to be broadcast on the big screen, and soon everyone's attention became riveted on the disaster once more. Some hoped to catch a glimpse of their professors, to know that they were okay. Explanations had to wait; the news was too overwhelming to avoid. It was happening live before their eyes.

They had not been back but ten minutes before Governor Alister's voice boomed throughout the campus. "Greetings students, professors. I am pleased to announce that everyone is back safely. No students were hurt by the explosion. We are getting cleaned up in the Infirmary at the moment. It was a bit dusty in there. My hair was singed a bit. I will give you a full report later tonight. In the meantime, will the nine students on the track team please phone your parents and let them know that you are okay and back at school? Thank you."

"Lindsey, you call, I can hardly speak right now, and I still have my track shoes on," Ashley whispered to Lindsey. Unfortunately, her cell phone was back in Des Moines. Pam lent her hers, and she hastily called her mother to tell her the news. It was a wise move, since they had all gathered at her house to watch the big race on the television, and everyone was terribly worried, though they trusted that Alister would not have let their children be harmed. Since the Whitewaters were right there too, Lindsey handed the phone to Amanda, who talked with her mom for a while, before handing it over to Fern, then Tom, and finally Jim.

Jim hung up, "Hey, Lindsey, your mom said that she would be letting the Blackburns and the Betts know that everyone is all right." Pam felt relieved. Lindsey smiled, handing the phone back to Pam. Emilio borrowed it next, while Jake had already borrowed a phone from a friend of his.

Jim undid Ashley's track spikes, while Lindsey made a quick trip to their room, Amanda joined her. A bit later, the girls ducked into the restroom to chance from their track outfits into their school clothes, rejoining the others to watch the news coverage.

Slowly the panicked first reports of thousands of dead gave way to more accurate reporting. The voice of Hugo announced, "Temporary emergency services have been set up in the parking lot. Our live cameras show many are taking advantage of the on the scene doctors. Officials have set up a temporary morgue in an undamaged locker room. The official death toll stands at five so far. Miraculously, the Orange County track team, who had just received their trophy, suffered minor concussion shocks and some scrapes and bruises trying to get out of there. According to their Governor, someone had placed a force wall between them and the blast, which saved their lives."

"The many wounded have suffered smoke inhalation from the blast or were trampled in the panic escape. Many are suffering from a loss of hearing from the explosion, though health officials have said that their hearing ought to return to normal within a few days."

"This just in, our reporters have just been contacted by Governor Alister Broadwell from his Bradbury campus. He claims that all students are unharmed. All somehow miraculously escaped the fiery inferno and blast. This runs contrary to the first reports, however, as our own video seems to show the entire track team being blown up. We will be running this footage once more shortly. See for yourselves or rather guess how Governor Alister Broadwell managed to get his students to safety in the blink of an eye. Also, we have many eyewitness accounts lined up next. Stay tuned for complete coverage. Now this word from our sponsors."

Shortly, Hugo returned. "Hugo back with breaking news of the bombing of the Des Moines Stadium. Security forces have just released the identity of the assailant. According to the Department of Law, preliminary findings show that a recently expelled student from Bradbury's School of Magic, one Phillip Royster, masquerading as Herbert, was solely responsible for the blast. He died instantly as he detonated the explosives. Stay tuned, as we try to find out more about this insane bomber."

Hugo continued his live coverage. Lindsey stared, as the footage of the actual explosion was re-shown. She noticed that there seemed to be other smaller explosions going off at the same time, right behind and around the team. She swore that she glimpsed the entire team falling downwards, but couldn't believe her eyes.

With the news now beginning to repeat, Lindsey decided to go check on the professors. She, Ashley, and Jim, who was not about to let Ashley out of his sight today, headed down to the Infirmary. "Good grief, what happened?" she asked. Alister was still covered in grey dust. Bits of dried blood spotted his face and from holes torn in his shirt and pants. The others had already been cleaned up. Doctor Caterwall was working on setting the right arm of Delius, who had broken it in the fall.

"The floor fell out from under us," Alister replied in his usual oblique way, "rather unexpected, by the way."

"Is Professor Cho Lin all right?" asked Ashley.

"Over here dear," she called out. Ashley, with Jim at her side, walked over to see her. Her head was bandaged. "Bump on my head. Nothing serious, though."

"Did the floor really fall out from under you?" she asked.

"Yes, it certainly did. I was helpless to keep my balance, I'm afraid. Fell and hit my head. Missed all the action. Woke up here," she managed a smile. "You've taught me a valuable lesson, my dear. I now value my arms more than ever before. It was sure strange, falling like that, frantically trying to use arms that were not there. I believe that I understand you far better now, Ashley."

"I was worried about you, professor. I mean I've always been this way so I'm used to it, but," she didn't finish her sentence. From the look on Cho Lin's face, she knew she didn't have to.

Huan Su entered from another room, drying off. "Well, hello. We got rather dirty. You were right, Miss Stokes-Compton. Dominus was out to capture you, but we foiled his plot. Timed explosions literally cut the very floor out from beneath us. We went crashing into the basement. I heard one Death Stalker specifically order three others to capture Ashley alive, along with Lindsey and to kill the rest of you students. Nasty fellow, this Dominus."

"But why should he be after me? Because I kicked him?" she asked.

"No dear," Cho Lin answered her. "Because of your Divination gift. Last time, he was apprehended only because Mabel Pruit was able to constantly figure out where he was going to be and when. We all believe now that he greatly fears that you will be doing the same in a few years' time. That, he cannot afford."

"Oh," she paused. "Does that mean he is going to keep on trying to get me?"

Cho Lin looked at Alister. Her eyes said, "We should tell her the truth," at least Lindsey thought so.

Alister said soothingly, "Oh no more so than Lindsey, I would expect. However, Ashley, as long as you always keep us informed as soon as you have premonitions, why, I expect that we will keep one step ahead of him." Lindsey noted that he used her first name; he was being very personal and not formal with her, as though she was a close friend. "Now then, I do believe that it is finally my turn to clean up. If you will excuse me," he smiled and headed into the shower normally used for emergency cleanups here in the Infirmary.

"We'd better get back to the others," Lindsey said.

"May I have a private word with Ashley, please," Professor Cho Lin asked. Ashley wondered what she could possibly want of her but followed her into a side waiting room.

"Ashley, I've learned just how precious you are. If you ever need anything, anything at all, just ask me. Promise me that you will ask if you need something and not necessarily while you are here at school."

She didn't quite know what to make of this, but promised that she would. Then, they headed back to the commons. Jim continued to have his arm around Ashley, though. Much of the crowd had finally left. Hugo was merely replaying the more graphic video footage taken earlier. A small caption announced the official death toll was now at a dozen.

Pam and Monique were both there, typing furiously on their computers. "You missed it," Pam blurted out. "Dominus! He came on and interrupted the MagNews feed. I've been taping the highlights of today for you all. He claims that—oh here, let me just play it back."

Monique had it queued up, and she played it for them. "Hello, Dominus Malefic here once more. Today, another great tragedy has befallen one of our national sporting events. I want to take this opportunity to state on the record that I had nothing to do with the insane boy who blew up the stadium, seeking revenge on his former school. In fact, if I am elected your President, I promise that nothing like this horror shall ever happen on my watch. Ask yourselves, what kind of a leader would allow this to happen? So many innocent lives were lost, so many injured. Remember this horrible tragedy when you go to the polls this fall. I promise you I will work hard to prevent any such bombings in our wonderful country."

"There, he is denying any involvement again! The evil scoundrel. We've been trying to see if we can find any connections to him," Monique stated angrily. "Pam might be on to something. Tell them love."

Pam blushed, "Well, I got to thinking, how did they get the bomb in there? I searched the security logs, and they did bring in bomb sniffing dogs. The explosives had to be on the ceiling; no wonder the dogs didn't find anything. It was twelve feet overhead, probably hidden in all the pipes and stuff, I imagine. However, the main bomb was in the trophy. That's what I'm working on now. You see, according to the Nationals' website, all the trophies are made by a Newark company called First Quality Trophies. I just came across something interesting. Look at this police report."

Newark, NJ. First Quality Trophies Financial Officer, Ben Smith, reported that their facilities had been broken into last night; the guard on duty murdered, one John Jerimiah. Ben discovered the break in and the body when he came to work at eight this morning. Four trophies bound for the National Track Meet were stolen. According to Ben, they will be remade and shipped in time for the presentation. Monetary loss estimate: $500.00. Autopsy: pending.

"Don't ask me how I'm able to view this police file," Pam stated. "Now, I need to find a way to pin this crime on Dominus and his men, find where they obtained their explosives, find witnesses to their appearance in the basement of the stadium, and we'll have Dominus!"

"Interesting, Pam. Man, am I ever starving!" Lindsey felt her stomach growl. None of them had eaten anything since around four and then only the energy drinks and bars. It was now closer to seven.

"Audrey thought that you all might have missed dinner. Sit tight. She's on her way with pizzas and sodas, best she could do on short notice on a Saturday night," Monique replied. "The others are cleaning up and will be down shortly. Party time soon."

A half hour later, the all the team members were gathered around a table in the commons. Audrey brought them four large pizzas, and all nine began devouring them, thanking Audrey repeatedly. She teased them, "Well, if you had been Brown Hall students who won the Nationals for us, why, you'd be having steak." Tom gave her a squeeze on her rump, and she giggled.

Sandy sat beside Tom, her fiancé. "I'm never going to let go of you again, Tom! I thought I'd lost you today."

"You can't get rid of me that easily, Miss Rains, soon to be Mrs. Whitewater," Tom teased her back, stuffing another slice into his mouth.

While they were all eating, Governor Alister again addressed the whole school. True to his word, he explained all that had happened in detail. He ended by praising the nine students for showing the world how to face adversity squarely, winning the Nationals for Bradbury, directly in the face of adversity. He also pointed out that the real Herbert Musk has been found tied and gagged in his office. He was otherwise in good shape. He promised Governor Alister a replacement trophy would be delivered to Bradbury's by Friday. Alister then stated, "If the trophy arrives on Friday, then we will hold a school wide assembly to honor our victorious track team." When he finished, Jimmy and the school bus arrived, bringing back all their personal items.

Friday, the huge trophy arrived. Alister had it placed in the center of the dining hall. When the track team arrived for the celebration and party at seven, the girls each found themselves given a large bouquet of red roses, a dozen each! One bunch was in a small pouch with a shoulder strap, especially made for Ashley. As Lindsey was handed her bunch, she noticed a tiny card. While she wanted immediately to peek at it, she resisted until the presentations were finished. A photographer took the team's picture around the trophy. Using digital methods, he soon presented them each with a copy.

Tom had each of them sign his copy, and his teammates loved the idea. Soon, they signed all nine copies. Then, Alister had Lindsey take the tenth photograph to the Admin Hall, while Tom and Jim lugged the trophy there. With pride, she pinned the photograph up next to her father's team, while Tom placed their golden trophy in the center of the room. Lindsey wiped a tear from her eye, as she looked at her father's photograph staring back at her. "I wish you could have seen us today, dad. Your little girl done good," she thought to herself.

Finally, the festivities were over, and the girls returned to their room. Lindsey suddenly remembered the tiny card. At last, she opened it.

To the Greatest Girl in the World. Deiter Cross.

Curious, she helped Ashley with hers, and together read her card. Ashley, Amanda, and Fern's all read the same.

To the Finest Athletes and Girls in the World. Deiter Cross.

"What's yours say," Amanda insisted on knowing. Lindsey showed it to her.

"Yours is different!" Ashley pointed out.

"I think Deiter may have a crush on Lindsey," Amanda proclaimed. Lindsey flushed, taking her card from Amanda's hand.

"I've never gotten flowers before, well, not quite like this," Ashley said timidly. "Shouldn't we send him a thank-you card or something?"

Chapter 24—End of Term

The warm days of May flew rapidly by Lindsey. Already, they were cramming for their exams. Saturday, May 14 came rapidly. Once more, they would get to visit Telluride, their last trip until the fall. All around town, the flowers were blooming; spring was fully here.

Andy and Lindsey spent much of the day walking arm in arm around the whole town. Neither wanted to catch a movie. They were grade B reruns anyway. Although they said little, words were not needed. Each enjoyed the mere presence of the other. They did, however, pick up wedding presents for Tom and Sandy.

In contrast, Monique and Pam first revisited the derelict house where Pam had been held captive. She was interested to see if it had yet been repaired. It had not, which Pam thought most strange indeed. After a little shopping, the two spent the long afternoon in the darkened movie theater.

Ashley and Jim spent the morning in the pool hall. In the afternoon, they walked to the small city park, where spring flowers were in full bloom. Jim spread out a blanket and laid down. Ashley lay next to him, resting her head on his shoulders, his arm around her. Neither said much. "I just want to lay here beside you, your arm around me, and look at the beauty of the mountains," she said. That's precisely what they did, except for sharing a few loving kisses.

The next week, Millicent Prague finally fully recovered from her ordeal. Professor Mary Ann allowed her to go home. However, Millicent sent a request for Ashley to come to meet with her briefly. "There you are, my fine young girl," Millicent said, as Ashley entered, a little uncertain why she was wanted.

"Mary Ann has pronounced me fit as a fiddle so I get to go home today. Before I leave, I wanted to again thank you, Ashley, for what you did for me. I have a little something that I want to give you to show you how much I appreciate everything you've done for me." She opened a small box, revealing a fine looking, small golden pin with an emerald set in its middle.

"This is for you," she said, pinning it to her blouse. "Wear it at all times. It is not a piece of jewelry, as you might think. It is enchanted so that no one can ever read your mind or read your thoughts. Take it as a gift from one Diviner to another. We must all do what we can for each other. There are so few of us in this world. If ever you need anything, do not hesitate to call upon me. I owe you my life."

Ashley was speechless. "Thank you. It's beautiful." She didn't know what else to say. She leaned forward, which Millicent took as a gesture indicating a hug. The older woman hugged her tightly, and Ashley even added to it with her leg.

"Wear it always. Don't give Dominus any chance to read your mind ever! Goodbye my dear." They hugged again, and Millicent left for home. Ashley returned to the commons to show Lindsey and her friends what she had been given. Pam promptly looked it up on the Net and discovered that similar items had been selling for nearly five thousand dollars. Ashley gasped and then swore never to be without it.

By the end of the third week of May, everyone had finally passed the last of their many exams. Kathy shocked everyone by pulling an A in chemistry, due in no small part to the constant aid from her friends, until her study breakthrough. She was elated, because it meant that she could take potion making next fall.

Then, it was time to work out their fall schedule of classes. "Eggads! How are we to jam nine classes into eight periods!" exclaimed Pam, as she began to work out her schedule for the next term. Lindsey looked at the list and agreed that it was not doable.

"We'd better all go see Professor Cho Lin at once," Pam declared. She dragged all her friends with her. Essentially, everyone had similar problems, too many courses, too little time.

"Ah, Miss Betts," Cho Lin smiled as she entered the immaculate office. "Oh, all of you?" she spied everyone else coming right behind Pam. "Ah, let me see, scheduling difficulties?" she grinned. She was used to this. It happened with every fourth year student. Their workload increased, because they would be fifteen and more mature.

"Well, yes," Pam said, rather surprised that she knew ahead of time why Pam was here. Perhaps she read her mind, she thought. "We have too many courses and not enough time periods."

"Surely, there are too many courses," Emilio pleaded. His proposed schedule was more than he had ever taken.

"Well, Emilio, you just barely made it into potion making, by the skin of your teeth, that is. Now let's see." She pulled up their tentative schedules on her computer. "Yes, I do believe that they are nearly the same."

"But there are only eight periods," Pam protested. "None of us want to give up our electives!"

"Oh dear me no, no. Nothing of the kind. However, I'm afraid that Kathy will lose her study hall this fall. Sorry. Your electives will take place at six, giving you all an hour for supper. I have arranged this with all of your elective teachers. Essentially, your schedules are all set. Here is the printout." She showed them their proposed classes.

```
 8:00 PE
 9:00 English
10:00 Trigonometry
11:00 Physics
 1:00 World Cultures and Foreign Language
 2:00 Alteration Theory II
 3:00 Potion Making I
 4:00 Spell Casting Grade 5
 6:00 Elective
```

"What changes do you wish to make?" she asked politely.

"Oh, oh, so I get Sleuthing II at six," Pam declared. "Well, then, I'm perfectly happy with mine now. I was worried that I would have to lose one subject, and I couldn't decide which to do without, you see."

Emilio groaned. "Nine classes! I'll have no time for anything at all!"

"Well, yes, fourth year is a bit challenging, but I'm sure that you will rise to meet the challenge," Cho Lin replied.

Lindsey could not tell if she was teasing him or was serious.

"I'm happy then," Andy spoke up, "as long as I get my archaeology class."

"What's this foreign language thing?" asked Kathy. "Can't we just use our magical spell?"

"It is proper that you make an effort to learn to speak and write another language of your choice. I know that you all tend to study together. I would suggest that perhaps you should all agree on which language to learn so that you may help each other with it." Cho Lin winked at Pam, who understood her implicitly.

"Excuse me, Professor Cho Lin," Ashley volunteered. She saw no way but to be direct. "Are you sure that I can actually do this potion making class? You know what I mean. I had an awful time with the chemistry experiments. Lindsey helped me immensely or I would never have been able to get the experiments done on time."

"Yes, Ashley. I talked at length with Delius about this. He assures me that you will be able to handle the physical side. Speed will not be an issue, rather accuracy will be." This satisfied the young girl. Cho Lin printed of the finalized version of their schedules and handed them out. They all returned to their dorm, chatting mostly about how much work fourth year promised to be.

Monique met them as they entered the commons. Grinning, she teased, "Discovered how hard fourth year is going to be?" Emilio gave his usual groan. Kathy replied that she had lost her valuable study hall. Pam began to understand why Monique had had to work so hard these last two years. "Don't worry. Fifth is worse still, and I just got my sixth year schedule, and it's next to impossible!" Emilio groaned as if his stomach were giving out. Pam chuckled at him. "They are going to work your fingers to the bones next year—that's toes in your case Ashley." Everyone giggled or laughed, but they knew next year would be no picnic.

Pam suggested that they all go get their books and spend the summer studying ahead so that when they returned in the fall they would be far ahead. Wanting no part of that at all, Emilio beat a hasty retreat to his room!

That afternoon, Andy received a letter from Colorado State University. "Yahoo!" he exclaimed and raced to show Lindsey his letter. "Look Lindsey! I've been accepted by CSU to be part of their summer school archaeology dig team. They are excavating some Anasazi ruins in Chaco Canyon—that was one of their premier sites. Best of all, look at this! I get paid too!" Andy was in seventh heaven the rest of the week.

"I know that I planned to spend the summer hanging out with you, but this is a chance of a lifetime. You understand, don't you?" Andy asked Lindsey.

"Sure, you have a golden opportunity. Go. You should go, Andy. Besides, my summer will be most likely spent changing diapers," Lindsey replied, relieving Andy, who feared to upset her with his change of plans for the summer.

"I was planning to work for your mom and be with you to help. Do you suppose she won't mind my taking off like this?" Andy double-checked.

"Sure, besides, it is for your own education. Mom would be horribly upset if you turned it down just to work around the ranch," Lindsey stated what she believed her mom would feel. Andy seemed relieved.

"I'll send you emails and pics, okay?"

"Great. I've never seen a dig before," Lindsey replied, wondering what it was that Andy would really be doing. Would he actually be digging in the dirt?

On Saturday morning, Tom called a meeting of the track and soccer team. "As you know, I'm graduating next week."

"And getting married three days later," Sandy teased him. She wasn't letting him out of her sight since he got back from the frightening Nationals.

"Yes, and that too," he grinned. "Let me say this. I've never had the pleasure of working with such fine people as you all have been. I'm extremely proud of each and every one of you. You are the greatest athletes I've ever known. Thanks for letting me be your captain." Lindsey thought he was spreading it a bit thick, but smiled. He had not worked them too hard, and they had achieved it all.

"Well, now I have to appoint next year's captain, as is

our tradition. Now I know what Becky meant when she said last year that the hardest thing is picking the next captain. Tradition says the older team members ought to get a shot at it. Thus, it goes to either Jake or Jim. I know that you all think I should favor my brother, you know, keep it in the family. We have a chance to have four captains in a row, you know. That would be something." Fern gave him a growling look. She didn't think that was the criteria for picking the team captain.

"Seriously, it ought to go to the one who I think is best qualified. I talked this over with both Jim and Jake. Jake has agreed to be your next Yellow Hall track and soccer captain." He sprung this on them when he knew they were not expecting it. Tom grinned; this was probably the last time he would get to tease all them.

"Congratulations, Jake!" Lindsey exclaimed, a bit surprised by Tom's announcement. He beamed the largest smile that Lindsey had ever seen on his face. The others congratulated him as well.

Tom explained, "Jim really doesn't want to be team captain."

"No way! I'm not and have never been a leader. It takes all the fun out of it. I want to play and have fun, not do all that worrying and such," Jim explained.

"Well, you are being honest, for once, Jim," Fern admitted. "He's right you know."

"Careful, sis, don't push me too far today, I might just have to call out the tickle fingers again," Jim teased her, but he felt good about getting the truth off his chest. He never thought of himself as being a leader.

"Again, remember, if Jake doesn't work out, you are free to elect whoever you want this fall," Tom added the required rule.

"Now it's our turn," Amanda broke in on Tom's meeting. "Tom, on behalf of this year's team, we all went together to get you a little memento to remember us all by. Fern, will you do the honors?" Fern grinned. She'd had a hard time keeping this a secret from her older brother.

She handed Tom a nicely wrapped, small box. "What's this?" Tom relied, his face flushing slightly. He opened the present. Inside was a photograph of his team with the first place trophy. The frame was 24-caret gold plated and heavy. His eyes watered and he tried to say thank you, but it was a bit mumbled.

"Now you can always remember us," Fern stated lovingly. She adored her older brother. "It's real gold too," she added.

On Sunday, Governor Alister asked both Lindsey and Ashley to come to his office for a brief meeting. "What can he want?" Ashley asked, as she and Lindsey walked across the campus. Heady aromas of the blooming flowers hung in the warm spring air. The grass was vividly green once more, a perfect day in late May.

"Dunno, must be important though," Lindsey replied. A bit later, they entered his office.

"Ah, there you are. Please have a seat. I have something to discuss with both of you." They did as he asked, though neither had a clue what he wanted to discuss with them. Lindsey wondered if some new news had just been discovered.

"As you know, next term you will be studying World Cultures and learning a language of another people. Every few years, Bradbury's plays host to some foreign exchange students, young wizards and witches from other countries. Norm high schools also do this as well. Next year, Bradbury's will be hosting a dozen students from the Utrecht School of Magic, in the Netherlands. These students will live with their host families during the summer and attend Bradbury's during the school year, spending the holidays with their hosts as well. Each student will need a mentor while they are here."

"Mr. Cross and his parents have already agreed to host Bruggen de Graffe. I have three Yellow Hall students who need host families and mentors: Hans and Katja van der Veer and Jeannette van Ravinstijn. All three will be fourth year students. Naturally, I thought of your family and the Whitewaters, because this would keep the brother and sister very close together. What would you two say to playing host and personal mentors to Katja and Jeannette?"

"Cool, way cool!" Lindsey replied without thinking.

"But what about mom? She's going to have a baby real

soon now," Ashley answered far more practically. She knew she was going to be facing almost insurmountable problems dealing with a little brother or sister. Perhaps Lena would not want all this additional responsibilities.

"I've already discussed this with your parents and the Whitewaters," Alister admitted. "Lena has assured me that she loves the idea and that more hands make less work for everyone. The Whitewaters are also enthusiastic about it. Since Tom is moving out—I understand that he is getting married and the two will be going to college—they have the room. My thought was to have Jim mentor Hans, and you two mentor the girls."

"Perfect! Especially since mom is all for it," Lindsey enthusiastically answered. "We can do it, Ashley, sure we can." Ashley grinned, and nodded her agreement, before she began to give it serious thought—what would a girl from the Netherlands think of having armless her be her mentor.

"Excellent, excellent. Thank you both. By the way, Ashley, Jeannette and you have something in common. She's the Editor of their school newspaper. Perhaps you can share ideas."

She thought that at least they would have that in common. "Good idea," she said.

"Good, I will relay the final plans to your parents and to the Whitewaters as well. They will be arriving at Denver's Stapleton Airport on June 11. Here is their flight plan." He handed Lindsey the computer printout. "All three speak fairly good English, I'm told, but that remains to be seen. I have a pamphlet that describes the program and the duties of the host families and the mentors. By the way, all the mentors will get a special benefit, our way of thanking you and your families for hosting these students."

"In late September and then again in mid-May, the foreign exchange students and their mentors will take weeklong trips to see the more famous sights in the US, from National Parks to big cities. Don't worry, during these weeklong trips, you will be fully excused from your classes and will not be held responsible for any material covered. I believe the professors will be conducting review sessions those two weeks."

"Wow! Fabulous," Lindsey declared, her eyes opening wide. "I've never been anywhere really, excepting here at school and the history trips and that short visit to Denver when you took me to the bank."

"Well, as part of our thank you, you both may submit suggestions on which places you might like to see as well. Professor Cho Lin will be arranging the trips, so get your picks to her by the start of the fall term. Again, I want to thank you both for taking on this added responsibility for our guests from the Netherlands."

Walking back to their dorm, Lindsey said, "Well, I never expected anything like this. Guess we will have some company over the summer. I guess if we don't understand them too well, we can always use our magic spell."

Just then, she spied Tom and Sandy walking arm in arm, out for a stroll. She realized that the two only had a few more days before they would be leaving the campus behind forever. Lindsey just could not imagine life without Bradbury's. Her whole world changed the day she entered these grounds. Now Tom and Sandy would not be here this fall.

"Excuse me, Tom, we were just talking with Alister, and he said you are going to college. I didn't know that," Lindsey said, unsure just what to ask.

"Yes, we've not said much about it, but we are both accepted at CSU in Denver. I'm going to study engineering so I can build things, and Sandy wants to become an elementary school teacher. We both got scholarships, so it ought to work out. Say, in your fifth and sixth years, you will be finding out all about colleges and careers," Tom explained.

"Yes, just get through the fourth year," Sandy added. "They just dump the homework on you like there is no tomorrow." Both Ashley and Lindsey grimaced.

Finally, graduation night came. Everyone cheered loudly for Tom and Sandy. Lindsey just couldn't imagine what life would be like without Sandy around. She'd always been there for her. Lindsey knew that she would certainly miss her.

After the lengthy presentation was finished, Governor

Broadwell said, "Now again, it's time to present the Bradbury's Distinguished Service Medallions. When I call your name, please come up here. As many of you know, these awards are given to those who have displayed uncommon devotion to helping our school in trying times or have given of themselves for the benefit of us all. The first award goes to Mr. Deiter Cross of Black Hall for his hurricane relief program, which many other schools of magic adopted, based on his program."

Black Hall students yelled and cheered as he proudly walked to the front of the dining room. "Next, for their successful thwarting of Dominus Malefic's hurricane control using the Crown of Moses, will Miss Pamela Betts, Miss Ashley Stokes-Compton, and Miss Lindsey Barron please step forward?"

Now it was Yellow Hall's turn to acknowledge loudly their own. "For diligently tracking down the location and thereby saving the lives of Millicent Prague and myself, displaying uncommon Tracker skills, will Miss Amanda Whitewater please step forward?" Tom stomped and yelled as loudly as he could for his older sister.

"Finally, so many others of you participated in the relief efforts, the rescue of the girls from Dominus, and even my own rescue, please give yourselves a big round of applause. All of you deserve a special acknowledgment." Indeed, all the professors joined him in applauding the entire student body. Then, Alister hung the medals around the student's necks, shaking their hands as well, but giving Ashley a hug instead.

The next day, the girls packed for home and spent most of the afternoon preparing for the end of term formal ball. After taking baths or showers, they took turns fixing each other's hair just right. All this fuss was new to Ashley. She had actually never really attended the formal balls at her previous two schools because no one had asked her to go. However, Kathy decided that Ashley was going to be her special project. "After all, you want to look gorgeous so you can knock Jim's socks off," she explained.

"Why does he need to lose his socks?" she asked, totally confused by all this attention.

"Silly, you want him drooling over how beautiful, how

great you look. Guys go nuts over pretty women. You want to look really special for him." Ashley was about to ask why she should want this, but decided better of it. She readily admitted that she knew next to nothing about male-female relationships and decided to do as Kathy suggested and see what the results might be.

"You are fifteen now, so you are certainly old enough to wear a little makeup, Ashley. Now I don't recommend wearing the gaudy cherry red lipstick that the girls in Red Hall wear. Instead, we need something more subtle, more demure, more suited to you. A little eye makeup will help too. Let's see what Kathy can do. Here, you can look through my Teen Glamor mags while I work on you. Let me know if you see any look that appeals to you."

"But I'm not glamorous like these models," Ashley protested, turning the pages with her foot.

"With makeup, anyone can be glamorous, if you know the right techniques," Kathy explained. An hour later, Kathy finished up, satisfied with her handiwork.

"Can I see now?" Ashley asked.

"No, not until we get you dressed. You have to see the whole look. I've matched your eyeshadow to your light blue dress." She helped Ashley don her fancy, silky blue, form-fitting dress that Lena had made for her. "There, let's see the whole look." She stood back looking Ashley over carefully. "Okay, have a look."

Lindsey, Amanda, and Pam also stopped to look at the result. "Oh my god, Ashley! You look gorgeous!" Lindsey exclaimed, shocked at how close Ashley resembled the teen models that Kathy had shown them.

"Wow! Oh wow!" Amanda added, genuinely impressed.

"Incredible! Kathy, you are amazing," Pam added.

"I, I, I look pretty, don't I," Ashley could scarcely speak as she stared at her reflection. Excepting for arms, she did look amazingly like the models Kathy had shown her. She had never thought of herself as looking pretty. She had many other words to describe herself; none was remotely close to pretty. "Thank you, Kathy. I need to learn how to do this for myself." Kathy beamed.

"Have you got time to fix me up a little?" asked Amanda.

"Me too, just a little maybe?" pleaded Lindsey.

Pam laughed, "This is going to become the 'model's bedroom' if you don't stop, Kathy." Everyone giggled at her tease.

Kathy finished with all them just in time to head down to the formal dinner and dance. "Really, we ought to be wearing heels. We are old enough now, I suppose. Maybe over the summer I can get my mom to buy me some. Let's stay in touch on it, and maybe we can all go shoe shopping," Kathy suggested.

Emilio was waiting for her and gaped at Kathy's appearance. "You, you look beautiful, Kathy."

Jim came over to get Ashley and nearly fainted. "My god, Ashley, you look ravishing!" She blushed, and he didn't let go of her all night long.

Henry Waldorf was likewise impressed with how great Amanda looked and pinned a corsage on her dress for her. Arm in arm, they made their way to the table.

Andy, dressed in his finest suede suit, met Lindsey. "Wow, Lindsey. Maybe I shouldn't go on this dig! You look, well, positively gorgeous."

The fancy dinner and formal dance seemed to last but seconds. It was ten at night when the girls finally entered their room. "How did the time go by so fast?" Ashley exclaimed. "Just a bit ago, we all left for the dinner. Now it's ten!"

"Did you see how Jim just could not take his eyes off of you all night long, Ashley?" Kathy asked. She'd joined them in their room to help take the makeup off of Ashley.

Ashley blushed, "Er no, I was looking at him all night." She admitted, though she said nothing about the loving kisses he'd given her.

They all chatted for another hour, before Kathy returned to her room. "All packed?" Lindsey began to wear her Floor Monitor hat once more. "After all, the bus leaves right after breakfast tomorrow."

Pam grinned, "Miss Floor Monitor, will you look at this for me and tell me what it means?" Pam had not said anything about her new appointment, wanting to surprise her friends.

Lindsey took the folder paper and opened it. "Oh! Cool! Gang, Pam is going to be a Floor Monitor like me next year. She's taking Sandy's place. Super cool!" A large satisfied smile appeared on Pam's face.

In the morning after breakfast, they climbed aboard their bus; they were heading home for the summer. Lindsey had much to ponder: Tom and Sandy would be getting married in three days; her mother would be having a baby any day now; and in eleven days, she would be going to Denver to meet her foreign exchange students. The summer promised much for her.

While Ashley had the same three things to ponder, she also could finally have time for herself. She was going home vastly different from when she had come. Last fall, she thought nothing about having no arms; she was antagonistic and easily fought back against any conceived insult towards herself. At that time, she had completely accepted herself as she was. Now, something had changed. She was sitting on grief that she did not know existed. She now wanted arms; she wanted to be like everyone else; she did not want to be so different, so helpless, so dependent on others. Worse, she now thought of herself now as a worthless cripple, something that she had never done before. It didn't matter in the slightest to her that others thought very highly of her. She knew the only thing that did matter was her own opinion of herself.

Then, there was Jim. Her heart skipped a beat every time she saw him. Though he doted on her, she could not imagine why he did so. If she were him, she certainly would be completely revolted by her sight. Ashley knew that she was a complete mess, but while at school, what with all the schoolwork and so many roommates, she had no private time. Now, maybe she could find a quiet corner to work this out. Maybe she could talk to her mother about it. Maybe Lena would have some answers, but Lena was going to have a baby. She'd have little time for Ashley. The mere thought of the infant brought on surges of helplessness in her mind. How could she do anything to help with a baby? She had no arms and in her mind, that was everything.

Lindsey's summer looked bright and cheerful. Ashley's summer looked more like a hopeless mess.
The End.

A Favor to Other Readers

How about helping other readers? Many readers rely on reviews to make the decision whether to buy a book. You can help them make their decision by leaving your opinions and viewpoint in a short review of the positive things of this book. Writing the review and expressing your opinion only takes a few minutes, and other readers will appreciate your efforts.

Click this link: Volume 3 The Crown of Moses
scroll down to Customer Reviews; click on Write a Review, and enter your review. Thank you.

Author Information

Visit My Amazon.com Author Page
Vic Broquard Author Page

Follow My Blog
Vic Broquard's Blog

Follow Me on Social Media
Facebook
Google+
LinkedIn
YouTube

Other Books by Vic Broquard

Without Warning (fantasy)

The Trident Series: (fantasy)
> Volume 1 The Trident and the Book
> Volume 2 The Trident and the Scepter
> Volume 3 The Trident and the Resurrection

The Adventures of Elizabeth Stanton Series: (science fiction)
> Volume 1 The Evolution of the Path
> Volume 2 The Great Messiah
> Volume 3 Of Kings and Queens and Troubadours
> Volume 4 Chaos in the Aftermath
> Volume 5 Power Plays
> Volume 6 Age of Exploration
> Volume 7 Abducted
> Volume 8 The Emperor and Empress
> Volume 9 A Job Worth Doing
> Volume 10 Degradation
> Volume 11 The Second Crusade
> Volume 12 When Worlds Collide
> Volume 13 Dark Ages

The Lindsey Barron Series: (fantasy)
> Volume 1 The Rod of the Apocalypse
> Volume 2 The Board of Governors
> Volume 3 The Crown of Moses
> Volume 4 Dominus for President
> Volume 5 The National Health Care Program
> Volume 6 States Justice
> Volume 7 Cross and Double-cross

Zoran Chronicles Series: (fantasy)
> Volume 1 A Dragon in Our Town
> Volume 2 Dragons, Power, Courts, and War

Planet of the Orange-red Sun Series: (science fiction)
> Volume 1 When Kingdoms Fall

Vic Broquard

The Return of the Wizards: Twelve Companions – The Making of Wizards (fantasy)

www.ingramcontent.com/pod-product-compliance
Lightning Source LLC
Chambersburg PA
CBHW070904260626
47162CB00007B/2553